Viking Bra

The last book in the Dra
Book 23
By
Griff Hosker

Published by Sword Books Ltd 2019

Copyright ©Griff Hosker First Edition

Cover by Design for Writers

Prologue

Ubba Ragnarsson was a bitter man. He had sailed to the Land of the Wolf to destroy the Dragonheart and claim the sword that was touched by the gods. He had hoped to better his father's achievements for his father, Ragnar Hairy Breeches, had raided Paris. He was now one of the richest Viking warriors and warriors flocked to sail with him. Ubba knew that his father's riches exceeded most of the so-called Saxon kings. Ubba had been not just defeated but destroyed. He had brought away just one drekar and, on the voyage home, ten more warriors had succumbed to their wounds. His hearth weru were dead and he knew that the men now with him were just taking him home. Once they reached Lundenwic they would abandon him. A man drew warriors to his standard when he won. When he lost then he would be left alone. Only Gangulf Gurtsson remained loyal. He was his foster father. He had been appointed by Hairy Breeches. He knew that he was the greatest gift his father had ever given him.

As the wounded drekar limped along the Tamese, Gangulf approached Ubba. Gangulf knew what the problem was. Ragnar Hairy Breeches did not like Ubba. Ubba was the son of his youngest wife and she had died giving birth to Ubba. Gangulf knew that Ragnar blamed Ubba for the death of the young wife who had been the prettiest of his three wives. Ubba had been unlucky and he had tried to outwit the cleverest Viking of his age. Gangulf waved away the helmsman, Siggi, and took the steerboard himself.

Gangulf was a good foster father but he had his own motives. He had a personal grudge. His hair, moustache and beard were festooned with small bones and tufts of his enemies' hair. He had filed his teeth to make them black. All of them marked him for what he was, a Skull Taker. "Ubba, what will you do now?"

Ubba shook his head, "What is there to do? We lost. These river rats will desert me as soon as we land." He looked at his foster father, "If you left me too then I would not blame you for I know I made mistakes."

"I will not leave you, Ubba. I swore an oath to be your foster father and I will keep that oath. We begin again, Ubba Ragnarsson. It may take a year; it may take longer but we find allies and we start to plan. You can become Lord of the Land of the Wolf!"

Ubba allowed himself a rare smile, "I admire your loyalty but it is misplaced."

"We need a better plan. I will speak frankly to you and I will be honest. That is my purpose. You tried to be your father. You thought to take a fleet of ships and take the Land of the Wolf that way. There lay the fault in your plan for that was a mistake. The Dragonheart has allies like Bergil Hafþórrsson and his brothers, Benni and Beorn. The way to take the Land of the Wolf is to build up an alliance. An attack must be made from many different directions all at the same time. To the north are the men of Strathclyde. To the east are the Danes of Jorvik and the Saxons of Northumbria. To the south are the Mercians and the Walhaz. All have reason to hate the Dragonheart. He acts like a king and they resent it. None have ever bested him. My plan is to use them and their mutual hatred for the Clan of the Wolf. If five armies attacked at once then there are too few warriors left to the Dragonheart to defend his land. He would either have to sit behind his walls and be picked off one by one or he would have to gather his men to fight each army. His men are good but even they cannot fight five armies."

The drekar was approaching the ruined Roman fort on the Tamese. It was where they would tie up and his men would leave him. Ubba was not a stupid man. He had heard the words and knew that Gangulf was correct. "But I have nothing!"

"Not true, Ubba, you have your father's name and you dared to take on the Dragonheart. There are other Vikings who wish to destroy the Dragonheart."

Ubba heard the venom in Gangulf's voice, "You hate him too?"

"He killed my father, Gurt the Silent. My father almost took Cyninges-tūn and came as close as any man to owning the sword. I swore vengeance. There are others like me. The Skull Taker

4

clan hate him. Although their power is destroyed there are warriors who lost kin fighting Dragonheart." The Dane leaned in and spoke conspiratorially, "Dragonheart is old! The Ulfheonar were feared but they are dead or have left him. His grandson Ragnar wishes to farm. His son, Gruffyd, does not know what he wishes to be, save that he will not rule the Land of the Wolf. He resents his father. Sámr Ship Killer is his heir and while he is a good warrior, he is young and he does not wield the sword that was touched by the gods. We weaken his power in his own land. His son and grandson have differences. We exploit them. Those who are close to him we weaken or kill. We isolate him until he is alone and weak."

"And the witches. Kara and Ylva? How do we defeat them?"

"We need to enlist the help of our own witches."

"We tried that and they were not strong enough."

"Then we find those who are strong enough. If we cannot find them then we use other means to defeat the witches. This will not be easy, Ubba, and it will not be swift but when we win then it is your name that men will remember. Think of years for this plan and not months. We build up our strength by raiding the Saxons. We seek warriors who are good at what they do. The wait will be worth it for you will be the man who killed the Dragonheart and took his sword. Then even your father will have to acknowledge your greatness."

"How much time?"

The drekar was drawing close to the quay. Gangulf shouted, "Steerboard oars in! Larboard, backwater!" As the drekar nudged into the quay and men leapt over the side to tie them to the shore, Gangulf said, "We start with a crew. We took some treasure which can be used to refit us and to feed the crew until we can raid. I know places which can be raided. They are Saxon halls and churches and we know we can defeat the Saxons. We gain warriors while we build up our treasure. Then we visit the Dragonheart's enemies. Within two years we will rule the Land of the Wolf and men will say that it was conquered not by the son of Ragnar Hairy Breeches, but Ubba Sword Stealer and your name will be remembered for all time!"

The thought of a name which accorded him fame and removed a reference to his father was the deciding factor. "I am decided. Today we begin to plan the end of the Dragonheart."

Dragonheart
Prelude

More than a year had passed since Erik Short Toe had died. It had been a sad year for me. I had lost many old friends like Karl, Asbjorn and Erik, my long-time captain. Aiden had gone to the Otherworld as had Uhtric, my servant of many years. My life would have been empty but for two who still lived in Cyninges-tūn and visited with me most days. Ylva and Sámr Ship Killer brought joy to me. Ragnar, Sámr's father, and Gruffyd lived far to the south. It was as though their lives and mine were unconnected. Ragnar seemed distanced from his son. Sámr had a stronghold across The Water from my home and he had a young family. He had a son, Ragnar, and his wife, Aethelflaed, was with child again. Their hall had been my first home. He would ride, most days, to sit and speak with me. He was keen to learn how to be Lord of the Land of the Wolf. The Clan knew that he was my heir. He was young but then I had attained power when I had been his age. He had good hearth weru led by Baldr Witch Saviour. It was Sámr who gave me hope.

In the last year, he had built a ship to replace, **'Heart of the Dragon'**. She had been destroyed in the attack by the son of Hairy Breeches. **'Úlfarr'** was not as large as some of the newer drekar. She had but eighteen oars on each side but she was fast. He and his hearth weru had spent three moons building her. He had taken his wife and child with him and that pleased his mother for Astrid loved children. His father, Ragnar, was an enigma. He no longer wished to fight and appeared happy to be a farmer. He seemed happy to live close to Whale Island with his wife and other children. He rarely visited me and yet there had been no falling out.

And then the news came that Elfrida, Wolf Killer's widow, had slipped away into the darkness that was death. She was a Christian but what I called a quiet one. My wife, Brigid, had been a noisy one. I had been very fond of Elfrida. She had watched over Ragnar and his family. She had tried to be as a mother to Gruffyd although he rejected her. There had, according to Ragnar, been no pain at the end of her life. She had simply not woken one morning and her face had upon it a smile. I hoped she was in the Christian heaven for if any woman deserved it, she did.

I saw Ylva each day for she lived in Cyninges-tūn. With Uhtric gone and just Atticus, Germund the Lame and Erik Shield Bearer in my hall, she visited to ensure that I was fed and well. She would never take a husband. I had thought her mother, Kara, would have been the same and would have remained unmarried but Aiden and she had been made for each other, *wyrd*! Kara had become increasingly ill since her husband, Aiden the galdramenn, had died. I wondered if she sought to join him in the Otherworld.

That morning in Einmánuður, Germund the Lame and I were practising with Erik Shield Bearer. He was a willing youth and as brave as they come but he had not been trained as a warrior. I was not certain how effective two old men would be to help him practise but we were better than nothing. We needed new blood. The last battle with Ubba Ragnarsson had cost the clan dear. We had lost many experienced warriors. There were just two Ulfheonar left besides me and Haaken One Eye and I were close in age. Aðils Shape Shifter was still younger and fitter than we but he lived with his wife and his sons in Lang's Dale. They kept apart from all others. I wondered why.

Erik was fast and he learned quickly. The first year of his training had seen him black and blue each night. Ylva's salve had been his salvation. Now he could avoid our blows and defend himself. He could even hit us with his wooden sword but I knew that he did not have the skill to survive for long in a shield wall. To be fair to the youth he was not yet big enough. He had put on weight and gained muscle since living with us. Germund could cook but it tended to be heavy, fatty dishes. Normally Atticus was the one who made our food and it was altogether finer. That particular morning he was absent collecting mushrooms from the woods.

Ylva and one of her women brought us some honeyed oat cakes she had baked. When I had been young, I had not had a sweet tooth. But when I was young, I had been a slave and there was no opportunity for sweetmeats. We stopped training immediately the women approached. A volva was a woman of importance. Ylva was fond of young Erik. It helped that he was most polite and in awe of Ylva.

"Thank you for these, my lady."

She laughed. She was now over thirty years but she still seemed like a young girl. Perhaps that was because she had not married. More likely, it was her power which waxed while her mother's waned. She ruffled Erik's hair, "I am not Lady Ylva, Erik. I am Ylva the volva!"

"You seem like a lady to me." He bit into his oatcake. "These are good." He hesitated before taking a second bite, "Are they bewitched?"

I shook my head, "No, Erik, and even if they were then they would help us and not harm us. We are lucky to have two such powerful witches in our home." Turning to Ylva I asked, "And how is your mother?"

Her face clouded over, "She is no better. I thought the winter chill would have left her but it seems to be in her bones."

"Did the steam hut not help?"

"A little but I fear it is something more serious. My father was the one who understood the workings of the body. It was he who saw your worm. It seems that we need the galdramenn that was my father. We do not see danger as clearly now as we used to. Of course, that could be my mother's illness too."

"I would have her healed."

She nodded, "As would I but I cannot see a way to do so."

"Have you used the steam hut to dream?"

"My mother is not strong enough." She looked up at me. "I miss my father and it is at times like these I realise how much he helped us for I seem unable to dream alone."

I smiled, "As he helped me." It was as though Aiden had entered my head. I cannot offer any other explanation. He was there and I heard his voice in my head. "I have often been to the Dreamworld. I could help you."

She smiled and placed her hand on mine, I was aware that Erik and Germund were stood with mouths open wide. I was speaking of entering the world of the spirits. It did not frighten me but it

9

terrified them. "It is a kind offer, grandfather but you are no galdramenn!"

"No, but I have crossed to Valhalla and returned. Kara is my daughter and Aiden was the slave I rescued. Those facts must count for something. And my mother and wife had powers. What have we got to lose?"

Her face became serious and as she spoke, I saw Erik and Germund clutch their amulets, "Because, grandfather, you have crossed to the other side once, that may be all that the spirits allow."

I held her hands in mine, "Ylva, I have done all in my life that I hoped. There is little left for me. If I can exchange my life for Kara's then that is a bargain I would gladly make. Sámr is now my heir and he has learned much. If I were to die then he could lead in my stead."

She saw the sense in that and nodded, "Sámr is not quite ready but I do not sense danger from our enemies. Germund, light the fire. I will go and tell mother. She can use her powers to help us."

"Erik, go and help Germund. You have used the steam hut, now it is time to learn how it functions."

Just then Atticus appeared. He had a wide-brimmed hat and a straw basket filled with fungi. He was whistling happily. We had had a year of peace and that made the Greek joyful beyond words. He was not a man of war. "I have some fine mushrooms. They will go well with the stew I put on the fire this morning." He was suddenly aware of the faces of Germund and Erik. "What have I missed?"

I pointed to the steam hut, "Germund, Erik, go and light the fire."

Atticus knew when I used the steam hut for peace. My tone and their faces told him that this was something altogether, in his mind, more sinister. He was a Christian and did not hold with such pagan rituals. He shook his head, "Just when I think this world is becoming civilised..." He stomped off into my hall.

Lighting the steam hut fire and then entering its misty world was not something which happened instantly. It was getting on for dusk by the time it was prepared and hot enough to use. Had Sámr been on our side of The Water then I would have invited him. Not only was he more like me than any other of my offspring, but he and Ylva also had a special relationship. I believed that Sámr had power. He had yet to use it but when he did then he would be more powerful than I had ever been. The difference would always be Ragnar's Spirit. The sword gave me powers from the god who had touched it!

The air was chilly with the wind off The Water and when I removed my clothes, I felt it. Inside there was a glow from the fire. I stared at the fire for that was part of the process of entering the Dreamworld. Ylva called it the Spiritworld. She entered the hut almost magically. One moment I was alone and the next she was next to me. She handed me a drinking horn. It did not contain beer or ale. Instead, it had a brew made by Kara and Ylva. I emptied the horn and continued to stare at the fire.

I saw shapes flare and then die. The flames were blue then yellow, white then red. Flashes of green glowed. I saw sparks rising and falling like stars. Some of the yellows glowed like the sun or shone blue like the moon. I was dimly aware that Ylva was chanting and then the potion began to take effect. I fell into a black chasm and all went silent.

I saw faces in the dark. That was all that I saw. There were no bodies attached to the heads but I recognised them. Asbjorn, Rollo, Beorn, Cnut. My old warriors smiled and then they vanished. I left the black chasm and I was beneath Wyddfa. I recognised it for it was the place where I had fallen into a cavern and found the rusty sword which now slept with Aiden. That was confirmed when Aiden rose from the ground before me. He was holding the sword but it was no longer rusty. It looked brand new. Its steel blade was so highly polished that it was almost silver, with a line of golden runes trickling sinuously along its length. It was half as long as a man's body and looked as though it needed two hands to hold it. The handle was adorned with a red jewel, the size of a grape. The red jewel looked like a ruby, an incredibly rare ruby. Also adorning the hilt were blue and green precious stones. The black ebony hilt was engraved with what appeared to be pure gold. Aiden gestured for me to follow him. He did not descend into the bowels of the earth. Instead, he led me up a path to the side of Wyddfa. Time passed and I had no recollection of its duration.

We reached a rock fall. Brambles had spun a web around it. Weeds and wild grasses sprouted from the cracks. Aiden plunged the blade into the earth and suddenly the rocks split and there was an opening. It was too small for a man to enter but Aiden reached his arm into it and pulled out a red stone. It was the twin of the one in the sword. It was then I saw, hanging from Aiden's neck, the red stone I had once given him. He had told me that it had magical powers. He handed me the stone and even as he did so the sword seemed to disappear and Aiden vanished into a fog.

The hut was filled with smoke when I opened my eyes. Ylva had gone. I heard a voice from outside the steam hut, "Grandfather, we have our answer and, once more, it is you who must face danger."

Dragonheart
Chapter 1
The New Drekar

We were back in my hall at my table. Atticus, Erik and Germund were listening to us attentively as we spoke. "I know I have to sail south and go to Wyddfa but I know not why. How does the red stone help my daughter?"

"That was the part of the dream you saw. My father spoke to me. You could not hear."

It suddenly came to me that my dream had been silent.

"The red stone has powers. The rocks you saw were once the entrance to the tomb of a great wizard."

I nodded. That made sense, "Aiden had a red stone. It is buried with him. Could we not use that one?"

"It belonged to him and its power died with my father. The stone you must recover is for my mother. It has powers for the red stones, the rubies, are the only ones which can be used by a volva or galdramenn." She smiled. "You need not go."

I looked her in the eye and spooned more of Atticus' stew into my mouth. "And if I do not go then Kara dies. She is my daughter and I said before that I would willingly give my life for hers but Wyddfa is many miles across the sea. I will need a ship and I will need a crew. Do I not put them in danger also?"

"You do but there are many men, especially here, who would happily journey south with you." She ate some of the stew herself, "This is delicious, Atticus."

My Greek was unhappy that I was to be leaving again and he sniffed, somewhat ungraciously, "It may be the Dragonheart's last meal! I am pleased it is a good one!"

Germund asked, "Have you dreamed him returning, my lady?"

"That I have not. If you go, grandfather, then you could die."

13

I smiled, "I am resolved. If I am in danger and about to die then I will send whoever is with me home. I will be the only one who will be sacrificed. When I have a crew, I will make them all swear an oath to leave me if their lives are in danger. I am old and my life does not matter."

Ylva laughed, "They will not agree to that!"

"Then they shall not sail with me." I would make them all swear on Ragnar's Spirit. None would break that oath.

The next morning, I visited my daughter. It was not simply a winter chill which had gripped her. She had trouble remembering things. It was most strange. She had forgotten that we once had two nuns who used to make cheese. She could not call to mind Karl the Lame. She seemed to remember me although she called me Aiden at one point. Her mind seemed to be in a fog and she was no longer Kara the volva. When I left, I knew that if I failed then she would slip into the fog and never return.

Ylva came with me to ride to Sámr's hall. He needed to know what I was planning. He was my heir. Erik Shield Bearer followed. Before I left, I asked Atticus to summon my warriors to my hall for the middle of the afternoon.

As we rode, I asked her, "Has she deteriorated in the past months? I have not visited her as often as I would have liked."

"She worsens each day. It began a month after my father died. It is as though she is dying a little each day. Her powers have weakened so much that it is hard to believe, sometimes, that she is a volva at all."

"Then my journey is even more urgent. When I have spoken with Sámr I will speak with my other senior warriors, Ráðgeir Ráðgeirson, Haraldr Leifsson and Sven Tomason."

"And what of Aðils Shape Shifter and Haaken One Eye?"

"I leave them here. I have interfered in their lives too often. They both deserve this time to be with their families. They would come if I asked but I shall not ask."

Sámr and Baldr Witch Saviour had not ceased improving the defences of their hall. The attack by Ubba Ragnarsson had come so close to succeeding that it had frightened my great-grandson. He had used the natural rocks to build a wooden palisade that even I would have struggled to devise a way to cross. Where his land met The Water, he had used stone and wood to make a wall as high as three men. He had a tower on each corner. Hawk's Roost was as powerful a stronghold as I had ever seen in the Land of the Wolf. Even Stad on the Eden was not as strong. He and Baldr Witch Saviour led just twenty warriors. Each night, six of them went without sleep to keep watch. When Sámr had told me of his plan I had smiled. It was the sort of thing I would have done when I was young. He had other men who followed him. They farmed the land around his eyrie. If danger came, he would sound his horn and they would bring their families and animals to shelter in his roost.

When we arrived, he and Baldr were stripped to the waist and sawing lengths of timber, "More building, Sámr?"

He shook his head, "Over the winter we realised that the towers needed a roof. This way we will be warmer when we watch and less likely to be skewered by an arrow plunging from the sky." He suddenly seemed to realise that Ylva was present. "Something is amiss?" He grabbed his kyrtle and threw it on.

"I have news, Sámr, and, as my heir, you should know all that I know."

He relaxed a little. "I feared you were ill again."

I looked at Ylva. She smiled, "Sámr has some powers, eh grandfather?"

Aethelflaed was some months into her labour. As with Ragnar, she bloomed. Sámr's son could now walk and was proving to be a handful. Sámr said after we had supped some ale, "My wife, if you would be so good as to take my son out to play for a while. The Dragonheart wishes to talk. He can chase the fowl around the yard. It seems to amuse him."

A slight frown passed over Aethelflaed's face and then she smiled, "Of course. Perhaps it will tire him out!"

When they had gone I said, "He is a handful but you are lucky to be at home while he is growing. I rarely saw my children."

"You have served the clan well, Great Grandfather, and now you can enjoy the evening of your life by The Water. As Ragnar grows you can play with him. I spent much of my childhood with you and it made me the man I am. I would have you do the same for my son."

I swallowed some of the ale. I did not drink so heavily as I once had but this was a good ale. Aethelflaed knew how to brew beer. "I would that were true. I am here to tell you that I have to go to the land south of Ynys Môn. I will be sailing as soon as I can gather a crew and a ship. I tell you this because you are my heir."

His face grew dark, "Why? Do you wish adventure or are you determined to die?"

"Neither, Sámr Ship Killer, I go to save the life of my daughter, Kara."

Sámr looked from me to Ylva, seeking confirmation, "It is true Sámr. My mother has an ailment I cannot cure. There is a stone which lies close to where the ancient sword was found and the spirits have said that only the Dragonheart can fetch it. Believe me, if there was another way, I would have chosen it."

Sámr was, despite his youth, the most thoughtful of all of my offspring. He was the most like me. He measured his words carefully. He thought before he spoke. It was one of the many reasons I had chosen him as my heir. He nodded, "'*Úlfarr*' needs a voyage and I will take you. We need another half of the crew. I would not leave my land devoid of warriors. Baldr Witch Saviour can watch over my land while I am gone." Baldr Witch Saviour had been sent by the gods. We had found him clinging to a piece of driftwood. He was not Norse. Germund the Lame told us that his people were horsemen who raided the lands north of the Empire. He was the son of a leader and he knew how to command.

This I did not like, "You are my heir. It is dangerous to put all of our eggs in one basket."

"Perhaps, but the spirits have decided this course of action. We ought to trust in them. Ylva will not be going and if I should fall in Gwynedd then she can raise Ragnar and he can rule the Land of the Wolf."

"You are my heir!"

"And Ragnar is mine." He smiled, "There, it is settled! You wish to leave soon?" He was decisive and I knew I would not be able to sway him. This was *wyrd*.

"I would quit Cyninges-tūn tomorrow."

His face fell, albeit briefly, and then he nodded, "It is good. Long goodbyes are always harder."

Ylva stood and hugged Sámr. She looked at him as though he was her child. She would never have a child and Sámr was as close to a son as she would have. "The Dragonheart chose his heir well." She took my hand, "Come, we have much to do!"

The Norns were spinning. This was so sudden that I had barely had time to think and yet I found myself becoming excited as we rode back around The Water. This would not be war. I would not need to draw my sword. We could sneak around the island the Saxons called Anglesey. It was now the heart of Gwynedd. Since King Rhodri had defeated Gorm the Great he had fortified the island. In doing so he had taken his eye from the mountainous heart of his land. That was understandable. Anglesey was his breadbasket for it produced wheat! His miners toiled in the last gold mines further south but at Wyddfa there were few defences. We could sail up the river and the walk to the place I had seen in my dream was less than half a day. With luck, we would be back in the Land of the Wolf within three days. Ragnar would barely have the chance to miss his father.

Ylva seemed to read my thoughts, "Grandfather, I did not dream your death but since my father died and my mother became ill, I do not see as far as I once did. I have more power here in the Land of the Wolf but I cannot see what will happen beyond the sea any more. When my father chose to die, he cut a thread. My mother's is frayed. You need to be careful."

I smiled, "As I will. I know that there might be danger. I hear the Norns spinning. I saw the stone. My aim is to hold the stone and then my daughter will live. You, of all people, should know that is all that we can do."

When we reached Cyninges-tūn I left Ylva. She would see to her mother. Erik and I went to my hall. We walked our horses, "Lord, will I be coming with you?"

"You have not been with us for long, Erik Shield Bearer. On such a voyage as this, all men are asked if they wish to come. There is no expectation from me that you will follow me."

"I wish to come. I know that I have little experience and that I may not be of much use to you." He shook his head, "I cannot even take an oar! However, I should like to come."

"Even though you know you may not return."

"Aye, lord."

"Then you have courage and a good Viking heart. The Allfather likes that. I have one and that is why I am named Dragonheart. I believe that I have been saved so many times because of it."

Despite his misgivings, Atticus had prepared food for the warriors who would attend. My hall was large but, of late, just a handful of us rattled around inside. When the men of Cyningestūn began to arrive, it filled and became a living beast. There were forty or more men who had sailed with me before and another fourteen who had been too young the last time. There was a buzz of conversation and anticipation. I sat, as was my wont, on my chair. I now used a cushion. It was a small affectation but none seemed to mind. Erik stood at my right side. The sword that was touched by the gods lay in the centre of the table and was surrounded by food. I saw the younger warriors surreptitiously touch it as they pretended to reach for food. All Vikings wished to hold the sword for it linked them to the Allfather and to me. They thought it brought them luck. In the heat of battle life and death were determined by such margins.

I looked up at Germund the Lame who banged on the wooden floor with his staff. All went quiet.

"I have a voyage I wish to take. I need twenty warriors to row my great grandson's drekar to…"

I got no further for there was a clamour as men stood, waved their arms and raised their voices.

I looked up at Germund the Lame who, this time, not only banged his staff but shouted, "Silence for the Dragonheart!"

The noise subsided but they still stood before me. There was a breeze in the room as the door opened. "I need a mixture of warriors who have sailed with me before and younger bloods who wish adventure. I am not certain that I can promise the latter but…"

A voice came from the rear, "But it is likely that the Sisters will have something planned for us, Dragonheart!" The men before me parted and there stood Haaken One Eye. "You did not think to leave me behind, did you?"

"But how…?"

"Ylva sent word last night that you were planning something. I know not yet what it is!" Rubbing his hands together he said,

"But I am ready! I have lived in a woman's world this past year and need to sail with flatulent old men like Haraldr Leifsson and Sven Tomason!"

I smiled for the whole room erupted. Haaken had always had a way with words and with men. His humour in dire straits was often the difference between success and failure. I was happy. I chose the men I would take carefully. I needed a mixture of experience and youth. I did not take Haraldr Leifsson for he had a family and his son had recently made him a grandfather. He was not happy but then again none of the ones I did not choose were happy. They all wished to sail with the Dragonheart. They knew there would not be many such voyages left in me. When the men and Ylva left us Haaken remained. "Will I need my mail, Dragonheart?"

I laughed, "If we have to fight then things will be desperate. I do not intend to wear mine. A helmet and my sword will have to suffice. Climbing Wyddfa will be hard enough without being encumbered with iron!"

"Good! I had no intention of wearing mine either but I did not wish to embarrass you! This will be a treasure hunt and no more. Now is the time for the likes of Erik here to do the hard work while we elder statesmen watch them labour."

Erik shook his head, "I have no skills yet, Haaken One Eye. I shall watch and learn."

"A good idea except that the Norns sometimes have a web or two they wish to spin. Dragonheart is a particular favourite of theirs. They like to make his life interesting."

"And that is not helped, Haaken One Eye, by your taunting them as you do!"

He was not put out by my words. He grinned, "When I am in Valhalla Odin himself will wish to hear how I managed to annoy them and still survive! The Norns might cause mischief here but in the Allfather's hall then I will be a hero!"

I nodded and smiled, "That you will."

We sat and supped ale. Atticus fussed around us. Normally he would spend the evenings either playing chess with me or teaching me more about the Greeks. I had learned, not only about their philosophers, like Socrates, but their scientists, men like Archimedes and Pythagoras. I enjoyed them for they were interesting men and they had knowledge which seemed almost like magic.

I pointed to Erik, "Erik here has shown us some skill in singing. He often makes up songs and the like."

Erik blushed as Haaken turned his one eye to stare at him, "You would be the one who takes over from me?"

Erik shook his head, "My creations are fragments only. I would appreciate lessons from you, Haaken One Eye, in the making of a saga."

Haaken laughed, "Then I too have a purpose on this voyage! I shall make a copy of myself. It is not right that when I go to Valhalla to entertain Odin there will be none left here in the Land of the Wolf to sing my songs!"

Shaking his head, Atticus rose, "You will be walking. I will fetch the staff we have been making, lord. It needs a leather thong. You will need it if you intend to climb a mountain. And perhaps some ear muffs so that you do not need to suffer Haaken One Eye's bleating."

Haaken shrugged and raised his horn in a good-natured way. I pointed to the west, "I climb Old Olaf!"

"This Wyddfa sounds a different prospect. The staff I made is now well coated with oil and is strong."

I nodded, as he left to fetch it. The staff reached almost to my shoulder and was made of hornbeam. Where I held it, the staff had a natural knobble at the end. For most of its length, it was thick as a child's arm. It was a substantial staff and I knew that I would need it.

Haaken smiled, "He is like your mother!"

"Aye he is, but he means well. He has taught me much."

"And tomorrow, Dragonheart, you and I will, once again, sail with children. I wonder if the old warriors will be watching us?" With those thoughts in our head, we retired and my dreams were filled with the warriors who were now in Valhalla.

'Úlfarr' was a fine vessel. She had only sailed twice and had that smell of new drekar which took me back a lifetime ago and the memory of my favourite ship, *'Heart of the Dragon'*. It also brought back sad memories. My captain and his family all lay dead. This would be the first time since... I could not remember when I had sailed with someone new. Ulf Long Sight was a

captain who had sailed with my grandson Ragnar when he had still raided. Now that Ragnar had abandoned the sea and used his old drekar as a hall, Ulf Long Sight was keen to serve Sámr. It was a perfect arrangement, Ulf could teach Sámr how to sail. Josephus had done the same for Erik Short Toe. While Sámr and the crew went over the ship, I rode with Erik Shield Bearer and Haaken One Eye to visit my son and grandson. It was courtesy. They had visited me but once since the battle we had fought here. I think that Gruffyd blamed me for bringing war to the land in which he lived. Probably Ragnar felt the same.

I visited Gruffyd first for he lived further from the sea. Mordaf, his eldest, was happy to see me and when I told him of my plans, he was desperate to come with me. I saw from my son's face that he did not wish it and so I said no. It hurt me as much as my grandson. It seemed my lot to be estranged from most of my family. Kara, Ylva and Sámr were the only ones of my blood with whom I felt comfortable. That was the work of The Norns.

Gruffyd asked, "There may be danger?"

"When you are a Viking and visit a neighbouring land without permission then there is always danger. Why?"

"What if something happens to you and to Sámr Ship Killer? What happens to the Land of the Wolf then?"

I sighed, "Then it will not matter to me for I will be dead and my chosen heir will also be with me in Valhalla. I am guessing that my heirs will continue to live in the land I have created."

He nodded but Mordaf said, "Do not die, grandfather! I wish to voyage with you!" I saw his father scowl.

"There may be another journey left in me after this one but I am not certain." As we rode west I wondered about my son. Mordaf now had his own hall and a family. Was Gruffyd cutting him off too?

The visit to Ragnar was a much easier one. He was pleased to see me. Since he had ceased to be a true Viking, he had become a much happier man. He and his wife, Astrid, were well suited and Ragnar enjoyed farming. He was skilled. That is not to say he couldn't fight if he had to but he had no desire to do so. Sámr's brother, Ulla War Cry, belied his name for he was a farmer too. The meeting with my grandson was a happy one. I saw that he did not resent me as my son did. He understood the reason for my voyage. It was for Kara and family was all.

As we headed back to the drekar Haaken said to me, "If you were both to die, Dragonheart, then it is obvious to me who would raise his standard as jarl, Gruffyd!"

"Probably!"

"And that would be a disaster for the clan. Your son has too much of his mother in him!"

Haaken was the only one who would risk such comments. I allowed him that for he had known Erika first. That explained his opinion and I knew he was right. Brigid had been a Christian and had delusions of grandeur. She had always wished me to be King of the Land of the Wolf. That I would never be but my son Gruffyd would and the clan would not suffer that. King Gruffyd would destroy all that I had created.

When we reached the river, the crew were all aboard and the sail was ready to be lowered. I was able to admire her lines. She was lean and she was hungry. The wolf, which was the carved figurehead, was the wolf which had saved Sámr when he had been a child. Sámr had put some of his own blood on the figurehead when it had been carved to make it his blood brother. Sámr understood the significance of such gestures. Úlfarr would be watching from beyond this world and that wolf's spirit would be in the drekar.

Sámr stood with a foot on the gunwale and a hand on the backstay, "Come, Great Grandfather Dragonheart! The tide does not wait, even for you!" I laughed and climbed aboard. It was another journey and another chance for the Norns to spin a web. How would they entangle me this time?

Dragonheart
Chapter 2
The Walhaz

It had been some time since I had been at sea and I had forgotten how much I missed it. I had not been born a Viking and my first voyage had been, to say the least, traumatic. Taken as a slave by Vikings and with others from my village, the first days had been an ordeal. Some of my fellow captives threw themselves overboard but I did not. I decided then that any life was better than death and I made the best of my life as a Viking slave. In the last few years, that philosophy had helped me cope with tragedies and disasters in equal measure. The word 'philosophy' would have been alien to me then. Even twenty years earlier I would not have understood it. Thanks to Atticus and the education he gave me I was now aware of far more. My life had changed immeasurably. What would I have been like if I had not been taken from the Dunum?

I stood with Haaken at the steering board. Erik Shield Bearer was at the prow, looking ahead. The crew was a mixture of men and boys from my stronghold and Hawk's Roost. The majority were young warriors and just ten of the crew, all from Cyninges-tūn, had experience. I did not think there would be much danger on the expedition. Despite the fact that King Rhodri of Gwynedd had defeated Vikings some years earlier, I knew that my great grandson's ship could outrun anything we found. The approach to Wyddfa was through forest and untamed high land. We would not find warriors. As a precaution, before we had left Úlfarrston I had made them all swear, on the sword that was touched by the gods, that if I fell, or was wounded, they would not try to save me. The priority, if we found it, would be the red stone and after that Sámr's life. I was unimportant. They had not been happy, especially Sámr but I refused to let any board who did not swear the oath. All knew the power of the oath. It explained why there was a sombre mood aboard. It was only Haaken and I who were in a lighter mood.

That lightness was reflected in the contents of our chests. Without mail and spare weapons, they were the lightest they had ever been. We had been able to bring spare boots and warmer clothes. We were warriors who now enjoyed comfort. I just had my sword and my dagger, Wolf's Blood, as weapons and, of course, I had my helmet and comforter. It was for practical purposes. We had a rock fall to dismantle. The helmet was there to protect my head, not from a sword or a spear but a falling rock. Old men thought of such things!

We passed the island of Man. An island which was much fought over, it was a haven for pirates who acknowledged no leader. I suppose they were the true Vikings. Bergil ruled Dyflin and I ruled the Land of the Wolf. There was a King of the Danes and, it was rumoured, a clan in Norway who were trying to claim the title King of Norway. The islands had their own jarl and in the Land of the East Angles, Aethelward was beginning to be ousted by the increasing number of Danes. The men of Man remained aloof from all of these peoples. They raided anyone! Haaken and I watched the island slip by. It was part of our past and we both wished it to remain that way. I touched my horse amulet. Prince Butar had died there as had my mother. I would not reconquer it now and that was a regret. It had been there that my sword had been struck. Man would always be part of me.

With a benevolent breeze, there was no need to row and Haaken and I spread our cloaks upon the deck and took an afternoon nap. There might have been a time when I felt embarrassed about such a thing but no longer. The pleasant motion of the drekar rocked us gently to sleep.

We were awoken by the cry from the ship's boy, Olaf, perched on the yard and mast, "Ships to larboard! Three of them!"

We had napped enough and we both leapt to our feet. Our eyes were no longer what they had been and we were reliant upon others to tell us what lay upon the horizon.

Ulf snapped, "A proper report, Olaf! Viking? Saxon? Walhaz?"

There was a delay in his answer. Olaf would be cuffed when he descended. Ulf was not known for his patience; no drekar captain was.

His voice drifted down to us. "They are not Viking. I think they are Walhaz. They have oars and there are armed men."

I heard Ulf growl to Sámr, "If I have to ask him the number of oars…"

Almost as though he had heard him Olaf shouted, "There are ten oars on each side!"

We were bigger than any one of them but we would be outnumbered if they chose to gang up on us. I would not offer advice. I was a passenger. This was Sámr and Ulf's decision.

"Can we outrun them?"

"Aye, we could." That was all Ulf said. He was letting Sámr make a decision. My great grandson looked up at the pennant to gauge the wind and then glanced down the boat. The men had not rowed and this was an opportunity to see how they worked together. I saw him nod as he made his decision. "We make out that we are heading to the south and west, for the south Hibernian coast. The wind is with us and even if they use their sail, we will be faster. When they are committed to following us and they have tired a little we man the oars and turn to sail through them. We arm the ship's boys and have six of our men with bows. We will trust in the skill of Erik Bollison and his shipbuilders and pray that both Odin and Ran support our endeavours!"

I nodded when he looked at me for it was a good plan.

Ulf shouted, "Get yourself down here, Olaf, I want every sheet and stay checking. I do not want to hear the snap of a sail! Get to it!"

As soon as Olaf was down from the yard Ulf pushed the steering board over. The wind was now astern of us and we flew making the sail billow. Sámr had had a wolf's head stitched into it. With a black head, red eye and tongue it was striking. It echoed the ship and the land from whence it came. If they did not know before, the Walhaz now knew that we were from the Land of the Wolf and they had been given the only warning they would get. Perhaps their King's victory over Grom had emboldened them. Whatever the reason they were willing to risk a clash with us. I saw Baldr and Sámr go to their chests and take out their helmets,

25

swords and Saami bows. I had left mine at home. To be honest, one of the wounds I had suffered in the battle with the Danes had made pulling a bow harder than it used to be. I would watch the archers loose their arrows. Haaken and I did don our helmets. The Walhaz had good archers. It would have been foolish to risk a lucky arrow.

We were extending our lead but the Walhaz were wise to our move and they spread out to catch us if we turned or in case the wind changed. They thought they were driving us on to the Hibernian shore. We were now in Ulf and Sámr's hands. They had to choose their moment perfectly to make the turn. Haaken and I watched the three ships which were trying to capture us. They were not as narrow as a drekar but they were as long. They had a sail and the three of them now allowed their sails to be unfurled. Slightly smaller than our sails, they were not as good but it meant they could ease the rate of the oars and begin to catch us. The waves were not huge but all four ships, theirs and *'Úlfarr'*, crashed into waves sending showers of salty spray down the decks. Each time a ship dipped the helmsman lost sight of the sea ahead. He had not said anything but I knew that Ulf was waiting until all three hit a wave at the same time and then he would make his turn. Their reaction would be slower. When they rose they would see, not the steering board, but the side of the drekar and it would be heading away from them. More importantly, the crew would be rowing and a Viking crew, especially a fresh one, could out row any other ship.

"Ready your oars but keep them run in until I say!"

"Aye, Captain!"

Baldr and Sámr had chosen their archers and they lined the larboard side at the stern. There was a temptation to warn Ulf when the three ships were about to hit a wave but he was captain and even the Dragonheart did not interfere with his orders.

Ulf glanced astern, "Oars out! Prepare to come about! Hard a larboard! Now row!"

Haaken had a spear in his hand and he marched down the deck banging the shaft on the decking and he began a chant! It was, of course, one of his. The wolf cave was the place we were heading. It was the most appropriate chant he could use.

The wolf snake-crawled from the mountainside
Hiding the spell-wight in cave deep and wide
He swallowed him whole and Warlord too
Returned to pay the price that was due
There they stayed through years of man
Until the day Jarl Dragon Heart began
He climbed up Wyddfa filled with ghosts
With Arturus his son, he loved the most
The mouth was dark, hiding death
Dragon Heart stepped in and held his breath
He lit the torch so strong and bright
The wolf's mouth snarled with red firelight
Fearlessly he walked and found his kin
The Warlord of Rheged buried deep within
Cloaked in mail with sharp bright blade
A thing of beauty by Thor made
And there lay too, his wizard friend,
Myrddyn protecting to the end
With wolf charm blue they left the lair
Then Thor he spoke, he filled the air
The storm it raged, the rain it fell
Then the earth shook from deep in hel
The rocks they crashed, they tumbled down
Burying the wizard and the Rheged crown.
Till world it ends the secret's there
Buried beneath wolf warrior's lair

As soon as the oars bit we leapt almost over the waves. It was fortunate that I was holding on to the gunwale for the combination of the turn and the power of the oars had taken even me by surprise. When I recovered I looked astern and saw that only one of the ships, the one closest to us, had reacted quickly enough. The one which had been at the southernmost end made her turn and began to close with us. She was further east than we had been. Ulf and Sámr had known that we would risk coming closer to at least one ship and that one now began to close. The other two would be playing catch up. They would only catch us if the leading one slowed us down.

The crew had the rhythm and Haaken was able to come and join me. He smiled, "See, the sun begins to set in the west. All that we need is for darkness to come and we will escape these hounds. A pity, I would have liked to use my blade once more!"

"Haaken One Eye! The Norns!"

He laughed, "No matter what I say, Dragonheart, they will toy with you. When you are dead they will have to find another plaything!"

We were now close enough for me to see that they too had some archers on board. With the wind in their favour, they sent some hopeful arrows at us. They fell woefully short. They were still gaining for they had more wind. Once they turned, as we had turned, then they would be travelling at the same speed. I estimated that we had another six ship's lengths before they would have to turn. Of course, they would be with us in four ship's lengths. Baldr and Sámr nocked an arrow each and let fly. They had bows which were the most powerful I had ever seen and could outrange those of the Walhaz. I watched the arrows sail up into the air. They were not aiming at men; they had targetted the ship. The wind held them at the top of their arc and then they plummeted to the deck of the Walhaz ship. I had the luxury of being able to track their flights. The sun was in the south and the Walhaz did not have the same view. I did not see them hit but I saw the effects of the hits. The archers at the prow darted for cover. Baldr and Sámr sent another flight each.

Haaken went to the chests and returned with our swords. "I think we will be needing these before too long!"

He was right. We were going to be caught.

Ulf looked at us and shrugged, "We have a better chance against one than three."

Haaken One Eye laughed, "With Dragonheart and Haaken One Eye on board then we could take all of them! Who would dare face the sword that was touched by the gods?"

I saw the younger warriors looking up in awe at Haaken. He knew how to play an audience. He could also fight as well as any man I knew. I drew my sword. It was the right time. Raising it I shouted, "Clan of the Wolf!"

The crew all shouted as one, "Clan of the Wolf!" If the words carried to the men of Walhaz it would send shivers of fear down their spines.

The arrows which had been sent by Sámr and Baldr had had the effect of making their archers take shelter. Now, as they rose, they found themselves the target of our archers. The heartbeat's difference was crucial. Our arrows struck their archers while the Walhaz were still drawing. The leader could now be seen at the steering board. He wore a leather jerkin studded with mail. He held a shield and a sword which was shorter than the ones we used. The Walhaz were not known for their sword making. The presence of the sword beneath the mountain had always caused me a problem. It had obviously not been made in that land so why bury it there? I shook my head. I was daydreaming and it was a sign of my age. In the time it had taken for the thought to distract me the Walhaz had closed to within a ship's length.

Ulf said, "The gods must favour us, lord, for they are sending her to strike at our larboard side!"

I knew what he meant. If it had been approaching from the steerboard then he could have disabled us and we would have ended our days far from home.

"Stand by! They are going to strike! Larboard oars in!"

Ulf timed his move to perfection. He moved the steering board to the steerboard side just enough so that the Walhaz did not strike us hard, as their captain intended, but slid down our larboard side. Nor had he ordered his own steerboard oars in and we heard them shatter and splinter. The collision hurt the men who would try to swarm over us. Once they had regained their feet Sámr and his archers continued to rain arrows into the heart of the Walhaz ship. I leapt on to the gunwale and held the backstay with my left hand. I allowed the natural swing of our drekar to help me to swing out and hack across their forestay. The rope sheared and flapped in the wind. Their sail lost the wind. If they had not collided with us then I would be a dead man for I hung above the well of their ship with just a sword and a helmet to protect me. Erik Shield Bearer grabbed my shield and ran to protect my legs. I had not given him the opportunity to do more. Even though they were disordered, one Walhaz warrior leapt up the gunwale of his own ship. He swung at my left side. I was clinging on to the rope and I brought my sword around to block his blow. Haaken One Eye's sword hacked through both of the warrior's legs and he fell screaming between the hulls of the two ships. A Walhaz warrior whirled a grappling hook above his head. An arrow smacked him in the face and threw him to the deck.

I heard Ulf shout, "Out larboard oars and row before that bastard hits *'Úlfarr'*!"

The gap through which the warrior had fallen now grew. Our archers and the splintering of the oars had hurt their crew. The severed rope not only weakened the sail it also impaired their ability to manoeuvre their ship. Although the other two ships were closing we now had sea room. I could not help myself. I raised my sword and shouted, "Clan of the Wolf!" It was a mistake. Another word Atticus had taught me was hubris. The Norns were going to punish me. The Walhaz archer sent his arrow towards me. It smacked into my left hand, missing the rope by the width of a finger. Even had I been a younger man I could not have held on and I felt myself lurch over the blue and black sea. It was *'Úlfarr'* who saved me. She rolled to steerboard and I fell, not into the dark sea, but backwards to the deck. It was Sámr and Baldr who caught me. The sword that was touched by the gods was still in my hand. Haaken appeared, grinning, "Lucky! Dragonheart! Very lucky! I was about to compose your death saga!"

I laughed, "Not yet, Haaken One Eye!"

Erik Shield Bearer ran to my side with honey and vinegar. Sámr said, "Let us heal this, Dragonheart! If I were to return home without you then what would the clan say of me?"

Dragonheart
Chapter 3
Wyddfa

The arrow had pierced the bottom part of the palm of my left hand. It had not touched any bones although I knew that I would have to endure aches and pain in the cold weather. Sámr was not happy, "Great grandfather you are not here to fight! The only reason you are with us is that you and Haaken are the only two who now know where this rock filled cave lies."

I smiled at his impertinence. He berated me for all the right reasons, "Had I not done so then who would have severed the stay? They would have grappled us and then the others would have closed."

"Even so," he tailed off weakly for he knew I was right. He was torn. He was learning the dilemma of taking a drekar to war and leading men. He should have had fewer men on the oars and more men ready to repel boarders. I looked in his eyes and saw him learning. This was good. The Norns had punished me and taught my great grandson a lesson! *Wyrd*!

Ulf took us due south until we lost sight of the Walhaz ships. Then the oars were placed on the mast fish and we headed south and east using just the sail. Night would be upon us soon and so he reefed the sail. If the Walhaz continued their pursuit it would be harder to see us in the dark and we would not risk running into rocks at high speed. He wanted to reach the river at dawn.

Haaken knew how to tend wounds, especially mine, for he had been doing so for most of my life. He now took the time to instruct Erik Shield Bearer. This had been the boy's first battle at sea. I saw, in his white face, that he had been terrified. As he and Haaken bandaged my hand I said, "You did well back there, Erik! You tried to protect me."

"Had I done my job properly, lord, then I would not now be bandaging your hand. I should have been next to you!"

Haaken shook his head, "And then you would have been sleeping with Ran. Just because the Dragonheart is a foolish old man there is no need for you to be a stupid young one. You did the right thing. The Allfather has not yet decided that the Dragonheart is ready for Valhalla and the Norns are still playing as a cat with a mouse. When they are ready, they will cut the thread."

When my wound was tended, I went to stand with Sámr. I said nothing to him; I just wanted him to know that I was there to speak with. Haaken instructed Erik in the art of creating songs. If Haaken had had a son he would have done the same with him. Erik had been sent into our lives for many reasons and Haaken's beaming smile told me this was one of them.

Sailing on through the dark was also worrying for some of the younger crew. They would fear the darkness and the unknown. Both Sámr and I had confidence in Ulf. Good navigators could go for days without sleep. He would sleep once we reached the river. I found myself comforted by the presence of Wyddfa. We were drawing closer to it and, as we did so, I found the power of the holy mountain growing. I had a connection with it. I still did not know what that connection was but I felt it. Even the new wound did not hurt as much. All the aches and pains in my old body seemed to disappear. This was where Aiden had felt most comfortable. The grave of Myrddyn the wizard was almost a place of pilgrimage for Aiden and when we had walked into the cave then it had changed him forever.

Sámr wished to give me a sleeping draught. Ylva had given him a leather flask before we had left. She knew that warriors would be wounded. When we had parted, she had given the flask to Sámr and to me she had given a hug so powerful that I thought a bear had gripped me and when she had drawn apart there were tears in her eyes. All she had said, huskily, was, "Come back, grandfather. I still have great need of you. Do not take unnecessary risks, I beg of you." Now as we neared Wyddfa every moment of that parting was etched in my mind.

I shook my head as Sámr offered me the flask, "I need no draught for the pain is bearable and I would take in the power of this mountain. It feeds me, Sámr, it feeds from within!"

I did sleep but it was a peaceful sleep almost as though the mountain and the drekar had combined to sing a lullaby to me. I was awoken by an ache but that pain soon disappeared when I saw the sun rising over the mountain's craggy summit. Ulf and Olaf were the only ones awake. I knew that the navigator was enjoying the sunrise. It was always a magical moment. He had sailed through the night using a mixture of star sights and experience. A good navigator could feel the sea and smell the land. I walked over to him. Olaf moved apart. The extra watch was his punishment for failing to give Ulf all the information he had needed. He would not repeat the error.

Ulf nodded to me, "A fine morning, lord! I will rouse the crew and unfurl the sail soon enough but I enjoy this view."

"As do I and there is little hurry. King Rhodri now uses Anglesey as his fortress. He has forgotten his roots. He will pay for that. Wyddfa rules this land. She is the heart of Gwynedd. I am not Walhaz but I know the power the mountain exerts. My forebears lived close by. The cave lies on the southern side of the mountain."

"I studied the charts, Lord Dragonheart, but I know not where it is."

"It is the mountain we seek. I know where the cave lies. Get us to shore and I will find a path to take us there but it would be prudent if we landed at a river. Those ships which tried to take us will seek us out. Better if we are hidden, eh?"

"Aye, lord!"

Suddenly the sun flared above the mountain top. It seemed to crown it as though it was a king.

Ulf smiled and I know that my face reflected the joy I felt. Ulf said, "Now we can wake the crew! Olaf!"

Olaf cupped his hands, "Crew of the *'Úlfarr'*, rouse yourselves! We have come to land!"

Thus, the crew were greeted as they opened their eyes by the sight, not only of land, but also of a crowned King of the Mountains. It seemed to be a good omen and there were smiles all along the deck. The river Ulf found was not the same one we had used before. This one was not as wide but it looked closer to the mountain's base. It was deep enough and we sailed for almost three-quarters of a mile before it began to shallow and to narrow. We turned the drekar around before it narrowed too much and then stepped the mast. The river had curved and we would be hidden from the sea.

I gathered what we would need. I estimated it might take a day to find the cave. That meant we would have to spend the night on the bare mountain. We also took food. We then had a debate about the numbers we would need. Sámr wanted to bring half of the crew. I shook my head, "Haaken, Erik and perhaps four others are all that we need. The fewer the better."

"What if you and Haaken are attacked?"

I waved a hand at the empty land around us. The lower slopes were forested and there was neither sight nor smell of smoke, "And from where will these hordes of enemies come? I see none. The fewer the better for the danger lies with the drekar. That needs to be defended."

"Then I will come with three warriors. Baldr and the rest can watch the drekar."

"Good and remember your oath! You and all of those with you obey me!" His eyes flickered. "I can make you swear again!"

He shook his head. He did not like to be reminded of the oath he had sworn. "I will obey you! I do not remember you being this grumpy before, Great grandfather!"

I held up my bandaged hand, "Put it down to the wound." That was a falsehood, the wound did not bother me.

We took enough food and ale skins for two days. Erik Shield Bearer took his bow as did Sámr. We left and headed up the river. That would be the easy way to the mountain. Rivers followed the easiest route. Even as we began our march my eyes, although not as good as they had once been, were able to pick out the jumble of rocks, far in the distance, which I took to be the cave. I had brought with me the walking staff I had used to climb the Old Man the day before I had left my home. I always liked to see my land from its peak. I hung my helmet from my sword. Poor Erik was laden. He did not carry my shield for I would not need it but he did have a leather bag with food, ale skins and a blanket for me.

As we laboured up the rarely used path, Haaken grumbled, "I am Haaken One Eye and as famous as Dragonheart. I should have someone to carry my food!"

Erik said, "I will carry yours if you wish!"

I laughed, "Do not listen to his bleating, Erik. He has enough coins in his chest at home to pay for ten servants to carry his gear. He just likes to hear the sound of his own voice. Save your breath, Haaken One Eye, for the mountain."

"I only bring it up as I am certain I will have to carry you before too long, old man!"

"I will still be at the cave before you!" We both laughed. It felt good to be on an adventure, especially one which promised success. The air was fresh but the skies were clear. I could see Ynys Môn to the west and when, after a couple of hours of walking, we stopped for refreshments, I was able to turn and see the drekar in the river. We made much better time than I had expected. Perhaps it was the joy of being Dragonheart again and not a weary old man sitting in his hall playing chess with an old Greek. I idly wondered if I ought to raid again. Just as quickly I dismissed the thought. All that I would be doing would be endangering those with whom I raided. It would be arrogance on my part. I would be raiding purely for my personal pleasure. Men would die just so that I could feel the blood rushing through my veins. This adventure was enough. I could now see the cave; it was much closer than I expected. We would spend the rest of the day uncovering the stone, recover it and head back in the morning to the drekar. In a day or two, I would be home and Kara would have her stone.

My heart sank when we reached the rock fall. The dream had made it look as though it would be simplicity itself to shift a few stones and find the red stone. The jumble of rocks had weeds and scrubby shrubs growing from the cracks and some of the stones looked as big as a small house. How could we shift them? I could see now that we would not find the jewel quickly. It would not lie conveniently close. While the others made camp Sámr, Haaken and I walked to the foot of the fall. I remembered when the rocks had tumbled down sealing the tomb. When we came closer, I saw that there were not as many weeds as I had seen from further away. They were wild, tufty grasses and dandelion.

Sámr said, quietly, "The dream, Great grandfather, was it just that? Were the Norns teasing?"

I shook my head, "If I alone had dreamt then, yes, but Ylva did too and Ylva was in the world of the spirits. This will just require a little more work than I had thought."

"Then I will set sentries. This is a good spot from which to observe. We can see the mouth of the river, the drekar and even that trail which heads south and east. Let me know when you have devised a strategy."

I nodded, "Aye, Sámr."

Haaken and Erik had shed their loads and they joined me as Sámr and his men busied themselves. I walked to the fall of rocks. I put my hand to the grass, "In my dream, these were longer and there were far more weeds." I pulled the tussocky grass with my hand and its tenuous grip on the rocks allowed me to pull it free. I saw the gap between the two rocks. "I cannot see where to begin."

Haaken nodded, "As we would with any journey, by putting one foot before the other."

He took out his seax and ran it along the cleft between the two large stones. Haaken and I both had well-made weapons and his seax was no exception. He began to prise against the stone and, remarkably it moved for it was not one stone but a number of smaller ones. I took out my seax and I joined him, cutting away the soil and weeds from the other side. We both levered together and the stone popped out. I had once seen Olaf Leather Neck's axe hit a Dane's head so hard that an eye had popped out of his head. It was like that and there was a hole as big as Erik's head.

Haaken looked pleased with himself, "There!"

I nodded, "Now let us pull the grasses from around the base but be careful Haaken One Eye. Do not let your success go to your head! I would not have Wyddfa fall upon our heads."

Erik was able to clamber above us so that the three of us could all work in the same area. He perched precariously on the smaller rocks which lay above the base. Once we had cleared the grasses, we used our seaxes to clear the soil.

It was as we were doing it that Stig Sword Hand shouted, "Lord, I see the ships of the Walhaz. They are sailing along the coast."

I stopped what I was doing. This could jeopardise our chances, "Sámr, send two of your men back to Baldr. Warn him of the danger." I know I should have let him make the decision but he would be thinking of me.

He nodded, "Stig Sword Hand, leave just three men with the Dragonheart and me. If Baldr has to, tell him to get to sea and then return for us."

"No, Sámr, if there is danger then you will join Baldr. Keep watch and if they look to go up the river then you will get back to the ship and we will find our own way home."

"I will not leave you!"

I patted the sword which lay on the ground, "And your oath?" His head slumped. An oath was binding and he could not break it. "It may not come to that. Your drekar is hidden. This will turn out well! Come, Haaken, let us return to our work."

We now had more purpose. It was early afternoon and we all needed a break for food and ale but the three ships seeking us gave our task urgency. Sámr and the three men with him watched the four points of the compass while we three toiled. We could not have used the others to dig for we were like the Greek who cut me open in Miklagård. We were making an incision in the mountain and trusting to the dream. We began to remove the rocks carefully, one by one. We made certain that the one we took would not cause a rockfall and undo all of our work. Erik joined Haaken and I on the ground for we did not wish him to tumble and hurt himself when rocks fell. Haaken had been right. It was like beginning a journey, one step at a time. We removed the smaller stones and discovered that the stones beneath were just a little bigger. We had been toiling for an hour when we discovered a natural lintel. It was a huge rock the length of Erik's body and it was jammed across two huge boulders.

I said, excitedly, "We have a natural support. Let us take the stones from beneath." The stones beneath required all three of us to tug and pull them free but when we removed one, which sparkled with green and blue flecks, we felt a wave of musty air. There was a void.

I lay down and put my head into the hole. "Haaken light a fire. We need a burning brand." I was excited and when we are excited, we make mistakes. It was a mistake I made albeit a necessary one.

"Aye, come Erik fetch the flint."

I put my hand within the hole. My shoulders were too wide for me to enter and we could not remove any more stones for the ones at the side were enormous. This was the hole of my dream. The spirits had not lied. We would find the stone and my daughter's life would be saved! I cleared as many of the rocks away as I could while Haaken and Erik started the fire. They improvised a brand. No matter how much I cleared it I would still be unable to enter. Erik was the only one small enough to do so.

Sámr said, as the smoke rose from the fire, "Great grandfather, is this well advised?"

"Unless you can devise another way to discover what is beneath this pile of stones then we have to do this. So far, the dream is accurate. I believe that if Erik can get inside the entrance then he will be able to find the red stone quickly and we can leave. Just keep a watch for enemies."

One of his men said, "Lord, the three ships of the Walhaz have stopped and have lowered their sail."

I stood and went to him. I could see the three ships, they looked tiny but I could see faces. They had spied the smoke. "This may help us. They might investigate the smoke and by the time they reach us we will have gone."

I could see that Sámr was not convinced but he nodded. I was still the Dragonheart.

"Come, Erik Shield Bearer. Take off your leather jerkin. When I have looked within you can investigate. Are you happy to do this?"

"Go into a small hole no bigger than my body? Enter a tomb beneath rocks which have fallen once? Of course not, lord, but I will do it for I am oathsworn. It seems to me that this is my appointed duty and I will do it. Call it my rite of initiation into the clan!"

He had grown in the time he had been with us. "You need no initiation but I am grateful. Give me the torch!"

I dropped to my knees. They creaked and groaned. I held the torch before me and pushed it ahead. I saw that there was a cavity. Erik would only struggle in the entrance. As I moved the light from side to side, I saw coloured lights flickering and reflecting back at me. There were stones to be seen; however, I had no idea of the colour and I would have to trust my dream.

I stood and handed the torch to Erik. "You can leave the torch within. I see stones."

He took the torch and lay down using his elbows to insinuate himself into the opening.

One of the sentries shouted, "Lord, I saw a flash of light. It glinted off something to the east."

"Is it men, Einar?" Sámr was already drawing his sword.

"I think so. The light is in the distance. They will not be here any time soon."

"Great grandfather, we must hurry!"

"Sámr, if you have to leave then do so. There is little point in travelling all this way just to leave the stones buried under the mountain. Better not to have come at all. My daughter and granddaughter's hopes lie with us! I will not let them down! If you have to go, then go. We can make our way home across the land!"

Erik's voice echoed as he shouted, "I can see them, Dragonheart! There is a bag. The bag has torn! Urgh!"

"What is it?"

"There is a rat! It is dead."

"Pass the stones back and then get out. There is danger."

I will have to turn around, lord, and pass them out. Then I will crawl out. There is an opening above my head. I think I can turn."

"I see them, Great Grandfather. There is a line of ten warriors led by a warrior in a helmet!"

"We are almost there." I lay on the ground and saw, by the flickering light, Erik as he manoeuvred himself around. He did so carefully and then the light went as his head, shoulders and right arm still holding the bag filled the opening. He used his right elbow to crawl and drag himself out. The jewels were held in his right hand. He offered them to me, "Take them, lord, it will be easier to crawl if I can use my fingers."

I took the jewels. There was one red one, some blue ones and a few that were green. Perhaps it was Myrddyn, or the Norns or, more likely, Erik, having handed the jewels over became overconfident. Whatever the reason, with his head and shoulders out of the gap he screamed as I heard a rumble from behind him.

"What is it?"

"A rock has fallen and my leg is trapped!" His face showed the pain he felt. He shook his head, "Leave me, lord!"

"Hurry Great Grandfather!" Sámr began to kick soil into the fire to put out the tell-tale smoke which marked our position.

I stood, "Sámr, go." I handed him the ruby. It was the one I had seen in my dream. I put the others in my pouch. "Take this stone and give it to Ylva!"

"I will not leave you!"

"And you would have me desert, Erik? Desert my oathsworn? Do you not know me at all?" He looked up at the mountain. "Make a noise when you leave and those men will follow you. We will get Erik out; we just need time."

Haaken put his hand on Sámr's shoulder, "Dragonheart is right, Sámr. You are the future of the clan. This is the work of the Norns. We have a journey ahead of us but we have the sword that was touched by the gods. We will be safe." He grinned, "And I will have another fine story! Go!"

Nodding, Sámr put his arms around me, "May the Allfather be with you!"

I hugged him back, "And with you. The clan is in good hands. Do not fear for me. Get the stone, your crew and the drekar home and I will be happy!"

He handed me the leather flask with the potion, "You may need this!"

Einar shouted urgently, "Lord!"

"I come!" The four of them hurried off down the trail. The Walhaz would see them for their own trail intersected with the one Sámr would use to return to the drekar. Without two old men to slow them and with the slope in their favour, they would reach the river just after dark. Now, all we had to do was to find a way out of this dilemma!

Dragonheart
Chapter 4
The Long Road Home

"And just how do you propose to get Erik out of this situation, Dragonheart?"

"By being calm. Gather our gear together while I speak with Erik." He shrugged and began to pick up the ale skins, cloaks and blankets. "Erik, is it both feet which are trapped?"

"It is just my left one. My right is free. I think a rock has fallen upon it."

"Can you wiggle your toes?"

"What, lord?"

"If you can wiggle your toes then you can use your foot."

"I can wiggle."

An idea suddenly came to me. When he had been turning around, I had been able to see the ground before him, "Use your left hand and feel around the hole behind you. Can you feel a rock by your hip?"

"Yes, Dragonheart. It is the size of my head."

"Then we have a chance!"

I reached over and grabbed my staff. I made the mistake of using the hand which had been pierced by an arrow. It hurt. Haaken said, "What do you need a staff for?"

"Atticus once told me of a Greek called Archimedes. He spoke of using something called levers and pivots. I am going to test that theory. I am going to try to lift a rock."

"Then that will truly be magic and you will have become Aiden!"

"Erik, I am going to slide the end of my staff down the hole. Use your left hand to lay it on the rock which is the size of your head and then, when it touches your left leg let me know."

"Aye lord, but I do not understand this!"

"You do not need to understand it. If it works, we thank Atticus." I slid the smaller end of the staff down the hole. I felt it move as Erik touched it. Then he gave a yelp. "I take it that is your foot?"

"Aye lord."

"Then let us try. Keep pulling your foot and let me know when it is free." I leaned on the staff. There was some movement but Erik shook his head. He looked almost tearful. I kept forgetting that he had been just a boy when he had first come to us. I looked around.

Haaken shouted, "I can hear the sounds of fighting, Dragonheart. Sámr is in trouble."

"As are we. One problem at a time." I spied a larger rock. "Haaken, roll that rock here and place it close to Erik's head." Haaken had a sceptical look on his face but he obeyed. I had to lift the staff to get the stone underneath but this time the staff was thicker. "Now lean on the end with me."

I put all of my weight on the end. When Haaken added his I heard the staff creak and then saw the joy on Erik's face, "Lord, I can move my foot! I am free!"

"Crawl out. Haaken, we hold this until we see his feet." Erik Shield Bearer rolled clear and we released the staff and I pulled it out quickly. I barely made it in time for dust and small stones flew from the opening as more rocks fell.

"Haaken, see to the boy and I will see if we can follow Sámr to the ship!"

"We told him we would make our way across land."

Ignoring Haaken I went to the place Einar had used to keep watch on the paths and the sea. I saw, immediately, that the three Walhaz ships were sailing along the coast towards the river. I looked down to the trees. I could see, a tiny dot in the distance, the drekar. I could not see Sámr, nor could I see the Walhaz, however, as I looked to the east, I saw another band of armed men. I spied their spears. They looked to be taking the trail which, I assumed, the others had followed. If we attempted to follow Sámr they would catch us and we had an injured youth. We would have to make our own way home. I clambered down.

"Well, how is our hero?"

"His boot appears to have saved him from worse damage."
Erik had a good pair of sealskin boots.

"Can you stand? Here, use my hand to help you up."

He stood and gingerly tried to put his weight on the foot.
Although he winced, he was able to put weight on his toes. "It
hurts but it does not feel broken."

"Then leave your boot on. If we take it off, we may never get it
back on." I handed him my staff. "There are more men coming
and the Walhaz ships are heading for the river. Sámr will have his
work cut out just escaping the ships. We walk."

Haaken looked up at Wyddfa. We were on the lower slopes.
"Up there?"

"No, we head east. The Walhaz must have a settlement further
along but if it led to this path, they would have taken it. We find a
way around the mountain. Haaken, you will be the pack mule and
bring up the rear. Erik can walk between us and I will lead. I will
trust to my ancestors and this mountain."

I slung my cloak about my shoulders and took an ale skin from
Haaken. Erik took a second. It lessened the load. I saw that there
was a path which led around the mountain but it did not appear to
be man-made. If goats had made it then we were in trouble for
they could go where we could not. If, on the other hand, it was
sheep then there was a slight chance that we might just make our
way around. My only plan was to evade the Walhaz and then
make camp. I wanted to be on the eastern side of Wyddfa when
we did so.

We moved off. It was many years since I had done this but my
weekly climb of Old Olaf had kept me in good practice. I walked
slowly and watching for skittering stones, kept a steady pace. Erik
would be moving slower than an old man. As we were on the
south-eastern side of the mountain, we were heading away from
the setting sun. When the trail followed the contours and headed
north that gave me hope that we might evade our enemies but it
meant that darkness would fall soon. The last thing I wanted was
for us to attempt to walk along a path made by sheep in the dark!
That would invite disaster. We walked in silence save for the
occasional murmurs of pain from Erik. When we camped, I would
give him some of my draught. It would help him to sleep.

We descended a little; such a simple action irritated me for we would have to climb again. It sapped energy from already tired legs but, as we rounded a rock I saw a small patch of water. Had it been near to my home then I would have called it a tarn. A tiny stream descended to the east. The hollow was hidden and the sky was already darkening. In light of Erik's injury, I made a decision.

"We camp here!" I saw the look of relief on Erik's face. We reached the water and I spied a large rock. It looked like a man-made chair and before it was a slightly larger rock. "Erik, sit and elevate your foot." Haaken looked at me in surprise. I shrugged, "I listened to Aiden when he tended to men's wounds!" We made our beds and ate food. We drank some ale and then augmented our liquids by filling two of the ale skins from the third and then refilling the ale skin with tarn water. We had almost one hundred and eighty miles to tramp. We would have to be careful with supplies and ale. I wanted Erik to have food and ale before I looked at his foot.

"Erik, we could take off your boot and tend to your wound."

He shook his head, "It is an ache and not a pain. I have not yet risked putting my weight upon it but I believe I could if I had to. I can feel the boot tight about my foot. My foot has swollen. I like these boots and would not see them damaged."

He was right. The boot would act as a bandage. "Then take a swig of this," I handed him the leather flask with the potion. "It will help you sleep." He looked dubious, "Sleep is the best medicine. We have a long and dangerous journey tomorrow. We do not need someone who is tired."

He nodded and took a mouthful. He smiled. Ylva had a way of making her potions palatable. He handed it back and lay down. Even before I had put the flask in my leather satchel he was gently snoring.

"Haaken, this will be hard, let us see what we have."

We laid out all that we had. There were the three skins: two of ale and one of water. Eventually, they would all be water. There was a flask with the potion, a pot jug of vinegar and one of honey. We had a bag of dried venison. Ylva and her women dried blackberries and we had a pouch of those too. We still had some cheese but, as I looked at it, I realised that we would have finished it before we left the mountain. We had three blankets and our cloaks. None of us had brought our sealskin capes and I knew that would prove to be a costly error. We would have rain as we tramped north.

Then I looked at the weapons. I had my sword, my seax and Wolf's Blood, my dagger. Haaken had his sword and two seaxes. Erik had a short sword, a seax and my Saami bow. There were twenty arrows. Ten were for piercing mail while the rest were hunting arrows. Those ten might just keep us alive. When we reached Mercia, we would travel through the woods. That meant we could hunt game.

Haaken stood back and shook his head, "Not a lot, Dragonheart but when we were Erik's age this would have seemed like riches indeed."

I nodded, "We will need to ration. We can fill our skins with water. This mountain has many streams and tarns, we can use Wyddfa's water first. We have nine or ten days of hard marching. We divide the food into ten."

Haaken examined the venison, "Then that means we exist on one piece of dried deer meat a day. That is not a great deal."

"When we are away from danger, we can use Erik's helmet as a pot. If we add greens to the venison, we can make a soup which will sustain us."

Haaken laughed, "We will be travelling through Gwynedd and Mercia. Your idea of danger and mine must be vastly different if you think we will be able to light a fire."

"We have been set a challenge. Let us meet it!"

We began to pack away our supplies. I thought of Sámr. Had he and the ship escaped? If not, then this would all be in vain. I knew that I had created a problem for him. My older men would not understand his leaving me. I had not meant it so but this would be a test of his leadership. Thus far, he had been popular. Now he would have to endure dislike bordering on hatred. Every leader needed to know how to deal with that. He had a clan to lead and not all of the clan would support him. Perhaps that was why the Norns had spun the web they had.

I lay down on my cloak. It was oiled and would stop the damp from penetrating. I undid the bandages on my left hand and smelled the wound. It did not have an unpleasant odour. If it hurt,

I would have to endure it for the potion would need to be used for Erik. I had had worse wounds before. I covered myself with my blanket and closed my eyes. Even before I fell asleep, I heard voices in my head. They came from within the mountain. At first, they were mumblings and were indistinct. Then when I did hear them clearly, I had to concentrate for the accent they had made the Saxon they spoke hard to understand. There were two voices.

'You have done well, Dragonheart, and your journey is almost done. You are of my blood and my land is safe thanks to you.'

'Fear not for Sámr. You chose well in him. He will be safe and he will pass this test. Fear, instead, the men from the east. They plot and they plan. They seek to ensnare you. The last battle is coming and it will be a hard one. Your seat at the Allfather's table is saved but be in no rush to take it.'

'The Land of the Wolf, my land of Rheged, is safe in your hands, Garth, son of Myfanwy. Make it secure for Sámr and Ylva. They are the future.'

And then I drifted off to sleep. My dreams were filled with faces from the past. Warriors I had slain populated them. I saw Danes and Saxons, men of Om Walum and Walhaz. I saw them roll over my hills in uncounted numbers. They held, in their hands, bloody weapons. I descended into a deep black hole and I slept.

When I woke it was not yet dawn. Our little hollow faced east and I saw the thin line of light which heralded its rising. I shook Haaken awake. Erik was still asleep and we left him there. I stood and, as I made water, sniffed the air. If there were Walhaz around then I would smell them just as they would smell us. The food we ate and the clothes we wore determined our smell. It felt safe and so we prepared for our journey. We roused Erik and handed him some cheese, a slice of dried venison and the water skin. We would save the ale skin for the evenings as a reward for our toil. Haaken and I ate the same as Erik and drank from the same skin. Haaken then filled it.

"Well, Erik Shield Bearer, now is the time to test your foot. If you cannot walk then Haaken and I will need to carry you. I give you my staff. Your need is greater than mine. When we reach the forests of Mara and Mondrem we may be able to cut two more for Haaken and I. That should be a day away. Soon we will head downhill but first, let us see if you can walk."

Haaken and I held our hands out and he pulled himself up. His right foot took his weight and he just used the toes on the left foot to balance. I handed him the staff and we stood back. He slowly lowered his foot. I saw pain contort his face as the sole of his swollen left foot touched the ground. He gritted his teeth and then, bravely, took a step. I knew that each step was agony but he took five and stopped. He turned and gave a wan smile, "I cannot run Dragonheart, but I can walk. Perhaps I can keep up!"

"Well done, Erik. We keep the same formation. Haaken One Eye, keep an ear to the rear."

"Aye, Dragonheart. This will give me the chance to compose a saga. This proves, if nothing else, that Norns have a sense of humour. Two old men and a half-crippled boy attempt to walk through the land of their enemies. If we survive then this will be my greatest saga."

There were animals to be seen but we passed no people. Erik helped Haaken compose a song and I watched to the fore. This was the mountain of my blood and I felt at one with it. By noon we had descended to the ridge which marked the valley of the Clwyd. Here there were settlements but we were on the other side of the mountain from those seeking us. We were three cloaked and hooded travellers. Our helmets hung, beneath our cloaks, from our swords. I could speak Saxon and we would have to try to bluff our way through if we were questioned. A sudden breeze came from the south. I smiled. It would help Sámr on his way north. I would be happier if I knew he had reached the Land of the Wolf. Our journey was in our own hands.

We reached the Clwyd valley in the middle of the afternoon. We had spied the spirals of smoke which alerted us to farms. There were no towns or villages. Wrecsam lay to the east of us and St. Asaph lay to the west. The valley itself was without warriors and strongholds. It was why I had chosen this slightly longer route. We could spend the night on the far side of the valley and then head towards Caestir through the mighty forests which I hoped would hide us. We had not stopped save to drink some water. I knew that Erik would have severe hunger pangs. Haaken and I were old men. We did not need as much food.

We were forced to follow trails. Erik could walk, albeit slowly, but only on the flat. It was the trail which almost caused our downfall. We stumbled into a clearing. There was a hut. The wind, which was from the south, had taken the smell of smoke away otherwise we would have had a warning. Even so, we might have escaped had the dog, which guarded the farm, not bared its teeth and barked. A woman appeared at the door of the rude hut. She shouted, "Iago!"

I heard the sound of feet from my right. I said, "Keep your hands from your weapons."

A man of thirty or so summers appeared, he had a wood axe in his hand. He saw us and raised the axe. I showed him my open palms and spoke in Saxon. The Clwyd was so close to the land of Mercia that only those who spoke Saxon could survive. "We are travellers with an injured boy and we mean no harm!"

He seemed surprised that I spoke Saxon but he pointed his axe at me and said, "You are Vikings!"

"And Vikings can travel too." I lowered the hood on my cloak so that he could see I was an old man. "If we meant you harm do you think our swords would still be sheathed? I have coins and we would pay for food, and if you have it, shelter."

Two boys appeared behind him. They each had a hunting bow. I took them to be eight or nine summers. The man looked at the boys and then us. He took in our swords. It did not assuage his fear. Vikings were known to be cunning. However, he realised that I was right. The three of us could easily have taken him.

"What coins do you have?"

I always carried a purse with me. We had Saxon, Hibernian, Frankish and our own minted coins. I had both silver and copper. Moving my hands slowly, so as not to alarm him, I took out my purse and selected five silver pennies. They were Saxon. They had King Egbert's face upon them and they were in good condition. I held out my hand with the coins in the palm. He reached over and almost snatched them from me. He was afraid of us. He bit one. It did not yield. It was not a fake and he grasped them in his palm.

"This will pay for your food but I will not have Vikings sleeping under my roof."

I nodded, "You have a barn or animal shelter?"

He pointed, "We have a milk cow and it has a pen."

"Then that will suffice." I pointedly looked at his axe. "Do we have an understanding?"

He lowered the axe, "Aye. You shall have food."

Haaken had been listening and he said, cheerfully, "And ale! I have a thirst on me!"

The man allowed the ghost of a smile to appear on his lips, "Aye, and ale." He and his sons headed indoors. The woman watched us.

I saw that there was a tiny stream which led down to the Clwyd. It explained why they had chosen this site. Laying down our burden we went to the stream and washed. It seemed, somehow, to put the woman at ease as though our cleanliness was a sign that we were not truly barbarian.

"How is the foot, Erik?"

"It aches. I will be glad to have some potion this night."

"You have done well thus far."

He sat on a log pile, the winter wood for the fire, "I wonder if the drekar escaped." I mused.

I pointed to the north, "It is probably heading along the coast even as we speak. Sámr will be wondering if he ought to land and come for us. I pray that he does not. The Norns have spun. This is their web and we break it at our peril." I took off my cloak. "We will eat here, in the open. It is pleasant here."

"And if someone else comes? The Walhaz who hunted us for example?"

"Haaken One Eye, we both know that it will take time for them to pick up our trail. We will leave before dawn tomorrow for I have no doubt that when King Rhodri's men arrive this farmer will happily tell them all and then they will pursue us."

"Then perhaps we should slit their throats."

I saw the look of horror on Erik's face. Even though we spoke Norse, his eyes still flickered towards the hut where I could smell food being cooked. I shook my head, "I am of an age where the indiscriminate slaughter of innocents is abhorrent to me. We may be caught and that might well result in our death but I think the Allfather would prefer us to kill only warriors."

The woman and the boys brought bowls of food and a jug of ale with three wooden beakers. They laid them on the ground a pace away from us. The husband stood in the doorway. He had a bow in his hand with a nocked arrow. I smiled. We must have really terrified them. The boys hurried back indoors and then came out with three oat loaves.

I smiled at the woman, "Thank you, gammer." Her eyes widened when I used the word. It marked me as having Saxon blood.

"You are welcome." She hesitated, "What are two old Vikings and a lame boy doing here this close to Wyddfa?"

I chose to give her a version of the truth. "It is said that Myrddyn the wizard is buried in a cave close by. We thought to find it. Erik hurt his foot and so we are heading home."

"To the land of the Danes?"

"We go home!"

They could not differentiate between Norse and Danes. If the Walhaz sought us then I wanted their eyes looking east and not north.

She seemed satisfied and returned indoors. The ale and the food were both good. The fact that the food was hot was something we could not have expected when we began our descent of the mountain. Hot food sustains a man more than cold fare. We ate it all and used the bread to wipe the bowls clean. She looked inordinately pleased when she returned with her sons to collect the dishes.

"You enjoyed it?"

"That we did." I took out another two silver pennies. I gave them to her, "These are for you gammer. Visit the market and buy something for yourself."

She grabbed the coins and nodded, "You are not what I expected of Vikings. Are all Vikings like you?"

I shook my head, "You were right to be wary but if we had been Vikings with murder on our mind then all of you would now be dead."

She was a Christian and had a wooden cross. She clutched it and hurried indoors. I heard a bar being put in position. We headed to the cow byre. It was pungent but it was warm. We found a place which did not have dung and, after giving Erik the potion, we made our beds.

Haaken said, as Erik began to snore, "Should one of us stay awake? The man may have murder on his mind."

I laughed, "He and the dog will be sleeping behind the door and it is they who will be terrified of us."

We slept undisturbed and my mind woke me in what felt like the middle of the night. I went outside to make water and saw the sky becoming lighter. We had overslept. I roused the other two and we quickly quitted the cow byre. When we had been eating, I had spied the trail which led north. As we passed the hut the dog began to bark. They would know we were leaving. It could not be helped. All of us were in better condition than when we arrived. We had a chance now!

Dragonheart
Chapter 5
The Chase

We reached the forest not long after dawn. It was a vast forest and stretched across a land half as big as the Land of the Wolf. Crisscrossed with the trails of animals and hunters we had plenty of routes to choose. Erik was still in pain when we walked, but he was now able to put his weight on his foot. I knew that, eventually, we would have to risk taking off his boot to examine his foot. He was loath to do so for he feared losing the boot. We followed the game trail which descended towards what I assumed was a watercourse. It would lead to water of some description and we needed to refill the water skin. We still had two full ale skins. We followed the game trail for, although it was not as easy as walking along the man-made trails, we had less chance of meeting Saxons. We were now in Mercia and there would be thegns and warriors. They would fight first and ask questions later.

We stopped well before dark. The perfect place to camp by the small stream was too good a place to leave. There was enough cover to hide us and the stream had widened so that we could see fish. They were small ones but they could be eaten raw and we could save the dried venison for the journey after the Maeresea. While Haaken tried his hand at fishing I sat Erik on a rock.

"I will try to take your boot off. If it hurts too much, I will stop but we must see what the problem is. If your foot swells and we cannot replace the boot we will make a sandal for you." He nodded. I gave him Wolf's Blood. "Bite on the hilt. It will help you to bear the pain. This will hurt."

He bit on the hilt and I took the heel of his boot in two hands. This had to be done firmly and swiftly. When I touched the boot, I noticed that his foot did not seem as swollen as before. I pulled and saw Erik's eyes widen. It took a good tug but it finally came off. His foot was black. I hoped that it was not the blackness which necessitated amputation. I hoped it was the blackness of heavy bruising. I put my nose to the foot and sniffed. It did not smell as though the wound had gone bad and when I peered at the wound, I could see the blue and yellow of bruising. Three of his toes were broken. That was obvious for they were at an unnatural angle.

"You have broken toes."

"What does that mean, lord?"

I shrugged, "I think they need to be straightened and splinted but it may be beyond my skill. I am no Aiden. Put your foot in the stream. The cold will help the swelling to go down and I can look for something to splint your foot. I fear that you will not be able to put the boot on again any time soon." I handed him the boot and went in search of something to use as a piece of footwear. We had leather thongs but what I needed was a flat piece of wood. "Haaken, I will take the bow. I seek game and I need to find some wood to make a sandal. I think we will risk a fire. We passed no houses and we have walked miles. The only people who would be in the forest are charcoal burners or huntsmen and hunters will return home after dark. I leave you in charge of the camp."

"I am happy. It is many years since I fished."

Now I saw that the Norns had been spinning. There was enough light for me to hunt and to search for wood. The wind was still coming from the south and so I headed due west. That way I would be approaching either game or danger from the darkening east. I had an arrow nocked. I stepped over the stream and then looked for signs of animals. The forest was not silent. Trees, leaves and branches creaked and groaned. Birds and squirrels skittered in the trees and, in the distance, I could hear the sound of animals grazing. I could not see them. That was no surprise. The forest was their natural environment. I stepped carefully gauging each footfall. One of the deer, for I had found a herd, alerted me to their presence by moving. The fact that the animals moved towards me told me that I had not been sensed. I was hunting alone and that meant I would have just one chance for a kill. Whichever animal I managed to hit would have to be the target.

I drew back on the bow for I saw a lighter patch of reddish brown moving towards me. A bird further west suddenly took flight. It was not me which had scared it but it spooked the small herd and they raced towards me. I released at the nearest deer. It was a six-month-old fawn. It was just ten paces from me and the Saami bow was the most powerful of bows. It drove the arrow through the skull and killed it instantly. I was in danger of being trampled and so I waved my arms and shouted. If I was heard it could not be helped. The herd split and ran along the two sides of me. The fawn had died instantly. I slung it over my shoulder and nocked another arrow. If a hunter had heard me then I had to be ready. I made my way back to the trail I had left. I noticed something unusual as I closed with the path to the camp and the stream. I saw bones.

I laid the fawn down and made my way to the jumble of rocks. I saw the remains of a skeleton. It had been a man. I say man for there was a broken belt and, attached to it was a gnawed and chewed scabbard with a rusting seax in it. This had been a Saxon warrior; I knew not how long he had been there. In theory, it could have been there longer than I had been alive. I saw that there was a hole in the top of the skull. Someone had driven a weapon down on to the top of it. He had not been wearing a helmet. I spied a piece of wood which could have been the shaft of his spear. I knew that if I searched, I would find the spearhead. I was about to turn when a thought struck me. If he had a spear then he might have had a shield. I put the bow and arrow on the rock and dropped to my hands and knees. It did not take long. I felt around and found what had been a smooth piece of wood. I lifted up the remains of a small Saxon shield. It had not been well made and that was a good thing. Three pieces of wood were held in place by a fourth. I picked it up, slung my bow over my shoulder and hefted the fawn on my back. I had the makings for sandals!

I could smell the fire but only when I was within one hundred paces of it. Haaken had managed to find some dry wood. Erik still dangled his foot in the water. "We have meat and I can make footwear. Keep your foot in the water. Does it feel better?"

"Aye, lord and it is not as swollen."

"You will have to endure more pain soon. Are those fish cooked?"

Haaken nodded, "They are not very big but they will take the edge off our appetite until the deer is cooked."

"Good." I handed Erik the remains of the shield, "Haaken, divide the food. Erik, use your knife and shape this to that of your foot. Make it slightly bigger. The best way is to take your foot from the stream, stand on the wood and you will have the wet imprint of your foot. I will do the rest."

I first skinned the deer. I laid it with the bloody inside uppermost. Then I roughly butchered the animal. I put the heart, kidneys and liver on to cook. Haaken had laid the fish on the three pieces of wood Erik was not using and I greedily ate the fish while cutting the meat into chunks which would cook quicker. We had no salt, even so, the meat might last us until we got home. That would depend upon what else the Norns had spun! The offal soon cooked and I was able to put skewers made from branches through the deer meat to cook it. I cut the meat as small as I could to cook it quickly. I sliced up the heart, kidneys and liver. They were delicious. I gave the majority of the food to Erik, it was he who needed the food the most. He would have to endure pain when I broke his toes once again. I had worked out how to do this. I would use fresh deerskin. If we all made water on it then that would begin the curing process. I would use the offcuts from the sandal Erik was making to hold the broken toes in place. I would tie the cut piece of deerskin around the two pieces of wood. When it dried it would tighten. The last part would be to tie the wooden sole to the soft deerskin. I hoped it would work but he could not walk barefoot and I did not want him to try to put the boot back on just yet.

We ate, by the light from our fire, with Erik's foot dangling in the stream. We cooked all of the meat. Then Haaken and I made water on the deerskin and I used Wolf's Blood to cut out the piece I would need to cover the foot. When I was ready, we took Erik's foot from the water and I made him lie down. I gave him the sword that was touched by the gods to hold. "This will help but I will not lie. You will have to endure pain such as you have never experienced."

"I know!"

I bent his knee so that his left foot was flat against the deerskin. I carefully placed one piece of wood beneath the toes. The three broken ones were at an unnatural angle. "Haaken put your weight across his chest."

I took each broken toe and quickly straightened it. The first one, the largest of the three cracked. I heard a muffled cry from beneath Haaken's body. I worked quickly and soon all three were flat. They would never look normal again but they would heal. I put the other piece of wood on the top and then quickly tied, as tightly as I could, the thongs I had made.

"You can get up now Haaken." I took my sword from Erik's fingers. "You did well. When you go to battle this will stand you in good stead. I will wait until the morrow to fit your sandal. You have endured enough pain this night. Here," I offered him the flask. He took two swallows. I hoped that there would be enough for he would have pain until Ylva could heal him; if we ever reached home.

He was soon asleep. Haaken took the last of the deer meat we had cooked then he began to cover the fire with soil. While he did so I took off my bandage and looked at the wound in my left hand. It was beginning to scab over. I would risk using it without a bandage the next day. I had found it awkward to gut the fawn.

Haaken came over, "We have alerted our enemies enough. I know you said there were none nearby but that farmer will have told someone by now and all they need to do is look towards this forest and see this spiral of smoke."

"It is dark now. We will leave before dawn. I know we took a risk but now that his toes are set, he will be able to walk quicker. Two days from now, when we are north of the Maeresea, we can put on his boot."

"Perhaps." Haaken looked down at him. "I will say this for him, he is tough and brave. If the Allfather had graced me with a son then I would have wanted one like Erik."

"Be his foster father! I have raised sons, grandsons and great-grandsons. Erik can be the son you never had."

Haaken smiled, "Perhaps. Let us get north of the Maeresea first, eh?"

"There is something else, Haaken. When we were at Wyddfa I dreamed. There is danger from the east, I fear the Danes will return."

"We should have sailed after them when they came last. Dead men do not wreak revenge!"

He was right but it was too late for that now.

I woke before dawn. I made water and then began to gather up our belongings. I woke Haaken, "I will wake Erik and fit his sandal. Let us hope he can walk."

Erik murmured, "I am awake and I will walk, lord. I have held you up enough. Last night my dreams were filled with images of those at home and they were cursing me for being the cause of your loss."

"Erik, this is the work of the Norns! Here let me fit your sandal and then we try to walk."

The crude wooden sole was tied with leather thongs. Haaken and I had made holes for them to pass through. They held the wood firmly against the deerskin.

I held out my hand, "Let us try, eh?"

I pulled and he rose. He could not use the technique of balancing on his big toe and he had to put the weight on the wood. It appeared to work. He smiled, "It aches but that is all."

"Good, then we have over twenty miles to go this day. We cross the Dee and then the Maeresea. We now need to head east!" I handed him the hornbeam staff which had proved so invaluable.

The Dee would be an easy river to cross for it was shallow and there were muddy islands to break up our crossing but the Maeresea would prove more difficult. There was a ford which lay almost twenty miles from the sea. The Mercians guarded it. If we were to cross there then Erik would have to be able to fend for himself. That was more than twenty miles away but we had full bellies and Erik was more cheerful than at any time since the rock fell on his foot. We strode off.

When a warrior walks in a forest, he becomes attuned to the sounds. Birds could be heard in the distance, and then, as we came closer, they were silenced. It was in those silences that you heard the sounds from further afield and we were close to a tiny hamlet, almost on the banks of the Dee, when we heard dogs. They were far away but they were there, nonetheless. The men of

King Rhodri had followed us. I was almost flattered. They had risked Mercia and the Saxons who lived there. I knew that the river was just ahead; perhaps less than half a mile. I had no idea if we could cross it for I only had a vague idea where the ford lay but we would have to try.

I took the bow from Erik. He had insisted upon carrying it. "Erik, find the river. It is ahead of us. We need to cross it. Haaken and I will be behind you."

"I can fight!"

"And you can heed my orders! Find the river. This is warrior work!"

He hobbled off. He was moving better but he was still not fast. Haaken said, "How do we deal with them?"

"We run until we hear them. I stand in the trail and use arrows. You stay behind a tree and surprise them!"

"So we play the pair of mad old fools then?"

I laughed, "It has served us well up to now!"

We had allowed Erik some little time to get ahead of us and now we ran. I could now hear the dogs. They were much closer. I never liked killing dogs but, if we had to then I would. My life was unimportant but Erik was young. Haaken and I would do all that we could to keep him alive. That was the difference between a Viking leader and a Saxon. A Saxon king, prince or thegn would gladly sacrifice any who were of a lower status. A Viking leader would not. We owed our people as much duty as they owed us. That was our way.

The trail we followed was almost a road; it had a compacted surface. I could smell smoke. There were houses ahead and I hoped that they had no warriors within them! It was not for us but Erik was in no condition to fight his way to the river. The shrubs and trees which lined the trail had open fields on one side and what looked as though it had been an orchard on the other. Erik suddenly appeared. He was grey-faced for the effort had taken much out of him but he also looked happy.

"Lord, there is a hamlet just four hundred paces west but there is a ford. The river has an island in the middle. I think we could wade and then swim a little."

"Good! Then get across. We will be behind you."

He turned and hobbled towards the river which we could now smell. The dogs were much closer now. I nodded to Haaken. He ran to the largest of the trees. It had leaves and hid him. I took out the sword that was touched by the gods. The dogs would reach us first and then the men following. Dogs could always outrun men!

They were hunting hounds. Not as big as a wolfhound, they were big enough. I took a wide stance. In the distance, I saw five Walhaz warriors. Three had helmets, spears and swords. Two were the handlers and just had swords. I shouted, "Five!"

The two dogs spied me and they came towards me. They had teeth for tearing and they would kill me if they could. As with all warriors, canine and man, one was the leader and he came on ahead of the other. He leapt at me. I swung my sword and took his head. I was spattered by his blood. I immediately back swung and the second almost reached me but my sword hacked his body in two. I stuck the sword in the ground and picked up the bow and the arrow. I nocked it and aimed. In the time it had taken to kill the dogs and aim, the five Walhaz had come closer and were less than one hundred paces from me. Obligingly, they had all stayed together. I sent my first arrow at the chest of the leading warrior. It was an arrow which could pierce mail and he did not wear mail. It tore through his body and was only stopped by the fletch. I nocked a second and sent it at the second warrior. They had their shields around their backs and now tried to pull them around. My arrow hit the second warrior in the shoulder and spun him around. I picked up my sword as the three ran at me. The two dog handlers had faces filled with fury. I had killed their dogs. I slipped out Wolf's Blood as Haaken sprang his ambush and hacked across the chest of one dog handler. The sword tore through to his internal organs. I fended off the spear with my sword and drove Wolf's Blood up under the rib cage of the last true warrior. Haaken's sword sliced down and split the last Walhaz down his back. I sheathed my sword, picked up the bow and ran. We had pushed our luck enough. Whatever treasure the men had would stay with them. Our lives were more important.

Erik was on the other side of the river and we half swam and half waded across. We had passed the easy barrier and now we had to get to the Maeresea. We had lost the Walhaz, now we had to evade Mercians. The dead Walhaz warriors would be found and the Saxons would seek us! Before we set off, we rearranged the gear we carried. I handed the Saami bow back to Erik. He could use it. We cleaned our blades in the river, dried and then sheathed them. Once that was done, I took the lead. I had never been in this land before. I had sailed up the Maeresea but the land this far east of Caestir was a mystery to me. I would have to rely on the sun and my instincts. I would be navigating across an unknown land.

Dragonheart
Chapter 6
The Mercians

We headed east along the trail but this time I was acutely aware that there would be more people using the river trail and we would have to be very wary. The road led to the bridge. There would be merchants with goods to trade. The King's messengers would use the road. King Beorhtwulf warred against Powys but he needed his northern border secure. There would be armed men on the road. Each time we heard horses we took cover and we were lucky. The travellers who passed us were oblivious to our presence for we were well hidden. It did, however, slow us up.

I kept us north by east but I followed whatever trails we could. Sometimes the path I thought would go north and east turned back on itself and then we would have to go across country. That normally meant across fields and we risked being seen. There were isolated farms and huts. We steered clear of those. Erik's new footwear appeared to be working well. Certainly, he did not complain. It was coming on to dark when we found the river but we were still too far to the west. The river was too wide to be crossed. Darkness approached. As much as I wished to, we could go no further. We camped close to the water but we had no fire. We huddled close together in the miniscule clearing we had found in a patch of brambles. It afforded some protection and it hid us from view. It was twenty paces from the trail which ran along the river.

As we huddled together and enjoyed cold comfort Erik voiced his fears, "Lord, how do we get across this river?"

"There is a wooden bridge but there are Saxons who live on both sides of it. They would not allow three Vikings to cross in daylight."

"Then that will add another day for us. Each day increases the risk of being caught."

"I know Haaken One Eye. This is a web spun by the Norns is it not?"

Erik peered through the brambles, "Could we not build a raft lord? I know that here the river is too wide to risk a raft but see, there is driftwood which is caught on the bank. It need not be a large raft. Erik Short Toe told me that even a small piece of wood can bear a heavy weight. If we were to put our swords on a small raft, we could propel the raft across the river."

His idea had merit and he was right. We could even risk such a raft in daylight for we might be taken for a piece of driftwood. We could disguise it with foliage, "A good idea, Erik, but your foot might be a problem."

"It feels better and the cold water of the river might help. I will not hinder you. I have been the cause of enough trouble as it is."

Haaken shook his head, "No, Erik, you have been no trouble. There are three sisters who are responsible for all of our problems."

I clutched my amulet. It did not do to provoke the Norns.

We rose before dawn and continued east, along the river. We were getting closer to the bridge and that meant Saxons. It was noon when I saw the river narrow and, at the same time, the river trail became a better surface and turned slightly south. I saw why. There was a hill and a small palisade. The Saxons had a watchtower of sorts. I guessed it was to keep watch for Vikings but once more our luck held. As we watched we realised that the tower was unoccupied and I knew why. It had been some years since we had raided this land. We left the road and headed through a tangle of trees and scrubby bushes to the river. There was a beach and an overhanging willow shielded us from the palisaded watchtower and the road. Even better was the sight of some logs which had jammed against the bank.

"Perfect! We can make a raft or a vessel of some kind and float across the river. We do not need to use the bridge. We camp here. You two collect the logs and I will seek the bindings for the raft."

Haaken said, "You wish to risk crossing in daylight?"

I pointed to the river. "It might only be two hundred paces across but there is a current. Would you risk drifting in the dark?

See across the river, there is a beach there. We are going to head for that and we need daylight to do so." It was a risk but we had to take it.

I left my helmet and my cloak at the camp. I took out my seax. What I needed required cutting. When we had left the road, I had spied some ivy and some honeysuckle. There were no flowers yet on the honeysuckle and it would be easy to weave. I cut plenty of both and headed back to the camp. Erik and Haaken were still trying to drag logs to the beach and Erik was handicapped by his foot. If a ship came up or down the river then we would be spotted but I could not think of any other way to build a raft. I began to weave the ivy and honeysuckle into ropes. I made eight lengths. Both the ivy and the honeysuckle were tough, especially when they were woven. As I did so I smiled. Perhaps I was becoming a galdramenn for I was weaving and this spell might just be our salvation.

Noon came and went. We began to bind the logs. While we did so I had Erik cut down small branches and thicker twigs to help disguise us. We worked fast for I intended to cross before dark. We needed enough light to see the beach and yet we had to be hidden from the Saxons. I needed darkness to fall as soon as we reached the northern bank.

We ate while we could. We had already drunk one of the ale skins and so we drank water. We would not fill it here in this river. The Saxons were upstream and the quality of the water was in doubt. When we headed north and west, I hoped we would find better quality water. We risked loading the raft in the late afternoon and we disguised it. We took off our boots and laid them on the raft along with our food, weapons, helmets and cloaks. We even contemplated removing our breeks but decided against it. When we saw the sun lowering in the sky to the west, we slipped into the water. We had Erik between us. He wore just the deerskin boot. We would examine the foot before we left the next morning.

The river felt like ice, although, in reality, it was not. We pushed our improvised boat into the water. The current would take us downstream and so, to reach our beach we aimed the raft upstream. I was on the right and I kept watch for Saxons as Haaken and I kicked our legs to propel us. We had done a good job of disguise but the fact that we were sailing against the current would draw attention to us.

We had almost made it to the shore when Haaken said, "Saxon ship, heading upstream."

I turned my head and saw a small Saxon ship. It was about two hundred paces from us. Haaken had not seen it earlier. I could not blame him. He only had one eye but this could prove disastrous.

"Kick harder. Mayhap they might not see us."

It was a forlorn hope for I knew that we had been seen. We would not have a leisurely camp, as I had hoped. We would have to move as soon as we landed. When the Saxon reached the nearest settlement then the garrison would be alerted.

Once we reached the beach, we quickly emptied the raft and then pushed it into the river. The Saxon had passed us but if the captain reported the raft, they would search for it. The Saxon ship had not seen exactly where we landed. Any delay would help us. Haaken and I dressed quickly.

"Erik, do you wish to try to put on your boot?"

"Now is as good a time as any, lord." He untied the thongs holding the deerskin. The foot was almost black at the end where the toes lay. This time the toes looked almost straight. The splint might have worked.

Haaken suddenly said, "Put the deerskin back on for, if your foot is like mine, it has shrunk. The splints will keep the toes straight. You might have pain but your toes will heal."

Haaken was right. The cold had made my foot shrink too. Erik did as Haaken had suggested and replaced the deerskin. Then Haaken and I pulled on his boot. It did hurt the boy. I saw the pain on his face but he bore the pain stoically. He stood and winced when he put his foot down. He took a couple of tentative steps. He smiled, "It is easier than with the wooden sandal." He strapped on his sword, slung his bow and took his staff. "I am ready, lord!" He had courage; he was a brave Viking.

The ground rose to our left and we headed in that direction. Higher ground would help us for it would allow us to see our enemies. We headed into the last light of the setting sun. We now just had the Belisima and the Ēa Lōn to cross and we would be home. If the Mercians did not follow us then we had just four or five days before we would see the Land of the Wolf. We headed along the trail. The wheel ruts told us that it was used by people and we would, more than likely, have to pass a settlement. That could not be helped. We needed speed and travelling in the dark could only be contemplated upon a good road surface.

People did not travel at night. There was no need and it was always too dangerous to do so. That allowed us to move confidently. The path we trod was well worn and well used; during the day we would be seen and so we moved in the dark. We smelled the settlement before we stumbled upon it. It was the smell of animal and human dung. It was the smell of woodsmoke. I spied a stream and we headed down to it. It was shallow and we walked along the edge. In places, we had to wade up it but we were hidden. When I deemed we had passed the settlement we left the stream. We filled the empty ale skin with water and topped up the water skin. We had enough to reach the Belisima now. We had lost the road and, when we emerged from the undergrowth, I decided to look for somewhere to camp. By my estimate, we were two or three miles from the river. There were clouds and we risked becoming lost in the dark. I spied, ahead a wood. We had not passed through one nor seen one on our way from the river and so I determined that it had to be north of us. We made the safety of its eaves and worked our way in until we found a clearing. We made a cold camp.

Erik was soon asleep for I gave him almost the last of the potion. He was sleeping with the boot on and his foot would swell. It would hurt but, as Haaken pointed out, he had more chance of a life with toes which might work!

"Let me ask you, Dragonheart, while the boy is asleep. Was all of this so that Sámr could learn to be a leader?"

I did not answer immediately for Haaken, who knew me better than any man alive, had understood the way the Norns shaped my decisions, "I hoped that there would be some event which would make Sámr have to lead without me yet I did not and do not wish death. I would certainly not wish my oldest friend die just to prove a point. Nor would I wish this brave boy to die just to make Sámr stronger. I think the Allfather might have read my mind. We could not have left Erik."

"No, but we could have followed Sámr down the mountain. It would have been no riskier than this."

"When he reaches home, he will find others who question his decisions and question his authority. If we are spared, and I pray that we are, then that will show me where the cracks in my land lie. I have my suspicions but they are vague and indistinct."

"And if we are not spared?"

"Then Sámr will have to rely upon my advice from the spirit world."

Haaken nodded. He understood me and my motives.

I woke first. It seemed to be my lot for although the wound in my hand no longer troubled me, I suspected that some ache woke me early each day. Erik had the potion to numb his pain. I saw the sun appear and so I knew which was the east. I confirmed it with the moss on the trees which marked the north. While I knew where the east and the north lay, I woke the others. I wanted to begin our march and mark a line north and west. If nothing else it would bring us to the coast and if I saw the coast then I could follow the beach all the way home. The wood we had found was a large one. As we left it, I saw that there were ploughed fields and a farm. To the north and east lay a hill. A field boundary led to it and it was marked by a line of hawthorn. It would provide a windbreak for the crops. For us, it was sent by the Allfather for we could use it for cover. The problem was getting from the wood to the hawthorn and that would prove difficult for we had open ground to cover. It was as we ran that I heard a cry. I turned and saw a thrall pointing at us. A man sat astride a horse and looked at us. He was half a mile away but I knew, from his horse, that he was a thegn or a noble. We were crossing his land and he would want to know why. The die was cast. I knew that we had almost twenty or more miles before the Belisima. We could not stop again. Would Erik's foot hold up to the punishment it was about to receive?

The land over which we travelled helped us. There were farms and ploughed fields but there were also higher pieces of ground and small streams which were not an obstacle and gave us cover. Although it was harder work, I took us up the small conical shaped hill. In truth, it was not much of a hill. The path from The Water to Hawk's Roost was higher. What it did do was to give us a good view of the land around and there was enough undergrowth and rocks littering its slopes to hide us. Three men were hard to see.

Erik was in pain when we reached the top and sat in the lee of the little peak. "Have some ale. I will see if we are pursued."

Haaken gave him the ale skin and I looked, first east, where I saw nothing and then south. There I saw sunlight glinting from a helmet. I saw spears and I saw a man on a horse. There were just thirty men but that was ten times our number. They were two miles away. They would soon eat into our lead and we could not go any faster than we had been. I stared at them. My eyes were not what they were but I did not see mail byrnies. I saw that some men had spears but the others carried weapons which did not glint. These were not warriors as such. They would be led by a noble and his men, perhaps four or five of them would we well-armed. It was a small thing but knowing your enemy's strengths and weaknesses was never a waste.

I turned and looked west. There was nothing in that direction and I pointed. "We head there. We have the rest of a long day to prove that a Viking can run further than a Saxon."

As Erik nodded and gritted his teeth, I saw a warrior emerging. Erik was learning that a Viking often had to face overwhelming odds but he did not give in. He would keep up with the two old warriors even if it killed him.

As we ran down the slope Haaken began to sing!

The Dragonheart sailed with warriors brave
To find the child he was meant to save
With Haaken and Ragnar's Spirit
They dared to delve with true warrior's grit
Beneath the earth they bravely went
With the sword by Odin sent
Dragonheart and Haaken bravely roar
The Jarl and Haaken and the Ulfheonar
In the dark the witch grew strong
Even though her deeds were wrong
A dragon's form she took to kill
Dragonheart faced her still
He drew the sword touched by the god
Made by Odin and staunched in blood

Dragonheart and Haaken bravely roar
The Jarl and Haaken and the Ulfheonar
With a mighty blow he struck the beast
On Dragonheart's flesh he would not feast
The blade struck true and the witch she fled
Ylva lay as though she were dead
The witch's power could not match the blade
The Ulfheonar are not afraid
Dragonheart and Haaken bravely roar
The Jarl and Haaken and the Ulfheonar
And now the sword will strike once more
Using all the Allfather's power
Fear the wrath you Danish lost
You fight the wolf and pay the cost
Dragonheart and Haaken bravely roar
The Jarl and Haaken and the Ulfheonar

I joined in and sang with him. Erik did not know it but he tried to sing and when I saw him grin, I knew that Haaken's words were working. Singing helped you to breathe and we ran in rhythm. The same rhythm which aided us when rowing helped us when we ran. We ran down a slope but we ran together. The words inspired us. Haaken and I had been in the witch's cave and we had saved Ylva. It had turned Haaken's hair white and it was a defining moment in our lives. We had faced a Norn and we had not been defeated. That was a victory!

We could not see our pursuers and that meant that they could not see us. I led and I looked for a deviation which might throw them off the scent. They were like hounds hunting us and we were superior for we were the wolves! The song gave speed to our legs. I had no idea how much of a lead we had but the fact that it felt like we were leading was enough.

We ran and it was the steady run of men who knew they could run until the sun fell and then run some more. I did not know how Erik, with broken toes, managed it but it showed that he was a Viking! I did not glance back for that would avail us nothing. If they caught us then that would be *wyrd*. If I turned, they would see my face and know that we feared them. We did not. The ground fell and rose. We followed trails and greenways because they were the safest. We kept heading north and west when we could and north when we could not. We were forced to run through huddles of huts but our pounding feet and the swords at our sides told the Saxons who inhabited them that we were best avoided. They stayed within doors.

It was in the late afternoon and we had begun to climb towards the ridge that lay ten miles south of the Belisima when I heard the sound of hooves. They were not galloping but they were louder than the feet of the men running behind it. I could hear Erik's breath. It sounded laboured. Despite our age, Haaken and I knew how to run. We needed to find somewhere to fight. I saw that there was a rise ahead and a small wood. It was not even a wood; it was a copse of about ten trees but it could be used.

"We head for the trees. When we get there, Erik, nock an arrow. When I give the command then you send your arrows at those with weapons. Haaken and I will keep them from you. When all your arrows are spent then use your sword and die well!"

"Aye, lord!"

Haaken laughed, "And even better, if you can live well then you will hear the saga I sing of you, Erik Black Toes!"

"And that I will do!"

I reached the copse first and I dropped the ale skin, cloak and supplies. Donning my helmet, I drew my sword and stood between two beech trees. Erik ran through to the pair of trees behind me. I looked at the pursuers. They were half a mile behind us. We could have run further but there was nowhere better to fight. This was a good place to defend. We had the time to get a good footing and prepare ourselves. I held Wolf's Blood and the sword that was touched by the gods. I wished I had had my shield. It was not because I could use it to defend myself but because I could bang it and make the Saxons fear me.

As they formed a crude shield wall, three hundred paces from us, I raised my sword and shouted, in Saxon, "I am Jarl Dragonheart of the Clan of the Wolf! I wield the sword touched by the gods! I have slain Saxon kings and Saxon champions! Fill your breeks for all of you will die this day!"

Haaken chanted and banged his sword off his seax.

Ulfheonar never forget
Ulfheonar never forgive
Ulfheonar fight to the death
Ulfheonar never forget
Ulfheonar never forgive
Ulfheonar fight to the death

I was gratified when some of those who were at the rear of this pitiful attempt at a shield wall, stopped. The thegn dismounted and took his place at the fore of his oathsworn and three others who had shields. I heard him shout, "This is an old man! He is a Viking and a barbarian. We will kill him and put his head upon a pole! The priests will praise us for we do God's work!"

Erik had not understood any of this. Haaken said, "Do not worry, Erik! They are pissing their breeks. Aim true. The thegn wears leather mail. Choose a good arrow and he will die."

"Aye, Haaken, I will not let you down and I am sorry I brought you all to this."

"This was meant to be and the sun has not yet set. Our bones are still within our bodies and our hearts beat with Viking hearts."

The Saxon thegn pointed his sword and roared, "For God and King Beorhtwulf."

"Wait, Erik!"

The Saxons marched. The only shields they had were in the front rank and they were their best warriors. Only four of the second rank had spears and the rest had improvised pole weapons. There were six warriors and the rest were farmers. If Erik could disable three then Haaken and I had a chance. I wanted to give Erik the best chance and I waited until they were one hundred and fifty paces from us.

"Now Erik!"

He released too quickly. His arrow struck the warrior next to the thegn. The arrow hit his shoulder and disabled him but I had wanted the thegn out of the battle. The thegn raised his shield and Erik's second arrow thudded into it. His third arrow was his best. He hit a warrior in the face and he fell. When he hit the man behind then all semblance of a shield wall disappeared. His fourth arrow struck the right hand of another warrior. Three warriors were out of the battle. It was all that I had hoped. The warriors with the shields kept them in the air to avoid the arrows. Erik sent his next arrows at those without shields.

The six best warriors had been thinned and there were just three warriors to be feared who remained but Haaken and I had no mail. The thegn came directly for me. He rammed his sword at me and I deflected it with my dagger. I hacked at his leg with Ragnar's Spirit and was rewarded with a cry as I bit into his thigh with my blade. Haaken had two men to fight.

Erik was now too close to use his bow and he discarded it. He drew his sword and bravely stepped next to Haaken to defend my friend. The rest of the Saxons were emboldened for they saw just three men. They ran at us. They would surround us and we would die. This was the end of Dragonheart but it would be a glorious end. I would die with a sword in my hand. I would be with my oldest friend and my newest friend. My land was safe and secure with Sámr. I had left my land in good hands and it was a good day to die!

I lunged with my dagger at the thegn's eye. Perhaps he was distracted by his wound for my dagger entered his orb and he fell to the ground.

For some reason that enraged the two young warriors behind him and they threw themselves at me. They had no skill but there was a flurry of blows. I deflected most of them but then, as Haaken slew one of the thegn's oathsworn he fell and hit my left shoulder. I lost my balance and I fell. I lay with my arms outstretched as the two young warriors raised their spears to stick me like a pig. Even as I raised my arms to defend myself, I knew that I would be too late. I would die.

Sámr
Chapter 7
The River and the Sea

I hated to leave the Dragonheart. In fact, I was going to break my oath and stay with him but for a voice I heard in my head. I was about to refuse when I sensed a presence in my ear. I did not recognise it and it appeared to speak our words like a Walhaz but they came from inside the mountain, '*Leave him for he is the Dragonheart and the Allfather protects him. Save your ship. Save your men, heir to the Dragonheart.*' That decided me and I followed my three men as they hurtled down the trail. The worst thing we could do would be to relax. The three we had left at the rock fall were being sacrificed so that we would reach the drekar and save the life of the Dragonheart's daughter. It was ironical, we hurtled down the mountain like rocks in an avalanche. It was a rock fall which had begun this.

I heard shouts from the east. The Walhaz were closing for the paths converged. If we had delayed but a heartbeat then we might have been caught. As it turned out, one of the Walhaz, younger and fitter than the others suddenly burst from the trail to our left. Sven of the Water was leading and he whipped out his seax and gutted the young warrior before he even had time to shout. He did not pause. I drew my sword and dagger even though it was harder to run with weapons. If one had made it then the others would be close behind. I was the last man and I would be the one in danger. The afternoon was slipping by and I could hear feet pounding on the trail behind me. When stones began to skitter and scatter behind me then I knew they were closing. I yelled, "Whatever happens to me, keep going! Save the drekar! Have archers ready!" I knew not if they heard me and I doubted that they would obey me but I had tried. We were running through trees now and the trail twisted and turned down the slope. I saw, ahead, a thicker tree than the rest. Behind me, I could hear feet. As soon as I reached the tree I stopped and turned. I faced up the trail and saw two Walhaz warriors ahead of the rest. They carried spears. As they neared the tree and slowed to take the turn, I stepped out and brought my sword across the shoulder and neck of the first man. He shouted as he died. The second whipped his spear around and I blocked it with a backhand sweep of my sword. The head of the spear and the blade rang out as they clashed. The Walhaz shouted something. My dagger drove up under his ribs and he fell. I saw that there were more than fifteen men coming down the trail. This was more than the original number Stig Sword Hand had seen. I ran down the trail.

The short break had helped me to regain my breath. I risked sheathing my sword and transferred the dagger to my right hand. My fear now was that darkness would fall before I reached the open ground just above the river. If that happened then I risked either becoming lost or falling and hurting myself. I barely made the bank. I heard the river before I saw it. My men had obeyed me and I had run the last couple of miles alone. I was glad I had not worn my mail. Had I done so then I would have been caught already. I saw that the trail was not the same one we had taken up the mountain. Perhaps I had taken a wrong turning. The drekar lay like a beached whale some half a mile downstream. I ran. The river bank was slightly flatter but there were still rocks and I had to concentrate on finding a safe place for my feet.

I did not notice the eight Walhaz warriors who burst out of the trees to my right. They were closer to the drekar than I was and they must have followed the proper trail. Behind me, I heard a shout as more Walhaz emerged from the woods. I had to draw my sword again. I would have to fight to regain my ship. I ran as close to the river as I could manage. The water would protect at least one side when I fought, outnumbered. We were converging. The Walhaz were not running for the ship but for me. That saved me. They did not see Stig of the Water leading ten warriors from the drekar nor the other six I could see at the steering board with bows. It was a twilight darkness through which we ran. We could still see each other but details were blurred. I could not slow for there was another group behind me. I pulled my right arm back as I ran towards the Walhaz. My archers sent arrows towards the

Walhaz. They erred on the side of caution for fear of hitting me. One Walhaz was hit in the arm and his cry made them turn. They saw Stig and his men just twenty paces from them and they hesitated. In that hesitation lay hope!

Roaring, "Clan of the Wolf!" I slashed my sword across the middle of the warrior with a spear. As he jabbed with it, I used my dagger to flick the head up and my sword sliced into his side. Then Stig and my men hit the rear of the Walhaz. They were torn between me and the new enemy. I blocked a sword with my dagger and hacked with my own sword. It struck a shield. I was wearing my helmet. It had a simple nasal. I headbutted the Walhaz and he fell to the ground. I stamped on his face as I stepped over him.

I heard Ráðgeir shout, "Hurry, Lord Sámr. There are ships downstream!"

We were trapped. The archers scattered the ones heading downstream and the survivors from Stig's attack ran to join them. We were pulled aboard. Ráðgeir, who was now the senior warrior aboard, looked at me, "Dragonheart?"

"He commanded us to leave him and we obeyed."

"But he is…"

I held up my hand. Within I was a maelstrom and I did not need to be reminded that I had left my great grandfather behind. "I know who he is! He is my great grandfather and I obeyed him as you will obey me. We have to escape this web of the Norns." I held the ruby, "We have that which we sought. Let us not make his sacrifice, if sacrifice it is, to be in vain! Ulf how do we escape them?"

"It is low tide. We barely have a handspan of water beneath our keel. It is almost fully dark and we sail from the east. My plan is to sail quickly through them. We have not raised the mast yet and we will be hard to see. They have their masts and will find it hard to turn." He spoke quietly, "Trust to the men of the clan, Sámr Ship Killer."

"A good plan. Run out the oars! We trust to the river, to the ship and to the spirit of the Clan of the Wolf!"

I took an oar with Baldr. We now had more men rowing than when we had fled these same three ships. Ulf stamped on the deck to give us our beat. We were in his hands now. He would have to

74

judge his moments well. As we started down the incredibly narrow river, I wondered how the Walhaz would be feeling. We had hurt one of their ships and humiliated the others. We risked all in this bold move. Would the Dragonheart have ordered Ulf to do what we were about to attempt? I shook my head as Baldr and I pulled on the oar. The Dragonheart had taught me that all men were different. His son had been different from his grandson and I would be as different. I had made my decision and I would have to live with it. If that meant I was not to be the lord of the Land of the Wolf then so be it. I was my own man. I had sired a son and, possibly, a second. I had cast the bones and we would see how they fell.

It was a while since I had rowed. I knew that there would be a burn across my back when I thought I could row no more but I would have to push beyond that invisible barrier. Vikings could row further than their enemies thought. They could row faster than they expected. That was one of our secret weapons. Another was that we never gave up. I knew that we had drawn the pursuers from my great grandfather to us. They would climb the mountain when dawn broke to try to find them but the Dragonheart was the greatest Viking of his age, perhaps of any age. If there was a warrior who could evade them then it was him. As we stroked again, I thought of the voice I had heard. I worked out that it had to be Myrddyn. He had spoken in Walhaz. It was his tomb and he was the greatest wizard, ever! That he had spoken to me told me that I was destined for something more than an ignominious death in this obscure little river close to Wyddfa.

Ulf shouted, "Ship's boys, make your arrows count. Rowers you can sing for they see us now. When I shout, *in oars*, then be speedy else you might lose an eye!" Splintered oars were notorious for taking out eyes.

I began to sing! I sang the song of the sword!

> *The storm was wild and the gods did roam*
> *The enemy closed on the Prince's home*
> *Two warriors stood on a lonely tower*
> *Watching, waiting for hour on hour.*
> *The storm came hard and Odin spoke*
> *With a lightning bolt the sword he smote*

Ragnar's Spirit burned hot that night
It glowed, a beacon shiny and bright
The two they stood against the foe
They were alone, nowhere to go
They fought in blood on a darkened hill
Dragon Heart and Cnut will save us still
Dragon Heart, Cnut and the Ulfheonar
Dragon Heart, Cnut and the Ulfheonar
The storm was wild and the Gods did roam
The enemy closed on the Prince's home
Two warriors stood on a lonely tower
Watching, waiting for hour on hour.
The storm came hard and Odin spoke
With a lightning bolt the sword he smote
Ragnar's Spirit burned hot that night
It glowed, a beacon shiny and bright
The two they stood against the foe
They were alone, nowhere to go
They fought in blood on a darkened hill
Dragon Heart and Cnut will save us still
Dragon Heart, Cnut and the Ulfheonar
Dragon Heart, Cnut and the Ulfheonar

The words made us surge ahead. I heard Ulf laugh, "It is as though the Dragonheart, Haaken and Cnut were here amongst us! On my warriors!" Those like Ráðgeir and Sven who had sailed with my great grandfather rowed in memory of the great warriors with whom they had fought. The younger warriors rowed because they saw a chance for glory and immortality.

It was hard to sit and stare at Ulf. There was a temptation to turn and look ahead. It would have been fruitless. The prow hid our foes from us. This was what it meant to be a Viking. You trusted those around you. I heard arrows as they were released. Our ship's boys would be as insects, biting the Walhaz but their whistling arrows told us that we were close to the enemy.

"In oars!"

We were in a tidal race now as the river rushed to fill the space of the low tide. Baldr and I pulled the oar across us so fast that it seemed to burn our hands. Suddenly there was a crunch and a crack as we sailed between two Walhaz ships fighting the current and losing. We heard screams as oars shattered and splintered driving shards into men's skulls and bodies. Ulf had chosen the perfect spot to drive our drekar. The hull of *'Úlfarr'* ground against the side of a Walhaz ship. I was confident about my own ship. How would the Walhaz ship fare? Was she as well made?

"Out oars and row!"

We pushed our oar out and we rowed.

> *The storm was wild and the gods did roam*
> *The enemy closed on the Prince's home*
> *Two warriors stood on a lonely tower*
> *Watching, waiting for hour on hour.*
> *The storm came hard and Odin spoke*
> *With a lightning bolt the sword he smote*
> *Ragnar's Spirit burned hot that night*
> *It glowed, a beacon shiny and bright*
> *The two they stood against the foe*
> *They were alone, nowhere to go*
> *They fought in blood on a darkened hill*
> *Dragon Heart and Cnut will save us still*
> *Dragon Heart, Cnut and the Ulfheonar*
> *Dragon Heart, Cnut and the Ulfheonar*

We only sang until we saw the shadow of the land melt into the sea and sky. We stopped when we saw the three Walhaz ships attempt to turn. They fouled each other's rigging. There would be no pursuit.

"Steady now! When we are in the open sea we will stop and raise the mast. You did well. The Dragonheart would be proud of you!"

Baldr and I turned to look at the mountain which was a dark shadow looming to the north and east. Was my great grandfather still alive? We had honoured him but we had deserted him too. I felt no joy in this victory. We pulled away from the shore. Ulf would wait until we had clear water and darkness before raising the mast and the sail. I could feel the eyes of the older crew boring into me. They blamed me for the desertion. That it was unfair did not matter. They had sworn the same oath but it had been me and three of my hearth-weru who had abandoned him. I wondered if this was my great grandfather continuing his training of me?

Dawn found us to the west of Anglesey and Wyddfa in a sea which rose and fell with choppy, grey walls of water. I stared at the mountain and I wondered again if my great grandfather had survived? I had to believe he had and was still alive. In many ways, the winds helped me for they were precocious and changed direction from hour to hour. Ulf and his boys were kept busy as they adjusted the sail and the steering board. Sometimes we rowed and sometimes we sailed. It meant I could use the effort of rowing to exorcise my demons. The red stone seemed to burn in the leather pouch at my waist. I hoped that it would help Ylva's mother or all this would have been in vain. As we neared the northern coast of the island the Walhaz called Ynys Môn, I suddenly realised that even if the stone did not work then that had not been the purpose of the journey. The Norns and the Allfather were testing me. I would have to rule when my great grandfather died and this was preparation. The strange voice in my head had told me I was doing the right thing and, despite what Ráðgeir and the others thought, I had done the right thing! I found myself smiling. The Dragonheart lived. I now needed to work out how to rescue him. Then, as though a sign from the Allfather, the wind veered and our sail filled. It would take us home.

As we headed up the coast and passed the vast expanse of beach which lay north of the Maeresea, I wondered if we ought to land and seek the three of them out. Almost immediately I rejected the idea. It would be like trying to find a darker grain of sand on the beach. I guessed the three of them, if they were still alive, would cross the Maeresea upstream but by the time we reached it they could have passed or we could be attacked by Mercians. I had to get home. I had sworn an oath and a leader kept his word. It was what my great grandfather was known for. He kept his word.

It was dark when we entered the anchorage at Whale Island. The wind meant that Ulf was able to sail us in. Ráðgeir said, "We have fulfilled our oath, Sámr Ship Killer. Now we would like to sail south and find the Dragonheart."

"As would I but it is not as simple as that. If we sail too far south, we may miss him. I need to take the stone to Kara and consult with Ylva. We have a witch; we should use her. I will ride through the night to Cyninges-tūn. I would have you wait here. Baldr can explain to my father and to the Dragonheart's son. They may well wish to join us in the search for my great grandfather." Ráðgeir had a face which showed not what he was thinking. I had to exert my authority, "I am the Dragonheart's heir. All of the men swore an oath. I will not allow any to question my authority."

I held his eyes and he lowered his gaze, "We wait a day but, Sámr Ship Killer, this does not sit well with me. I swore an oath to Dragonheart long before I swore one to you."

"That I understand." I turned to Baldr, "Explain what has happened. I shall return as quickly as I can."

"You need someone to go with you!"

"I will be safe enough and I can ride more quickly alone." He nodded.

We kept horses at the port and I took one of the bigger ones. I dug my heels in and galloped into the night. I was not reckless for I knew the road well but I had never ridden as fast as I did that night. Since the attack by Ubba Ragnarsson, we had kept a good watch on the walls of Hawk's Roost and Cyninges-tūn. The gate was barred but as I was recognised it was soon opened. My horse was spent and I threw myself from his back and ran to Ylva's home.

She met me at the door, "I dreamed your return but I saw only you and your men. Grandfather?"

"We had to leave him at Wyddfa." I took out the stone and handed it to her. "He ordered us to leave. Erik was trapped beneath a fall of rocks and he would not leave him."

Closing her eyes, she gripped the red stone. I saw the concentration upon her face. When she opened them she threw her arms around me and hugged me, "He is alive. I do not see him in the Otherworld. My father comes to me and he has not seen the spirit of the Dragonheart. There is hope. Come inside and tell me all."

The words poured from me like a torrent from a waterfall. She nodded as I spoke. When I had finished she poured me a horn of ale as she considered her words. "You have done well. Ráðgeir and the others do not understand the Dragonheart. They think they do but they just see the face he chooses to show them! You and I know the real lord of the Land of the Wolf. Take a fresh horse and ride to your wife. She will need to see you. I will speak with my mother. This stone should help. If not, then the spirits have deceived us. I will come with you when you return to Whale Island. We will find the Dragonheart together." Her words filled me with hope for I would not be alone when I sought the Dragonheart. The grain of sand would be easier to find with a volva.

The night with my wife, although brief, was necessary for both of us. She had yet to give birth and I remembered from Ragnar's that this would be a difficult time for her for she would have the additional worry of my absence. As I lay in our bed with her, I prayed that the search for Dragonheart would not be a long one. He and Haaken were both old. They were tough warriors but the journey they were undertaking would be hard for those who were much younger.

Ylva and I did not reach the ship until the middle of the afternoon. I had never ridden so far in such a short space of time. Men were gathered at Whale Island. Rumour and gossip abounded. I realised that only Ylva and I knew that the Dragonheart was still alive. They all feared the worst and there would be others, like Ráðgeir, who would be critical of me and my actions.

Gruffyd and my father were waiting for us in my father's hall. I could tell that Ráðgeir had been stirring up trouble.

Gruffyd looked angry, "You left my father alone on Gwynedd! How could you, where is your honour?"

I forced myself to be calm. Dragonheart had taught me that, "Firstly, he was not alone. Haaken One Eye and Erik were with him."

"A boy and an old man!"

Gruffyd did not understand or perhaps he chose not to understand. "That old man is an Ulfheonar. Secondly, we had all sworn an oath and your father ordered me hence! I obeyed the Dragonheart. The stone he sought is now with his daughter."

He waved a dismissive hand, "Witches and galdramenn! They have always been a curse and no good has ever come to the clan from their interference."

Ylva's eyes narrowed. They now became the eyes of the wolf and her voice was filled with threat, "Go carefully, Gruffyd. You insult my parents and you insult me."

He faced up to her. He was a warrior but he was foolish to do so. Ylva was rightly named and was like a she-wolf who could use magic. "You threaten me with magic?" There was a sneer in his voice. They had grown up in the same village but their mothers had little in common with each other. They had never, truly got on.

Ylva had donned a sword when she had left her hall and her hand went to it. "I do not need magic to deal with you! You and your desire to gain reputation put the Dragonheart in more danger than Sámr. It was you sailed into the lair of the witch and remember this, Gruffyd, Sámr is the Dragonheart's heir, not you. It was he who was chosen by your father and he will rule the clan."

Gruffyd's mouth became a tight line and his eyes narrowed, "Perhaps and then again, perhaps not."

I saw my father about to speak. This was another test. Had my great grandfather known that this might happen? Or was this the Norns? I had to take charge for this was a test of my leadership. If my father spoke it would diminish the little power I clung on to. "Enough! Ylva is right I am the heir and you are right, Gruffyd, I did abandon the Dragonheart. I will now remedy that. Ylva and I will take *'Úlfarr'* and find him."

"I will come!" said Gruffyd somewhat petulantly.

"If you wish to come then take your ship but I return with the crew who sailed with Dragonheart." I looked Ráðgeir in the eye, "All of us owe it to the three men to save them. Am I right, Ráðgeir?"

"You are lord and I am sorry that I questioned you. I can see the Dragonheart in you and hear his words in your voice. We will prepare the ship."

Gruffyd had not finished, "My ship is not ready! You must wait for me."

Ylva laughed, "Wait for you? Why? Your mother was a Christian and that curse now manifests itself. You could have gone with your father. Why did you not?"

"He did not ask me."

"And ask yourself why? You and I are of an age, Gruffyd, we grew up in the same world but you have caused more trouble for the Dragonheart than any other in the clan. He risked all to rescue you twice! Follow us if you can but we wait for no man and certainly not for you!"

Ylva had power. It oozed from every pore of her body. Gruffyd recoiled as her words hit home. There was much I did not know but Ylva obviously did.

I looked at my father. He, too, had remained silent. He looked apologetically at me, "Take care, my son. You carry a great responsibility. I do not envy you but know," he looked over to Gruffyd, "that I am willing to stand by you in a shield wall and face any enemies who try to oppose you!" Battle lines were being drawn.

Gruffyd stormed out of the room. Mordaf looked from me to Ylva and, shrugging, left. I could not read his mind. I liked Mordaf but was he more like his father than his grandfather? Time alone would tell and I had more pressing matters on my mind.

As we boarded my ship Ylva said, "This is not over, Sámr. I read his mind. He means to do us ill and we must plan carefully for the future. The Norns have spun a complicated web this time."

By the time we had negotiated the entrance to Whale Island, it was dark. Ylva and I joined Ulf and Baldr at the steering board. We had half of the crew at the oars. The wind had veered but it still came from the south and west. Until we had decided a course there was little point in exhausting the crew. "Where to, Sámr Ship Killer?"

I looked at Ylva. A smile played upon her lips. She was playing the game my great grandfather did. She wished me to make a suggestion and then she could amend it. "The three we seek have had four nights to head north. I know not the condition of Erik. Perhaps he is not even with them. Despite what my great grandfather wished he might not have been able to save him."

"In your heart, you know that they will be together for I have not sensed my grandfather's death."

She was right. "Then they might have covered eighty miles. The Dee and the Maeresea are obstacles to them but they are resourceful. I would put them either on the Maeresea or north of it."

She turned to Ulf, "And if we sailed south to the Maeresea when would we reach it?"

"With this wind against, we would have to row. We might reach it by noon tomorrow."

"And then we would need to sail up it to discover them?" He nodded. "By which time they could be well north of the river."

Ulf stroked his beard and nodded, "And the river is a Mercian stronghold."

"Sámr, you know the mind of the Dragonheart better than any. If we cannot find him at the Maeresea then where?"

I could have gone to the map for confirmation but I knew a good place to intercept him, "The Belisima is the last river north of the Maeresea. It is twenty odd miles from river to river. If we were to sail along that river then we could take a party south to seek them. If we missed them then they would find the drekar."

She smiled. "We will not miss them. Once we are that close, I will read his thoughts and sense his presence. You have your route, captain!"

Ulf nodded, "Then, Sámr Ship Killer, take an oar for this will need us all to row."

I sat on my chest next to Baldr. Ylva stood next to Ulf. She had wool in her hand and she began to hand weave as we headed south. The witch was conjuring and that could only aid us.

Sámr
Chapter 8
A warrior comes of age

It was dark when we reached the Belisima and we were exhausted. We headed to the nearest beach on the southern shore and landed. We would begin our search in the morning. While the others fell asleep, I sat with Ulf, Baldr and Ylva.

I spoke for I had considered what the Dragonheart would do. Ylva was right I knew him as well as any save Haaken One Eye. "We need to get the drekar to the nearest ford. My grandfather will not try to cross the river here."

Ylva nodded, "Tonight, I will try to speak to the spirits and reach out to my grandfather."

"Do not tire yourself out, Ylva, we will need you and your power if we are to find Dragonheart."

"Do not worry about me, Sámr, I have power enough. The spell I wove as we rowed south can only help us in our search and tonight I will take a potion and I will dream."

Ulf asked, "How many men will you leave aboard?"

"Just six. That will be enough for you to escape to the sea if disaster strikes us."

Ylva smiled at my words, "Now you sound like grandfather. You are planning for disaster and hope it does not come. This is all part of a plan. We are too small to see the whole thing. I wonder if grandfather sees it?" We all looked south for somewhere, if Ylva was right, there were three warriors in the darkness trying to reach home.

The next morning, we sailed upstream until the river narrowed so much that we could go no further. Upstream lay Prestune. It was a small Mercian outpost but there would be armed men there. My great grandfather would avoid it. We turned the drekar around and then landed. Even Ráðgeir looked at me. I was the leader and this was my decision.

"We head due south. To the east of us is high and rough ground. The Dragonheart will not risk walking there with a wounded boy. Not only would the going be harder there are Danes there. Ylva, did you dream?"

She nodded and smiled, "I did and he is alive. More, I can tell you that there is no water between us. He has crossed the Maeresea."

"Then we head south. I want us in a line when we are able. Three men will be hard to see. A line of almost thirty men will be easier for them to see."

Baldr added a word of caution and said, "And just as easy for the Mercians."

"I did not say we would not have to fight. We may well have to but it is worth it, is it not, for the Dragonheart?"

Ylva nodded for I had chosen the right words and the men banged their shields with their daggers. We set off. The first part was uphill and then when we crested the side of the valley of the Belisima we saw the size of our problem. This was rolling land. There were farms but there were no vantage points from which to spy out the land ahead. Three men were not an easy target. I began to move faster and Ylva sensed my unease, "This is meant to be, Sámr. You and your men use your eyes and I will use my mind." She held up the piece of wool she had woven on the drekar. "This has some of the Dragonheart's hair. I took some of the fur from his wolf skin. This spell will tell me when we are close."

"Close?"

We were still marching quickly like a long line of beaters and Ylva explained as we walked, "It is like being in a dark cave with no light. You sense that there is someone within but you cannot see them. You know they are close for you can smell them and hear them. You put your hands out and then you find flesh. That is what it is like in the spirit world. I will know when he is close but you and your men must see him."

That comforted me but we still spied no one. We had been travelling for, perhaps an hour, when I saw a larger estate than any we had seen hitherto. It lay to the west of us and had a palisade. Ylva had not said that my great grandfather was close and so I dismissed the thought that he could be there. However, it was a Mercian farm and there would be warriors. We were in as much danger as the Dragonheart. We headed away from it as I knew that the Dragonheart would avoid Saxons if he could.

We were, perhaps, eight miles from the Belisima when I saw something which, for the first time, gave me hope. In my mind, I heard the Dragonheart's voice and I felt him. Ahead was a small rise. In the Land of the Wolf, it would barely be called a haugr but here it rose above the land and there was a small copse of trees on the top. I was about to draw my sword and order the line to head for the rise when Ylva gave a gasp, "He is close! I feel him!"

Drawing my sword, I turned and said, "Run, warriors of the wolf. The Dragonheart is close. Draw weapons!" There was the hiss of steel as swords were pulled from scabbards. We ran. I left my shield upon my back but drew my seax. The two weapons actually helped me to run.

As we neared the bottom of the small rise, I thought I heard a cry and then the wind brought a voice I recognised and the last refrain of a song I had heard many times.

Ulfheonar never forgive
Ulfheonar fight to the death

It was Haaken One Eye and if he was in the copse then so was my great grandfather. I now heard the neigh of a horse and the clash of weapons. The urgency of the situation made my legs eat up the ground so that I reached the top first. I saw Haaken and Erik, back to back fighting some Mercians but I ignored them for, lying prostrate on the ground lay the Dragonheart and two young Saxons were about to skewer him.

I roared, "Clan of the Wolf!" and hurled my seax at one of them. The Allfather guided my aim for the seax's handle struck one youth on the head and made the other turn to face me. My sword, sweeping down two-handed was the last thing he saw. My great grandfather used the sword that was touched by the gods to raise himself to his feet and he rammed Wolf's Blood under the rib cage of the second youth. Baldr, Ylva, Ráðgeir and the others had reached the top. I saw that the warriors were slain and all that remained were the farmers who held pole weapons. The five of them saw the warband of angry Vikings and, taking to their heels, fled. One managed to ride the horse that was there. I looked at the ground and saw a dead thegn.

There were no enemies left but the rider might fetch help. I sheathed my sword as did Dragonheart and I embraced him. When we stood apart, I said, "That is the last oath you make me swear! Had it not been for Ylva we would not have found you!"

Ylva kissed the spell and then put her arms around both of us. "We three are together, Sámr, and that is all that is important. Let us not dwell on what might have been."

My great grandfather turned, "Erik? Haaken?"

We looked and I saw that they were both alive. Erik had a wound on his arm. The Dragonheart said, "Ylva, Erik has a damaged foot and a wound. He is brave beyond words. Heal him."

"Of course. Come, young hero. Let us see if this witch can do more than the great Dragonheart."

Haaken came and embraced me, "That you found us is a miracle. The Dragonheart himself had no idea where we were going!"

I knew Haaken was wrong for the Dragonheart had been heading home. He knew where the Land of the Wolf lay. "I felt his mind, Haaken One Eye. Perhaps the years since we went to Miklagård have served some purpose."

The Dragonheart's eyes bored into me, "And you learned from this, Sámr?"

"Was that your purpose great grandfather? To test me?"

He shook his head, "Not my purpose but another's. You should know that I knew you would have difficulties." Ráðgeir appeared and was grinning. My great grandfather said, "I am guessing that this warrior berated you for leaving me on the mountain?"

Ráðgeir's hand went to his wolf amulet, "How…?" He dropped to his knees before me. "Forgive me, lord, I swear that I will never doubt your heir again."

I raised him to his feet, "It is no more than I did to myself. I doubted my decision but it was *wyrd* and I have learned much."

My great grandfather gave me a knowing look, "So?"

"This is neither the time nor the place. There is a Saxon hall between us and the drekar. We will have time to talk when we reach the Land of the Wolf." He nodded. "Ylva, can Erik walk?"

"He could but it would be better if he was carried." She pointed to four of my men, "You four collect the pole weapons and spears from the dead Saxons. We make a bier. Use the dead Saxon's belts and shield straps to bind them."

Erik said, "I can walk! I have walked from Wyddfa."

Ylva turned and I saw the power in her eyes and heard it in her voice. "And you may lose your toes. I am Ylva, the volva of the Clan of the Wolf. You will obey me." Erik heard the power too and, recoiling, he nodded. Ylva then smiled, "Good. When you are on the bier then we move and you are right, Sámr. I sense danger from the north and west. This fight is not yet over."

It was early afternoon when we began down the slope. We would not move as fast north as we had when we had come south for we had a wounded man to carry and I knew that the last of the Ulfheonar were spent. As we marched, with our three heroes protected by a ring of steel, I wondered if we would reach the river before dark. I kept glancing at Haaken and my great grandfather. They were keeping up well. Both were tough men. When I was their age would I have the will and the strength to do what they had done? I smiled as I heard Haaken composing his saga as we walked. It had been a prodigious feat and deserved a saga.

"From Wyddfa's top, the craggy cliff, The three warriors walked. what word next." He shook his head. "No matter, it will come. *Pursued by who wished them death They ran until they were bereft of breath*." I saw him smile, "That is a good one. I like that, bereft of breath!"

My great grandfather laughed, "Bereft of breath is one thing no one could accuse you of, Haaken One Eye! You never shut up!"

"I am an artist. I am above such things. Leave me to compose my greatest saga. Erik Black Toes and the last of the Ulfheonar."

"Have you forgotten Aðils Shape Shifter?"

He waved an airy hand, "Artistic licence and besides he now shuts himself and his boys up in Lang's Dale. He might as well live in another land."

It might have been a stroll around the head of the Water on a summer's evening had not the line of Saxons appeared ahead of us. There were thirty of them and they rose like wraiths. They had planned an ambush and we had walked into it. The wind which had helped us to sail from Wyddfa was now our undoing for it had carried our words and smells to them and had hidden theirs. It was a lesson too late in the learning. Ylva had been distracted by Erik but she had sensed danger. As she had said her mind needed our eyes and we had failed.

"Shield wall! Wedge! Baldr and Stig Sword Hand protect Ylva, Erik and…"

"Do not say Haaken and the Dragonheart, my great-grandson. We are the cause of all this and we will fight."

I nodded, "But without a shield, you will not be in the front rank! The two of you can be at the rear!"

Haaken said, "Good for it will give me the opportunity to find a better word than cliff."

"Fool!" I heard the affection in my great grandfather's voice.

I swung my shield around and, drawing my sword, beat upon it and began to chant.

The Clan of the Wolf have backs that are broad
All our enemies are put to the sword
When we roar and howl then fear
The Clan of the Wolf have teeth and we are near

"March!"

It was a small wedge. The rear rank with the Dragonheart and Haaken only had nine men but we were aiming at the centre of the double line. I saw that all of the Saxon front rank had shields and spears. The thegn in the centre and the two men who flanked him wore byrnies. My aim was simple. We would strike so quickly and so hard that we would break their line and, hopefully, kill their thegn. Our speed seemed to take them by surprise. I saw those in the second rank looking nervously at their neighbours. They had no shields and I knew they were working out where the point of the wedge would hit.

The thegn shouted, "Brace!" It was his only option. They could not build up enough speed to hit us and overlap our flanks. They were hoping that we would fail.

Our wedge, including the Dragonheart, were all chanting together. It was as though our voices were a weapon. Without turning I knew that Ylva, with sword drawn and spell in her hand, was adding her magic to our wedge. Battle was as much about belief and confidence as it was about skill. We believed we could win. The Saxons did not.

I held my sword before me and braced my left arm with my shield. Behind me, Sven of the Water and Einar had their shields in my back. They would propel me towards the thegn. His spear would come for my face. He would hope to either spear me or make me flinch. The two men on either side of him would do the same. One of the three spears would find my face. My sword, however, was an edged weapon. I would use it to try to stop their spears from skewering me. If it did not then my wife would have a scarred warrior returned to her.

The three spears lunged and I held my shield up while slashing across their shafts. One spear struck my shield and I hit the head of a second. The third gouged a line along my cheek. I felt the blood flow. I could not have stopped even had I wanted to. Thirty warriors were pushing me. My shield smashed into the face of the thegn. The Saxons behind him did not have shields to push into his back and brace him. He fell to the floor. My youth and my speed saved me for it would have been easy to fall and be trampled by the men behind me. I opened my legs and my right boot smashed into the thegn's face. I heard the bone crack and break. Behind me, the sound of Sven's sword as it hacked through the bones of the thegn's neck was the sound of victory. Without a thegn, the Saxons would flee. I lunged with my sword and stabbed a Saxon in the shoulder. Screaming in pain he turned and ran. There were no enemies before me and so I shouted, "Break wedge!" Turning to my right I backhanded a Saxon who had also just turned to flee. My sword struck him just below his ribs. The edge sawed across his side and his entrails poured forth like a nest of baby snakes. Einar and Sven of the Water hacked and stabbed the thegn's oathsworn. I heard a roar as the Dragonheart brought the sword that was touched by the gods, two-handed across the neck of a mailed Saxon. His head was half severed. The rest ran!

My warriors despatched the wounded. The Saxons had lost six men in our first attack and that had broken them. I saw that those fleeing half carried another eight who were wounded. Two of my men had minor wounds. It was inevitable as we had sharp weapons and warriors could not be careful when they hacked and slashed. The battle had cost us time and was something we could not change. We hurried north, to the river. None of us were entirely certain where we had started our journey and when we reached the river, I saw that we were just half a mile upstream from the darkened shadow that was *'Úlfarr'*. We were all weary and I knew that the Dragonheart and Haaken would be in a worse condition.

Once we were all aboard, I said, "Ulf, is the tide right to leave?"

He shook his head, "It is low tide and I would not risk the ship on this river. There are sandbanks. Besides we have to raise the mast. Better to leave at dawn. We can anchor in the middle of the river if you fear a night attack."

"I am not sure what I expect but we have had two attacks already and it would be prudent to take precautions. Anchor us in the middle."

"Aye, lord. A wise decision," I heard the respect in his voice. My great grandfather's lessons were paying off.

The Dragonheart was quite concerned about Erik. I saw him frowning as he spoke with Ylva, "Has my clumsy work crippled the boy?"

"You have done the best that you could. But I will have to break the toes when we return to Cyninges-tūn. Only a healer could have done more than you did. He will not be crippled but Haaken may be right. Erik Black Toes would be a more suitable name for him than shield bearer."

"Why?"

"He will not be bearing your shield again, grandfather. This was a test for Sámr, was it not? I know that you did not plan it that way but it has been a worthy test. He will lead the clan now. Your shield can be hung up and Ragnar's Spirit will just be used for show."

"You have dreamed?"

"I need not dream to know this." She looked at me, "Sámr, you had better tell him of the words that were exchanged at Whale Island before we left."

Even as I opened my mouth to speak Dragonheart said, "Gruffyd."

"You knew?"

He shook his head, "Knew is the wrong word. Let us say that I dreaded this. Since he was rescued from the land of Om Walum, I have felt us growing apart."

I shook my head, "You saved him and Mordaf."

"His mother was a Christian. He spent longer with her than with me when he was growing up. He married a Christian. I think he blamed me for his incarceration." He shrugged, "I do not think I was to blame for it was he chose to go to the land of Om Walum but he has twisted it in his head. What was it he said?"

I was reluctant to say what had happened. Ylva had no such qualms. She shook her head in irritation, "He questioned Sámr's right to rule and accused him of deliberately abandoning you."

"He did not go as far as that, Ylva!"

"I read his mind, Sámr. He meant it."

The Dragonheart asked, "And what did your father say for I assume he was there?"

"He said he would fight alongside me."

"Good!"

Ylva said, "It will be interesting to see if your son has sailed south, grandfather. He said he wished to come to find you but Sámr would not wait."

"Then that will, indeed, tell us much." He stretched, "And now I am ready for sleep. I thank you all for coming for us. The Norns have not yet decided to cut my thread but they had the knife ready this time. I fear they have more planned for me."

Haaken and Erik were already asleep and my great grandfather joined them. I could not imagine how things might have turned out if Haaken One Eye had not been with the Dragonheart. Ylva took my hand and led me to the prow. The ship was named for Úlfarr the wolf, which had saved me and it seemed the right place to talk. The crew who had remained onboard watched along with the ship's boys but they moved to give us the space to speak.

"We need to plan, Sámr. Gruffyd has changed. Grandfather was right. His son's Christian links and origins added to his fear of witches makes him dangerous. He fears and hates me."

"I do not like this, Ylva. He is family and he is of the blood of the Dragonheart."

"And sometimes blood can be bad. You have a great responsibility now, Sámr. The clan is in your hands. I can help you but you must make the clan strong for I fear there are enemies gathering. Like it or not the end of the time of the Dragonheart approaches and there are many who see you as weak and would take the land from you. The Dragonheart has dreamed and he seeks to keep the dream from me. If we were attacked from without then what would Gruffyd do?"

"Fight?"

"For us or against us? I know him better than you and I do not know. He is clever and devious. He might choose to help our enemies defeat you in the hope that he could then defeat them later."

"That is a dangerous game to play."

"When you seek a throne then every game is dangerous. Think on my words. When we reach Whale Island there will need to be a decision. I will be behind you and I pray that you make the right one."

Sámr
Chapter 9
Homecoming

We were not attacked in the night and the wind, still from the south made rowing unnecessary when we headed home. I had time to stand and think. What would the Dragonheart have done when he was my age? I almost laughed aloud for when he had been my age, he and the clan were fighting for a foothold on Man. There the enemies were easier for they were not family. I had found it hard to believe Ylva but I trusted her. She had always been on my side and, despite my youth, supported me as a leader.

"You are troubled, great-grandson."

It was not a question. It was a statement from the one person who knew what I was thinking. I turned, "Aye great grandfather; this chalice I hold is a poisoned one, is it not?" He nodded. "No matter what I do I will cause a schism in the clan."

He put his arm around my waist. He spoke quietly, "Choosing you as my heir was not an easy decision. I love all of my children and grandchildren." I looked at him in surprise, "Aye, even Gruffyd, but you are my favourite. I know that should not be said out loud but I am honest and I am never foresworn. I did not want to choose you for I knew that the decision would result in a harder life for you. The spirits chose you and you are right. It is a poisoned chalice. Do you wish to walk away?"

I knew that if I said yes then he would understand and there would be no disappointment but I had been brought up to respect the clan and the land. I had been given the opportunity to continue to do that which my great grandfather had begun. "No."

"Then you must fight for the clan and if that means taking on Gruffyd and those who support him then so be it."

And at that moment the future of the clan changed, he was talking of war and a war between Vikings. More than that it might become a war between family! I saw that certainty in his eyes. He said, "I am sorry, Sámr. There is no other way but it may not come to war. You are clever as, I think, I am. We may be able to use strategy to avoid war." That was all he said. I do not think he knew how we would achieve this miracle but I trusted him and his judgement.

I was largely silent as we sailed gently up the coast to the Land of the Wolf. I think that everyone on board was lost in their own thoughts. One positive to take from it was the fact that the young warriors had all been blooded and emerged unscathed. They had fought the Walhaz and the Mercians; both had been defeated. The Danes were a stronger foe but it boded well for us. We had a couple of Saxon byrnies we had taken. In addition to which, my great grandfather had jewels we had rescued from the cave. We could pay our weaponsmiths for their work.

When we reached Whale Island, I saw that all of our drekar were in port. Despite the words of Gruffyd none had left port. Gruffyd now lived further east than he used to. I wondered if I was doing him a disservice. Perhaps he had travelled overland to rescue his father. I would discover that when I spoke with my own father. Even though it was late when we arrived people were waiting for us. The story of the Dragonheart's latest adventure must have spread like a contagion for the quay was lined with folk who wished to see if he was alive.

When the Dragonheart raised his hand, the whole quay erupted. Would I ever enjoy such love and affection? Speaking to Haaken I knew that my great grandfather had always been held in high regard. I knew there was a faction which did not wish to see me rule. Such was the burden of leadership. Ragnar stepped forward and all parted. He and his grandfather embraced. They spoke but it was private. I did not intrude. I saw the Dragonheart nod.

Ylva slipped her hand through my arm, "I will head to my home with Erik. I need to begin to heal his foot. I will send a message to Aethelflaed."

"I can come with you."

She shook her head, "You and grandfather need to be here. There are words to be said and actions to be taken. If I am here then it will be like pouring pig fat on a fire. I will have my own battle but it will be a time of my choosing."

We stepped on to the quay. Well-wishers clapped me on the back. I had promised to bring him back and I had.

Ylva smiled, "You have many allies. Do not dwell on the enemies. There are always more of those than your friends." She turned and shouted, "Fetch my patient!"

I waved Baldr over, "Send our men back to Hawk's Roost. You and I will return with my great grandfather."

He gave me a wan smile, "And Nanna will have to wait an extra night."

"I fear, my friend, that it will be ever thus."

We followed my father and the Dragonheart into the hall. Haaken walked with us. He said, quietly, "I hear that Gruffyd has been beating his shield?"

I nodded, "I can handle it."

"That is not in doubt but a word of advice, be ruthless. You do not leave an adder close to your bosom. The Dragonheart had a worm and it was cut from him."

"I will speak with him when we are all in a more reflective mood. Words were spoken in anger. We have all calmed down now and Dragonheart is safe. I would not have him wander again."

Haaken stopped Baldr and I, "Has he told you of the dream?" I shook my head. "He dreamed, at Wyddfa, that the Danes came again. We all know that Wyddfa makes the Dragonheart dream and the dreams always manifest themselves in truth. Beware the men from the east. I agree that the Dragonheart should stay at home now but the war which comes may not be of our choosing."

"Thank you, Haaken, you have ever been the Dragonheart's friend."

I saw sadness and pride in his single orb, "Until death, Sámr, until death!"

We entered the hall. My father used it whenever he was in Whale Island but his real home was the farm to the north of the port.

I turned to Haaken, "Your lives are closely intertwined, Haaken."

Haaken smiled, "And for that, I am eternally grateful. Think how dull my life would have been without him." He nodded towards the fire where there was a slave with a jug of ale. "And now, if you will excuse me, I have a thirst!" His brief moment of sadness was gone. He was Haaken One Eye.

As he left me, my mother, now grey-haired but still beautiful, rushed over to me and hugged me. "We are all so proud of you."

"I could not have lived with myself had we lost the Dragonheart. It was a close-run thing."

She nodded, "And has Aethelflaed given birth yet?" Mother preferred domestic issues to military ones. It was why she and father were so happy. He was no longer a man of war and that suited them both.

"Not yet but it will be soon. I will leave as soon as I can. You must come and see Hawk's Roost when the new babe is born. We have made many improvements."

"And I shall for I know that the time we have together is precious and should not be squandered." She led me to the table where my father and great grandfather sat speaking. Haaken was close enough to be summoned if needed but he was giving them the space that they needed. Baldr was still with me. I knew that his thoughts were far to the north and I felt guilty for I was keeping him from his family but just as Haaken One Eye was my great grandfather's staff, so Baldr would be mine.

I allowed my father and the Dragonheart the chance to talk. Baldr peered around and said, "I do not see Gruffyd nor Mordaf."

Shaking my head I answered him, "Mordaf is not the problem. He never has been. It is his father we worry about. I know you need to get home, as do I, but I must speak with him and clear the air. If there is a threat from the east then we needed to be ready for it."

"I cannot believe that they will repeat their mistake! They lost heavily the last time they came."

"And yet they were within a whisker of victory. Had Bergil Hafþórrsson not arrived we might have lost. I can see why they would seek to take this land. If they have the land of the Wolf then they can threaten Mercia as well as Northumbria, Strathclyde and Hibernia. At the moment their ships have a long sea voyage to reach these lands. That is why I believe that they will come by land. Once they take the Land of the Wolf then they will fill the seas with their drekar. We have seen how weak Mercia is. When we marched south, we saw few strongholds and Haaken told me that they passed almost none north of Caestir. The world could soon be Danish!"

Dragonheart waved me over and I left Baldr. He wandered over to Haaken. My father beamed, "You have done well, my son. We have spoken of the future. I meant what I said. I will stand in a shield wall with you."

I shook my head, "That is not what we need." I saw Dragonheart smile as I spoke. "My great grandfather has dreamed that the men from the east will come. I believe so too but I do not think that they will come by sea. I think they arrive over land and we need Whale Island and Úlfarrston to be as two fortresses which can hold off an attack and make the enemy bleed. We did well last time but they will have learned. Ketil's men, Ráðulfr Ulfsson's men and the men of Cyninges-tūn are the warriors who will fight the invader! When I reach my home, I will prepare for the attack."

Dragonheart clapped me on the back. "Did I not tell you that he had grown."

My father nodded, "Dragonheart just said, almost word for word that which you did. What happened at Wyddfa? Did the two of you become one?"

I just smiled. I loved my father but I was the product of Dragonheart's mind. Dragonheart spread an arm and said, "Haaken, Baldr come and sit here. There are no secrets between us. We have crossed too many rivers together for that."

Haaken nodded, "And I will swim no more! It is undignified." We all looked at him quizzically and he explained how they had made a raft to cross the river. Once started Haaken could not stop and he regaled us with his tale of the journey. My great grandfather rolled his eyes at times and I recognised the embellishments which were added.

When he had finished Dragonheart said, "And now that we have skirted around the subject of my son, we should cease dancing and look at the problem."

My father said, "He and Mordaf returned to their halls east of the river. The two had words before they left. One of my warriors heard the argument. Gruffyd felt that Mordaf had not offered him enough support. Things became heated. They did not leave together."

Dragonheart nodded, "Oda has been good for Mordaf. As much as I like Ebrel she is like Brigid was with me. She adds nothing to him as a man. Your grandmother, Ragnar, Erika was my right hand."

Haaken nodded and fingered his amulet, "Aye, she was the best of women and the Allfather took her too soon."

"Tomorrow, Sámr, we will head home. But we will ride first to Gruffyd. We need the air to be cleared." I saw Baldr smile as my great grandfather used the same words as I had.

I nodded, "And when my new child is born, I will visit Bergil Hafþórrsson. He knows more than we do. He may have news of Ubba Ragnarsson. And when I have all that I need I will visit the Eden and Ketil's stad."

The Dragonheart went to the wooden desk which had once stood in his own hall until he had had a new one made. Now it was used to store maps for use by sailors leaving Whale Island. He unrolled one. It was the Land of the Wolf. There were patches of blue, which were the stretches of water. He jabbed his finger at the largest one, "And what of Windar's Mere? I know some, like Ketil, think it is cursed and it may well be but we need a presence there for it holds the key to the back door of our land. There are people there. There are farmers and the like but there is no leader. There is no stronghold."

I nodded, "There are two who could do this but the one I would ask to leave Cyninges-tūn and become jarl there is Haraldr Leifsson. He is a rock. When I returned to my home, he was the one who never questioned me. He follows orders and fights as well as any. I know he is getting old but he has wisdom and experience."

Dragonheart nodded, "And I concur. We have a palisade, a ditch and we have men who can watch each night. Haraldr is the man who can do that!"

Haaken nodded, "And I will go to see my wife and my daughters. If there is to be a last battle then I will spend time with my family."

I shook my head, "You and great grandfather will not be fighting. You have fought for the last time."

Haaken looked sad, "Then you know neither of us, Sámr, for if there is blood to be shed for this land then we two will be there. Since we first stood back to back in Norway the Norns have deemed it so. That is how it will end." He smiled, "But your mother brews a fine ale and so tonight I will drink more than I should for I deserve it!" He stood and headed to the barrel.

Rising, Baldr smiled and said, "I will see that he finds his bed safely. Goodnight."

I sat and spoke with my father and great grandfather long after Haaken and Baldr had gone to bed. We spoke of Wolf Killer, my grandfather. I learned much that night. I learned of the division between Dragonheart and Wolf Killer yet it was different from that between Dragonheart and Gruffyd. Wolf Killer had wanted to prove himself. As the two spoke I had an insight into the reason my father had taken a different path. Meeting my mother had changed him and he had become a gentler man. The two of them seemed to make peace. They spoke of the past and the home to the south and east where Wolf Killer had been ambushed and died. I heard the regret in Dragonheart's voice that he had not been able to save his son. I thought of my own son, Ragnar. I would do all that I could to keep him safe. My great grandfather had had a lifetime of regret that he had not managed to save his son and grandson.

On the way north Ylva had tended to the arrow wound in Dragonheart's hand. He gave a wan smile and held his scarred left hand, "This now aches and I think it tells me to go to bed. I am happy that we had this talk, Ragnar. I see that the air is open between us. The clouds have scudded away. Let us hope that the task with Gruffyd will be as easy. Good night."

My father nodded to a servant who followed Dragonheart. He would ensure that he was safe. Then, turning to me, my father said, "My grandfather will not be able to break down the wall which Gruffyd has built. It has deep foundations and was begun by Brigid. As the leader of the clan, you will be the one who has to beard Gruffyd and, for that, I am sorry. Ulla War Cry has chosen my path but you, my son, have been selected for a harder journey. You will need vision and fortitude. I am not the warrior you will be nor half the warrior my grandfather was but I will offer advice. Surround yourself with men like Haaken. They will not be Ulfheonar but they do not need to be. You need stout men in whom you can place complete trust. Your instincts are good for the blood of my grandmother flows through your veins. It is good that you have Ylva, she is a link to the spirit world and the leader of the Clan of the Wolf needs the help of a volva. I live here in the south. The power of the Land of the Wolf is not as strong here but The Water and your home is at the very heart of it. I believe that when the last battle comes that the land itself will come to your aid."

"I hear all that you say and you are right. The burden I bear was not chosen by me but a warrior does not abandon his path. You were not chosen, I can see that now. I am still young and I still have much to learn. The Dragonheart thinks I can fill his boots but I cannot. The gods have not touched me but I can keep and hold what the clan has built. We lost Man but we shall not lose this land."

He clasped my arm, "Good. You are not blinded by power. Your mother and I will visit with you. She would like to be there at the birth. She thinks it will be a girl."

I laughed, "My mother has become a volva?"

"No, but Astrid Mother was always at one with the cycle of life. She was born to be a mother and I thank the Allfather that she was brought into my life. You do not mind a daughter?"

"So long as the bairn is born healthy, I care not. I have seen what girls can achieve. Kara, Ylva and my mother are good examples. Goodnight."

There were just three of us who rode south and east the next morning. The Dragonheart was grateful for the horse he rode. I also watched him as he looked around, taking in every detail of the land. We passed old deserted farmsteads and he spoke of the men who had farmed there. We paused at the shipyard. Erik Short Toe's death was still a raw wound. I knew what he was doing. He was saying goodbye. When he and my father had spoken it had been almost like a testament. I hoped that Gruffyd would accept the hand of peace which would be offered.

As we neared Gruffyd's home Dragonheart reined in, "I know that you are my heir and I have given the reins of this land to you,

Sámr, but I beg you to let me speak to my son first. I know that I have not been a good father. A good father does not allow the mother to try to change the nature of a boy!"

I nodded and then pointed at the ditch, earthworks and palisade. "He has made a strong home. This would be a good model for the rest of our lords."

"Aye, the Stad on the Eden is a strong one too. Ketil is lucky for the Romans gave him the foundations but Haraldr needs something as strong at Windar's Mere. The Roman fort there is not as strong as it should be."

We dug our heels into our horses to continue the last half a mile to Gruffyd's home.

I half closed my eyes to try to remember the Mere. "As I recall is there not, halfway down the mere, a piece of high ground? As I remember it has an island just before it which could be used as a refuge and a bastion."

My great grandfather nodded, "Aye, there was a farmer, Beorn Bull Keeper who lived there; he had been one of your grandfather's warriors. He married a Saxon and lived there. He died when the Skull Takers came and the farmstead lies empty. You may be right and that might be a good stronghold. Haraldr Leifsson will want a new start. The folk who followed Asbjorn will need to be secure." He shook his head and then patted my hand, "You see, Sámr, my mind is not what it was. It needs new eyes, younger eyes to see that which is there before us. It would be perfect for the road from the south passes through it. Lying half way down the mere and with the island close by, Haraldr can control Windar's Mere." He laughed, "Windar was a good man but lazy. He liked an easy life and he just built upon what was already there and Asbjorn saw what he expected to see. His son, Eystein, promised much but he is young and, unlike you, does not seem capable of learning lessons. Well done, Sámr!"

Being praised by the Dragonheart was the greatest accolade a man could have.

We had seen just a single man on the gatehouse as we approached but there had to have been others for the gates were opened by half a dozen men. None were mailed but all were well armed. As he dismounted my great grandfather said, "Expecting trouble, Einar Sword Hand?"

"No jarl, but we live on the edge of the Land of the Wolf here. It pays to be vigilant." He smiled, "I am pleased that you are safe. Many of us wished to try to save you. I am pleased that Sámr Ship Killer did so."

I learned much from that conversation not least that not all of Gruffyd's men shared his opinion of me.

Einar led us to the hall. Gruffyd had had a fine chair made for himself. It looked like a throne and next to it was a smaller one. Of Ebrel, his wife, there was no sign. I had not seen Mordaf either. Gruffyd did not rise. His eyes glared at me and then he turned his gaze to his father, "I am happy that you are safe, Dragonheart." He waved a hand and two servants came with a chair for the Dragonheart. This was all planned. He would make Baldr and I stand. The chair upon which Dragonheart sat was lower than the throne of Gruffyd. My great grandfather caught my eye as he sat and gave a slight shake of the head. I was to ignore the insult. I nodded, subtly.

"Of course, father, there was no need for you to travel to that unholy mountain of the Walhaz. Prayers to God would have healed my half-sister."

"So, you are now a Christian. I know your mother had you baptised but I thought, at heart, you were like me."

"A pagan? I think not. Paganism will destroy the Land of the Wolf but you have already determined its end by naming a stripling as your heir instead of your son."

Dragonheart said nothing at first. He nodded and then said, quietly, "And would you be Lord of the Land of the Wolf?" I noticed he emphasised the word 'wolf'.

Gruffyd's eyes widened, "You would offer it to me?"

"If I did then how would you rule?"

He smiled, "You have never chosen a title but we are as mighty as Mercia, Wessex and Northumbria. This should be the Wolf Kingdom. We should have a cathedral and be the Kingdom of the Britons! My wife would be Queen. That is how it should be for she was born a princess!"

Dragonheart nodded, "And those who do not wish to be Christians? The majority of the Clan, what of them?"

Gruffyd jabbed a finger at me, "Like this lover of witches? They would be converted for their own good."

"And if they would not?"

"Then they would die."

Dragonheart took his sword and scabbard from his belt and laid it upon his knees. "And this sword? Ragnar's Spirit, the sword that was touched by the gods, what of this? It is a symbol of our beliefs and of the clan."

"It would be destroyed."

"And that is why, my son, I could never have you as heir for you would destroy the very foundations of the clan."

"Then why did you come here today?"

"I came to show you that I am alive for you said you wished to rescue me."

He jabbed a finger at me, "I did not want you to be rescued by a stripling boy!"

Dragonheart's voice was quiet and sad, "The truth is, Gruffyd, that you did not wish me rescued at all. You wanted my sword and me to be lost in the land of the Walhaz and then you could try to become King of…" he waved a hand, "the Britons!"

Standing, Gruffyd became angry, "You have cost me my son! Mordaf has left me and it is your fault, you and this boy. Leave me now! I have done with you!"

"Before I do, I give you a warning. There are Danes who are coming. I have dreamed. You and your stad are strong but they stand in the path of the Danes."

Gruffyd laughed, "A dream? Paganism! We are strong here and if the Danes come… well, let us see if they do, eh?"

It was not the result I had hoped for but my great grandfather did not seem discomfited as we left. He nodded, "Well, I have lost him and now I see his ambitions. His wife was a princess and would be a queen. His mother's influence is now clear. I could have done little about it. I married Brigid and this is my punishment."

"You do not seem unhappy."

"I can do nothing about this nor can you. Gruffyd has made his own bed. The good news is that Mordaf is not of his father's mind and therein lies hope. More, there are men who follow him, like Einar, who do not share his views. We will ride to Mordaf and we will spend the night with him."

We headed towards Bogeuurde. It was as far south as any Viking lived. It might have been a dangerous place but that the high divide rose like a wall behind it and the Mercians had made their northern boundary the Belisima. The Ēa Lōn was a river Mordaf could use. We passed isolated farms as we headed ever upwards. There were few of them. These were the hardy Vikings who chose not to live in large settlements. They were independent. Many had fought with my great grandfather and they came to speak with him. They helped to guide us to Mordaf's home.

It rose on a piece of rock which rose from a jumble of other rocks seemingly spread by the gods. They necessitated its size. It had a wooden palisade and a single warrior hall. Mordaf and his wife Oda lived with his handful of warriors. This time the greeting was warm. Mordaf rushed from his hall and threw his arms around his grandfather when he dismounted,

"You are alive!" When he had hugged him, he ran to me, "Thank you, Sámr. I am sorry my father said what he did. He has changed."

"You did not do anything for which you need to apologise. We would, if you would have us, stay the night."

"Of course, although we just have one hall!"

The Dragonheart laughed, "As do I. It will do and I am anxious to meet your wife!"

"She is inside feeding the bairn. He eats for two!"

"You have a son!"

"Aye Sámr, I would have told you at Whale Island but it did not seem the time. His name is Úlfarr for when he was born, we heard a wolf howling,"

"A good name for the Land of the Wolf."

I smiled for although Mordaf was young he had a sensible head upon his shoulders. His wife, Oda, was pretty and looked to be about fifteen summers. I knew that she and her family had lived in this part of the world and knew how to fight for what they had. The Mercians and the Hibernian raiders had learned to respect them. The baby was, indeed, huge.

Dragonheart smiled as Oda tried to rise, "Sit, for you are a mother and the work you do now will make a warrior. I am

Dragonheart and I welcome you to the family. This is Sámr Ship Killer who is the new leader of the clan."

"You are both welcome. I am sorry that our home is small."

"Do not apologise. We have no delusions of grandeur."

Mordaf looked at me and said, "Then you have visited with King Gruffyd?"

"Aye, how long has he been like that?"

"Since before we were taken in Om Walum. I was young then and did not see it. By the time I did he was no longer the father who had raised me."

When Oda had finished feeding Úlfarr she handed him to my great grandfather, "Give him your wisdom, lord, for even here, in the south of your land, we all revere the name of Dragonheart."

I then saw a side of my great grandfather which had only recently been revealed to me. He held the babe tenderly. He touched foreheads and whispered in the boy's ear. He had done the same with Ragnar. I wondered if he had done that with me? He was a complicated man.

That evening we ate at the long table in the hall. Mordaf only had eight oathsworn warriors and all were young. None had byrnies but their helmets, swords and shields were good ones. The helmets had all been taken from enemies that they had slain. I waited until Oda went to put Úlfarr to bed before I began my tale. I told them of the rescue of my great grandfather and the Saxons we had slain.

When I had finished the tale I added, "I think this shows their weakness but that weakness may hurt us. Another may come to fill the void. You do right to have a strong home but how many men can fight?"

"More than you see here. Oda's family live closer to the coast. They fish on the river and they farm. Oda has four brothers and Oda is the youngest. Her father leads fifteen warriors. Then there are the farmers who live close by. We can field forty odd men."

I nodded, "Then you should know that Saxons may not be the only danger." I told them of Dragonheart's dream and my suspicions. "So, you can see why the loss of your father's men hurts us. Much is on your shoulders, Mordaf."

"And I am of the Dragonheart's blood. I have not yet done as much as you, Sámr, but the witch and the cave did not affect me as much as my father. I still believe in the old ways. Oda's mother is a volva and she has powers herself. We will stand and if you need our aid then we will come."

My great grandfather spoke, "We will not need that. We just need you and your warriors to slow down an enemy. Stay behind your walls with your animals and deny them food. Sámr will meet them further north with our army."

"You have planned that far ahead?"

I smiled, "We have spoken and our minds are as one. I do not say we will win but we will do our best!"

Dragonheart
Chapter 10
A new child and a new lord

We reached Cyninges-tūn two days after leaving Mordaf. We were both in a more positive frame of mind. Gruffyd had made us think that all was black and it was not. Mordaf was a new hope. Erik, now named, Black Toes, had a crutch and he hobbled to greet us along with Atticus, Ylva and a much healthier looking Kara. My reunion with Kara was as though we were alone in the world.

"I owe you a life again, father. You went to Hibernia and Ynys Môn to save me when I was a child and now when I am an old woman you risk your life for me. Was ever there a better father?"

I smiled, "What else should a father do for his child? I am glad that you are well."

She clung on to my arm, "I fear that, while I am well, I will never be the force I once was. It is now down to Ylva."

"And that is good for we must all pass on the burden to the next generation." I turned to Sámr, "You and Baldr should get back to your families. I am safe now"

Sámr hugged me, "And I would have you stay safe. I will ride to speak with Ketil and Ráðulfr in a day or so, and then I will go to Dyflin."

"Spend time with your family first. Wait until the bairn is born then your mother and father will be here to watch over your family while you build up the alliances, we shall need to defeat our enemies."

"Thank you, I now understand the sacrifice that you made for so many years. Will I have a son who will fight me?"

I laughed, "I know not. I thought I was doing a good job and raising sons who would wish to follow me. Perhaps they did but not in the way I hoped. You can only do your best with Ragnar.

The Norns spin and they weave. They plot and they plan. We are like the insects who find themselves sticking to their webs. Live life, Sámr. I have few years left to me. I just want to see your children grow. I wish to hear them say my name and to sit them on my knee. I would like them to hear one of Haaken's tall tales and I would see them happy. All else is down to you."

Erik said, "I am much better now, lord, and Ylva says I can return to your hall tomorrow."

"Take all the rest you like. Thank you, Ylva."

"There are no thanks necessary. He is a Viking with a true heart. He risked his life for my mother. In my eyes, he is a hero."

When they had returned to their hall Atticus said, "And are you back for good now, lord? There will be no more ridiculous adventures."

"Aye, you annoying old man. I will be here but you should know that your lessons paid off."

"My lessons?"

"We used a lever to get a rock from the top of Erik's foot. Archimedes and his engineering worked. Sometimes you can be quite useful!" Although he said nothing, I could see that I had pleased the old Greek.

"I will fetch you some ale!" He disappeared to the ale barrel.

Germund the Lame came in, "He fretted and worried about you, lord, especially when he heard you had been left behind! I too am pleased you are home."

"Do not get too comfortable, Germund, war is coming."

He nodded, "And this will be my last one but it is good to know that when I fight, I will be fighting for my people. When I fought for the Emperor it was for money, it was for gold. When I was young that was important but now, I can see that it is better to fight for your beliefs. You gave me a life here, lord, and I am grateful. I did not think I could be so happy. I hope I survive this war but if I do not then I will go to Valhalla content. I will have fought on the right side for once rather than the one which paid me."

It was the most I had heard Germund the Lame speak at one time and he was right. I had never fought for gold yet I was a rich man. Successful warriors always were but I had not fought for coin. No man had ever hired me. I had chests of coins and jewels which I needed to give away. I had grandchildren and great-grandchildren who would benefit from my riches. It was then I remembered the other stones.

I took the leather pouch and emptied them. I took out one of the blue ones. I would keep that one for blue stones were Odin's stones. I would give the other blue one to Sámr and the green to his wife. Green was a stone for a woman. I would take my blue stone to Haaken Bagsecgson. I had some gold coins and he would be able to melt them down to make a mount for the blue stone. I would wear it around my neck. I had the wolf charm, but Odin's stone would add to my protection.

Atticus brought me some ale and he looked at the stones. "Was that what it was all about, lord? Some jewels?"

I sighed. This would be a long debate. I swallowed some of the ale. It was good, "This is fine ale, Atticus. Did you brew it?"

"I do not brew ale but I know the alewives who do. They like it when I speak with them for I am polite. It appears to be a novelty!"

"No, Atticus. Vikings just speak plainly and we do not dress up our words. We say what we feel and if something displeases us then we say so."

"That is uncivilised."

"Like going to a mountain to retrieve stones yet the stones have already begun to heal my daughter. How do you explain that, Greek?"

"I cannot but there will be a rational explanation."

I drank some more ale. I was enjoying this debate for I could sense that I was winning. "Then explain how my dream told me exactly where to find the stones. Erik crawled into a small space and found them immediately."

He pointed an accusing finger at me, "You put the boy's life in danger for the stone! He may yet be crippled."

"No, he will not. Ylva has said so and you are on shifting sands, Atticus. You cannot explain it. This does not fit in with the miracles of your White Christ."

He sat in the chair he used when we played chess, "And Germund says that there will be war..." I nodded. "Here?"

"I fear so. We were not ruthless enough when the Danes last came. We should have followed them and slaughtered them and then we would be safe."

I did not believe that. We were a clan with too many enemies. Strathclyde, the Walhaz, Mercia, Wessex, even Northumbria, all hated me and my clan. The difference was that we knew the Danes were coming soon. Ubba's father had reaped a great reward in Paris. He had taken great quantities of gold. He would have men eager for more glory and what greater glory was there than the taking of the Land of the Wolf and the sword that was touched by the god? Ragnar's Spirit was like a flame which drew the moths and insects to it.

"But you will not fight."

"Should I stand and let others defend my land, my home, my family? I am nothing without them. Aye, I will fight and before you ask, yes I might die." He just stared at me as though he could not believe the words I had said. I realised that I had been harsh. "But you need not fight. We will win. Many of us may die but we will win and you will have a place with Sámr when I am gone. His son and his new child will need to be educated. I am sure that is why the Norns sent you to me. Our threads are bound together."

He stood and shook his head, "Young Ragnar Sámrsson may be but a babe yet he talks more sense than you already! I will fetch food!"

I laughed as he left. The verbal duels were good. They kept my mind sharp. Germund the Lame joined me and we discussed the ale. Atticus could never understand how we could derive so much pleasure from fermented water. We never praised his food in the same way. The truth was his food was often too fancy. Germund and I were Vikings and preferred plainer fare. His food was enjoyable but it did not make our spirits rise like a good ale. When Atticus brought in the food, I saw that he had catered for Germund and me. It was plainer fare and he had managed to acquire some wheat to make wheat, oat and rye bread which he knew I enjoyed. The meal was a calf's foot and some of the meat from around the shin of an old cow. It had been cooking all day with onions and wild garlic. The meal was one of my favourites for my mother used to cook it for me. The gravy was almost gelatinous and the meat so tender that even a warrior with no teeth could eat it.

"Atticus, you have excelled yourself, eh Germund the Lame?"

"Aye, lord, warrior's food!"

Atticus gave me a thin-lipped smile, "A simple enough rustic dish, lord. I am pleased it meets with your approval." He was happy. We had servants to clear the table and wash the pots. Atticus and I played chess. Perhaps my mind was sharper than normal for I managed to beat him. Atticus never liked that and we played two more games just so that he could show that he was superior. I did not mind.

Erik returned the next day and Atticus fussed over him as though he was his own son. I had given Atticus a dilemma. He was annoyed with me for having placed Erik in danger but also grateful that I had saved him. I left Atticus to make Erik comfortable and I took the gold and the stone to Haaken Bagsecgson. He was more than happy to make the piece for me.

I took gold from my purse to pay for it but he shook his head, "There will be gold left over from the piece, lord. This will be an honour."

"There is something else I wish you to do for me," I explained exactly what I wanted. On the journey north, the idea had been born and grew and now I gave it birth by speaking it.

"This will not be a quick commission, lord."

"So long as I am still alive when it is done then I will be happy."

"I will let you know when I need to have you return to my workshop."

I smiled, "I am going nowhere!"

I took a turn around the settlement before I visited with Kara and Ylva. Every person who lived within the wooden walls was known to me. I had known some of their parents and grandparents. These were not farmers. These were the folk who made things which others needed. There were women who sewed fine clothes. There were tanners and cheesemakers. Of course, farmers and their families also made cheese and sewed clothes but as our warriors all raided, they had coins and what better way to spend them than by visiting Cyninges-tūn. Once Windar's Mere had had such trades and a market but the last war had ended that.

They now travelled across the Hawk's Head to trade and to buy. Even as I headed to the hall of women, a farmer and his family came through the gate. It was Aude who lived by Torver which lay to the south of The Water. We had a good life and I would not see it changed. He stopped to speak with me, "We heard of your adventure, lord. The Allfather favours you."

"It is the land he favours, Aude. And your family grows?"

"Aye lord, they grow and they prosper. Soon I will be a grandfather and that is good." We walked together towards the centre of the stronghold.

Ylva must have seen my progress and she was waiting inside the door to the hall. It was still the same as it had always been. There was one long room and the women who lived there shared everything. It always felt special to me for most of the women were volvas. A warrior could feel power as soon as he stepped under its lintel. With Aiden gone there were few men who came inside. I would have to ask Erik how he found the experience.

Ylva led me to the fire where her mother sat with a wolf skin around her shoulders. It was one I had killed many years ago. Kara still looked older than she should but she now had colour and her eyes were bright once more. She held out her hand for me to hold. Ylva had placed a chair next to my daughter's.

"Now that you have had a night in your hall, father, we can talk of other things. First, I am sorry that my illness prevented me from helping you."

"You and Aiden did more than enough in former years. We both know that this is the work of the Norns."

"Aye. We do and it is not over yet?" I shook my head, "Sámr is up to the task?" There was the hint of a question in her words.

"I know he is. It is hard watching him. It was the same when I watched you and Wolf Killer try to walk for the first time. Your mother kept telling me that your falls were necessary but I always tried to help."

"You should know this, grandfather, he will make mistakes but he needs to learn."

Kara looked at me, "And you, father, need to learn to watch and not reach out to steady him each time he stumbles. Now is the time for both of us to enjoy this land. My illness is a warning that my time here is coming to an end. My daughter now has more power than I ever had. I can enjoy The Water and Old Olaf's craggy face. I can speak with the women of this house. I can walk amongst the folk who live around my home and discover them."

"And I, too, will do that. I learned, when on this latest trial from the Norns, that I can no longer do all that I would wish. I was just lucky that the warriors who came against me were poor. If it had been Ubba Ragnarsson then I would be dead."

Ylva shook her head, "And when he does come you will be behind a wall of shields and spears. It will be Sámr who faces the foe. All that the Clan needs is your sword and the knowledge that you live."

"Aye, the sword." It was back in my hall but it was as though the weapon had a life of its own, an existence for we spoke of it as though it was alive. "Should I give that to Sámr? It is a powerful weapon."

Kara and Ylva surprised me. I expected a decision or an answer at the least from one of them but both looked at each other. Ylva said, "We have spoken of this and can find no answer. The sword was your sword and the god touched you. The sword draws those who wish to own it like moths to a flame yet it is a symbol. We cannot give you an answer. When the time comes then a decision will be made."

I left and doubt filled my head. If Ylva did not know what to do how could a befuddled old man make a considered decision? As I was walking towards The Water Stig Sword Hand rode through the north gate, "Dragonheart, Sámr has sent me to summon his mother and father. He says that his wife will give birth within the week."

I nodded, "I will tell the volva!"

I returned to the House of Women and told Ylva. She nodded, "We will travel there today. She is a healthy woman and it should be a birth without complications. I hope Astrid and Ragnar are ready to travel as soon as they hear the message or they may miss it. We will take The Water."

"When the child is born then I will attend. I would not wish a curse to be upon the birth."

Ylva laughed, "Not that a man could serve any purpose at a birth save to get in the way."

114

"Besides I have work to do." Ylva frowned and I spread my hands, "I need a lord for Windar's Mere. I will visit with Haraldr Leifsson and ask him. That is not dangerous, is it? Sámr has his hands full as it is."

She leaned in, "But do not go alone."

"This is the Land of the Wolf and Haraldr lives close to the tarns and the haugr."

"And your enemies are gathering. What if they sent a killer? Take Germund the Lame. When you were away, he was restless. He wished to be with you and share your danger."

I took Germund, not because I was in danger but I knew that my granddaughter was right. He needed purpose and riding with me the couple of miles north would not hurt. Of course, Erik wished to come too but Ylva had been adamant that he needed at least half a month off his feet and Atticus would ensure that he obeyed her. I took my sword and I went to my chest of treasure and took a large bag of coins. I handed it to Germund the Lame.

The farm of Haraldr was not far away. There was a jumble of humps and bumps which surrounded a shallow and silt filled tarn. In summer it was plagued by flies and the humpy ground made ploughing almost impossible. I had never understood why Haraldr and his wife Gytha had chosen such a home but he appeared happy there. His family lived there in a sprawling settlement. Perhaps that was the reason. We rode around the head of the water and then took the trail which wound up the hills. I suppose that one reason he had chosen this as his farm was the fact that it was close to my home and yet he could be alone with his family. He kept sheep and cattle which grazed around the tarn. It was shallow enough for them to wade almost to the middle in hot summers and to keep cool.

Haraldr and his wife came from their home to greet me. It was not a hall. He had just two slaves and they lived in a small hut. The rest of the huts, which were used by his shield brothers, were on the top of the small bumps and lumps. Haraldr's farmhouse was just ten paces long and four paces wide. She bobbed her head as her husband greeted me.

"Lord Dragonheart, this is an unexpected pleasure. Is there trouble? Do you need my sword?"

I shook my head, "No, Haraldr, but I need you."

Gytha shook her head, "Husband, where are your manners. Lord Dragonheart should be inside and away from the sun. Come, lord, I have some freshly brewed ale. Sven, see to the horses!"

I smiled. In war, Haraldr was fearless but here, in his own home, his wife ruled. The slave hurried to obey and Haraldr spread his arm for us to enter. "I am sorry, lord. Gytha is right."

The house was simply furnished. There was a table and four chairs. Haraldr had made the chairs. I thought back to my wife, Brigid, she would never have sat on such crudely made objects. My son Gruffyd had inherited her ideas for his throne had been beautifully carved. When I had been a slave with Old Ragnar, I had been content to sit on the floor before the fire. I did not mind the finish of a chair so long as I did not get splinters!

The ale was good and I said so. Gytha was a true alewife and proud of her beer, "I toast the barley, lord. I think it gives it a better flavour. The tarn may not be the best for fish but the water makes good beer. I will leave you to speak with my husband and I will prepare food."

"No Gytha, we need no food and what I say concerns you." A frown creased her face and I smiled to appease her worry. "It is nothing bad I can promise you." She nodded and held her husband's hand. They were close. "You have a good home here, Haraldr and you are happy."

"Aye, lord, I wished to live close to Cyninges-tūn to enable me to be at your side when you need me. My sons and daughters are happy here."

"And if I asked you to go further away?"

His face fell. "Have I offended you, lord?"

I shook my head, "The opposite. I apologise, Haraldr, I am a clumsy old man. I should speak more plainly. I need a lord to rule the eastern side of my land. Ketil and Ráðulfr rule the north and the northeast, Mordaf the south-east but since Asbjorn died then the east lacks a lord. Eystein Asbjornson has learned much but you have more experience."

Haraldr nodded. Like all Vikings, he did not know how to speak anything other than that which was in his heart, "Asbjorn was a good warrior. I was sad at his end. You would wish me to rebuild Windar's Mere?"

Eystein and the men who lived along the Mere were now dispersed and lived alone in their farms. I had hoped that Eystein would have taken on the rebuilding of his father's domain but he had not. It was another reason I had chosen Haraldr.

"No, I wish you to build a new home further south. You remember the farm of Beorn the Bull Keeper?"

"Aye, the Danes slew him and butchered his mighty bull."

I nodded, "His farm lay on a small hill. It is close to the island. I would have you build a stronghold there. You could still have your cattle. Beorn chose it because it suited his animals. I would have you become Jarl of the East and lord of that land." The two of them looked at each other and I saw Gytha nod. Before Haraldr could accept I went on, "Do not answer hastily, Haraldr. When I was at Wyddfa I dreamed that the Danes were coming back. If they do then the Mere might well be the route they choose to enter my land. There will be danger."

Gytha smiled, "Lord Dragonheart, when last they came it was Cyninges-tūn which was attacked. My husband and I do not fear danger."

"I will be honoured to accept, Lord Dragonheart."

"Good. Would you wish me to come with you and explain to Eystein?"

He laughed, "If I cannot bend Eystein to my will then I should not be lord. The Dragonheart has given me the land and I will take and hold it."

"You will need hearth weru."

"I have shield brothers. They will come with me. You have given me the land and I will use it well."

"Germund." Germund handed over the coins. "Good warriors need payment. You will need to build. Use this coin. You are lord of the Mere and all the land which surrounds it. That land is rich. I know that you will be a good ruler but build well. When the Danes come, I do not want them to ravish the Mere. Your task is to blunt their spears and swords so that Sámr can defeat them."

"He is a good warrior. He is young but he has a wise head. When I heard that Ráðgeir questioned him, I was angry. Sámr swore an oath!"

"Good, then I leave all else to you. Yours is the last gift I give. Once Sámr's new child is born then the Dragonheart will enjoy The Water."

Gytha squeezed my hand, "And it is rightly deserved."

Ragnar and Astrid reached Cyninges-tūn the day after I had returned from Haraldr's. They had left home as soon as Stig Sword Hand had delivered his message. Astrid took charge. "Husband, stay here with your grandfather. We will have enough men under feet as it is. I will send for you and the Dragonheart when the bairn is born."

Ragnar beamed and spread his arm, "And that will be no hardship for Atticus is a fine cook."

My Greek beamed with the flattery and gave me a look which said, *'I told you so'*.

After Astrid had gone, I said, "Your flattery will come back to haunt me. That insufferable Greek will crow about it from now until Samhain!"

"But his food is good! Even my mother liked it and she knew her food."

Elfrida had been a good woman. I missed her. I became a little sad for I would never see her again. I would see Erika but Elfrida had been a Christian. She would be with the White Christ and I found that hard to accept. I had not said goodbye to the wife of my first born and would never get the chance to do so. At my age such things were important.

I decided to make up for that by speaking with Ragnar. We spoke not of Danes and wars nor sons who rebelled against their fathers. Instead, we spoke of the Land of the Wolf, of Ulla War Cry, of his daughters, Ada and Astrid. We spoke of his land and how he was reclaiming what had been a forest. He had become a farmer. Once a warrior he could still fight but some men were like that. They found a different direction that was peaceful. It was rare in Vikings and I think the reason for Ragnar's conversion was twofold: his father and brother's murder had scarred him and his mother had been a woman who loved to see things grow. When he married Astrid then Ragnar was, in effect, lost to the shield wall. I had been too busy to notice. My eye looked within and not without. Now that Sámr would be my heir then I had the chance to listen to those around me. I found that, far from being bored, I was fascinated by his efforts.

Atticus brought in the food and he and Germund joined us.

"Grandfather, I hope that you do not think that because I look to the land, I have neglected the bondi and the warriors of Whale Island and Úlfarrston."

"Have you?"

"No, I still have warriors who are happy to fight in a shield wall as am I. It is just that those who live in the land of Pasgen and of me prefer to fish and to grow things but once each sennight we meet and practise with bows, sword, shield and spear. My men are all well-armed. We can muster more than a hundred spears and we count ten byrnies!"

"That is good but, remember, you just defend your walls. Our world is changing. The Danes grow while our numbers remain constant."

"And you had but two sons."

I shrugged, "The Norns spin and I am content. I have but one daughter left to me and a son who is estranged. Perhaps that was the price I had to pay for Ragnar's Spirit. I am lucky, Prince Butar had no children and Haaken One Eye has no sons. A man should be grateful for what he has."

It was good to talk to the father of my heir. We drank and ate well. Even Atticus appeared in a good mood. We rose early and walked around The Water and Cyninges-tūn. We ate a good lunch and then, in the middle of the afternoon a boat arrived. Baldr was at the helm, "You are summoned, Lord Ragnar and Lord Dragonheart. Aethelflaed has given birth. It is a girl. She has been named Ylva Sámrsdotter."

"And the babe and the Mother are well?"

"They are lord."

"Then let us not tarry!"

Sámr
Chapter 11
Distant war drums

When my daughter was born there was no question of naming her anything other than Ylva. The birth had not been easy. All had expected the child to be born quickly and she was not. But for Ylva the baby might have died and that would have destroyed my wife. Ylva saved her and my wife.

As Aethelflaed nursed the red-faced baby I said, "Once more, Ylva, I am in your debt."

"Our threads are entwined. What happens to you affects me, it is *wyrd*." She drew me aside. "Since I have returned to Cyninges-tūn I have dreamed."

"The Danes?"

"And more. There were faces I saw which I did not know. The sooner you visit with Bergil, the better. I will suggest that your mother stays with Aethelflaed. It will be good for them both. You can return to Whale Island with your father and take a ship to Dyflin. Bergil is a good friend and he has sharp ears. He may know more than my vague dreams. This Dane uses witches too."

"But what of Ketil and Ráðulfr? The Dragonheart wished me to speak with them too."

"And so you should but you need to find out all that you can before you speak with them. Haraldr will soon be taking over at Windar's Mere. That gives you a warning."

My father and great grandfather both looked ecstatically happy when they strode through the gates of Hawk's Roost. I had wondered if they would be disappointed in a girl. My father embraced me first and said, "Well done"

"I did nothing!"

"You fathered a daughter and as my grandfather knows that can lead to great things. Kara and Ylva should show you that.

Ylva Sámrsdotter can be the heart of this land just as Ragnar Sámrsson can be. Now let me see this new member of the clan."

I led him through to Aethelflaed. I saw that the Dragonheart hung back. When I returned to the main hall I said, "You could have come with father."

"This is his moment. I am composing myself and my thoughts. I will not see your daughter grow to be a woman. I must plant the seeds in her head now. My words will be chosen carefully so that when I am in the Otherworld, she will recognise my voice."

I did not like the way he was talking. "Do not talk that way! You will have years yet to watch her grow and she will know your voice from the stories you tell her."

He nodded but I saw, in his eyes, that he did not believe my words. He went to hold Ylva, my daughter, when my father had enjoyed his moment with her. I saw the Dragonheart's forehead touch my daughter's and then he spoke in her ear. She did not cry and appeared content. When he handed her back to Aethelflaed the baby was asleep. He did not tell me what he had said.

The first day of Ylva Sámrsdotter's life was hectic and passed in a blur. My wife was exhausted. Ylva said that she would sleep in the same room in case Aethelflaed needed for anything. I was relegated to the warrior hall with the men. It was probably a good thing for we wet the baby's head. That is Viking for becoming drunk. It was easy to do for everyone raised his horn to speak of my daughter and we all drank when they did so. Atticus said that the Romans called this a toast. We had many such toasts.

The Dragonheart's was the most poignant toast and the one which moved my father to tears, "Here is to Ylva Sámrsdotter, may she be the light of the clan and a joy to her grandfather, may she live as long as she wishes and have all the happiness that the Land of the Wolf can bring. She is named for the wolf and she has the heart of a hero for she is Ylva Sámrsdotter!"

All cheered and banged their horns on the table. More ale was spilt than drunk. Aethelflaed had anticipated the wetting and over the last fortnight, she had had much ale brewed. We would not run out.

Ylva and Kara left the next day for Aethelflaed had recovered well and my daughter was healthy and showed no ill effects from the long birth. Before she left Ylva said, "Do not tarry here. Your wife is well. Let your mother enjoy being a grandmother. She and Aethelflaed have not had enough time together yet. This will make them as one. A mother and a grandmother who think as one are a powerful force. Get to Dyflin. You are now a leader and with it comes a greater responsibility than fatherhood."

I spoke with Aethelflaed and she understood. My mother did not and it took the intervention of my father to calm her down. I left the next day with my father and great grandfather. Baldr remained behind to guard my home and I took just my hearth weru. We would use a crew from Úlfarrston to sail the short stretch of water to Dyflin. When we took horses at Cyninges-tūn I saw that my great grandfather and father desperately wanted to come with me to Dyflin but they knew that I had to do this alone. Atticus' face, in contrast, was joyous. He had his lord in his hall and that pleased him.

As we rode south, I used my father to sound out ideas. "You say that many of those who live and work on your lands fish and farm?"

"Those are their main occupations. Why?"

"I am just musing. Bear with me, father." He nodded. "And we still have ships which sail and trade?"

"Aye, the men of Úlfarrston are natural traders and the offspring of Leif Tryggvasson and Lars Siggison still ply the seas as their grandsires did. Why?"

"Few of us go to sea to raid these days. Many do as you do but the seas are filled with enemies. I fear that our knarr and snekke may be attacked by the pirates of Man or taken by the Walhaz. I would have each ship which leaves have warriors aboard. They would not be there to sail but to fight enemies."

"That would eat into the profits of the captain. The men would need to be paid."

I shook my head, "You told me that you already have a practice each sennight. We extend that. Every man who reaches the age of fourteen summers promises to give three moons to serve on a knarr. They will learn about the sea which is in our blood and they will learn to fight." I could see he was not convinced. "It is too late to initiate this plan this sailing season. What if the Walhaz were to come? Or the Danes? Who would warn us? If they see a knarr they would attack it. I have seen how good are our archers. With half a dozen archers on board a knarr then they would have a chance to escape. If nothing else they could row and bring word of the danger." He nodded. "I do not expect your men to be an army which stands as a shield wall but I would have them guard our southern border, the sea."

"Then it shall be done!" He gave me a strange look. "You think that we can simply sit behind our walls and defeat the Danes? The last time they came they were so close to success that we almost lost the Land of the Wolf."

"I know and that is why our new strategy builds on what worked then. You held them here in the south and that allowed Dragonheart to bring men from Cyninges-tūn. This time we ensure that our borders are safe and then bring an army big enough to defeat the Danes." I shrugged, "Like your grandfather, I am not happy about fighting this war at all but there are too many places they could invade. We need to choose a place where we can fight them and that will be outside the walls of one of our strongholds. Since the last attack, they have all been strengthened. What we do not have is enough men and Gruffyd's vacillation does not help us. Mordaf needs his father's men to give him a chance."

"Surely Gruffyd will help his son!"

"Father, you have spoken to Gruffyd. Is he the same man he was ten years ago? I was still a child then and perhaps I was wrong but I thought he was a better man than he has shown lately."

Father was silent and that silence was eloquent.

When we reached Whale Island Ulf was still working on the drekar. "You need to go out again?"

"Just to Dyflin."

He looked relieved, "That she can do but I have sheets and stays to replace. Each time we fight there is wear and tear. We can do that when we return. And a crew?"

"I have ten and my father will supply another ten. We go on a peaceful errand."

"Then let us hope that there are no pirates out there for such a small crew might be at risk."

Ulf Long Sight never exaggerated and I heeded his warning. "We leave at dawn."

123

When I entered my father's hall I said, "I would have good archers on the drekar and plenty of arrows. If any have the Saami bow then choose them. Ulf Long Sight is being cautious and it is no bad thing."

He smiled, "I had already done so. Besides. the best archers make the best rowers."

I did not take an oar this time and I wore my mail. Ulf Long Sight was being careful and so would I. I had ten hearth weru with me and six of them had mail. If we hit trouble then the seven of us would be at the fore. I looked up at the sail. The wolf's head marked my ship as a drekar from the Land of the Wolf. We would have to furl the sail before we landed. They would soon discover who I was but I needed to slip ashore and speak with Bergil and his brothers.

The wind was from the north and west. It meant we would not need to row until we neared the coast but the wind was both wet and cold. I had my sealskin cape with me. I looked at Leif and Lars, two of my younger hearth weru. I saw that they were shivering. They had no capes. I had with me, some coins and if the market in Dyflin was open I would buy them both one. A leader did that for his oathsworn. I would not buy them mail for that was a purchase a warrior made himself. In battle, it was a sign for those you fought of your skill. The better the mail the richer you were and that meant the more men you had killed. I had been given my first byrnie but my new one had been paid for by me. It was the best that gold could buy. I had had it treated with charcoal so that it was like the Dragonheart's. It looked black. It also resisted rust better.

It took most of the day to reach Dyflin. We furled the sail when we saw the smudge of the coast and rowed the last few miles. The rain which had fallen all day had finally ceased but I could see more clouds to the west. We would have heavy rain but a swifter journey home. The ship's boys saw no ships other than traders. There were no pirates on the horizon. As usual, the longphort was busy. Ulf spied a drekar leaving the longphort and he headed for the berth it left. I saw a drekar and a knarr from Orkneyjar. There was a Norse dragon ship. There was also a Dane. That signified nothing. Ubba Ragnarsson was but one

Dane. I spied at least one Wessex trader and there were four other ships which could have come from any port.

As Ulf nudged us into a berth I said, "I will just take Stig, Einar and Leif. If you need to make any purchases then that is fine. I will send word if we are to stay the night."

"Be careful. I know that Bergil is a friend but this is a den of thieves. Stay away from the quiet areas."

"I have been here before, Ulf."

"Aye but then you were not the heir of the Dragonheart."

His words were a stark reminder of my new position. I nodded and left the ship. When I had been here with my great grandfather he had been recognised and all men had stopped and stared. At the moment I was a young warrior with expensive mail and I was largely ignored but the word would soon spread. The other captains at the longphort would ask about me and once I was announced at Jarl Bergil's hall then there would be no hiding. I took the decision. We passed through the market and I stopped so that I could buy Leif and Lars their seal skin capes.

Some traders had packed up already. Inclement weather often meant repairing to an inn or tavern for the day. I saw that one seal skin trader remained and showed no sign of packing away. We wandered the other stalls picking up daggers and weapons or examining adornments for weapon belts. It was while we were admiring a baldric that the owner, a Saxon, said, "You four likely lads must be getting ready for the raid, eh? You have come to the right place. I have the best weapons for they are Saxon made and we make the most sought-after blades." He tapped his nose. "I also have some spells I can sell to you. No matter how good a warrior you are if you are going into the Land of the Wolf then you have a witch to face."

Stig was experienced enough to keep a straight face but I saw Lars and Leif look up in surprise. I handed them a purse, "Go and buy yourself seal skin capes. We will find you."

I saw the hint of an argument and then they saw my face and nodded, "Aye, lord."

The Saxon looked surprised, "You are a little young to be a lord. What is your name, sir?"

I leaned in, "You know, Saxon, that Ubba Ragnarsson would not be happy if I told you my name. His plans are supposed to be secret."

I put enough of a threat in my voice to make him recoil. "I am sorry, lord. My tongue runs away with me but it is common knowledge in every other port I have visited. It has given me a good trade. I visited the Walhaz, Mercia and Veisafjǫrðr before I came here. These are my last three blades and I brought twenty. I will have to return to Wessex before I can sail to Alt Clut. Can I interest you in them?"

I shook my head, "I have a fine blade. Remember, Saxon, watch your tongue."

I waited until we were well away from the stall before I spoke with Stig. "This is worse than I thought. Every enemy in the western world must be coming here."

"The man may be wrong, lord."

"He has sold seventeen swords. He is a business man. He might be wrong about many things but what he buys and sells will not be amongst them."

We found Lars and Leif. They handed me my purse and showed me the capes. Lars said, "Sorry, lord, we could not disguise our surprise."

"From now on do not call me, lord. It attracts too much attention. Let us find Bergil and hope that he can give us more accurate information. I cannot believe a conspiracy of so many people who hate each other."

Stig said, "Unless they hate the Dragonheart worse than each other."

With that worrying thought in my head, we went to the hall of the Jarl of Dyflin. The two guards at the door were going to refuse me admittance until I used my name. As soon as I did their attitude changed and they parted to let me enter. Bergil was seated at a table with his men and his two brothers. After the battle with the Danes, the two brothers, Benni and Bjorn, had returned to Dyflin. They still had farms in the Land of the Wolf but they had been raiding with Bergil. The three were reputed to be three of the richest Vikings. I counted on the fact that they owed all that they had to my great grandfather. If they had joined the conspiracy then all hope was gone.

When they looked up at me, they each had a guilty look upon their face. Bergil stood. There was not the usual smile, instead, he waved his men away, "Go to the warrior hall, I need to speak alone with these men." His men showed little surprise and left. I recognised a few of them for they had served with the brothers before. "We were just talking about you. Word came that your drekar had arrived in port. Sit, for we have much to talk about."

I sat and took the horn of ale which Benni proffered. My hearth weru helped themselves. "I came here to find out about the plans of the Danes and I have discovered much already. Does the look on your faces tell me that I need to fear you also?"

"No, Sámr Ship Killer, for we are loyal to the Dragonheart. Did we not prove that when I came to your aid last time?"

"I am not the Dragonheart and it is no secret that he has named me his heir. You owe me nothing."

"The Dragonheart is dead?"

"No."

"Then so long as he lives you do not need to doubt us." The words slipped out without Bergil meaning to utter them and they told me much about their thoughts.

"But you are saying that the oath dies with my great grandfather."

They all looked at each other and guilt was all over their faces. I was angry but I forced myself to keep it inside. Did we have any allies left at all? I had come here thinking to enlist the support of the brothers now it looked as though I would have to persuade them not to join in the attack against us. I stayed calm. The worst thing to do would be to threaten or cajole. We needed their knowledge and help.

I just nodded at them and then spoke. If they were expecting anger and vitriol then they were disappointed. The disappointment was in my voice. Afterwards, Stig Sword Hand said that my voice sounded sad and old. "Tell me then of this conspiracy so that men of true hearts can fight against it."

Bergil looked hurt as though I had stabbed him with a dagger, "We did not say that we would fight against you, Sámr!"

"Nor did you say that you would help me. Time is pressing, Bergil, and I have a great grandfather who expects me to save the Land of the Wolf from this threat."

He nodded, "Ubba Ragnarsson has spent the time since he ran with his tail betwixt his legs planning the downfall of the house of the Dragonheart. King Rhodri of Gwynedd was the last to join the alliance. He has King Beorhtwulf of Mercia who will bring men from the south. He tried to get the Hibernians to join him but they just argued amongst themselves about who should come to attack you. King Dumnagual of Alt Clut has said that he will help the Danes when the Danish attack draws the men of the Eden south. The Danes will come over the High Divide at Einmánuður."

I nodded and then said, "And what about Veisafjorðr? What of the Vikings there?"

This time Bergil's eyes widened, "How....?"

"I am young but I have ears and I have a mind."

"Haraldr Beer Belly will not attack until the Dragonheart is dead."

He was silent. "And what of Man? What do they plan?"

"They slew the Dane who came to ask them. They are unpredictable. The Danish ship, *'Crow'*, lost five men before they fled. The men of Man sought to take their ship. They sailed from Man to here and asked us to help. They left as you arrived."

I remembered the ship. I had not looked too closely at it and now I saw that had been a mistake. "And you, the Hafþórrsson Brothers, who owe all that they have to the Dragonheart and the Clan of the Wolf. When were you approached?"

The guilt on their faces seemed to eat into them and contort them. Bergil said, "It was three days since when the ship which visited Man and then Veisafjorðr came here. We told the emissary that we would not fight the Dragonheart. We were offered coin and the land of Mercia between Belisima and the Maeresea. We still said no."

"And then you visited Haraldr Beer Belly and the men of Veisafjorðr." They nodded. Each of them looked as though they wished to be anywhere but before my gaze. "I will not say I am not disappointed, for I am. You have had days to send a message to the Dragonheart. If I had not come would we have found out the danger when the Danes attacked?" I waved a hand as though to rid the air of the image before my eyes. "And so I ask you, will you come to the aid of the Clan of the Wolf?" I pointed at Benni and Beorn, "Will you fight for the farms which were given to you?"

"If we do then the men of Veisafjǫrðr and the Hibernians will take Dyflin from us. If the Dragonheart wishes to come to Dyflin then we will give him and his family refuge."

How these men had changed. They had been true and loyal once but my great grandfather had given them Dyflin and the power had changed them. They did not wish to lose that which they had. I shook my head, "I do not think that my great grandfather would wish to end his days in a rat hole like Dyflin surrounded by men he cannot trust." Again, their faces showed the pain my words caused them and yet they had no argument. "I have a counter proposal." The pain was replaced by curiosity. "I offer you Anglesey." It was not mine to give but I knew that it was there for the taking. I had seen the Walhaz and knew that Bergil and his men could defeat them. "Join with the men of Veisafjǫrðr and some of the Hibernian kings. Sail to Anglesey when the new grass appears. There is little else in Gwynedd which is worth having but their island of Ynys Môn is rich and fertile. You could add it to your lands." I saw them considering. "That way you could sleep easier for you would have kept your honour."

"We did not say we would abandon you. We came to your aid last time."

"Dress it any way you wish Bergil but you and your brothers cannot look me in the eyes and deny any of this, can you? Had I brought Ylva and she had looked within you then what would she have seen?"

It was the threat of Ylva which worked. They clutched their hammers. "Yours is a good suggestion, Sámr. We will visit with Haraldr Beer Belly. He was unhappy about attacking fellow Vikings."

"And yet he would have done so." I stood, "One more thing, if there is any other news we should hear then, for my great grandfather's sake, send it immediately! Tarrying as you have done makes me think that you conspire against us!" They were all older than I was but my eyes burned with anger and my voice had a veiled threat.

They nodded and chorused, "We will."

I paused at the door, "And when this is all over, I pray you visit me at my home. We will see if we can come to some arrangement for if we are to be neighbours then I would have neighbours that I can trust."

Bergil nodded, "You have grown, young Sámr Ship Killer. We will do as you ask and we will speak with you when the battle and the war is over. I will send a messenger to tell you when the island is ours."

Lars started to speak as we left the hall. I held up my hand, "Not a word until we are on the ship. I am angry and I have controlled my tongue for long enough. Do not tempt me!"

When we neared the drekar I saw men gathered around the gangplank. My hand went to my sword. Then I saw that Ulf was laughing. "Say nothing until we are aboard." As we neared them, we were seen and the crowd parted to let us through.

"Here he is. This is Sámr Ship Killer, the heir to the land of the Wolf."

I saw that the crowd was actually just twelve men. Our crew had come from our drekar to speak with them. They were warriors. They had swords and leather byrnies. They had good shields which lay on the quay with their war gear. They had helmets which, although well made, showed signs of wear.

I nodded to them and the largest warrior stepped forward. He had a wolf skin about his neck and he had, not a sword but a fighting axe. He looked to be in his twenties. "I am Naddoðr of Beinn na bhFadhla. My brothers and I came here on a trading knarr. We seek a new lord."

"And Bergil of Dyflin is your new master?"

Naddoðr of Beinn na bhFadhla shook his head, "His drekar is being repaired and there is no chance of raiding. We were going to head down the coast when we saw your drekar pull in. When we heard you were from the Land of the Wolf then we thought to ask you if you wished to have eleven good swords and," he held up his fighting axe, "Pict Killer."

I was suspicious. I tried not to show it but I wondered if this was part of Ubba's plot. Did he plan on having these men inveigle themselves into places close to us and then kill my great grandfather and me? They certainly looked like warriors.

"Why did you come in a knarr and not in a drekar?"

He smiled and I looked into his eyes. I saw no deception but then when Bergil had first come to us he had had the same look. In fact, Bergil and Naddoðr looked to be very similar in appearance. "If we had a drekar, even a snekke, then we would have raided." His face clouded with shadow. "My father died and my elder brother took over the clan. He used our drekar to bury my father."

"That is a good end for a warship."

"True but my father would not have wished his ship to end that way. He was a true Viking. We came to the island from Norway and he did not stop raiding until the end of his days. He had seen but forty summers when he died raiding Alt Clut."

Alt Clut, the Norns were spinning.

"You have been in this town for long?"

"A sennight, Sámr Ship Killer. Why do you ask?"

I leaned in so that only he could hear me, "Then you have heard of the plan of Ubba Ragnarsson. You know what is about to descend upon the Land of the Wolf."

"I do."

"Then why would you choose to join what appears to be a lost cause?"

He smiled, "Even on Beinn na bhFadhla we have heard of the Dragonheart and the sword called Ragnar's Spirit. The men I lead have no families. The family men all stayed on Beinn na bhFadhla. I am the eldest by many years. Most of the men I lead have seen less than twenty summers. They wish to be Vikings and I wish to lead them. I do not think that yours is a lost cause. I have spoken with Ulf Long Sight and he is certain that you will win. Give us a chance. What have you to lose except for twelve men who wish to live like true Vikings?" Despite my best efforts, I could not truly hide the doubt in my eyes and he said, "You think that we will be as knives in the night? You think us killers." Before I could answer he took out his amulet. It was the Hammer of Thor, "I swear that we will fight for you and we will not flee. We have courage and it is Viking courage."

I heard no voice in my head other than my own but I believed him. "Then join us and welcome. Bring your war gear aboard! Ulf, when can we sail?"

"On the morning tide!"

I turned and handed a purse to Stig, "Then, Stig, go and buy food and ale. This warrior has rekindled my faith in Vikings."

That evening we ate well. Dyflin could be a rough and ready sort of place but the alehouses around the longphort served good food and ale. We were not disappointed. Naddoðr's brother sounded a little like my father. He did not wish to raid and was quite happy to stay on his island. From what I learned I deduced that their father had not been a good war chief. He took on enemies who were easy to defeat but they did not reap the rewards they might have had they raided further afield. Naddoðr was keen to learn how we acquired such good mail and weapons.

"We have a good weaponsmith and we pay for them with that which we take from our enemies. I fear, Naddoðr, that you have come at a time when we are assailed by foes and enemies."

He seemed quite happy at the prospect, "Then we will slay them all and become as rich as you."

The depression I had suffered since the meeting with the three brothers began to lift. We talked until late and I discovered that I liked Naddoðr. He had raided and fought many times under his father. It seemed the enemies he had fought had been the Picts and the men of Strathclyde. It explained why he and his men did not wear byrnies made of iron. Their enemies had been poor. That did not mean they were not good warriors but Ubba would be bringing mailed men to fight us. As we sat and ate on the quayside and Naddoðr told me his tale in full, I began to plan. My suggestion to Bergil had begun an avalanche of ideas. We had no need to sit and wait for the onslaught to overwhelm us. Ubba had come up with a sound plan but it was a cumbersome one. It relied on timing. Bergil's attack on King Rhodri would upset those plans. I hoped the jarl of Dyflin would honour his word. It was ironical that the men we mistrusted the most, the men of Man, had actually aided us. I did not think it was for the right reasons. They were just murdering pirates but the Norns had indeed been spinning. I would take the war to our enemies. The plan was vague but once I had spoken with my great grandfather and Ylva then I would have it formulated.

Sámr
Chapter 12
The War Chief

We had twelve more hands to crew the ship although, with a wind from our larboard quarter, we still would not need to row. Ulf had made some good purchases including some rope. We made our own but good rope was always handy. His ship's boys were coiling it as we headed east towards our home. Olaf was at the masthead and it was he shouted, "Drekar to the north and west."

I looked astern. Naddoðr nodded, "That is the Dane who left yesterday before you arrived. I did not like the captain. He was a squint-eyed dwarf."

"*'Crow'*?"

"Aye, do you know her?"

"I know of her. Arm yourselves. She thinks to take us but we will turn the tables on her."

"But we are the same size and equally matched!"

"Not so. They think I have a smaller crew. When they saw us arrive, we had a skeleton crew. They know not about you. Besides this messenger will be taking the news back to my enemy and if I can stop the message reaching him then I gain an advantage."

Nodding he went to his war chest. "Then we begin to become rich men this day!"

"Keep your men hidden until I give the command. I would not have him slip away."

I hoped that none of his young warriors would lose their lives. They were young and taking on a Dane was harder than the half-dressed barbarians they had fought. Even the leather byrnie Naddoðr and his men wore was better protection than the painted skin the Picts seemed to like.

"Ulf, keep this course. Sail a little more slovenly. He will try to come for the steerboard side."

"Do not worry. I can take him."

"Ship's boys take your bows with you. Bowmen have your bows ready. Let us make them think we are ill prepared. Do not don your helmets until we board them. I mean to take this ship." The crew old and new all cheered. They were in high spirits and that was good. A battle at sea was never an easy thing and the Danish captain must have been supremely confident to attempt such an attack. While I had been inattentive, the previous day, he had been the opposite. He had lost his leader and this would be a way to ingratiate himself in Ubba Ragnarsson's good books.

I glanced astern. I had not yet donned my helmet and my youthful face would encourage the Dane. I saw that our loose sail work had allowed the Dane to close. She was directly astern of us. He was trying to unnerve me but I knew which side he would use to make his attack. The closer he came to us then the easier it would be for him. He would take our wind and inexorably reel us in. We had open sea ahead of us until the Land of the Wolf, Mercia and Man. He had all the time in the world to make his move and take the young warrior whom the Norns had thrust before him.

I kept glancing astern of us. They would think that I was nervous when I was not. I was judging the moment when we would unleash our arrows. Normally we would have sent a shower at them when they were four ship's length away. I saw that the Dane had anticipated that and he had the men at the steering board covered by shields.

Ulf murmured, "A little closer, you Danish whoreson!"

They were now just a length and a half behind us. A few desultory arrows rattled on to our deck. The Danes were never very good with bows. They still used hunting arrows and hunting bows.

"Naddoðr, your men and my hearth weru will board. Be ready! You take the mast and we will take the steering board."

"Aye, lord!"

"Stig, have the grapnels ready on the larboard side."

"Aye, lord!"

Ulf shouted, "Be ready to come about!"

I donned my helmet and drew my sword. "Bowmen, rain death!" The arrows soared into the air. The Danes had become lax and their shields were no longer above them. The arrows hit their bowmen and some of their warriors.

"Now!" Ulf put the steering board over so sharply that we almost spun around. The Dane was now on our larboard side and, as our drekar went into the wind we stopped, almost as though we had hit a wall. Stig Sword Hand and my hearth weru put our newly purchased ropes to good use. They threw them at the Dane which was less than six paces from us.

"Raise the sail!"

Our archers continued to send flight after flight into dazed Danes who had suddenly been outwitted. Normally a captain knows when he is about to be grappled and he has men with axes ready to sever the ropes. It was he who had been expecting to hurl hooks at us. The men with the ropes lay on their deck, bleeding from the arrows in them. Stig Sword Hand and my men used the cleats on the gunwale to haul the two drekar together.

I ran to the forestay. The hearth weru who did not have a rope to haul were gathered there. I saw that ten Danes had been struck by arrows but their captain was busy trying to organise a defence. The trouble was he still had a full sail and the wind was trying to push him south and east. *'Úlfarr'* was like a giant sea anchor. His crew were trying to get their sail down and prepare for battle.

Our hulls had yet to bump when I heard a battle cry and Naddoðr led his young warriors over the narrowing gap to land at the mast of the Dane. I had to wait a few more heartbeats and then, as Stig Sword Hand and the grapplers tied off the ropes I leapt, with Leif and Lars close behind me, on to the Dane's deck. The Norns had been spinning. As we hit their hull, one of the Danes who had been rushing to repel us lost his footing and slipped. I landed on his back. He had a leather byrnie. That gave him little protection and I heard his back break as I landed. A mailed warrior is a heavy weight!

Drawing my dagger in lieu of a shield I ran straight at the steering board knowing that my men would be close behind. Naddoðr had described the Danish captain well. He was like an ugly goblin. That gave him an advantage for I was much taller and he would have better balance on the pitching deck. The two ships were beam on to the wind. Ulf would be using our steering board and all of his years of experience to turn the two ships but that would take time. The beginning of this battle would be largely down to luck.

The archers we had brought had been trained by my father and they continued to rain death on the Danes. Even as I ran to the Danish captain an arrow smacked into the face of the warrior who guarded his right and a second hit the warrior holding the steering board. Ulf now had complete control of both ships. As was usual in sea battles warriors fought not as individuals but gathered to defend the important places. Naddoðr was attacking one knot of warriors at the mast but the hearth weru and the mailed warriors were at the steering board and faced us. A few had shields. The Danish captain was one but many were like me with two weapons. Combat would be swift and deadly not to say brutal. I was glad that I was wearing my mail.

I feinted with my sword and the Dane raised his shield. I lunged with my dagger. His small stature meant my dagger went towards his shoulder and not his gut. His sword came up to block the blow and he scored a hit on my left hand. I saw him grin as his blade came away bloody. He had first blood and some warriors thought that would determine a battle. The Dragonheart had told me that last blood was always the deciding factor.

Ulf must have made a move with our steering board for the deck suddenly canted as he tried to turn us. Some warriors slipped and slid down the deck. My feet were well apart for I was preparing a second blow. Lars' opponent was a big man and he had fallen to one knee. Lars brought his sword up to strike the Dane under the chin. Lars was young but he was strong. His sword tore off half the face of the luckless Dane and his blood spattered the Danish captain. This time I was committed to my own blow and my sword was coming down towards the Dane's shoulder. He was bringing his shield up when he was spattered by the blood and brains from the man to his left and that slight distraction made his movements a heartbeat slower than they should have been. His shield only half blocked the blow and the weight of my blade and my arm hit his helmet. He was wearing a skull protector but I saw that I had dented his helmet and he reeled backwards. His size saved him for he kept his balance but only at the loss of two paces when he stepped back.

I moved into the space he vacated. Lars was with me and we had now broken their wall of warriors. As our archers laid down their bows and poured over the side the Danes were outnumbered. I contemplated asking them to surrender then I remembered that our failure to be ruthless the last time we had fought them had resulted in this new threat. There would be no quarter!

A ship's boy from the Danish ship launched himself at me from my left. He had a small axe in his hand and I was forced to flick my hand up to deflect the blade. The Danish captain saw his opportunity and rammed his sword at me. I was young and I was quick. I turned. The sword hit me but it was a glancing blow along my mail. Sadly for the young ship's boy, his movement brought him close to the combat and as the Danish captain withdrew his sword, he tore open the Danish boy's belly. The boy screamed as his guts poured on to the deck. I swept my dagger towards the face of the Danish captain. All around me, we were winning but, so long as their captain lived, they would fight to the death. My dagger tore across the nose of the Dane. Raising my sword, I stepped forward. This time the blow to his helmet, his sliced nose and the fact that he was having to move backwards all contributed to his demise. My sword hacked across his neck and bright blood spurted and arched across the stern.

Lars was being pressed by two men. This was not the place for honour. I rammed my dagger into the back of one and slid my sword up under the ribs of the other. The captain's death tore the heart from the surviving Danes. Five of them, none of whom were mailed, hurled themselves overboard. To remain on their ship would result in their death. In the sea, there was a chance that they might live. I turned to survey the carnage. The Danes had all died. We had not escaped unscathed. Erik of Torver lay dead. I had lost one of my hearth weru. Two of the men who had followed me from my father's home would also never return home. Naddoðr had lost two also but, in the grand scheme of things, it was a victory and our losses were negligible. In addition, we now had a Danish drekar. More importantly, we had denied Ubba Ragnarsson news of his attempt to build an alliance against us. The unknown was a dangerous place for any leader. Until I had visited with Bergil we had been in that land. The news I had had from Bergil was unpalatable but we now knew the size of the problem. I had plans to thwart our enemy but I needed to get home and speak with Ylva and my great grandfather.

The decks of both ships erupted as every man and boy began chanting my name, "Sámr Ship Killer!" over and over. This was my victory. With a small crew, I had beaten, alone, an enemy who should have defeated me. It was a start! Naddoðr of Beinn na bhFadhla and his men sailed our new drekar, now named *'Danish Crow'*.

Before we untied his new ship, I said, "You said you would serve me. If you do so I give you this ship and ask that you help to fight for my cousin, Mordaf!"

He nodded, "Lord, already we are richer. I will do all that you say. We are your men until death!"

I left Naddoðr and his men to examine and, if needs be, repair *'Danish Crow'* at Whale Island. I took horses and rode with my hearth weru for Cyninges-tūn. I barely had time to tell my father what I had learned. He promised to send word to Mordaf and Gruffyd. I was not certain what the son of Dragonheart would do but I had done what I needed to. I had warned him of danger. As we reached the southern end of The Water, I sensed Ylva's thoughts. They had been a vague tickling in my mind from the moment we had landed but, as we rode up the road, I heard her voice. She knew I was coming. I tried to formulate my thoughts and tell her of the victory but I could not transmit them to her. My great grandfather had told me that Aiden had been able to speak with his daughter and his wife even though they were many miles apart. I was not a galdramenn. Perhaps I did not have that skill.

As we galloped through the open gates, I saw Ylva and my great grandfather waiting for me. Erik Black Toes was with them as were Atticus and Germund. While most would want to know of the battle, Atticus would examine me for wounds. When he saw my bandaged hand, he would frown and scowl!

I was not disappointed. Shaking his head, he said, "I thought, my lord, that this was a peaceful expedition?"

I shrugged, "No one told the Danes that!"

My great grandfather said, "Make yourself useful, Atticus. Food and ale. Ylva will see to the wound while we talk for I can see that there is much to talk on."

I nodded and we headed towards the hall of women. While Ylva began to take off the crude bandage I began immediately. Time was a luxury we did not have, "There is a conspiracy and it is far bigger than we could have dreamed. I fear that the clan is in grave danger."

We sat before the fire and Kara and Ylva saw to my hand. While they dressed the wound, I told them all of my news. Atticus came in halfway through. He was sent back to prepare food for us. When I finished, my great grandfather shook his head, "I would not have expected this of the brothers."

Ylva's face showed her feelings quite clearly. She was angry, "We should have known that something was wrong when the two brothers who had farms here did not return. They have been seduced by the riches of lordship. I will not forget!"

"Granddaughter, do not forget that Bergil came to our aid the last time."

Her eyes blazed with a cold and dangerous fire, "You have always had a kind heart, grandfather. It will be the undoing of you. The debt the brothers owe you can never be repaid." He nodded. She whipped her head around and said, "So, Sámr, what is this plan you have in your head." The scowl had gone and was replaced by a smile.

"You read my thoughts?"

"We are becoming more in tune with each other. When you neared The Water, I tried to speak with you but you know not how to control your powers. We need to use the steam hut. You have a plan and you seek our opinion."

"Aye, that is it."

Kara smiled and came over to kiss me on the forehead. "And I am not completely healed yet. I need to sleep. I will retire."

"Come Ylva, Sámr, we will go to my hall. Atticus should have food prepared and I think better seated on my chair with Ragnar's Spirit close by."

Once in his hall, I felt more comfortable too. The house of women was a house of healing. The Dragonheart's hall was a place of planning. Atticus and Germund sat at the table as well although neither spoke.

"Dragonheart, when we last had a threat from Alt Clut you went with the men of the Eden and gave them a warning of the consequences of attacking us."

"You would have me do the same again?"

I shook my head, "They had the one warning and that is all they get. I would take men from Cyninges-tūn and sail in our two drekar to Ráðulfr's stronghold. I would use his men and those of Ketil Windarsson. We attack Alt Clut and subjugate King Dumnagual."

I saw Atticus' eyes widen while Germund grinned and nodded. My great grandfather said, "A bold move but Alt Clut is a hard place to take."

"I know. We would land to the seaward side and then use one of the drekar to sail upstream and draw their attention. We storm the walls while they look at the river. When we take their hall I would take hostages for their good behaviour."

Ylva gave her approval, "That is bold and the men of Strathclyde are not Danes. I take it this would be before Einmánuður?"

"It will have to be well before Mörsugur for at Mörsugur I intend to take men from Mordaf and my father and raid the Saxon strongholds on the Maeresea and the Belisima. I would, during those first months of winter, destroy all the Saxons who live to the south of Mordaf."

My great grandfather supped his ale and nodded, "That would make the King of Mercia think twice and if Bergil and the men of Veisafjǫrðr attack Anglesey then he will fear an attack on Caestir. Clever."

Even Atticus nodded, "Those games of chess have worked, lord."

"And the Danes?"

I turned to Ylva, "They are the one enemy we cannot attack for their centre is far from us. We would need a fleet. I just hope that my plan will keep them blind. When *'Crow'* does not return Ubba Ragnarsson has a choice. He can do nothing or he can send another ship north to confirm that his alliance has worked. Naddoðr is keen to raid. I will give him a crew and he can patrol the seas south of Man. If the Danes send another ship then he can take it."

Ylva smiled, "The Norns have indeed spun. Had this warrior's brother not destroyed a drekar then you might have been taken and we might have been blind to this threat."

My great grandfather said, "And your family? You are in great danger of doing that which I did and abandoning them for long periods."

"I know. When we are done, I will ride home. My wife and I need a long conversation but my two raids will not take long. Alt Clut will be over in less than a sennight and Mercia will need just a fortnight. As for the Danes? I will be there with them defending my home when they come. We make this stronghold and mine capable of holding off the enemy for a month! When you appointed me heir you knew this day would come."

"I did but I hoped it would not."

Ylva kissed the Dragonheart on the top of his head, "Grandfather, you are a plaything of the Norns and the gods favour you. No matter who becomes your heir they will be the battleground for gods and Norns."

I headed home to Aethelflaed and my grandfather's words were still ringing in my ears. Was I creating problems for myself when Ragnar grew to be a man? Riding around the head of The Water I passed the tarn which Haraldr had farmed. He, his family and his hearth weru had gone. The tarn was abandoned. Would he be able to build a stronghold before the Danes came? Had I doomed him and his family to the same fate as Asbjorn? My head felt it was spinning around there were so many questions within. Stig Sword Hand and my men were silent. Hearth weru learned to gauge the mood of their leader. They knew there was nothing they could say to help me. These problems were my own to solve.

Baldr had been on the gate to my home and he descended the ladder to greet me. "It went well?"

I gave him a wan smile, "Let us say it was interesting and the Norns have been spinning. Ubba Ragnarsson is coming. I must speak with my wife, Baldr, but tomorrow I will rise early and speak with you. We have much to do."

Baldr knew me as well as any and he nodded, "For one so young you bear a heavy weight."

"And you should know that we never choose our own path. We just tread the one we are given carefully. There are traps and pits all along the way."

My wife was in the chamber we had made at the end of my hall. It was close to the fire but there was a single wall which came halfway across the hall and afforded us some privacy. Aethelflaed's face lit up when she saw me. Ragnar was having a nap and Aethelflaed put her finger to her lips. Ylva was suckling. I leaned over and kissed my wife on the forehead. I sat on the edge of the bed and looked at my family. I was lucky and I knew it. To have two healthy children and a wife who had borne them both without ill effects was not something which every family enjoyed. Many women died in childbirth. Many more children died in the first month of their life. I stroked my wife's hair. She was also young but she was strong. When I had rescued her from a fate she did not deserve she had endured great danger. I did not doubt that when I left her alone, she would be strong enough to cope. It was just that I felt guilty about it.

Ylva fell asleep on the breast and Aethelflaed laid her down on the bed next to her brother. She took my hand and led me towards the fire. The others in the hall saw our movement and left the hall. They gave us space. There were always jobs outside which needed completion. She kissed me and hugged me. She stepped back and looked at me. I knew what she was doing. She was looking for wounds. I held up my bandaged hand, "This is the only wound, my love, and it is a simple cut. Ylva has healed it."

She nodded and led me to the table where she poured me a jug of ale. "Then you had to fight?"

I nodded and sat. I pulled her on to my knee and, as I supped the ale, I told her all including my fears for our land. I was honest with her. I knew that my father was ever that way with my mother but my great grandfather had had to keep certain matters from his second wife, Brigid, and I knew the result of that error.

Aethelflaed had reason to both hate and fear the Danish threat. She nodded, "We will fight them." She touched the end of my nose with her finger, "Even though I know this means that you will be away from my bed and your family!"

I kissed her, "I do not wish to do so."

"I know, you goose. I married a warrior and a leader. I am the daughter of such a man. I know what you have to do." She stood to refill my horn. "I love this home. The trees which surround it are mighty and tall yet they began as tiny saplings. The time you are missing with your children is but a tiny speck of time. They are saplings. You will be here to watch them grow. You seek not to make our land bigger. Your quest is to keep it safe. When our enemies are dead and their bones lie bleaching in the sun then we will enjoy peace in this idyllic land. By the time Ylva can walk then we will have peace."

I looked at her in surprise, "Are you a volva now?"

She laughed and her laughter was like the beck which tinkled down to The Water, "No but I know you. You have a plan to defeat these foes and you have told me when the Danes will come. For my part, I will lay in stores of salted fish and meat. We will prepare Hawk's Roost to withstand an attack by these Danes and they will bleed upon our walls."

"You are the best of wives!" Just then there was a whimper as Ragnar woke up. I stood, "I will go and greet my son!"

Two days later Baldr and I rode, first to Ketil's stad and then to the Stad in the Eden. I took both leaders into my confidence. Ketil was older now and war had taken its toll. "I fear, Sámr Ship Killer that this battle will be one led by my son Windar Ketilsson. I am not the Dragonheart and my body has been broken too many times."

I nodded, "And you will do as the Dragonheart does. You will guard the walls of this stronghold. This is the time of the young warriors. You, Haaken One Eye, my great grandfather, all built this land. Now it is our time to make it secure."

His son was happy to follow my banner and he promised to bring two boat crews. He had no drekar and so we would have to sail the ships his men would use from Whale Island. That would not be a problem. We would have double crewed ships. They were not enough to fight a sea battle but we had no intention of doing that.

Ráðulfr Ulfsson was eager to raid the men of Alt Clut, "They are deceitful men! They do not have the courage to face us beard to beard and would rather be a knife in the night. This is good! We will be ready and I can bring the crews of three drekar."

Ráðulfr had just one drekar but he and his people had five knarr. We would use those to transport the men. Baldr and I left and headed home. I went out of our way to visit with Aðils Shape Shifter and his family. His sons were good warriors and I wanted them with us. Aðils had not fought since the battle with the Danes. He ruled Lang's Dale like his own fiefdom. He and his sons farmed along with their thralls.

He looked older and grey but his eyes were still sharp. His sons were all powerful warriors. "You have grown, Sámr Ship Killer. How is the Dragonheart?"

"He now enjoys peace. I am the one who will rule the land of the Wolf."

"Good! You will be a good leader." He took us into his hall where we enjoyed ale. His sons offered us no greeting.

I told him of Wyddfa and the stones. He clutched his amulet when I retold the tale of the cave and the flight. Then I spoke of the threat from the Danes.

"You wish us to fight?"

"It is not a case of wishing, Aðils Shape Shifter. When the Danes come, they will destroy every vestige of the Clan of the Wolf."

One of his sons, Beorn, spoke for the first time. I noticed that he wore animal skins. He had the look of an Ulfheonar and I knew that the Dragonheart viewed Aðils as the best of the Ulfheonar. He would have trained his sons well. "The Lang's Dale is remote. Even if the Danes conquered the rest of the Land of the Wolf then they would soon tire of trying to wrest this from us."

I saw Aðils flash an irritated look at his son, "I will come to Cyninges-tūn and fight alongside the Dragonheart no matter what my sons do."

I nodded. I was disappointed but I hid my disappointment. "A good leader never orders a man to fight for that lays in disappointment. I thank you Aðils Shape Shifter. It is good that you are loyal." I stared at Beorn Aðilsson. We could have used the skills of him and his brothers but Aðils Shape Shifter would be a mighty asset.

We rode to Cyninges-tūn. I saw that my great grandfather's right hand was bandaged, "What is wrong great grandfather?"

"Nothing, I was just careless with a blade."

I looked in his eyes and saw the lie. He had to have a good reason and I did not pursue the matter. I went on to tell him all that I had done. He smiled, "You have done well, Sámr, and, like you, I am disappointed in the sons of Aðils Shape Shifter but you are right. One volunteer is worth ten pressed men. And now you prepare for war?"

"Aye. Ask the men of Cyninges-tūn to be ready to leave within a sennight. We gather at Whale Island and then sail to the stad on the Eden. I will ride home and thence to Mordaf. He needs to prepare."

My great grandfather hugged me and said, "I am sorry to have inflicted this upon you. If I could then I would bear the burden."

"I know."

He pointed to Ragnar's Spirit, "You could use the sword if you wished."

Shaking my head, I said, "We both know that would be a mistake. The sword was given to you by the Allfather. I am happy with my blade. I will miss having the power of the sword with us in battle but this is now my time. I will need to find a way to fight my own battles and to win them. The Dragonheart has done his part. Now is the time for the blood of the Dragonheart to do theirs."

He suddenly looked old and sad, "And I pray to the Allfather that the cost will not be the blood of my family. Their bravery has already saved this land more times than enough."

Even as I headed back to my home, I heard the wind blowing from the east. It was a cold wind and it heralded the coming of the Danes. I was beginning a war early in the hope that I could save our land. Were the Norns ready to cut my thread as they had that of my grandfather?

Sámr
Chapter 13
Alt Clut

With my home protected by half of my men, I took the remainder and the warriors from Cyninges-tūn to Whale Island. I had sent a rider to warn my father and the shipwrights to prepare the drekar for sea, I knew that Naddoðr would have **'Danish Crow'** ready and that Ulf would have ensured that all was in order on **'Úlfarr'**. We would just need **'King's Gift'** and **'Ran's Breath'** to be prepared and we could sail north. None of the drekar would be fully crewed. Ráðulfr had more men than he could carry in his single drekar and Haaken Ketilsson needed oars for his whole warband.

My mother returned with us. She would have stayed with my wife and children longer but she had other grandchildren closer to Whale Island. It was a wrench for her. She was a hardy woman and she rode next to me without complaint.

"My son, you have a good wife and you have been blessed with healthy children. You should try to spend more time with them."

"Meaning I should war less?"

She put her hand on mine, "This war has not been decided by you, my son, I know that. Many people would say that you do not need to attack the men of Strathclyde but I know that is not true. You cannot wait for an enemy to attack. People will die if you do nothing. I know what you do is right but I still fear for you and your family. I am lucky. Your father is a good man. He stays close to home but that is because the Dragonheart has made the sacrifice. That is now your burden."

We had spoken for the rest of the journey of the hopes she had for all of her children. She knew that Ulla would soon marry and there would be more grandchildren for her. That would keep her closer to Whale Island for longer. Although she was able to ride well, we did not reach my father's home until dark. The men went to the drekar. Many would sleep aboard. The captains would put them to work early and that meant we would be able to sail quickly.

Ulla War Cry surprised me, "Brother, I would come with you on this raid."

"You need not. I will have many good men with me."

"The blood of the Dragonheart is in my veins too. I may not wish to raid but our father has told me of the danger we face. I am just one extra sword but that single sword may make all the difference."

"You could come with me on the raid on Mercia."

"I will, if the gods spare me, do that also." He smiled, "Father says it will be a short sharp campaign and that means I can be back to watch my animals and to plant my crops. Besides, there will be treasure to be taken and I will be able to afford a wife."

"You can afford a wife now, little brother."

"I am the brother of the Lord of the Land of the Wolf, the woman I marry will expect more of me than if I was just Ulla War Cry son of Ragnar!"

I saw then the burden that my title created.

With small crews, the four drekar seemed to skim the waves as we headed around the coast for the short journey to the Eden. Even though it was short and we made good time, negotiating the waters of the Eden meant we did not reach Ráðulfr until late afternoon. I was both pleased and surprised by the number of warriors who awaited us. Many oars would be double crewed. Almost a third of the warriors had mail byrnies and they had the look of seasoned men.

As Ulla and I sat with Baldr, Haaken and Ráðulfr I realised that this would be the heart of the army which would defeat Ubba. The other leaders like Naddoðr and Ráðgeir were also at the long table and they listened. Haraldr Leifsson was not there, neither was Ketil. They were building their defences. When the Danes came, they would bear the brunt of the attack.

"If the gods and the Norns will it then we can negate the attacks planned by Ubba on our flanks. It may even deter him from coming."

Naddoðr shook his head, "No, lord, he will come. We were not in Dyflin long but we heard the words from the Danes whom we slew on *'Crow'*. Ubba Ragnarsson has made this a blood feud. He has a foster father, Gangulf Gurtsson. We heard his name mentioned by many Danes. He advises Ubba and he, too, bears a grudge against the Dragonheart and the Land of the Wolf. Ragnar Hairy Breeches became rich when he raided Paris. The Danes feel that they are in the ascendancy. Ubba Ragnarsson has to remove the stain on his honour. When he fled with his tail between his legs, he lost face. They will come."

Now I knew why the Norns had sent Naddoðr. That tiny gem of knowledge was crucial. I had hoped that the Danes might not come if they heard that their alliance was in tatters. That had been the opinion of Atticus although my great grandfather had argued with the old Greek.

"Then if he comes, he will come for my great grandfather and will attack Cyninges-tūn. Your men, Haaken and Ráðulfr, will be the hammer to strike at the anvil which is Cyninges-tūn. If Ubba decides to lay waste to the lands which lie to the east of Cyninges-tūn then we will have plenty of time to gather. Naddoðr, Mordaf is our weak point. You will patrol the seas off Whale Island but when the Danes come then you must help Mordaf!" He nodded."

Haaken Ketilsson said, "Then you do not think he will take the time to lay waste to the east."

"No, I do not." I knew that the southern approach to my great grandfather's home was now unguarded and that was why Naddoðr was so important. I could not rely on Gruffyd to stop an enemy coming. The river and Úlfarrston would be a barrier and so the only approach I could see would be to the east of the river and then up the two sides of The Water. "I think he will attack either me or Cyninges-tūn first. It is hard to hide a huge Danish army but they would simply destroy the isolated farms. If we hear of any enemy in our lands then I will light the beacons my great grandfather had built after the last war. If they are lit then you and your men will have two days, at the most, to reach us. I believe we could hold out that long but they will have learned the last time of our defences. This Gangulf Gurtsson who advises Ubba will have devised some plan to circumvent our defence."

Ráðulfr had an old and wise head upon his shoulders, "First, young Sámr, let us teach Dumnagual the folly of allying with Danes."

I nodded, "You are right. This is our plan. We disembark most of the men just two miles west of the stronghold. They will march east while I will take two drekar and slip past them in the dark and land to the east of their walls. We attack at night from two different directions."

Naddoðr was new to this and he asked the obvious question, "How do we time the attack? If we attack piecemeal then we risk failure."

Baldr said, "Not so. The men of Alt Clut do not keep a large garrison. They rely on their rocky position and the river to keep them safe. I have spoken with the Dragonheart too and know that we have rarely raided them and they have few other enemies who could attack them. They will not expect an attack."

"Baldr Witch Saviour is right, Naddoðr. The ones who land to the west of Alt Clut will have a longer journey. There will be a difference in the time of the two attacks but it should not weaken it. When they send men to one wall the second warband can attack the other." I put my hands on the table and stood, "We kill every warrior but I want the King and his family leaving unharmed. We take hostages."

Ráðulfr banged the table and shouted, "Aye, and all the treasure that he has accumulated!"

My men all banged the table and chanted, "Sámr! Sámr!" They were ready for war."

We left at dawn. The current down the Eden helped us and then we used the winds from the west to edge up the coast of Strathclyde. We were unworried about being seen. We would travel faster than any horse for a rider would have to ride far upstream from Alt Clut to cross the river. We did not row for there was no need. We wanted night's cloak to hide us as we rowed up the river. We stopped in the estuary and took down the mast and sail. Men donned mail. Some, especially the older warriors, applied cochineal or charcoal to their eyes. My great grandfather and his Ulfheonar had done this. It terrified our enemies but I had not adopted the habit. When we were all prepared then the oars were manned. Baldr Witch Saviour and I also took an oar. This would be a hard pull up the river.

Ráðulfr knew the river best and he and Haaken Ketilsson led the way. They would land and then Ulf would lead Naddoðr and his drekar to our landing site. I would leave the oar once we passed Alt Clut. As we rowed towards the darkness of the east, I felt the power of the drekar which, in turn, was the power of the warriors. Even without a chant, we were all in rhythm. Ráðgeir had the stroke. He was the oldest warrior on our drekar. Baldr Witch Saviour and I were at the prow. I was able to watch the heads of the warriors as they dipped forward and then came back. It was as though we were one being. We were not a wooden vessel propelled by men; we were a war machine and we were perfectly in tune. The smooth wood of the oar had been made so by the men who had rowed before me. Despite the cleaning of the drekar, there was blood in the wood of the decks. That blood was a reminder of the ones who had gone before and we would never forget them.

I saw the white hand of Ulf rise and that told me that the other drekar and knarr had pulled off to land their warriors. We were now the lead boat and instead of watching the men before me I watched the land slip by to the north of us. Ulf edged us slightly closer to the shore. There was a risk we might be seen but I doubted that the men who watched the walls, if there were any, would be watching the dark river. It had been a generation or more since the Dragonheart had raided. I had not even been born. The threat of a Viking attack had receded.

As we closed with the land the smell changed. The river cleansed the air and now, as we closed with the settlement, the stink of man struck me. We were nearing the fortress. It had been a stronghold since the time of Myrddyn and when we neared it, I saw it rise above the river. It was a formidable fortress and therein lay its weakness. They thought they were safe. I nodded to Baldr and we lifted our oar from the river and slid it inboard. Ulf adjusted the steering board to compensate for the slight loss of power on the larboard side. Baldr hefted the oar on his shoulder and headed down to the mast fish. The sight of him walking down the centre of the drekar told the rest that we were close to our target. I picked up my helmet and stood at the prow. I would be acting as a ship's boy now. I peered to look to my left. I was looking for a landing site. Baldr Witch Saviour was still on his way back when we passed the last stone wall and I saw, ahead of us, a patch of lightness which suggested a beach. I waved my left arm. The drekar began to shift closer to the shore. Ulf was making too much of a turn and I signalled him to straighten. He did so and I pumped the air to tell him we were on course.

Baldr joined me and I heard a whisper slip down the drekar, "Larboard oars in!" It told me that Ulf had seen the beach and was heading for it.

My work was done and I slipped my shield over my back and then donned my helmet. I used the dragon prow to pull myself up and hold on to the forestay. I balanced on the gunwale. I saw that the patch of beach was little bigger than our drekar. Naddoðr would have to use our drekar as a bridge to land his men.

A second whisper came down the ship, rolling as it was passed from bench to bench, "In steerboard oars!"

I jumped when we were approaching the beach. I landed ankle deep in the water and a heartbeat later Baldr joined me. I ran up a slight slope and drew my sword. I would not need my shield yet but if there was an enemy ahead then I could despatch him. I quickly found a trail which headed downstream and up through the woods. That would be the route to the stronghold. Although my men were quick and worked fast, securing two drekar and landing men over the two of them took time. I had to curb my impatience. The noise, as men splashed into the water along with the jingling of mail sounded inordinately loud to me but I knew the river would mask some of it.

When Naddoðr joined me, I raised my sword and jogged off down the trail. Baldr followed behind me and we ran in single file. It was good to stretch my legs and I knew that I had the easier task for there was no one before me. The trail climbed steadily and I smelled the smoke from the fires burning in Alt Clut. The men of Strathclyde had cleared the land before the walls and I saw the thinning of the trees. It was as we approached them that I heard a single cry from the west and then the sound of a bell in the night. Haaken and Ráðulfr had begun their attack.

Ráðgeir was behind Baldr and as soon as I cleared the open area, I heard him hiss, "Spread out!"

Baldr and I ran to the gate. There was no shout from the walls. The stone gatehouse was supposed to be manned but the bell had drawn the guards to the far side. No faces peered over the top and Baldr and I opened our legs to race to the protection of the gatehouse. The killing ground now became an avenue for attack. As soon as we reached the wall Ráðgeir said, "You four, shields!" I sheathed my sword.

Four tall warriors took two of their shields and they made two steps for us to use. Baldr and I moved away from the wall and, as more of our men joined us, we ran at the shields and when we touched the shields with our feet we were propelled into the air by our warriors. I grasped the edge of the stone parapet and used my feet to clamber up. I had just drawn my sword when I saw a light from an opening door and two men appeared. I did not wait for Baldr nor did I swing my shield around. I ran at them roaring, "Clan of the Wolf!" To my men, it was a war cry but to the men of Strathclyde, it was terrifying confirmation that Vikings had come. The first man hesitated and that cost him his life. I held his right hand with my left as I rammed my sword up into his rib cage. The second warrior managed to swing his sword into my side. Although he connected with my mail he did no harm and Baldr's blade hacked into his neck

Throwing the body to the side we raced down the stairs to the gate itself. Men were belatedly coming up and one of them swung his sword at my legs. I jumped in the air and my feet hit him in the chest. We both tumbled down the stairs but his body broke my fall. I rolled away from the axe which came towards me and it hit, instead, the dying man beneath me. Baldr slew the axeman and I rose to my feet and ran to the gate. Ráðgeir would be leading more men down the stairs but Baldr and I needed to open the gate. We lifted the two bars and swung them open. Behind us, I could hear the cries and screams as the battle raged on the western side of the stronghold.

Naddoðr's grinning face greeted me and he led his men past us to run into the heart of the stronghold. Ráðgeir shook his head, "Lord Sámr, you have a shield! Use it!"

Nodding, I swung it around aware of how lucky I had been. I owed Baldr Witch Saviour a life. We ran through the wooden buildings. People rushed out; had they thought about it they would have been safer inside. My men obeyed their orders. Women and children were spared, men were not. It was night time and the men who foolishly tried to fight us were slain quickly for they had been sleeping and were unprepared for battle. My warriors despatched those who opposed us so that when we approached the King's quarters, I was at the fore with my hearth weru around me. King Dumnagual's bodyguards had been good warriors once but he had kept them as guards around his person. He had not been to war and despite their fine mail and weapons, they were fat and unfit. More importantly, my men were young and hungry. The four men who filled the door to prevent us from gaining entry tried their best but it was not good enough.

I blocked the first sword blow with my shield and my quick hand darted in to slice into the thigh of the warrior who collapsed in a bleeding heap as his tendons were severed. Baldr and Ráðgeir slew another two and, while the last of the bodyguards were slain, the rest of us ran towards the private quarters of the King. Naddoðr and his men burst from a side door and tore into the last of the bodyguards. The King and Queen held their children before them. I saw that his son was almost ready to shave yet he still had puppy fat. Neither the King nor his son held a sword in their hands.

I walked up to the King, dropping my shield to the ground as I did so. "You have conspired with Ubba the Dane. You have broken your promise to the Dragonheart and betrayed his family!"

He looked at an adviser who cowered next to him. I heard the man stammer a translation. The King put his hands together and jabbered at his translator.

"The King apologises to the Dragonheart's men. The Danes were persuasive. This will not happen again."

I nodded, "Quite right. Who is that?" I pointed my sword at the overweight young man.

The translator frowned and then said, "That is Malcolm, the King's son."

I turned to Baldr, "Take the prince. He is now our hostage." As Baldr secured the protesting prince I said to the translator, "If your King betrays us again his son will die and I will come north and blind every man and take every woman as a slave! I will slaughter every animal and burn every town, house and farm! Do you understand?"

The translator translated and the King, looking petrified, nodded. His son began to weep.

I turned to Ráðgeir, "Search the hall and find every piece of gold, silver and copper that you can. This is a day which the men of this land will rue for many years."

I saw the translator speaking in the King's ear. My great grandfather had tried diplomacy but it had not worked. Now we would try terror and destitution. Ulf entered the hall. His mail was bloody. "Ulf, take this prince as a hostage. If the men of the north cause you trouble again send a hand back as a warning."

"Aye, lord. This was a good raid. We lost but four men. If you wish we could rule this land for they are not men!"

I saw the translator listening. "That may be something for the future. Let us see if the King can rule his land and be at peace with his neighbours." I saw the translator whisper in the King's ear. My message had been delivered.

We stayed until the evening tide. We had much to take. We commandeered four cargo ships to carry the treasure back. That had not been my aim but it would make us stronger and the north weaker!

Sámr
Chapter 14
Mercia

The journey home, even with the wind, was slower for we had lumbering cargo ships and knarr with us. All of us were laden. The warriors we had fought had fine weapons, mail and helmets. The treasure went to the warriors who had slain them. They also owned purses which bulged. These had belonged to the guards of the King who were well paid. The kitchens and storerooms had been raided and they had yielded other riches. The animals from Alt Clut: the goods, fowl and the like all were taken aboard. It would be a hard future the King and his people faced. He had gambled and lost. We had divided the booty at Alt Clut and I did not need to take my drekar up the Eden. With *'Danish Crow'* as our consort, we sailed slowly down the coast. I was anxious to return home for, within a short space of time, I would need to leave for my war on Mercia. At the back of my mind was a nagging doubt that the three brothers from Dyflin would not do as I had asked. If they did not it would not be disastrous. King Rhodri and his men were not seamen. They would have to come by land and would have the same problem as the Mercians. They would be travelling across land which had been stripped of food.

I stayed but one night. Naddoðr and his men were building themselves a hall close by the shipyard where Erik Short Toe and his family had died. They used one of the captured cargo ships. Dragging it ashore they removed the prow and the stern post before inverting it. After cutting a hole for a door they had an instant hall. They would use it for their home when they were not on patrol. Baldr and I led our men north. It was as we did so that Baldr came up with an idea and a refinement which I had not thought of.

"Lord, I am a horseman and there are some of our warriors, not many but enough, who can also ride. I nodded. Riding was Baldr's heritage. "If I mounted them then I could head south from Mordaf's hall and draw the eyes of those thegns who live south of the Belisima. We could run from any Saxon band which outnumbered us and destroy any settlement which was undefended by a wall."

I liked the idea but I had learned to reflect before I answered. He would only have twenty or so men. I knew that we had horsemen but their numbers were few and as only Baldr would be mailed then that meant that they could not fight Saxon housecarls. The idea, however, had merit. With a hundred or so men sweeping from the south, any attack which drew warriors from facing us was to be applauded. In addition to which he would be our eyes.

"It is risky, Baldr, I would not take you from Nanna and your children."

He smiled, "Do not worry, lord. I am no longer a reckless youth. You have changed and taken on the mantle of the Dragonheart and I, too, can become a leader who knows when to fight and when to decline. I know our purpose. We make the land between the Maeresea and the Belisima a wasteland."

As we rode along The Water, we refined his plan and chose the men he would take. He would have to train them. The fact that they could ride was only half the battle.

We had taken treasure for Cyninges-tūn. The men had provided more than half of the warriors we had taken. As our column approached our walls the people flooded from their homes to greet us. The miniscule losses meant that the cheers were even louder than they were normally. It was my name they chanted and I saw the pride on the face of my great grandfather as he stood with Germund the Lame and Atticus atop the gates of Cyninges-tūn. I did not look at him. I looked at the ground. When the Danes came, they would have places they could use for cover. Farms and houses had sprung up outside of the walls. The people would be safe inside the palisade when an attack came but their homes would be a hostage to fortune. I hoped that my great grandfather had planned for that.

156

Passing through the gates the Dragonheart descended the stairs and his name was chanted by the warriors I led. More than half of them were his. They had fought for me but it was he who had trained them. Ráðgeir and the others surrounded him to tell him of the battle. I dismounted and Ylva walked over to me. She beamed at me, "I can see it went well. Come, we will speak while the Dragonheart receives the accolades from his men. You will have many years for such accolades."

I looked at her and she shrugged. I had learned, over the years, to hear the words which were unspoken. She was telling me that he would not have long left on this earth. Kara had ale for Baldr and myself. They had good alewives in their hall and I quaffed half. The road had been a long one from Whale Island. I told them what we had done and the taking of a hostage.

"That is clever, Sámr. The Dragonheart did not do that and I wonder if such an act might have kept some other enemies at bay."

"We both know that it would not have worked with the most dangerous of our enemies, the Danes."

"You are right and they have ever been our bane. I hope that this will be our last battle. If we can bloody them enough then they may stop."

"We let just one drekar escape last time. How much blood must there be?"

Her eyes were hard as she answered me, "None must survive. This army must be slaughtered so that their families wait in homes, far to the east, looking for warriors who do not return. Then we have a chance!"

We joined my great grandfather and his men who crowded around him to tell him of their exploits. He looked old but, as we approached, I saw that his eyes were still the same. Beneath the white hair and wrinkled skin was still the young warrior who had forged a clan and taken a land. The men parted as we approached and Ráðgeir shouted, "And here is the new Dragonheart! As fierce and fine a warrior as I have ever seen, Sámr Ship Killer!"

My great grandfather put his arm around me, "Then I am happy for I have an heir who can keep this land safe and my work here is done."

As we went into his hall I said, "Do not speak like that! You still have much work to do."

Atticus sniffed, "He has done all that is expected of him, lord. Let him lay down his burden and enjoy the sunset of his years here in this valley."

My great grandfather shook his head, "Greek, be silent. Your people are not warriors!"

Atticus opened his mouth to answer and then thought better of it. He shook his head, "Come, I have food and ale prepared."

As we ate, I expanded on the brief battle of Alt Clut and I told Ylva and Dragonheart of my new plans. I saw the worry on my great grandfather's face and in his eyes but he was nothing but supportive. He gave me advice about fighting a land campaign. I knew it was not the same as raiding. Sea raiders always had the security of a ship to which they could return. A land raid meant that if the enemy reacted quickly, they could cut us off from the sea. He told of the raid on Wessex when hundreds of Danes had been slaughtered despite having won the battle. The wily King Egbert had cut them off from their ships and, like a wolf attacked by a pack of dogs, devoured them piecemeal.

"I know the dangers but your words of your journey north gave me the inspiration, Dragonheart. Three of you managed to evade the men who lived twixt those two rivers and when we found you, we were able to slay many."

"But remember you wish not just to annoy the Mercians, you wish to draw them into battle to prevent an attack from the south."

"And that is why we head north to the Belisima. The band I lead north to harry the Mercians will be small. I want them to think that we are just one crew who have lost their drekar. I want them to mount an attack and to follow us. That is why we begin our raid less than twenty miles from the stronghold that is Caestir. There they have an eorledman. I want him to raise the fyrd and to follow. I intend to have Pasgen ap Raibeart and his men waiting at the Belisima. Our wooden ships will give us a floating fortress if one is needed."

Ylva smiled and put her hand on mine. "You will not need that wooden wall for you and our men have Viking bravery. You have the heart of a wolf. You are not Ulfheonar but if you chose to be one then you could do so."

Dragonheart nodded, "Ylva is right. Only the sons of Aðils Shape Shifter have your skills."

I shook my head, "The days of the Ulfheonar are gone. I need to stand on a battlefield beneath a banner. I need to show our enemies that I am a leader."

I did not spend the night with my great grandfather for I was anxious to return home to my family. I would be leaving soon enough. My son was now able to recognise me. He ran at me as I entered the gates. His running was still awkward. I worried that he would trip and fall but he managed to reach me and throw himself into my arms. His words were not clear and so I compensated for my lack of understanding by squeezing him and saying, "How is my little warrior?" He jabbered an incomprehensible reply.

I had not been away for long but Ragnar had changed in that time and Aethelflaed had many tales to tell of both of my children. It was trivial and mundane but I loved it. My wife and I put our weary children to bed and then sat before the fire in my hall. My wife was a clever woman and our union had grown from war. She understood what I did. We spoke until her eyes, too, began to droop. I took her to bed and I was content.

I left for Mercia just seven nights later. My men and I would spend two days at Cyninges-tūn and Whale Island before our little fleet set sail for the Maeresea. I spoke with my father while we awaited Mordaf and his men.

"I have many more volunteers for you, my son."

I smiled, "You mean they do not fear to go to war with someone who is younger than the mail they wear?"

He had the good grace to laugh. "I confess that there were those amongst my men who thought you too young but your rescue of the Dragonheart and the victory at Alt Clut have convinced them."

"And have we had news from Dyflin?"

He shook his head, "You would not expect word yet. The brothers and their allies need secrecy. You told them when you wished them to attack?"

I nodded, "Aye, but since our words, I am not confident that they will do as I ask. If they do not attack then we will still have two enemies to face."

"Bergil will do as you ask if for no other reason than I am certain he is embarrassed about having one so young outshine him. He will do this if only to increase his reputation and Anglesey is a rich jewel."

"Perhaps."

Pasgen ap Raibeart, the son of one of Dragonheart's drekar captains, would be vital to our plans. His people were a mix of those who had lived here in the time of Rome and our people. They were not natural raiders but they were good warriors. Raibeart ap Pasgen had been the first to choose the sword. He had been wounded in the last war and now guarded Úlfarrston. His son was keen to emulate his father. I spoke at length to them both.

"We will sail together and leave you at the Belisima. I want you to clear the south bank of that river and rid the land of any enemies. Then you will prepare a wall of spears. I hope to draw the men of Mercia and destroy them in one battle."

Raibeart was experienced and I saw him rubbing his wounded leg as he spoke, "You are putting your head above the palisade wall, Sámr Ship Killer. I do not doubt your ability but you go with perilously few men."

"Aye, but I go with men who are not afraid and that is half the battle. Saxons expect Vikings to be reckless. When we turn and flee then they will take our youth and fear as signs that they can destroy us. Whichever leader comes from Caestir he will hope that he does his king's bidding. He will think to destroy us and make their attack on the Land of the Wolf easier. This will have the opposite effect. When Anglesey is taken then the Mercians will fear an attack up the Dee. I hope, in one fell swoop, to destroy two enemies and that will leave just one."

Raibeart nodded, "And the most dangerous one at that!"

I nodded and I heard the Norns spinning.

I said farewell to Baldr. He had ten men with horses which would make their way south. He was happier on a horse.

It was not a huge fleet which left Whale Island. Only my ship, with a full crew, would travel to the Maeresea. I would have sixty warriors. Most were from Hawk's Roost, Cyninges-tūn with the others from Mordaf's home. Naddoðr and his men would come with me. I had seen how good they were. As we headed out from the anchorage and, with a wind come from the south and east, we were forced to row. As we had many new men on board we sang. I know not why but I chose the song of the sword which now lay buried with Aiden. It seemed right somehow.

The wolf snake-crawled from the mountain side
Hiding the spell-wight in cave deep and wide
He swallowed him whole and Warlord too
Returned to pay the price that was due
There they stayed through years of man
Until the day Jarl Dragon Heart began
He climbed up Wyddfa filled with ghosts
With Arturus his son, he loved the most
The mouth was dark, hiding death
Dragon Heart stepped in and held his breath
He lit the torch so strong and bright
The wolf's mouth snarled with red firelight
Fearlessly he walked and found his kin
The Warlord of Rheged buried deep within
Cloaked in mail with sharp bright blade
A thing of beauty by Thor made
And there lay too, his wizard friend,
Myrddyn protecting to the end
With wolf charm blue they left the lair
Then Thor he spoke, he filled the air
The storm it raged, the rain it fell
Then the earth shook from deep in hel
The rocks they crashed, they tumbled down
Burying the wizard and the Rheged crown.
Till world it ends the secret's there
Buried beneath wolf warrior's lair

We stopped when the crew had the rhythm but, as I stood with Ulf and Mordaf, I heard the men at the oars. The song had put them in the right mood. They bantered and they joked; they were in the right frame of mind to raid. As the Dragonheart had told

161

me, that was half of the battle. Ulf nodded at the boats astern of us, "We have so many rowers on board that had we continued to sing we would be at the Maeresea already and the other drekar would be far behind."

"We will need those ships before this is over."

"Lord, are you not taking on too much? I know this is a large crew but you have forty miles of Mercia to cover."

"The Dragonheart did it with a wounded boy and an old man. I am not a fool, Ulf. Mordaf and I are of the blood of the Dragonheart and we are not attempting anything which he did not do when he was our age. If we fail then so be it but I do not think we will fail."

Ulf sighed, "You will raid the settlements along the river first?"

"Aye and you can sail home with the booty we garner. Bring back another crew south to the Belisima for we must win this battle. The Dragonheart is sending down men from the two stad to the north. There were volunteers wished to join us."

I saw that Mordaf was troubled and so we went to the larboard side. When we were alone, he said, "Men come from the north and from all over the Land of the Wolf but not my father. What game does he play, Sámr? He is my father and I do not understand him."

"From what I can gather he is a troubled man and always has been. When you almost died close to Syllingar he blamed the Dragonheart. We both know that was unfair but he is a complicated man."

"I fear that he seeks a crown. He seeks to rule the Land of the Wolf."

"Then he is doomed to failure. No man rules the land, not even Dragonheart. The land allows us to live there and it protects us. The moment a man tries to control it his endeavours will come to nought!" My words sank in and Mordaf saw that he would have to be his own man. It was the start of the change in Mordaf and it was a good one.

We reached the Belisima in the middle of the afternoon. I waved at Pasgen ap Raibeart as he led his ships upstream. We continued down the empty coast. One reason that this part of Mercia had been untouched was the lack of settlements. There was nothing along the coast. Sand dunes and pine forests were all that could be seen. Beyond dunes and trees, the land was flat and fertile but the forests seemed to act as nature's palisade. The sea was also shallow and we had to keep well away from shore. At low tide, the bones of unwary ships could be seen.

Mordaf and I prepared for war. He was less experienced than I was and so I helped him to prepare. The Dragonheart had perfected the best defence. He had fought for so many years that he had forgotten more about raiding than we would ever learn. We both wore, above our shifts, a simple but effective, padded byrnie. It helped to spread the weight of the mail and absorbed blows. Then I helped him to pull on his mail byrnie. He would not remove it until we reached our home. I was more used to it than he was for I saw his face as the weight came upon his shoulders. We both had byrnies with a ring which fitted over our middle finger. It gave protection to our hands. We would not use the device until we were ready to fight. Finally, we fitted his belt with sword and dagger attached. Our helmets and shields would have to wait until we were ready to go ashore. By the time I was ready we were approaching the mouth of the estuary of the Maeresea.

Erik, one of the ship's boys called down, "I see the mouth of the river. There are some huts just down from the sea."

"How many?"

"Three."

Ulf, as he began our turn, looked at me and I shook my head, "They will not harm us and they are not worth the risk of landing. We keep to the plan and head for the bridge."

I saw the relief on Ulf's face for we were losing the light as the sun set behind us. This was a tricky river. There were few settlements until we reached the bridge and the northern shore was both muddy and treacherous. His ship's boys would have to watch carefully as we edged our way the few miles to the bridge. We knew, from Haaken One Eye and the Dragonheart that there was a settlement before the bridge but it was on the southern shore. I had contemplated attacking it but dismissed the idea as warning might be given and the bridge settlement defended. We would be seen but we would reach the bridge before any warning. Of course, it meant that the lord of Caestir would know of our presence. That was all part of the plan for I wanted him to summon his hundred. We needed him to come north and deal with us.

The river began to narrow and the wind brought with it the smell of man to the south. A flicker of light in the night showed us where the southern settlement was. Not all of the huts were within the palisade. As we passed it, we heard the sounds of alarm. We had been seen and they were preparing for an attack. By the time they discovered that they were not our target we would have passed them and be closer to our real objective. While the wind did not help our progress, it helped identify the Saxons and young Haraldr Ulfsson came running down from the prow. His father had taught him well, "We can smell the Saxons, captain! Galmr says he can see some sand."

Ulf nodded, "You have done well. Return to the prow and tell the larboard oars to withdraw."

There was a ripple of noise as Haraldr headed up the drekar. Men slid their oars back aboard and, after stacking them on the mast fish, began to don byrnies. The steerboard side would give us the power to reach the shore. Mordaf and I went to the larboard side and saw the lighter patch of land which marked the beach. I took my shield and hung it from my back. I left my helmet hanging from my sword. I made my way to the prow where the warriors who had not had to don mail waited. Haraldr and Galmr, the two ship's boys, were perilously perched on the forestay with a tethering rope in their hand. They would leap ashore first.

I saw that the beach was just large enough for the drekar. I spied an opening in the undergrowth which suggested a path. I had been on enough raids to know that you used all the information you had to ensure success. I would make for the path and see if there was any danger. As soon as Galmr and Haraldr splashed into the river I followed them. The water came up to my waist! I struggled to the shore, aware that the drekar was not far behind me. I left my helmet on my sword hilt for I needed my ears. The path was now clear to see and was well worn. I guessed women from the nearby farms used it to wash their clothes. I reached the top and found that there was a wide path, almost a cart track, which paralleled the river. I could see, in the distance, a church. It looked to be more than half a Roman mile from where I stood. Across the field, I saw a single hut. It was less than four hundred paces from where I waited for my men.

Ráðgeir joined me. He had his helmet in his hand. "Send five men to the farm and see what you can get. I will take the rest to the settlement."

"Aye lord."

Mordaf and his hearth weru joined me as did my own hearth weru and Naddoðr. "I will lead. Keep close. Mordaf, when we get close to the settlement, take your men and secure the church before they bury their valuables."

"Aye, Sámr!"

I donned my helmet and swung around my shield. I began to jog along the river path. It was wide enough for five men abreast. I ran with Stig Sword Hand and Sven of the Water flanking me. I could see the huts and wooden walls of the settlement ahead. The walls would be a deterrent only. They were just above the height of a man. They might have stopped us had they been manned. I saw no white faces ahead; they were not manned. The gates would be closed but we knew how to surmount such walls. We came to a fork in the path and I knew, instinctively, that the second path led to the church. Perhaps it was a monastery of the White Christ. I waved my sword to signal Mordaf to head for it.

We were just thirty paces from the rough-hewn walls when there was a cry in the night. The men Ráðgeir had sent to the farm had been spotted. It mattered not. Einar and Leif ran from behind us to reach the walls. They had to jump over a shallow ditch to do so and then they braced themselves against the wall. I jumped the ditch while they were securing the shield I would use as a stepping stone. We would not be able to take a running jump at the wall. I clambered on to the shield and they raised me up. The shout in the night had woken someone for I heard voices from within. I stepped on to the top of the palisade and jumped down to the ground below. As I had expected the fighting platform was close to the ground.

I scanned the ground ahead of me. The huts were not laid out in a regular order. There was one just five paces from my shield arm and another twenty paces from my sword. I ignored both and ran, instead, down the slight slope towards the river and the gate I knew would be there. I saw a large building ahead. Behind me, I heard Stig Sword Hand and Sven of the Water as they hurried to catch me. They would be cursing me for not waiting. They were my hearth weru and oath-bound to protect me. My risk was calculated. Men would be rising. Any who came forth to face me would not be mailed and I was. The hall would belong to the thegn of the settlement. He would have a handful of warriors who were his bodyguard. Even as I spied the gate a light from my shield side showed me where the door of the hall had been opened. I had raised my shield by the time the warrior with a shield, helmet and sword burst out. His eyes widened as he saw my helmet and shield. Both marked me as a Viking.

He made a fatal mistake. Instead of engaging me immediately he turned to shout, "Vikings!"

The turning was reactive and it cost him his life. I swung my sword at his middle. He was facing the wrong way for his shield to save him and his sword was of no use as he was too slow to block my strike. The sword ripped through the linen and into his gut. The edge of my blade was sharp and it grated off his ribs before tearing him open. I shouted, "Naddoðr and Ráðgeir, secure the hall!" Without breaking stride, I ran to the gate. Only half of my men would have gone to the wall. The rest would be waiting outside the gate. There were two gatekeepers. The brazier by the gate told me that they had been warming themselves there instead of standing a watch. They had leather byrnies, helmets, spears and shields. When they saw me, they raised their shields and stood close together to give mutual protection. I slowed to allow Stig Sword Hand and Sven of the Water to join me.

It was three against two but the two Mercians had spears. They were not warriors and they were not young. I took the initiative and punched my shield at the two spearheads. They smashed into my shield and I swung my sword overhand as Stig Sword Hand and Sven of the Water hacked into the men's thighs. They followed up with a sword thrust across the Saxon's necks and the Saxons fell dead. As my hearth weru pulled away the bodies I lifted the bar on the gate. Doing so I noticed that it was a single one and not particularly thick. A shield wall of warriors could have broken it. I would bear that in mind if any of the other villages we found were protected by such a gate. We drew back the gates and my men cheered. I saw as I did so, the first rays of the sun in the east. Behind me, I heard the cries of the dying warriors and the cries of women.

I turned and ran back to the hall. I saw the dead man I had killed in the entrance. Inside there were five Saxons left and Ráðgeir was wounded. Two more of my men lay dead. I shouted, "Fall back and leave this to Sámr Ship Killer and his hearth weru!"

The six men who had been engaged obeyed me and stepped back. The Saxons were going nowhere and fresh blades and warriors would end it quicker. I saw that Einar Red Shield was wounded. I would not underestimate this thegn and his oathsworn. Stig Sword Hand and Sven of the Water stood on either side of me with Leif and Einar Haraldsson next to them. We were all mailed and we stepped forward as one. The fighting had already cleared a space and the Saxons were before the fire. Behind the fire cowered their families. I held my sword above my shield. Our shields were bigger and better made than the Mercians. I could see the damage my men had caused on the Saxon shields. I headed for the thegn. He was a little younger than my father. His round helmet was old fashioned but looked to be well made. His sword was equally old and notched from the fighting. Saxon swords were better than most of our enemies' weapons.

The thegn began the fight by swinging his sword at my head and punching at the same time with the metal boss on his shield. I countered by lifting my shield and angling the lower metal rim to face him. I took his sword strike across the middle of my shield but his punch was a strong one and he forced me back on my left leg. Stig Sword Hand was there and I almost tripped on him. This thegn knew his business and was using his experience and the confined space to defeat me. I kept my sword behind my body. I would make him wonder whence the first strike would come. He thought he had the advantage for my move had forced me back and holding his shield before him lunged at my face and neck. He struck downward. This time I angled my shield so that the blade slid down the shield. I heard it rasp from the nail heads and the metal boss. His edge would be duller and his blade notched even more.

I went on the offensive. I stepped on to my right leg and I lunged, not at his body but at his thigh. He was not expecting the blow and he was tiring. His shield, which was smaller than mine, slid down too slowly to stop the hit. He merely deflected my sword so that the tip slid down his breeks, opening them, and sliced into his leg. The tip jarred against the knee cap and he winced. I pulled my shield arm back and punched, aware as I did so that Stig and Sven had dispatched their opponents and the thegn was isolated. My shield hit his sword and sword hand and he had to step back towards the fire. As he did so Einar slashed at the face of the Saxon he was fighting and he fell screaming into the fire. Burning, the warrior ran towards the women and children, all of whom screamed in panic. The sound distracted the thegn enough for me to swing my sword at head height. There was no one to impede my swing and my sword slid over the top of his shield and into his neck.

As the dying thegn fell backwards into the fire I heard a woman scream, "No!"

Leif ended the life of the last Saxon. I stared around at the charnel house and saw no more warriors. We had won. My men began beating their shields as the women wailed and mourned their dead.

"Stig Sword Hand, take from the dead and search the women. Find this thegn's treasure and have it taken to the river."

"Aye, lord!"

I stepped outside and saw that dawn was now breaking properly. The women and children of the settlement were being herded by my men into an animal pen which had been emptied of the animals.

Ráðgeir said, "We have summoned Ulf, lord, and taken the animals to the bridge. What do we do with the captives? Do we board them too?"

I shook my head, "We do not need slaves. Just watch them. If there are carts then find them and any horses. We will use them to carry our food as we head north."

Just then I heard a shout from behind me. It was Mordaf and he was followed by some monks carrying treasure. He looked in good spirits, "We caught them as they were rising. If raiding with you is always this successful then I should like to do it again."

I laughed, "The Norns have spun and we have been lucky thus far. Load the treasure on the drekar and then put the monks with the women and children."

As he led off, I turned to Einar Haraldsson, "Have our dead and wounded boarded on the drekar."

"Aye, lord!"

By the middle of the morning, we had taken all that we had to take. The village was empty. The sacks of grain and animals, not to mention their pots, pans and ale, were on the drekar. I returned to the captives. The woman who had screamed when I had killed the thegn did not sit like the others but stood with the man I assumed was the abbot. She glared defiantly at me.

As I approached her, she shouted, "Do not think we will go into captivity peacefully, Viking. We will bite, scratch and fight you!"

She spoke in Saxon and I was unsure if her words were meant as a rallying cry for her people or if they were truly meant for me. "You are not going to be taken back to our land, my lady. Take your people and cross the bridge. Caestir is not far away. You can make it there by nightfall if you leave now."

I had taken her by surprise and stunned her into silence. The Abbot said, "You will let us go?"

"Of course."

"And can we bury our men?"

"No. You leave now or I shall make you all captives! Go now and go quickly!" I pointed to my men who were drinking and I played on their fear of us as barbarians. "Now is the time to leave for we shall celebrate and we are men!"

That was enough of a threat and the Abbot quickly ordered the monks to help the women and children. The last to leave was the thegn's wife and her eyes glowered hatred at me. I heard her curses as she left. I had been cursed by real witches and a follower of the White Christ could do nothing to hurt me.

Mordaf and I followed with our hearth weru. They crossed the bridge and I waited until they had disappeared before I went over to Ulf. "You can leave now. I intend to burn the bridge and then rest. We march north in the morning."

He smiled, "They will see the fire and assume you burn the village. You are clever, lord."

"We will burn the village but that will be when we leave!"

I saw that Mordaf looked a little nervous as my drekar slipped down the river. We were setting off through Saxon land in an attempt to draw them to battle. I was confident but I could see that he was not as he was worried we might be trapped.

"Do not worry, cuz, she will make the sea quickly. The wind and the current are with her and the same wind will take her home."

Mordaf was younger than I was and he said, "I was not thinking about the drekar, Sámr."

I smiled, "I know. You are worried that we will be trapped and captured or slaughtered. Your time in Om Walum and Wessex has made you fearful but you need to trust the men of the clan. We rescued you and we will not let you come to harm. This is not reckless and we do what we do for a purpose."

He looked around to see if any other had heard, "How do you know such things? Are you a galdramenn?"

"It is written on your face and it is understandable. Let me put your mind at rest. We will set fire to the bridge. The Saxons who are heading south will see it and they will take the news to the eorledman at Caestir. He will hurry north for he will think we have burned the village. By then the bridge will no longer be here and he will have to take his men east to the next bridge. That gives us one whole day to raid the land north of us. Baldr will join us tomorrow and, with his horsemen, we can keep watch on the Saxons. Now get your men to find as much combustible material as they can. The bridge should burn well!"

By the time the sun began to set the bridge was blazing. There were stone pillars but the bridge itself was made of wood. We ate and watched as the fire consumed the river crossing. We kept guards but that night was a restful one for us. The second fire was begun in the morning when we fired the settlement. This time there would be nothing left. The church, the monastery, the walls and the halls were all made of wood. The Mercians would have to begin again.

Sámr
Chapter 15
The Saxon Thegn

Baldr found us when we were just five miles north of the burned bridge and village. We had followed the road we found. Two farms had been discovered. The people had fled but we found some fowl that they had forgotten to take and some more sacks of wheat. We took them loaded on the carts we had taken.

Baldr reined in. He looked comfortable on the back of a horse. When I rode, I looked like a sack of barley! "Well met, my lord! We saw the smoke in the sky. It was like a beacon drawing us to you."

"It is good to see you, too, Baldr Witch Saviour, for now, we have eyes again. What lies ahead of us?"

"There are farms but we saw the people who lived in them heading across the fields. There is a palisade and a hall twelve miles to the north-west of you and they are heading there. There were bells tolling warning them of our presence. The fire let them know that the wolves were loose in the sheepfold."

"And to the northeast?"

"I do not know; we have not had time to explore there yet."

"Then leave one horseman to take us to the hall you found. Take the other horsemen and find what lies to the northeast and then keep watch for the men of Caestir."

"Surely it is too early for them to be close, lord?"

"Yes, but what if they have horses too? We need them to be tired when they catch up with us. We will attack the hall you found as soon as we arrive."

Baldr nodded and left Siggi Haldisson as our guide. Baldr gave his instructions to his horsemen and they divided into two groups. They were our secret weapon. The Allfather had sent Baldr to my great grandfather for a reason. He was to help the clan by giving us something other Vikings did not have: a horseman.

The land was flat. That made marching easy but prevented us from having a good view of the land ahead. Baldr had told us that the settlement was not on a knoll or even a man-made hill. It was just on a marginally higher piece of land. It had been built, I guessed, as a refuge in case of raids such as ours. When we were within five miles or so we heard the church bell tolling. It was not the day they worshipped the White Christ and was rung constantly; it was a warning bell. That suited us. It meant the farms would be abandoned and the livestock would all be gathered in one place. We were slightly slower than I would have liked but that was because we carried supplies. If we had to, we could disperse the ale, water and supplies and abandon the carts but I would keep them as long as we could. We would reach the settlement shortly after noon. As soon as I spied the wooden wall, less than a mile ahead and surrounded by fields and farms, I sent Siggi Haldisson ahead to see how many gates there were. He was mounted and would be able to evade capture.

Mordaf, Naddoðr and Ráðgeir walked with me and I discussed my plan with them. "They will be watching from their walls and will see our approach. How many bowmen have we?"

Ráðgeir understood the question. Every Viking could use a bow how many good ones did we have? "Twenty-three."

I nodded. I had estimated twenty-five. Perhaps two of the bowmen had been wounded or killed and were now on the drekar heading home. "That will leave us with twenty-five warriors. I intend to make a human battering ram. We will form a column five men wide and five men deep. Our archers will clear the gate and we will simply run and hit the gate."

Ráðgeir shook his head, "That plan is doomed to failure, lord."

"Because the gate will be too strong?" He nodded. "Not so. The one I opened at the Maeresea had a single bar and the wood was not particularly thick. The Saxon defences have not been tested. However, if it does not break after two charges then we will withdraw and I will come up with another plan. We could always use fire."

"Fire arrows are difficult to use, lord."

I sighed. Ráðgeir was looking at the horn half empty, "Then I will devise another plan. It is good that one of us can think of ideas, eh Ráðgeir? It is always easier to pick holes in another's plan rather than come up with one of your own."

He flushed, "I am sorry, lord. I wish only for success."

"Then let us try my first plan and see if the Allfather smiles upon us!"

We stopped two hundred paces from the walls. If they managed to send any arrows at us, they would have no power. I wanted to examine the defences as closely as I could. Ráðgeir spread our archers out in a long double line. I walked to within a hundred and fifty paces of the walls. The Saxons hurled insults at me and my parents. One man put his backside over the walls and showed me his bare arse. I ignored their bravado. I saw that they had men all along the wall before me. Siggi would tell me if the other walls were equally defended. There were just thirty men on the wall I could see and, perhaps, eight boys with slings. As I could only see the heads of the boys and the top of the chests and heads of the warriors, I assumed that the fighting platform was not a high one. The walls themselves were little taller than a tall warrior. I counted just eight metal helmets. The man who had the best helmet looked to have a byrnie and he stood over the gate; making him the thegn. The light shone through the gate and I saw a single bar. I had seen enough and I turned my back to head to my men. I heard a shout from Mordaf and then heard the arrow as it sailed through the air. I felt it as it struck the shield which covered my back.

I saw my men pull back on their bows and I shouted, "Hold!" I stopped and, taking off my shield, turned. The arrow had barely penetrated the leather covering of my shield. I pulled out the arrow, it was a hunting arrow, and, breaking it, spat on it and threw it to the ground. Holding my shield before me I turned and walked back to our men. No other arrows followed.

Mordaf shook his head, "That was reckless, cuz! A second arrow might have been luckier!"

"Not so, Mordaf. The arrow barely penetrated the wood. I wear a mail byrnie and I was further away than when he had hit my shield. If the first one did no harm then the second would have been doomed to failure. Now we know their range. It is where I threw the arrow and they will see that we are not easily frightened." Cupping my hands, I shouted, "Make camp and light fires." Ráðgeir joined us. "When Siggi returns then we attack. Have the bowmen sit and rest. Make sure that everyone eats and drinks. I want the Saxons to think that we will try a siege."

Siggi returned as the first pieces of a pig were fried on the fires. The smell of cooking pig always made me hungry. Leif gave me the first hot slice and I ate it while Siggi reported to me. "There is another gate to the west lord but the path from it is narrower than this one. I counted ten men on the other three walls and none wore a helmet."

I nodded, "You have done well. Water your horse and have some food." When he left us, I said, "There may be fifty or more men within the walls. There are less than forty on the walls but there will be older men who can be called upon to fight and there will be others out of sight. We will be outnumbered but they will not be warriors. When the men have eaten, we attack. I will go and speak with the bowmen."

The bowmen had all eaten and stood as I approached. "When we form our human ram, I would have you go to the arrow I broke. That is the extent of their range. I think we can send our arrows further." They all nodded enthusiastically. Ráðgeir had chosen well. "Your first arrows must all go as one. After that select any target you think you can hit. You need to leave a gap for us to run through."

Peder was the eldest of the bowmen. He was one of my father's men and wore a mail byrnie. "Do not worry, lord, the gatehouse will be a death trap."

I walked back to the rest of my men. There were about two hours of daylight left. I could have waited until dark but I wanted a swift victory. I hoped that they would be off their guard. They might be expecting a night attack. They had seen us eat and would not anticipate that we would rise and attack immediately. When I reached my men, I turned. I saw fewer men on the walls. They were taking the opportunity to eat and to make water.

Swinging my shield around I said, "Rise! We attack!"

I was in familiar company in the front rank. Stig and the others were like pieces of my mail. Ráðgeir and the most experienced men of Cyninges-tūn were behind me, Naddoðr and his men behind them. Mordaf and his men made up the last rank. I raised my sword and, as we jogged, began to sing! It was my grandfather's song and seemed appropriate. It was fast and only Mordaf and I knew it. Dragonheart had taught it to us for he had been proud of his son, Wolf Killer. The fact that just two voices sang it did not diminish it for the rest of my band banged their shields with the hilts of their sword. It sounded like the song was punctuated by thunder which rolled towards the Saxons.

The Angry Cubs and the Wolf Killers Bears
Sailed together, through dangers shared
Through battles hard against their foes
They forged a link, a bond which grows
Cubs and bears forged from steel
Cubs and bears to no man kneel
When Egbert came they held their walls
When others fled they still stood tall
With Ironshirt and Wolf's blood
They drove the Saxons through the wood
Cubs and bears forged from steel
Cubs and bears to no man kneel
And now they sail, brothers in arms
Protected by the volva's charms
Cubs and bears forged from steel
Cubs and bears to no man kneel
Cubs and bears forged from steel
Cubs and bears to no man kneel

As we approached my bowmen, I saw them pull on their bows and as we passed them, I heard the hum of the strings as they released and then the whisper of wings as the arrows soared towards the Saxons. With our shields before us and all wearing helmets, it would have taken an incredibly lucky hit to cause an injury with the arrows the Mercians used. Some of the Saxons tried and in doing so paid the ultimate price. As they aimed their weapons twenty-five arrows fell and it was the archers and slingers who perished. Our speed meant that by the time the second arrows were sent we were less than one hundred paces from the walls. I heard cries as arrows hit Saxons. Inside I could hear the strident cries of men being ordered to defend the walls.

I shouted, "Lock shields!" We had done this against other shield walls but never against a gate. Our five shields overlapped each other and I felt Ráðgeir's shield in my back. Had I not sung the chant we might have risked tripping over each other but our feet hit the ground at exactly the same time. I would have the easier task for my shield would hit the gates where they joined. The danger would be going too fast and falling and I fought the temptation to do so.

The gates were just ten paces from us. I raised my shield slightly so that if there were splinters, they would not hit my eyes. We hit the door and it sounded like Thor's hammer on an anvil. It made my ears ring and my left arm was jarred but I heard a crack.

I shouted, "Back five steps! It is breaking."

Walking backwards was harder than charging but our bowmen prevented the Saxons from hurting us. We had to strike quickly or else they would brace the gate with timber and, perhaps, men. We stopped and I shouted, "One, two, three; go!"

This time some large stones were dropped from on high. I heard a shout from behind me as one hit one of my men. Then we smacked into the gate and it burst asunder. Before us were half a dozen Saxons. They held hammers and planks in their hands. All six fell as they discovered that hammers and wood were no match for Vikings with swords! When we had fought at the river, we had awoken the men but here they waited for us on the walls and our sudden entry meant that they tumbled from the wall to face us. I saw that these were old men and boys.

As Ráðgeir slew one of the mailed warriors with contemptuous ease, I shouted, "Surrender and you shall live!"

Even with their blood fired up my men halted swords midstroke. The Saxons looked at us in amazement. The man I had seen on the walls wearing a good helmet was obviously the thegn for I saw that he had a richly decorated sword scabbard. He looked younger than I had expected. He shouted, "Why should we go into captivity? Better to die here than endure Viking slavery!"

"You can leave and go to Caestir. Your lives will be spared."

"How do I know I can trust the word of a Viking?"

I took off my helmet and sheathed my sword, "Because we both know that we outnumber your fighting men and we are better warriors. If we chose then all of you could be slaughtered."

I saw him look around and take in the fact that he now had less than thirty men most of whom were farmers armed with wood axes and without shields. He too took off his helmet, "Then why attack us? It is surely not for the paltry takings which Orm's kirk has to offer. Our church has no gold and our only treasures are the children we raise."

"I am Sámr Ship Killer and I am the heir of Dragonheart of the Land of the Wolf. Ubba Ragnarsson has suborned your king, Beorhtwulf. He intends to make war on the Land of the Wolf. I would have you take a message to your King or the Eorledman who holds the north for him. We will defeat Ubba and if Mercians come to fight us then this will be the fate of Mercia. We have left you alone up to now, have we not?"

I saw the young thegn's face as he considered my words. He nodded, "Aye, you have."

"Then take my offer and leave for we will either have more blood this day or you will leave!"

The thegn was no fool and he nodded, "We will leave. How long do we have to pack?"

"You leave now with what you carry on your backs. You, thegn, may keep your sword. The rest can take only their spears and seaxes." I turned, "Clear the gate so that they may leave!"

I nodded to Stig Sword Hand. He shouted, in our language, "Hearth weru guard the hall and the church. Let none enter!"

The thegn saw my men move and he said, "We will do as this Viking says. I did not lie, Viking, our treasure is the blood of our children."

He sheathed his sword and swung his shield around his back. He led his bodyguards towards the gate. Ráðgeir looked pointedly at the swords in the hands of the Saxons. They dropped them at his feet. A young Saxon woman, wearing finer clothes than the rest, carrying one babe and holding the hand of a young boy went to the thegn's side. They waited while the rest of the folk of Orm's kirk trudged by. I saw that there were two priests and they were helping the wounded.

"You may have the carts for the old and the wounded. Mordaf, go and empty them."

The thegn's eyes widened, "You are a strange Viking. I can see that you are the heir to Dragonheart for all Mercia knows him to be less barbaric than the Danes."

I nodded, "And yet your king chose Ubba over the Dragonheart. Use your words, Mercian, to persuade your king to mend the error of his ways. He has misjudged the moment. There are easier victories closer to home."

We watched them head south as Baldr led my horsemen along the same road the Saxons were taking. He dismounted in the gateway. Shaking his head and smiling he said, "I can see there is a tale here and I would hear it while we eat for I am weary beyond words. I have never ridden as far in one day!"

"Close the gates! Prepare food! Search the buildings. There will be treasure to be had!" As my men hurried to obey my commands I said, "Then first pay for your food with the news we crave. Mordaf, join us!"

"First let me and my men see to our horses, lord. They have served us well this day."

The hall of the thegn was not as large as the one by the Maeresea but there was food ready to be cooked. Leif had taken it upon himself to begin preparing it. Mordaf fetched some ale as I took off my shield and sword belt.

"The Saxon was right, cuz, you are surprising. "Why did we let them go? Will their men not fight us again?"

"They may but how many men did we lose this day in this skirmish?"

"None but Benni Galmrsson has a bloody coxcomb from that rock."

I nodded, "And if they do fight us again will these Saxons be confident or will they be so fearful of what we will do to them that they might hang back? They might tell those in the shield wall with them of our prowess. They will talk of the accuracy of our archers who slew men with mail. They will tell of our terrible swords which killed all they struck and they will speak of a wall of iron and steel which battered down a wooden gate! We did not need to kill them. Our purpose was not to come here to take captives and treasure. It was to draw a Mercian army north and to destroy it."

Baldr came in, "I hope there is ale for me, lord, for I have a thirst which could drink The Water dry… if The Water was made of ale!"

I smiled and turned back to Mordaf, "The fate of the Land of the Wolf hangs in the balance. There was a conspiracy of enemies come to take it. Alt Clut is neutralised. I hope that Bergil and his brothers have dealt with the Walhaz and that leaves just the Mercians and the Danes. Let us hear Baldr's news."

Baldr had emptied one horn and, after smacking his lips, wiped the foam from his beard, "They are coming but they are just five miles north of the river. Those folks you let go will meet them but it will not be until the morrow. They look to have two of their hundreds. Only their lords, there were four of them, ride horses. We counted just twenty men in mail."

"And are there more settlements?"

He shook his head, "Isolated farms only."

Ráðgeir had come in and listened to the last part. He sat and poured himself some ale, "And we have many animals to drive north. You were right to let them go, lord, for we found pots of coins buried in their huts and they had gathered all of their animals in one place. I will learn to keep my big mouth closed for you are the Dragonheart's heir and he has chosen well."

"How far, Baldr, to the river and our drekar?"

"As the crow flies or the horseman rides less than sixteen miles but it will take you almost a day to reach it with the animals Ráðgeir says we have gathered."

"Then we head for the river and your horsemen can be two miles behind us. If the enemy close with us then we can have a warning."

Baldr asked, "And now, tell me how went this strange day?" When I had told him he nodded, "And we fire this burgh?"

"No, for if we do then they will know that we have left. I wish them to think that we are the barbarians they believe us to be. If they see no smoke, they will think we are still here and hurry to catch us drunk and asleep. It will add to their journey and make them weary. I have no doubt that the men we freed will join them and that means they will outnumber us even with Pasgen ap

Raibeart's men. I know not the effect of the Dragonheart's strategy on Ubba Ragnarsson. We need to do our part and then be ready for a Danish onslaught."

"You think he will still come?"

"Aye, Mordaf, no matter what we do vengeance will burn in his heart. The thwarting of his plans might inflame him even more. We do not fear the Danes but we know that we cannot fight four enemies at the same time. There will be a last battle and the outcome will be close."

Sámr
Chapter 16
Preparations for War

We reached the river in the late afternoon. I sent Baldr to find the Saxons who were following us. Pasgen and the warriors we had left at the river to prepare our defences had done well. He and his men had dug a ditch and planted stakes. The ditch was cunningly concealed at the bottom of a slight ridge just before the river. An approaching enemy would see just a line of spears as they neared the ridge and when they began their attack would discover a hidden obstacle before them. Pasgen had brought many archers with him. Although not as good as my bowmen, they had good weapons and they used the same sort of arrows as we did. We loaded the drekar with the animals and the treasure we had gathered. While Mordaf told Pasgen what we had done and the enemies we would face I spoke with Ulf, my captain.

He smiled when he saw that we had survived almost intact, "We reached Whale Island easily. We met a knarr from Dyflin. Bergil Hafþórrsson sent word. He and his allies are sailing to Anglesey. Even now the men of Gwynedd will be assaulted. I sent a message to Lady Ylva and the Dragonheart. The strategy works, lord."

I shook my head, "Do not tempt the Norns. I am pleased but I still fear that the threads we see are only part of the web sent to entrap us."

Baldr rode in after dark, "They are camped at Orm's kirk, lord. Your trail is clear to see and they have sent scouts out. They will be here by noon."

"Good, then we will be rested and prepared." I waved over my captains, "Ráðgeir, on the morrow plant stakes in the bottom of the ditch and have the men use the ditch to make water and empty their bowels. Better there than in the river. Naddoðr, your men will cut down more of the undergrowth and place that on top of the hidden stakes."

That done I went down to the river. I had with me one of the crosses we had taken from the church at Orm's kirk. The thegn had been less than truthful. The cross was made of silver and was valuable. I waded into the Belisima and held the cross aloft. I would make a blót. "Allfather take this cross and give us victory tomorrow. The Dragonheart is your chosen one. Help me to keep the Land of the Wolf safe from all enemies." I threw the cross into the middle of the river. As it hit the water the clouds, which had been threatening rain, suddenly parted and a shaft of light lit up our camp. I took that as a sign that the Allfather had listened to my words.

I returned to the fire and explained my plans to my leaders. "Pasgen, I would have you and your bowmen form up on the high part of the ridge. Ráðgeir, Naddoðr and Mordaf, we will be lower down the slope closer to the ditch and we will make a double shield wall. Baldr, I want you to take your horsemen and ride upstream. When the enemy is engaged with us, ride to their rear. They will have baggage, priests and, hopefully, a religious emblem with them. Attack those at the rear and we will suck the heart out of this Saxon army."

Mordaf asked, "That is it? We sit and wait for them to attack?"

"Were you not listening, cuz? We let them strike first and we whittle them down with arrows. We kill their best warriors with our swords and then when their priests are threatened, we will attack."

I saw Pasgen and Ráðgeir nod their approval. Mordaf shrugged, "I am learning, cuz. Now I see why, in the past, my father and I have not fared as well as you and my grandfather. You do things differently."

I said nothing. There was already a divide between Gruffyd and his son. I did not want to widen it. His father had not listened to the Dragonheart. I knew that my great grandfather had taught Gruffyd the same as he had taught me. I had listened but his son had not.

We had sentries posted to give warning of the approach of the Saxons. We had made a wooden bridge across our ditch and after they had rushed to warn us of the enemy, we removed the willow and we waited. As soon as our men were in place, I inspected our lines from the Mercian side. They would see a line of bowmen facing them. They would only see us when they reached the high ground above the stakes. That was well within the killing range of our bowmen. When they were there Pasgen would launch his arrows. What happened after that would depend upon this Eorl. We had discovered, from what the men of Orm's kirk had said, that he was called Wigmund and was the nephew of the King. Caestir was an important burgh and this Wigmund might see himself as a future King of Mercia. A victory over Vikings might garner him a crown and a throne. He might be reckless.

We were silent and still as we waited. Our shields were ready and most of our men had spears. We heard the Mercians before they reached us. They were singing and I recognised some of the words; it was a song of the White Christ. I did not know how they expected such words to inspire them. They spoke of their god as a lamb; a lamb was for eating!

Pasgen shouted, "They are almost at the high ground, lord. Soon you will see them!"

"Prepare!"

We would be within bow range of the Saxons. I doubted that they would be ready to loose arrows quickly but it did not do to be careless. I saw the standard first. It was a blue flag with a yellow diagonal cross. Then we saw the lords and their horses. As they crested the rise they looked down and saw us.

I yelled, "Now, Pasgen!"

A hundred arrows soared. Horses and men who were slow to raise their shields were hit. I heard the cries as the arrows tore into their unarmoured bodies and then a Saxon horn sounded. The horsemen who were still mounted dismounted and the Saxons flooded down the slope towards us. In their blind rage to get at us, for we had slain their standard bearer, they did not see the ditch; they were too busy negotiating the stakes. We were just twenty paces from the spike-filled ditch. The undergrowth which Naddoðr and his men had used masked the deadly spikes. When men began to cross the hazard I shouted, "Brace!"

The men who crossed successfully and attacked us were their best. They were mailed and they were well trained. The less experienced ones found the stakes and spikes. They screamed as the wood tore into feet and legs. I recognised the young thegn from Orm's kirk. He led men to the west of their line. Their Eorl, for he had the best armour and his shield bore the same device as the flag, came at me. We were a solid line while they came at us piecemeal. I saw two of the Eorl's bodyguard hurrying to flank him. The Eorl held a spear and ran up the slight slope towards me. He had a full-face helmet and that gave me hope for he would not have a clear sight of me.

Seeing that I only held a sword he lunged at me with his spear. He was below me and I blocked the strike easily. His feet struggled for purchase on the slippery ground and he made the mistake of looking at the earth to find a better path. I brought my sword from on high and struck his helmet. It was well made but I dented it. He must have worn a protector beneath for he did not fall. Swinging it to the side, he rammed his spear at my leg. He was slightly unsighted and although he hit and tore my seal-skin boot the spear merely grazed my leg. I would need a new boot! I brought my shield down hard and the metal rim shattered his spear below the head. He drew a fine sword as he stepped closer to me. I had chosen the flattest piece of ground I could and his head rose as he stepped closer. I could not see his face but I did see blood trickling down his chin. Head wounds were tricky. I had hurt him but I knew not how seriously. He punched at me with his shield to allow himself a swing. His bodyguards had reached his side and Stig and Sven were engaged with them. I could focus my attention on the Eorl.

All along the line, men were fighting. I saw as I swung my sword at the Eorl's head, that Pasgen was still sending arrows over to thin out the unarmoured fyrd who followed the Eorl and thegns. The men they were targeting were the farmers and the poor of the land. They had small, simple shields and no helmets and they were dying. Their numbers meant nothing. My blow was blocked by the Eorl's shield. He lunged upwards at my face. It was a tempting target but the blow could be avoided. I moved my head to the side and brought my shield up. I rapped his hand with the metal edge. Unlike my mail protected hands, his were bare and he would have numbed fingers. Swords needed dexterity and a numbed hand was a weakness. I brought my sword from behind me as he withdrew his sword for a second strike. As he lifted his shield to block the blow, I completed the swing with my sword. It was a powerful strike as it came from behind me and all of my weight was behind it; the edge of the blade cracked into his shield. I would have taken some of the edge off my sword but he was now vulnerable. I swung my right leg and, kicking, connected with his face. His arms spread as he lost his balance. He tried to step back but there was blood on the ground and he lost his balance and tumbled down the slope. His fall took out two of the fyrd.

I disobeyed my own orders and ran after the Eorl. I swung my sword at one of the fyrd who foolishly tried to hit me with his scythe and I hacked through his right arm. I punched the other in the face with the boss of my shield and he fell unconscious. I reached the Eorl as he struggled to his feet, "Surrender and live!"

"I will have you boiled in oil, barbarian!"

He put all of his effort into a swing at my head. As I raised my shield, I heard a cry from the south. Baldr had struck. The Eorl made the mistake of flicking his eyes around. With a full-face helmet that meant moving your head. My sword struck just below his helmet and above his byrnie. My sword had been blunted slightly but it broke the skin and the weight of my strike broke his neck. He fell at my feet! I raised my sword and took his head. Pulling off his helmet I lifted the skull by the hair, "Saxons, your leader is dead!"

The men at the top of the rise must have seen Baldr and my horsemen at the same time as I took the head. There were still enough Saxons fighting us to give them a chance of victory but the fyrd had had enough and they fled. I heard a voice. I recognised it as that of the Thegn of Orm's kirk, "Mercians, fall back! We have lost!"

Some of the Eorl's oathsworn fought on and were slain but the majority ran back up the slope. When he reached the top the Thegn of Orm's kirk turned, "Viking, you have won this day. I will visit the King and give him your words but come not again south of the Belisima! I will make my home so strong that the next time you come your men will bleed upon its walls!"

I took off my helmet, "Keep Mercians south of the Belisima and I have no need to cross it! Think on my words. You know I speak truly!"

He nodded and led his men away.

I turned, "See to our wounded and dispatch the Saxon hurt. Mordaf, come with me."

I crossed the ditch; there were dead bodies which I used as a bridge and we climbed up the slope. I saw that Baldr and his horsemen led captured horses and a chest. They were heading towards me, away from the fleeing Saxons. I estimated that half of the Saxons remained but their backs were to me. They had enough men to have defeated us. I did not think they could have done so for we were better warriors but I was grateful that they had fled. We had a bigger battle to fight and that would be a battle for our homeland.

We left the next day. Baldr and his horsemen gathered even more animals. Mordaf and his men took their share and they walked back to their home. It would be a shorter journey than going by sea to Whale Island and then heading east. We spoke alone before he left.

"Sámr, know that I am loyal but I cannot say the same for my father. If he turned against you and the Dragonheart, I would be torn."

I nodded, "And I do not envy you your choice. You make your own decisions but if you do choose to fight against us know that blood will mean nothing. The land and Dragonheart are all. I have been given a burden to bear and I will do so no matter what."

"I know and I swear that I will not fight against you or the clan but I am not certain if I could fight against my own father."

Perhaps I was becoming a galdramenn for when I looked into his eyes, I saw his heart. He would not fight with his father. He was about to make a decision which I knew I would not have to make.

"Farewell Mordaf, it was an honour to fight alongside my kin. May the Allfather be with you."

The voyage home took a day for we were laden with booty and animals. Ulf had taken the dead home after our first raid and we buried those who had fallen at the Belisima to the north of the river. If their graves were despoiled then the Saxons would pay.

Our people had kept a good watch and my father had been summoned as our drekar negotiated the narrow entrance to Whale

Island. I descended first to the accolades of those who lived by the sea. My father frowned and asked, "Mordaf?"

"He is well but he took his animals directly to his home. He fought hard and he is now a warrior. We have an understanding."

"And the Saxons?"

"We burned their bridge over the Maeresea, killed the Eorl of Caestir and laid waste to the land south of the Belisima. I do not say that the Mercians will not attack but they will not attack for six months and I sent a warning to their King. They may seek vengeance but more than two hundred of their men were hurt. I believe that they will see Gwynedd as an easier opponent. Now that the men of Dyflin have kept their promise then we worry about the Danes but I do not underestimate them. Their grand strategy may have failed but we lost men in our campaigns and the Danes will come." I looked at my father and could not believe the words which came from my mouth. I was advising my father. Our positions had reversed! "You are ready for an attack?"

He nodded, "We learned our lessons from the last time. We and the people of Úlfarrston now have double ditches. We have wells and we have towers. Food is laid in and men and women know that they will have to fight!"

There was a confident mood in the stad. That may have had something to do with the fact that we had had success so far and there were only a few families who had loved ones to mourn. Those families received a larger bounty and so they accepted the loss for all those who had died would be in Valhalla. They had died with a sword in their hand.

Naddoðr came to speak with me, "Lord, I know that you wish us to patrol the seas and then fight for Mordaf but you will need us to fight the Danes. We could supplement your men. We are good enough, are we not?"

"You are more than good enough and nothing would please me more than to have you and your men behind my walls but Mordaf has the smallest garrison. If he were to fall then the road to Hawk's Roost and The Water would be wide open."

He nodded, "I pray to the Allfather that you are safe." Mordaf's father had much to answer for. If he could be trusted then Naddoðr and his men would be able to fight further north. The sisters had spun. It was *wyrd*.

We rode up The Water. Each time I made this journey I felt a sense of satisfaction but since Ylva and my great grandfather had dreamed I had also endured a feeling of dread. It was such an idyllic place that I did not want to lose it. I saw now, as Old Olaf was reflected in The Water, that my great grandfather had prepared me well. When I had sailed with him to Miklagård, Cyninges-tūn was just a place where the Dragonheart lived. Raiding and visiting exotic places seemed far more exciting. Since I had married and knowing that the Dragonheart had a short time left in the Land of the Wolf then all of that paled into insignificance. If I never raided again nor saw a new city it would not worry me. I now knew what was important. I now understood what I had to fight for. I found myself smiling. The change had been subtle and was a mark of the greatness of Dragonheart. I would never be a shadow of the Dragonheart but I would have to try to take his place. It was an awesome challenge.

"You are quiet, lord."

I nodded, "Aye, Baldr. I wish that Ylva had the power to freeze time so that what we have now we always have and that it never changes. I do not want to lose a single person." I pointed to the stand of trees which had sprung up next to The Water, "I want to see those trees grow high enough to touch the sky."

He gave me a sad smile, "As did I and then my family was taken and I was made a slave. I would hate to lose paradise a second time."

I shook my head. I was thinking only of myself, "I am sorry Baldr. I have been lucky, I know that. I have had adventures and the love of my family. You were torn from your family."

"Aye, lord, but when I close my eyes," he tapped the side of his head, "and when I sleep then they are here and I can hear their voices. When I dream, I see them and they come to me when I least expect it. They watch Nanna and me and they are content. I live their lives for them."

"Then you take the men back to Hawk's Roost. I will take a boat across The Water. I would speak with my great grandfather."

I had even more to think on as we approached the open gates of Cyninges-tūn. My great grandfather was not there to greet me and that worried me a little. Ylva did meet me and she smiled at me even before I asked the question, "Grandfather is well. He is with Haaken Bagsecgson. Haaken One Eye has come to visit and they have been with the weaponsmith all afternoon. I did not think to bother him. He and Haaken One Eye were like two young boys. They even kept Erik Black Toe from them. He was sent to Hawk's Roost to help your lady. They are plotting something and wish it to be a secret. Come, we will go to his hall. Atticus and Germund the Lame are the best to speak to about his health."

My fears resurfaced, "He is ill?"

She shook her head and linked my arm, "No, but he is old. All those years ago he hid his illness from all of us. I have not sensed any danger but we will speak to those who see him daily." She saw my look of disapproval and read my mind, "I also have a mother who has been unwell. She recovers but slowly. Do not think to chastise me, cuz!"

"I am sorry. I meant no offence."

She smiled and squeezed my arm, "And none taken. You have a great weight upon your shoulders and you are still young. All of us are proud of what you have achieved and I have dreamed and know that there is more to come."

I turned to look at her. That meant I was not yet destined to die.

She shook her head, "Ask me no more for it is dangerous to know too much about our future. Know this, I shall be there watching over you and I will guide you as my father guided Dragonheart." She left me at the door of the hall, "I will fetch them for they will both be anxious to know what you have done."

Atticus beamed as I stepped through the door, "You live and you are whole! That is to be celebrated!"

Germund the Lame shook his head, "He is a Viking! A wound marks him as a man!"

I smiled, "And I am glad to see you. While he is absent, tell me how is the Dragonheart's health?"

Atticus reflected but Germund grinned, "When I am his age I would be half as healthy!"

Atticus shook his head, "He is in better spirits than he has been for a while. He has not had to fight and for that, I thank you, Sámr. I know that you have taken that load from his shoulders. If I was to try to define the difference it is that he is at peace. It is hard for me to say but my master seems in tune with the land.

When he thrives so does the land and vice versa. I do not yet understand it but I shall. Germund, go and light the fire in the steam hut. Lord Sámr may not smell himself but I find it hard to bear the reek of sweat, blood and God alone knows what else!"

I bowed, "And I am not offended, Atticus, and I know that I smell. Before you go, Germund, help me take off this mail. It seems I have worn nothing else for months and it weighs upon me."

After he had taken off my mail and gone to light the fire Atticus asked, "Will you be staying the night?"

"As much as I would enjoy your company I will stay to bathe, dine and then talk with the Dragonheart. Have a boat made ready to take me home. I need to see my family."

Atticus smiled. He had gentle eyes and the most understanding nature of any man I had ever met, "And that marks you for a true man. You are so civilized I find it hard to believe that you are truly a Viking!"

I shook my head and took the ale he proffered. "I am like my great grandfather, Greek, I am an enigma and therein lies the hope for the clan. Our enemies do not understand either of us!"

My great grandfather and Haaken One Eye arrived back before I had finished my first horn of ale. They had a conspiratorial look about them. My great grandfather hugged me, "Another victory I hear! I have made the right choice!"

Haaken also put his arms around me. He had been drinking heavily for I could smell it on his clothes as well as his breath, "And I need all the details. It is time we had sagas about the young and not the shrivelled up poor john that we celebrate!" Poor john was the dried fish which we ate when there was nothing better left in the larder!

"Speak for yourself. Do you stay the night, Sámr?"

I shook my head, "Germund has lit the steam hut and then I need to get back to my family."

"Of course, of course, what am I thinking. But you will eat with us?"

"I will."

"Good, then we will join you in the steam hut. Atticus, the meal will be a good one?"

"They always are, although some people," he glared at Haaken, "are normally so drunk that they cannot taste the fine food I prepare!"

"The food I crave, Greek, is the food of words!"

Smiling Atticus said, "Then perhaps you should learn Greek!"

He went off to fetch more ale and Haaken said, "Why do we suffer that old fool?"

"Because he is like us, Haaken, a remnant of the past and when we go to the Otherworld this world will fade a little."

Haaken's mouth opened and closed, "I should have said that!"

My great grandfather laughed, "Don't worry, you will!"

Would Baldr and I enjoy such a closeness when we were old?

The three of us went to the steam hut and I told them all. My great grandfather nodded, "Then it is just down to Ubba and his Danes. What are your thoughts, Sámr?"

"We cannot know whence he will come. We must wait behind our walls. After the success of Baldr and his horsemen, I have a mind to use boys on ponies as messengers. We have plenty of horses and Baldr has identified boys in each stad who can ride well. We have at least six in each stad. Whichever one is attacked they will send their riders to the others to warn them of the danger."

I saw them both thinking. Drunk or sober Haaken One Eye had a good mind. He said, "That is a good plan but how does it help us? If they attack Ketil and he sends to the other stad for help we risk leaving them undefended if we go to their aid."

"I know. I have spoken with Mordaf and my father as well as Pasgen ap Raibeart. When we receive the message, we do nothing for two days. Each stad must hold out for two days."

"Two days can seem like a long time, great-grandson."

"I know but my father and Mordaf are well prepared. They have food for a week and strong walls."

"And my son?"

"My messenger was sent away. Gruffyd would not hear my words."

"So be it. Then I have lost another son."

I saw the sadness in his eyes and it hurt me for there was nothing I could do about it.

"One more thing, Great Grandfather. No matter what happens you do not go to the aid of any other stad! You are the target of Ubba. If he attacks other places first it is to weaken you. I am across The Water and I will watch your hall."

He suddenly looked at me, "You will not wait two days!"

"If you are attacked, Dragonheart, then I will come to your aid as soon as I hear your horn." Sámr was showing his skills as a leader for he was happy to argue with me.

"But you have the fewest men."

"Remember, apart from yours, they are the best trained. Our leaders all know a secret word I will send if my orders are to be broken. Only they will know it and only I can send it. If you are attacked first then it means it is unlikely there will be other attacks." I smiled, "You have made me your heir. You must live with those consequences."

"Aye," he looked sad.

It was late when Arne the Fisher took me home. I had had plenty of wine but I was not drunk. I was happy. I had dined with the two greatest warriors who still walked this earth and I was privileged to do so. When I walked into my hall and looked at my sleeping family, I felt that I had been gifted a life which was offered to few mortals. I would not let it go easily.

Dragonheart
Chapter 17
The Blade and the Wolf

When Sámr left for Mercia I was unworried, although I could not discern the reason. I just knew that he would come home without a wound. Since I had been to Wyddfa I had almost seen what men thought; the mountain had changed me. Perhaps it had unlocked a power which had lain dormant inside me. Ylva and her mother were the exceptions for I had no idea what went on behind their eyes except that I could hear their thoughts when they wished me to. I also had dreams and now they were every night. I saw Sámr as a man with his son Ragnar by his side. I even saw him sailing to destroy a fleet of Danes off our southern coast. As Sámr was full grown in my vision this had to be the future. I also felt as though the Land of the Wolf was filling my veins with... for want of a better word, I thought power. I woke early without aches and pains each day. I had no burning in the chest when Atticus made me rich pastries. I was able to practice each day with Erik and Germund without having to stop every few strokes. In short, I felt as though I had been reborn in Wyddfa.

I was no fool and I knew that this was the work of the Allfather but the Norns still had enmity for me. They were spinning and weaving; they were plotting my end but that did not concern me. What they did would come no matter what I did. I was now the oldest Viking that any knew save for Haaken One Eye. If I died the next day, I would have had a fuller life than any save my oldest friend. He came to stay with me the day after Sámr left to raid in the south.

He shrugged when I asked him why, "My wife is with Yngvild who is with child again. I know that it will be a girl once more. We both know, my old friend, that you and I have few years left. I would rather spend them with you when I can. You are planning something and I would be part of it." I gave him a sharp look. Did he read my mind too? "Come, you cannot fool me."

I held my finger to my lips. "Erik, Haaken will be staying for a while. Why do you not go and stay with Aethelflaed? Her husband and Baldr are gone and although there are guards for her, she will enjoy your company."

The young warrior's eyes narrowed, "What is going on, lord? Why do you send me away? I am here to guard you."

"And that is why I send you now for Haaken can do that for me and besides the Danes are not yet come and they are not due here for some time or Ylva would know. We have upset their plans. They will still come but Ubba Ragnarsson will have to modify his cunning devices."

Apparently satisfied, he nodded and mounted a horse to take him around the head of The Water. After he had left us, I took Haaken by the arm and led him to the workshop of Haaken Bagsecgson, the weaponsmith. His sons were busy working but the master weaponsmith was in his own workshop which was hidden by a seal-skin curtain. I could hear him working as we neared him. He stopped, guiltily, when we entered.

"I have brought your namesake to show him the progress on the work."

Haaken Bagsecgson smiled, "It has been hard keeping the secret. My sons are curious."

Haaken One Eye shook his head, "What is this, Dragonheart? Do you need another weapon and why should it be secret?"

I saw that Haaken Bagsecgson had hidden his work beneath a cloak when we had entered and so I continued to tease my old friend. "Do you remember Wyddfa?" He nodded. "We found stones other than Kara's Hope. I noticed that they were identical to the stones on Ragnar's Spirit."

"I saw the coincidence too, but what has this to do with the finest weaponsmith since Bagsecg Bagsecgson?"

I saw the weaponsmith go to pull back the cloth and I shook my head, "It planted an idea in my head. We were sent to Wyddfa for Kara's Hope but there were other reasons. Sámr is ready to be lord and I am happy for him to do so but Ylva has told me that Ragnar's Spirit can belong to no other but me. He needs a sword." I nodded to Haaken Bagsecgson. Like a magician, he whipped off the cloth to reveal an almost identical copy of the sword which was touched by the gods.

The weaponsmith nodded, "When I was consulted by the Dragonheart, I was both honoured and fearful. How could I attempt to do that which was asked? I slept on it and then my father came to me in a dream. He told me that I had to make it and so I agreed. The Dragonheart's blood was used to temper the steel and I copied it exactly all save the last part. If the god wishes to strike this sword then he must send a storm. I am just a man."

I patted him on the back, "You are more than that, Haaken Bagsecgson, you are a master weaponsmith!"

Haaken put his hands towards the blade and then pulled them back, "This is truly remarkable. I have seen Ragnar's Spirit more than any other man and I would find it hard to see a difference."

I smiled and picked up the blade. "There is a difference and this is my addition." It was dark in the workshop and I turned the blade so that the light from the fire shone upon it. When I did so the runes which Haaken Bagsecgson had begun to etch could be seen. "When Haaken is done they will say, '*I am Dragonheart, ordered by the Dragonheart and made by Haaken Bagsecgson'*."

I handed the blade to Haaken who nodded as he ran his fingers over the blade, "And this is for Sámr?" I nodded. "He truly is your favourite. I will compose a song for this blade. You are right, old friend, it is not touched by the gods but it is almost as magical for it has been born from your mind and with the will of the Allfather." He laid the blade down reverently, "And no one else knows?"

I shook my head, "None save Ylva. She came and wove a spell when the blade was almost done." I laughed, "She is a clever and a deep one. She lies as though born to it. She wishes the surprise to be complete. She sees Sámr as a young brother. When I am gone then she will watch over him."

Haaken One Eye gave me a sharp look, "You have dreamed your own death?"

Shaking my head, I led him from the workshop, "This is not the place to speak of such things. The weaponsmith has not finished. I do not want the blade to have such negative thoughts."

"Aye, you are right for it is a living thing. When I touched it, I heard its voice. It is small but it grows."

Once outside we headed for The Water. There was a rock on which I liked to sit. I could see across to Erika's grave and Hawk's Roost. When we were seated there I spoke, "We both know that when the Danes come, they will come for me. I know all of Sámr's plans and they are well made. There will be tricks for we know that Ubba is advised by a cunning warrior, Gangulf Gurtsson. There will be subterfuge and deception. There will be attempts to distract us but we both know that they will, ultimately, come here for me. That upsets me for there will be people who will die because of me."

"That would happen no matter where you were."

I had thought about this, "And I debated going to the top of either the Old Man or Úlfarrberg but I know that others would follow me to protect me. No, I have decided to make my home so strong that Ubba and this Gangulf will lose many men trying to take it. That will buy Sámr time to gather men and to end this but I will fall." I tapped my chest, "They call me the Dragonheart and the dragon's heart knows the truth. I am like the old wolf who leads the pack for one last battle. I know that I will die but I am content. I have seen the future. Sámr now has a son, Ragnar. I cannot foresee his future but the next generation is safe. It is why I have been spared so long. It is why the Allfather had the doctor in Miklagård save me. Sámr was with us and Baldr was sent to us. The Norns spin but the Allfather does all that he can to counteract those vindictive witches!"

I smiled as Haaken's hand went, involuntarily, to his amulet, "Then I will stay here by your side until that time. The Dragonheart will not die alone. It is a lifetime since we stood back to back with Old Ragnar. I was chosen to be with you until the end."

"And your family?"

"Will understand. They of all people know our bond. They see this old man who has lived a long time and they see a purpose in my life. They are grateful to have had me as long as they have. So, old friend, how do we thwart this ugly Dane?"

We walked around my stronghold and worked out together how to do so. I had already formed ideas and Haaken refined them with me. The next day we began our work. We had another ditch dug and I ordered the construction of a sluice gate so that we could use the power of The Water to make a river around our walls when we were attacked. The beck to the north of the stronghold was deepened and its banks made steeper. The day we spent walking my walls made me feel young again. It had been many years since I had looked so hard at my home. After Ubba had been defeated the last time we had thought of improvement but time had passed and we saw no threat. Now I knew that what I did would live beyond me. When I was in Valhalla the work Haaken and I began would outlive us. That was good.

Over the next days, while Sámr was away dealing with the Mercian threat, Haaken and I drew up plans. We included Atticus in our discussions. He was no warrior but he was a clever man and was well read. He would not condone war but he was more than happy to defend people. He and Germund used their knowledge from the east to present ideas we had not yet thought of. Each day we visited with Haaken Bagsecgson to see the progress on the sword. The working of the runes was taking almost as much time as the making of the blade but he wanted them etched perfectly. He used copper from our mines to inlay the runes. They would make them stand out.

Ylva met us there and said, "I have dreamed and Sámr is on his way home." She took out a piece of cloth and unwrapped it. There was a scabbard which she had obviously made. "I have used some of my hair and that of my mother to weave a spell into it. There are tiny fragments of red stones, chips from Kara's Hope, which are also in the sheath. The sword may not be as powerful as Ragnar's Spirit but the scabbard is the strongest. It will keep Sámr safe from wounds; so long as he wears it then he can never be wounded."

I kissed her on the forehead, "Then this is truly a great gift."

"And when do you present him with it?"

"I thought to give it at Yule. When the days are short and the nights are long; when the sun is a dream and snow rules this will be a light for the land."

Ylva beamed, "And that is a perfect day. The Danes will come but they will not risk the High Divide in winter."

Haaken One Eye was curious, "How do you know? Men have crossed in winter before."

She linked her arm through mine, "Dragonheart is at home. He has not left this land since he sought the red stone. Each day he is here increases his hold over this land. His power spreads. He does not know it but my mother and I can see, through the spirits, the borders. This winter will be a wolf winter and that is appropriate for the last of the wolf warriors. Men may try to cross but the Mother and the land will conspire to destroy them. The thaw will be such that there will be great flooding. We need to prepare our people for that eventuality."

I nodded, "And the preparations for flood defence will also strengthen our stad. *Wyrd*."

Ylva nodded, "I told you, grandfather, you and the land are one. So long as you are here, the Clan of the Wolf will prosper."

I turned and stared at her, "Then what happens when I die?"

Ylva always had an enigmatic look but in that moment her face became a veil through which I could not discern anything. She merely said, "Trust in the spirits and the Allfather!"

Haaken One Eye, Ylva and I were with Haaken Bagsecgson when Sámr returned. We would have rushed out to greet him but the weaponsmith had summoned us. The blade was done. We laid the blade and the scabbard together. Haaken One Eye said, "This is *wyrd*. I finished the saga last night."

Ylva nodded, "Then stay here and sing the song to the sword. I will greet Sámr. Come when you are done."

When she left the three of us stood while Haaken One Eye sang the song of the Dragonheart Sword.

Born of blood from Viking Slave
With steel forged 'neath Olaf's brow
And The Water, deep and slow
Made for one, a warrior brave
The sword protects Úlfarr's land
Long beyond the Dragonheart's time
When the hills he no longer climbs
This blade will lead the wolf's band
With witch's spell to seal the steel
The sword will be a shining light

There to help Sámr's clan fight
The enemies its touch will feel
As heads are hewn and warriors slain
As foes unnumbered try and fail
To end the Dragonheart's heroic tale
With magic sheath he will feel no pain
Born of blood from Viking Slave
With steel forged 'neath Olaf's brow
And the Water, deep and slow
Made for one, a warrior brave
The sword is now the Dragonheart
Named for the one there from the start
And Haaken too, he played a part
In the tale of the Dragonheart

To say I was touched would be an understatement. To cover my embarrassment I joked, "And I see you had to get yourself into the tale!"

He laughed, "Aye, well I was there from the start. I tried to weave Cnut into it too but…"

"Cnut would understand. Come, let us greet Sámr. Curb your normal loquacity, Haaken One Eye, and keep this a secret." He nodded and looked unusually serious. "Haaken Bagsecgson, I leave the sword and scabbard with you until Yule."

"Fear not it will be safe. I am honoured to have been part of this."

After Sámr had gone Haaken and I got drunk. It had been a momentous day. Sámr would not leave the Land of the Wolf now until the battle had been fought and won. Ylva's words had told me that he would grow more powerful right until the day I died and that was all that I could ask for.

When Atticus went, reluctantly, for more ale, Haaken said, "Let us make our end a good one, Dragonheart. I have hopes that Erik Black Toe may well turn out to be a wordsmith too. He can never achieve that which I did but he can try. I would like a good song about our end."

"You have written one already. I still hear the words of the Dragonheart Sword in my head. Our end may be a good one but it will cause pain. Not for us as we shall be in Valhalla, but for those who remain it will."

Erik came back from Hawk's Roost the next day. As much as he had enjoyed the company of Nanna and Aethelflaed he was obviously happy to be back in my hall. We used him to help organise the men who would be needed to make the changes to the strongholds. We had two large halls and many small homes. My hall and the women's hall could accommodate all the women and children who lived in the stronghold or close to it. They needed to be defended. Although Sámr had said he would come as soon as I was attacked, for he could see us, I had to assume the worst and that he would not reach us for two or even three days. We had just forty men to fight on my walls and that included old men like Haaken One Eye and Germund the Lame. We had boy bowmen and slingers but the forty men were the ones who would fight sword to sword. The walls and the gate would fall. Many Danes would bleed but they would, eventually, get inside. We needed to make two fortresses of the halls.

We had our men dig two deep ditches around each hall. We had our carpenters make two bridges. There would be but one way into the halls. When an attack came then the two bridges would be pulled up in front of the doors to make a double door. The ditches were dry but they were as deep as a small man. One side was steep and at the bottom, we planted metal and wooden spikes. The metal ones were made from the poorer quality weapons and mail we had taken from Alt Clut as well as the slag from our own mines. Nothing was wasted. We already had a double gate at the gatehouse. In addition, we added holes from which we could drop stones, darts and boiling liquid on the attackers. We missed Aiden's wizardry but Atticus and Germund made up for it with their knowledge of Miklagård and the Byzantine fortresses.

An arduous job was to put a roof over the fighting platform and the towers. Our archers could still release arrows but our men would be protected from arrows and stones sent from beyond our walls. Any sent into the air would hit the roof. We put turf on the roof. It was living and so would slow down fire. The double ditch around our walls was deepened. Now that it could be flooded, we could use longer stakes. They would not just incapacitate, they would kill.

As Haaken Bagsecgson had finished my sword he turned his attention to making darts, spearheads and arrowheads. The darts were the most important weapon he made for they could be thrown by anyone. With a weighted tip and a long spike, they were easy to make and would be deadly. The whole of Cyninges-tūn, save the most infirm, would fight on the walls. Once the walls fell then they would be the first to be sent to the halls. The days grew shorter as Yule approached but the work did not relent. This would have been the time when men carved bone and wood or made sheaths and scabbards. Those activities would have to wait until after the attack.

Word came, a sennight before Yule, that the Danes were recruiting more warriors to attack us. They knew that their secret was a secret no longer and had abandoned all pretence. The lure of the sword that was touched by the gods and the rumour of a fictitious mountain of gold hidden by Myrddyn in the Land of the Wolf were spread. If Ubba Ragnarsson could not have reliable allies then he would have plenty of desperate men. Bergil and his brothers, along with the men of Veisafjǫrðr had kept their word. They had taken Anglesey and were now raiding Gwynedd and Caestir. Mercia was now helpless to join in an attack. With the hostages at the Stad on the Eden, only the Danes remained as a threat and Ubba was making up for a lack of allies by buying the services of desperate men.

Sámr had not been idle. He had visited all of the other stad and leaders. Haraldr had the one which was in need of the most work. Ketil sent some of his men down from the north to help. The three northern stad were the strongest. Two of them were Roman and made of stone. Mordaf's felt like the most vulnerable to me for he had the smallest garrison. He had shown himself to be loyal and I prayed to the Allfather that he would not pay the price for such loyalty. I was glad that Sámr had left Naddoðr and his men there. They had proved themselves to be stout and reliable. Even Ráðgeir had been impressed. I considered riding to speak with Gruffyd but I knew that would be of little use. We now had riders in place and the young, soon to be warriors, were keen to show the new leader of the clan of their worth. He had just visited me to inform me of his progress when Ylva's prophetic words came true. The first snows of winter came. It was not the small flakes which melted as they landed, it seemed that the gods had rolled the snow into giant balls and within a short time the land was completely white as though the Allfather had laid a blanket upon the world. Baldr and Sámr had to return home by boat. Our halls would be separated by a short piece of water but it might as well have been an ocean. When he was ten paces from the shore, he disappeared in a flurry of white.

I turned to Haaken as we headed for the warmth of my hall. "We have finished the defences just in time. Let us see if Ylva's predictions were true."

Haaken suddenly started, "The sword! You did not give Sámr the sword!"

I frowned. It was not yet Yule but we could have given him the sword a little earlier. "It is too late now and, besides, it is not yet Yule. The weather may improve in a day or so. We do not know if this is the wolf winter yet so let us not worry yet."

He nodded, "And the Norns are ensuring that I cannot get home to see my family and my first grandson!" He shook his head. Word had come that Yngvild had given birth to a boy, Haaken! "All those girls and the first time one bears me a boy I cannot see him."

"The Norns, Haaken, the Norns!"

I confess that I had thought she might be wrong. A wolf winter usually began in Ýlir but as Mörsugur passed the snow grew deeper and the air colder. I began to fear that we had not laid in enough supplies. It was Atticus who put my fears to rest. "Lord, we laid in supplies for a siege. Your enemies cannot come in this weather or, if they do, then they will come as skeletons. Whenever it thaws, we will have more than enough time to lay in fresh supplies."

Just then I heard a wolf howl. It was far to the north and east, closer to Úlfarrberg but Atticus clutched at his cross. I smiled at the Greek who was terrified of wolves, "Fear not, my friend, I have never known the wolves to descend to this valley no matter how bad the winter. Our people who live in remote places may need to worry but we can deal with wolves." I pointed to my two wolf cloaks which were hung on the walls. "Haaken and I are two of the last wolf warriors. I fear no wolf!"

The Norns were spinning.

The snows stopped and even as clear skies greeted us so did an icy blast which had turned the soft snow into hard, craggy rocks. The air froze before our faces. Yule had been and gone. The sword now rested in my hall but we dared not risk a ride around The Water. What had been the road to Sámr's was now a snow-covered wall. There seemed little point in having men spend energy trying to cut a way through when there might be a thaw. Besides which, the snow wall was a barrier against the Danes. The next days saw the temperature plummet and the howls of the wolves grow closer. They were becoming more desperate for food.

It was when The Water froze that we saw the true scale of this Wolf Winter. Ylva had visited us almost on a daily basis. She ensured the entire population of Cyninges-tūn was well. She smiled at my face, "You are desperate to give the sword to Sámr. He knows not that he has the gift coming to him and he will not be worried. This delay is for a purpose and remember the snow and ice guarantee that the Danes will not come. Each day makes our young boys a little older and closer to the time when they can use their slings and bows to defeat the enemy. There is purpose in all of this."

Atticus snorted, "Boys with stones!"

Ylva was a clever woman and she was more than a match for Atticus' quick tongue. "As I recall, Atticus, there is a story in your holy book about a boy with a sling who kills a mighty champion? The Dragonheart was a boy when he used his small bow to kill his first wolf and to save old Ragnar. Do not disparage young boys."

Despite her words, over the next days, I fretted. The sword seemed to speak to me. It wanted to be in Sámr's hands. Haaken One Eye did not help. He too was desperate to sing his song for Sámr. We had kept the gate clear as men still needed to go to the woods to collect kindling and wood. Until The Water froze, they had visited their nets for fresh fish. One morning Haaken, Erik and I went out to The Water and we saw that Arne the Fisher and his sons were standing forty paces from the shore. They had cut holes in the ice and were fishing.

I shouted, "Is that not dangerous, Arne?"

He laughed. "No, lord. So long as you keep well apart the ice supports you. Young Arne, my eldest, even made it to the other shore. I have never seen the ice as thick."

The seed was planted. I did not know it, as we headed back to the warmth of my hall but the Norns had spun and inside my head, an idea, like a young sapling in undergrowth began to sprout and grow. As we ate our evening meal, a few pieces of dried salted meat with a dried bean and dried mushroom stew mopped up with oat bread, I looked at the chest which contained the Dragonheart sword. When the Danes came Sámr might be attacked first. The sword and scabbard were enchanted and, once Sámr had them, then he could not be wounded in battle. He needed the sword. Just at that moment a wolf howled. It sounded to me like it was just north of Torver's Waite. It seemed to speak to me. I had to get to Hawk's Roost.

"Haaken, what say you and I try the ice tomorrow and walk over to Hawk's Roost?"

Erik and Haaken grinned. Haaken banged the table and said, "Anything is better than waiting here in this white prison cell!"

Atticus placed his hands on the table and looked appalled, "Are you mad, lord? Have I used the magic mushrooms by mistake? Why risk the ice, the cold and the wolves?"

Germund sat back and drank some of his ale, "Because, my Greek friend, the Dragonheart has something hidden in yonder chest and he is desperate to take it to Sámr." I stared at Germund. How did he know? He smiled, "When you are quiet and reflective, lord, you look at Ragnar's Spirit. You have looked at the chest in the same way for the last moon. I have not looked within for if you wish a secret then so be it."

I nodded and stood. I went to the chest and opened it. I took out the sealskin covered scabbard and sword, "This is the Dragonheart sword and it is a gift for Sámr."

Germund the Lame was a warrior and he sighed, "Lord it is the twin of Ragnar's Spirit. Is this magic?"

"I hope so but it is not yet touched by the gods."

Haaken said, "Now we have to take it for the secret is out."

"But the ice, lord!"

I nodded, "I tell you what, Atticus, we have some fowl who live. I will take one and make a blót before we cross the deepest part of The Water."

My answer did not satisfy the Christian but he knew that the fact I was making a sacrifice meant I was going to do it. He shook his head, "Then sacrifice Gurt for the old cock no longer knows when it is dawn and when it is the middle of the night! I am fed up of being woken up!"

I nodded, "Then give Gurt a good meal tonight and tomorrow we will rise early and cross The Water."

Germund looked sadly at the sword, "I would come with you, lord, but I would slow you up."

Gurt, perhaps, knew that he was not long for this earth. He woke the hall in the middle of the night. Atticus blamed the extra food but I knew that we were meant to rise early. We put the animal in a sack, which quietened him and Erik, well wrapped in a cloak, carried him. Haaken and I were Ulfheonar once more and wore our wolf cloaks. I carried the Dragonheart sword. When we stepped outside the hall the cold hit us like a blow from a war hammer. The icy air made my chest hurt.

"You cannot leave in the dark, lord!"

I pointed to the sky. The moon was a large one and a red one. We called it a wolf moon and I believed it was a sign that we were meant to cross. "The moon makes it look like day. I can see Arne's ice holes. This is better for we will have longer to spend with Sámr. We will return tomorrow. Tell Ylva not to worry."

Atticus shook his head, "The Lady Ylva will not be happy!"

I grinned and felt like a boy again, "And that is why you will tell her and not me." I waved Erik and Haaken to the side of me and stepped on to the ice. We all had good seal skin boots and they were warm. Even so, the ice beneath our feet was so cold that I knew we would have to hurry. Gurt was silent. He was old. I hoped that the gods would accept such a sacrifice. It was a worthy one for the alternative would have been that he would have been in a pot and we would have enjoyed him as a meal. The sword in my arms and the one on my belt seemed to weigh me down and, as we approached the middle, I wondered if I had taken on too much. Even as I thought it the Norns were spinning.

I spied a shadow on The Water. A couple of clouds had appeared and flitted across the red moon. It was after one such cloud that I saw the shadow and the shadow moved. The hairs on the back of my neck began to prickle and I stopped. I said, quietly, although in the silence of the night it seemed like a shout, "Hold, there is danger!"

I laid down the Dragonheart sword and drew Ragnar's Spirit. I knew not what this was but it might be Danes come to slay me. Had the Norns spun and tricked me? Had they lured me across The Water to end my life? Perhaps Atticus had been right. Then I heard the growl and knew what it was. It was a wolf. The shadow grew two eyes which looked as red as the moon. I heard a cluck from Erik's sack, Gurt heard it too. I had not killed a wolf since before Úlfarr had saved us from the assassins. I sheathed my sword.

"Erik, bring Gurt to me and pick up the gift."

I heard the terror in his voice for the wolf was approaching slowly. "Aye lord."

Haaken One Eye said, "He looks lean and hungry, should we not slay him, Dragonheart?"

"It is a wolf moon and we are wolf warriors. This is *wyrd*. If this is to be the end of Dragonheart then what better end? But I do not think that this is my night to die."

Erik handed me the sack and I began to walk towards the wolf. I loosened the fastenings on the sack and held the bird by the neck. I did not want it to begin to crow. I spoke and aimed my words at the wolf, "I am Dragonheart, the wolf warrior. I have slain wolves before now but I will not kill you. You are hungry and have young to feed. If you try to kill us then you will die and they will go hungry." All the time I walked I stared at his red eyes. I could see into them and they told me a tale. Something spoke to me through the wolf. Was it the spirit of Erika, my dead wife? I seemed to understand him. His growling drew my attention to his muzzle and his body. His teeth were bared and I could see his ribs. Even though he was emaciated he was still crouched and ready to fight. He was a true wolf and had fed his young and his mate at great cost to himself. "I have here, Gurt. It will give you a meal. Soon this ice will go and you can hunt." I stopped and, dropping the sack, took out Gurt and held the old bird out, offering it to the wolf. I realised that the bird's silence had been because he had died. Either the cold or my fingers had ended his life. I was just four paces from the wolf. If he chose to leap at me and fasten his teeth around my throat then I would die. Haaken and Erik would end the life of the wolf but that would not matter because I would be dead. Since that moment long ago when the Viking dragon ship had taken me from the Dunum all that had happened to me had been determined by the gods and the Norns. That gave me peace. If I was to die then it was meant to be. It was *wyrd*.

I was not afraid of the wolf. A wolf had saved Sámr. I took another step and laid Gurt on the ice. "Take this, Lord Úlfarr. If I can I will send more food for you and your clan but I believe that this night was meant to be. This will be the end of the wolf winter. I shall never see a wolf again, not in this life. I know not if they have wolves in Valhalla but if they do then we will speak once more." I saw that his hackles were no longer risen and his teeth no longer bared. I put my hand on his head and closed my eyes, A voice in my head said, *'There is a place waiting for you in Valhalla, Dragonheart.'* I opened my eyes and saw, in the eyes of the wolf, Valhalla. I stood and turned my back on him and headed back to the sword. I did not turn until I reached Erik. When I did so there was no sign of either the wolf or the meal.

I took the burden from Erik. "Let us not tempt the ice further. Stand apart."

The cloud had shifted and we were bathed in moonlight. I saw Haaken shake his head, "Walking at your side gives me so many stories that I will not have time to sing them all."

I nodded, "Aye, Haaken One Eye, but this I know. I have seen my last winter. I looked into the wolf's eyes and saw my death. Let us get to Sámr and then to my hall. This winter is ending!"

Dragonheart
Chapter 18
The Danes are coming!

We reached Sámr's gates when it was still dark and there was not even a hint of lightening in the sky. The sentry on the wall, Einar Haraldsson, stared down at us, "Are you ghosts? Are you the spirits of the Dragonheart and Haaken One Eye?"

I looked at the other two and laughed. Our cloaks and beards were rimed with frost and we looked white. We could easily have been mistaken for spirits.

Haaken shouted, "We are not ghosts yet, but if you do not open the gates and give us hot ale and honey then we soon will be!"

Aethelflaed was up as she was feeding Ylva Sámrsdotter. Sámr was shocked when he saw us, "Has Cyninges-tūn fallen? What made you risk the ice?"

I smiled for my treasure was still secreted. The sealskin around the sword hid its true identity, "Come, let us go to the fire and have warm ale. We have made it across the ice and we now have time but I will return home this day."

"This day? Why?"

"Because the thaw will come soon and with the thaw the threat of the Danes."

Haaken nodded, "And besides, I have the tale of Dragonheart and the wolf to tell you!"

Sámr's face changed from shock to intrigue. We went to the fire and puddles appeared as the ice on us melted. The poker infused honeyed ale coursed through my body. I could not remember the last time I had enjoyed hot ale as much.

Sámr frowned when Haaken had finished his story "You were lucky and also foolish!"

I shook my head. Haaken's tale had been from his perspective. I had looked into the wolf's eyes. "Sámr, the wolf spoke to me. I think it was Erika's voice I heard. The thaw will come soon. Our ditches will fill with meltwater and that will add protection to our homes. The Danes will come and when I go home, I will speak with Ylva. She must dream for the voices in my head tell me that the Danes are ready to come. Ubba has a mercenary army to feed and the wait hurts him. Men will start to desert and he will come sooner rather than later. We do not have the time I thought."

"Then why make the journey?"

"Ylva has told me that Ragnar's Spirit cannot be wielded by another but you need a sword and more, you need a special sword." I unwrapped the weapon. "Here is your enchanted sword. Ylva and my daughter have spun a spell on the scabbard. It will protect you and the sword, the Dragonheart Sword, will protect the land after I am gone!"

Sámr gave me a sharp look but before he could speak Haaken had begun to sing. He had worked on the first version of the song and this one was longer!

Born of blood from Viking Slave
With steel forged 'neath Olaf's brow
And The Water, deep and slow
Made for one, a warrior brave
The sword protects Úlfarr's land
Long beyond the Dragonheart's time
When the hills he no longer climbs
This blade will lead the wolf's band
With witch's spell to seal the steel
The sword will be a shining light
There to help Sámr's clan fight
The enemies its touch will feel
As heads are hewn and warriors slain
As foes unnumbered try and fail
To end the Dragonheart's heroic tale
With magic sheath he will feel no pain
Born of blood from Viking Slave
With steel forged 'neath Olaf's brow
And the Water, deep and slow

Made for one, a warrior brave
Though time will pass and bodies die
The sword will heal a clan's great pain
Dragonheart's spirit will live again
His body deep in the earth will lie
The sword is now the Dragonheart
Named for the one there from the start
And Haaken too, he played a part
In the tale of the Dragonheart
The two great warriors, Ulfheonar
Defy the Danes with the clan's great power

I saw tears in Sámr's eyes. He held the sword but he looked at me, "You have dreamed your death."

Shaking my head, "Not dreamed but I saw Valhalla and that is enough."

"And this sword?"

"Was tempered with my blood. Hairs from my beard are in the steel. This is the Dragonheart Sword for, when I am gone, it will house my spirit."

He handed the sword to Baldr and put his arms around me, "I do not want to lose you."

"And you will not. My body is old but when it is gone the heart of the dragon will beat in yours through the sword." I leaned in and said, in his ear, "so long as you have the scabbard then you can never suffer a wound. It will not make you immortal for there are many ways to die but it will not be in battle. This is my gift to you." I stepped back. I looked at him and nodded. He held my stare and nodded back. He understood, "And now, fetch us food and let me see Ragnar and Ylva so that I can etch their faces in my memory."

While we ate, I sat first with Ylva, while she was awake, and then Ragnar. I spoke to each of them quietly and said the same words. "I am your grandsire. I will never see you grow for I am old beyond years but when you are grown and hear that voice in your head then that will be me. When you are in danger call for the Dragonheart and I will come. This is my pledge for you are my blood and you are the future."

The sun would have been up an hour when we left except that a blanket of white and black clouds filled the sky. There were now clouds above us and so we could not tell. The air felt warmer and we knew that the thaw would just be days away. I would not risk the wrath of the Norns a second time and so I bade my family farewell.

"I will see you when the battle is fought and won, Dragonheart."

"I pray to the Allfather that is so. Aethelflaed, my great grandson chose well. You are like a jewel we have found. I thank you."

She burst into tears and threw her arms around me. She sobbed, "Do not go! Stay here and we will protect you!"

"No, for I am the lodestone which draws the enemy. I am what they seek but Haaken and I will not go quietly into the Danish night. Fear not for all will be well. The night will become darker and blood will flow but the wolf has told me that the clan will prosper and that is all that matters; I am just the tool of the Allfather."

We headed across the ice. In the daylight, the journey did not seem so long or perhaps we hurried more than we had during the night. Atticus and Germund were waiting for us along with Ylva. While Atticus looked fearful, Ylva looked joyous. She had seen the wolf!

She hugged me, "You looked into the eyes of the wolf and heard the voices." I nodded. "The thaw is coming as is the last battle."

"My last battle."

She nodded and then whispered, "Fear not for I will be at your side. I too have a sword and, like Haaken One Eye, you will not face this foe alone."

The thaw did not come for a fortnight. The weather warmed but the ice was so thick that the thaw seemed imperceptible at first. Then, when it did start it was like a flood across the land and my people thanked me for the defences we had made against the Danes. The ditches we had dug to protect against man now absorbed all of the meltwater. They filled and slightly overflowed and that was good; the sides of the ditches would become muddy and make it harder for an enemy to cross. We had no need to use the sluices. Atticus smiled for their design had been his. He beamed, "We can easily keep them topped up. By summer we will need to drain them but until then they serve a purpose."

"As do you, Atticus. When we found you in Lundenwic I could not have imagined the effect you would have on my people and my life."

He looked somewhat abashed, "Lord, you saved me from a life which I did not enjoy. There were times when I considered that most unforgivable of sins; I thought to take my own life but I did not and I thank God that you came. This life has given me a family and a sense of purpose. When you have rid us of this Danish threat then this will become a place of peace and hope."

I did not disillusion him. He would not believe my dire predictions anyway.

Haraldr Leifsson had taken his responsibilities seriously as had Ketil Windarsson. Both had sent scouts out to the High Divide as soon as the snow had melted. At the end of Gói, both of them sent messengers to tell me that travellers had spoken of a Danish horde gathering to the north-west of Jorvik at an ancient hill fort called Stanwyck. That was at least five days' march away from us but Sámr did the right thing. He warned all of the clan of the threat. He included my son, Gruffyd. Until he actually betrayed us, he would be treated like the rest of the clan. Ragnar also sent word that there had been a battle close to Caestir between the Mercians and the Walhaz. Many men had died but the battle was inconclusive. The gods favoured us for that strengthened the hold Bergil and his brothers had on Anglesey and guaranteed that there would be no threat from the south.

Ragnar sent a message to us to tell me that if we sent riders, he would not wait two days. He would bring his men and those of Úlfarrston to our aid immediately. It was not for me to tell him no. Sámr was now Lord of the Land of the Wolf and the plan was his.

Once the news reached us, we sent riders to warn the nearby farms and the people who lived remotely that they should be ready to seek shelter if the horde came close. It was a surprise, therefore, when two days later Aðils Shape Shifter rode into Cyninges-tūn. He looked much older than the last time I had seen him. To me he would always be the youngest Ulfheonar and would be the one who melted into the undergrowth and disappeared. Now he had flecks of grey in his hair and in his beard.

"I did not expect you, Aðils Shape Shifter. When we spoke to your sons, they said they did not wish to fight."

"And they did not speak for me. We have had harsh words, Dragonheart, and it pains me that they have not followed me to fight at your side. When this is over, I will need to change them. I thought the isolation of Lang's Dale would be good for them but it was not. They are good warriors, as good as me, but they lack the heart of a true Ulfheonar for they do not respect the pack, the rest of the clan. That saddens me."

I nodded, "While you are here then speak with Ylva she has a way of seeing into men's hearts."

He nodded and when Haaken appeared he grinned, "And, of course, it will be good to fight alongside Haaken One Eye again so that I can hear what a great warrior he is!"

"I have much to tell you as well as a new song which you have not yet heard! Atticus, ale!"

Somehow it felt right to have the last of the Ulfheonar gathered together. I was sad about the problems Aðils Shape Shifter was having with his sons but we did not live in a perfect world and I had seen how the best intentions could go awry. After Aðils Shape Shifter had approved the song we ate and I heard more about his sons. I frowned as I listened for if we won then Sámr might have problems with these warriors. The sons and the men they led would be something he would have to deal with when he ruled alone.

The next day we took him around our defences and he saw an immediate problem. "Dragonheart, you have forgotten the markers for the archers. You have good bowmen but they need to know the range. I will mark the range around your walls with white stones."

I nodded, "Thank you and is there anything else we have overlooked?"

He grinned and looked like the young warrior we had not been able to find on Man when we had hunted him, "No, and there are many things I would not have considered."

I gestured towards Atticus who had heard the words and was preening himself. "If you are to have a Greek then you should use him!"

Once he had seen my defences then Aðils Shape Shifter gathered all of the bowmen from my stronghold. He was, quite simply, the best bowman I had ever known, He could not improve their skill in such a short time but he could improve their technique. When Aðils Shape Shifter had put the markers in place he taught them how to use their breath along with their strength and soon all of them were able to hit the markers.

I turned to Haaken, "Even if Aðils Shape Shifter is not with us when we fight the battle, he has already done enough to give us an edge."

"He has!"

Erik looked unhappy and I wondered if he resented the intrusion of another of my old warriors, "Lord, what do I do when we fight? I am not Aðils Shape Shifter nor Haaken One Eye. Even Germund the Lame, for all his infirmities, is a better warrior than I will ever be."

It was Haaken who answered, "Erik Black Toe, you watch the Dragonheart's back. Every foe who comes will try to kill him. Do not think of honour. Use your sword and your dagger to stab, slash and emasculate every warrior who comes close to him. If you have to stab them in the back or ram a sword to take away their manhood then do so. So long as the Dragonheart lives then the clan will survive." I saw him put his arm around Erik's shoulders, it was the touch of a father. "We do not matter. No man will try to kill us above all others but they will do so with the Dragonheart. Hold on to your weapons, Erik, and, if you die, then I will be in Valhalla to welcome you."

"But you are Haaken One Eye, and cannot die!"

He laughed, "Of course I can but when I die then I know that I will have saved the Dragonheart for a few more strokes. In all of the battles we have fought, no matter how perilous, it has been Dragonheart who has won them all at the end. We may both die but if our sacrifice saves the clan then it is worth it. We are old and we pass the clan to Sámr, Baldr, Mordaf and to you. Take care of it!"

Each day I practised with Germund, Haaken, Aðils and Erik. It was as much for them as it was for me. Aðils Shape Shifter had not fought for some years. We all knew that we would be the target for the Danes; our wolf cloaks would mark us as Ulfheonar. Each day that the weather improved increased the chances that the Danes would be here sooner. Erik was growing stronger but he was not a full-grown man and I feared for him. One day, as Ylva watched the other four practise I said, "I do not want Erik to die in this battle, Ylva. Can you enchant him?"

She shook her head, "He was sent to you by the Norns and they are the ones who have spun! He has already played an important part in your life and he is not yet done." She squeezed my arm, "Think of yourself, grandfather!"

I gave her a sad smile, "After all these years I am not certain that I know how to do so."

She nodded, "I have dreamed and they are coming. I see a host to the east of the Great Divide."

"Then they do not come by sea?"

Smiling she said, "You are too good a warrior to fear that. Ubba tried that last time and now the seas between Anglesey and Hibernia are closed to him. It is too early in the sailing season for him to come from the north. He comes by land!"

When the riders came, they rode from the south and east, Haraldr Leifsson sent them. His rider told us that a mighty host was heading from the east. They were to the north of his new stronghold on Windar's Mere. The messenger, named after the former Jarl of Windar's Mere, Asbjorn, was a clever boy of eight years. The message he recited was word perfect.

"Lord, the riders our jarl sent had to take the southern route for the Danish host fills the land to the north of us." I nodded and the boy briefly closed his eyes to focus his mind. "Jarl Haraldr says that there seem to be ten or more boat crews. His scouts counted a hundred men in mail. Danish scouts approached our island but they were slain. My lord says that Ubba Ragnarsson leads them." He beamed when he had finished.

"Good." I had, in my boot, a seax. I reached down to take it out. I gave it to him. "Here is for your diligence." His eyes widened. I had many such knives in my hall but he would treasure the blade given to him by the Dragonheart. One day, long after I was dead, that seax might be used in battle and Asbjorn would remember the gift. "Now tell me, the other riders who came with you, when do you think they will reach their destinations?"

Gripping the handle of the seax he concentrated again, "Olaf was heading to Hawk's Roost. He should be there by now for he came up the eastern side of The Water. The two who went south will still be travelling but they should be there by the middle of the afternoon. I fear that Beorn and Cnut who went to Jarl Ráðulfr and Jarl Ketil, will not reach those lords until well after dark."

"You have done well. Atticus, feed the boy and give him a bed. Asbjorn, you can return to Jarl Haraldr on the morrow."

When he had gone, I summoned Ráðgeir. "Have our riders readied then sound the horn. Battle is upon us."

"Aye, lord."

Erik, Haaken and Aðils joined me, "Make certain that the ditches are filled with water. Have the fishing boats moored in The Water. Burn the houses which lie outside the walls. I want nothing remaining to give the Danes comfort." The folk who had lived in the houses had already removed everything of value. They understood the need to sacrifice their houses. We would rebuild them when the battle was over.

They both nodded. Haaken said, "They are not attacking Haraldr. That is interesting."

Shaking my head, I said, "I think the scouts they sent might have been to decide if they could attack it. Haraldr has learned well from the fall of Asbjorn the Strong. This Ubba wants me and Haraldr has made his home so strong that the Dane fears he will lose too many men. Erik, go to the farms on the slopes of Old Olaf. Tell the people there to come into the walls. Do not take no for an answer."

"Aye lord."

They hurried off to obey my commands and my six young boys arrived. They had seen the arrival of Asbjorn and their eyes told me that they were ready to risk the wrath of the Danes to help the clan. Even the young had Viking bravery!

"I want you to ride to every farm and home. Do not worry about the ones on the slopes of Old Olaf. Erik will speak with them. Tell them the Danes come and they must bring their animals and families here to Cyninges-tūn. Ride until the sun has passed its zenith and then return. We will need brave warriors like you upon our walls!" They were words only and there was no magic in them but I saw that they had an effect and the six boys' backs stiffened and their eyes blazed. The clan needed them and they would not let it down; more, the Dragonheart had asked them and that made them special. They vaulted on to the backs of their ponies and they rode.

Even as Ráðgeir went to the tower to blow the cow's horn I heard the horn from Hawk's Roost. Sámr had received the message, now we would have to see if the plan we had conceived would thwart the Danes. I went into my hall, "Germund, fetch my mail and my sword!" Until the threat was gone, I would wear my mail. I had not worn it for such a long time that I wondered if my ancient body would bear the weight. I heard our horn sound the alarm. Each horn sounded different. The farmers would begin their preparations and my messengers would direct them to our stronghold. The ones who lived the furthest away would make their own decision. I suspected that the ones who lived on the far side of Old Olaf or up Lang's Dale would wait. I hoped that would not prove to be a fatal delay!

As Germund hurried off to my chest, I saw Asbjorn eating the barley bread, cheese and salted meat Atticus had brought. I walked to my wall and took down Ragnar's Spirit. His eyes widened. I saw the unspoken question in his eyes. "Would you like to touch the blade?" Unable to speak he nodded and wiped his greasy fingers on his breeks. I took the sword over and removed it from its scabbard. I placed it before him and Asbjorn put two hands around the hilt. I smiled for I knew what the effect would be. It was as though Asbjorn had been plunged into an icy bath. His eyes widened in shock and he almost dropped the blade. I had expected it and my hands caught it before it could fall to the table.

"Sorry, lord! It burned as I touched it." He looked at his hands to see if a mark had been left.

"Do not worry, Asbjorn," I sheathed the sword and hung it from my baldric, "the blade was touched by the gods. Even now, many years after the storm, I can still feel the shock of the thunderbolt from the god!"

Germund came in with the mail. I saw him smile. He knew what had happened. Asbjorn supped some of the small beer and asked, "Will we win, lord?"

I was putting on my padded kyrtle and before I could answer Germund said, "We are the Clan of the Wolf and we are led by the greatest Viking the world has ever seen. I have fought for the Emperor of the East and faced greater foes than these Danes. We will win." He looked at me as he held the byrnie above my head, "Not all of us will live to see the victory but that matters not. The clan will live and young warriors like you, Asbjorn the pony rider, will remember what we did and when the next threat comes, and come it will, then you will be there to defend this land."

I had not heard Germund speak as much in a long time. It made Asbjorn sit a little straighter. He would remember those words. I held my arms up and the byrnie, held by Germund, slipped over them. When I felt the weight on my shoulders, it did not feel as heavy as I had expected. I took my baldric and strapped it on. I took Wolf's Blood and fitted that scabbard to the baldric. Finally, I went to the chest by the fire and took out two more seaxes. I slipped one into each boot.

Asbjorn asked, "Why do you need so many weapons, lord? You have Ragnar's Spirit."

Germund laughed, "A man can never have too many weapons! Take my advice, Asbjorn, have a good sword, a strong spear, a well-made shield and then as many other weapons as you can carry!"

I left my hall and went, with Germund, to the gatehouse. Ráðgeir and some of my men were already there. They had not yet put on their war faces. They had manned the walls even though there was little likelihood that the Danes would arrive any time soon. My arrival meant that I was now in command. Darts, arrows and spears were neatly stacked in small wooden barrels. There were barrels of ale and water along with a ladle. Fighting was thirsty work and we could refresh ourselves; the Danes could not. There were bowmen in the two towers and, along the fighting platform, warriors were arriving to take their allotted places on the fighting platform.

When I approached, Ráðgeir said, "We will go and don our mail, lord."

"We have time. Asbjorn and the riders sent by Haraldr know the byways and greenways of our land better than the Danes. We man our walls but it is in the night when we shall have to be vigilant."

They hurried off leaving just Germund and me with the bowmen in the towers. The gate faced south and we turned to look east. Germund pointed his spear. "It is Hawk's Roost or Pennryhd which will bear the first attack."

I shook my head, "It will be Hawk's Roost. If they wished to attack Ketil or his son at Pennryhd they would have crossed further north. I just feared that they would strike at Mordaf for he is the most vulnerable. I think that Sámr's attack on Mercia has saved his cousin."

"Might this not be a ruse to draw our eye to the north and east?"

"Ubba is with them and ten or more boat crews means that there could be more than six hundred warriors. Ragnar and Mordaf can deal with a few boat crews but, in my head, I do not see another attack."

Ylva's voice almost made me jump, "And you are right to think so. I have dreamed, grandfather. You have good instincts. This army is the only one."

I saw that she had strapped on a sword and wore a short mail byrnie. The sword had been her father's. The sword which lay with Aiden was the one I had found in the submerged cave. Like Germund and me she had not yet bothered with a helmet or shield. Strapping on a sword always made the wearer feel ready for war. "And you will fight here?"

"Ubba has no witches this time. The last time he used them they were betrayed by the Dane and none will serve him. I can use a sword and I would be at your side when we fight."

"I do not want to risk your life."

"It is mine to risk. I am a Viking shield maiden and I have the same courage as my cousin, Sámr. Should I cower in my hall like a Christian priest when the clan's warriors are dying?"

She was right and so we stood and watched as our mailed men clambered up the ladders. Haaken and Aðils were amongst the last to do so. They had walked every part of my stronghold and ensured that we were secure. I saw Arne the Fisher and his sons carrying their last boat through the gate. The rest were moored in the middle of The Water. They came through the gates which were then slammed shut. They would only be opened when the farmers and my riders returned. We were at war.

Dragonheart
Chapter 19
The Last Battle

The last farmers arrived just after dark. Ráðgeir watched them carefully as they entered for we were wary of Danish scouts who might have tried to infiltrate our stronghold. While their families were accommodated in our halls the men stood along our walls. We had a hundred and two men to defend the walls and thirty boys who could use a sling or, in some case, a bow. The sixty extra had little mail and were largely farmers but all had fought for me or raided with me at one time. They would do. I had already calculated, with the aid of Atticus, that if we gathered every warrior in the Land of the Wolf and faced the Danes shield to shield, we would outnumber them. That would not happen as it would mean stripping our defences. The Danes outnumbered the warriors who manned the five strongholds we had in the north. Gruffyd was the one who could have made the difference. It was sad that I could not count on my son.

The days were now almost the same length as the nights. As the sun set behind Old Olaf and plunged The Water into darkness, we heard the first cry from Hawk's Roost. The horn in Sámr's home sounded three times and then stopped. That was the signal that they were under attack. Those hours were the hardest I ever endured for I knew that my blood was being attacked by overwhelming numbers. Sámr's home had better defences but there were less than sixty warriors to defend it. Could he hold out until Ketil, Windar and Ráðulfr reached him? I had to trust in our plan. We had known that we would face such numbers. The sounds of battle drifted across The Water. They came in waves. We heard the clash of steel and we heard cries. Sometimes the wind took the noise away and it seemed as though the battle had ended. Then there would be a flaring of noise and an eruption of shouts. Men were dying.

I turned to Ráðgeir, "Have two in three of the men sleep and rest. This will be a long night."

"Aye, lord."

Ylva said, "I have a potion which will keep us awake."

Erik asked, "Will you not rest, lord?"

I looked at Erik and then glanced at Ylva, "I have slept in my own bed for the last time, Erik. You should sleep."

"No, lord, you did not leave me at Wyddfa. I will stay with you until…"

"Until I tell you to go and then you will obey me!"

He nodded.

The fighting seemed to end not long before dawn. The potion which Ylva had given us had worked and we were all wide awake. Everyone but those around me had had some sleep and been fed. Bleary-eyed we stared across to Hawk's Roost. We could see the lower gate and that appeared to be intact but the main gate was on the northern side. Had it fallen? Perhaps my great grandson read my mind or, more likely, Ylva had sent her thoughts across The Water for a horn sounded twice. Sámr told us that they lived still.

Aðils shouted, "Stand to! Watch for tricks." This was always the cry at dawn but today, knowing the Danes were across The Water, it was even more significant.

I hurried down to the gate. Asbjorn waited there with his pony. "Asbjorn, I want you to ride back to your lord. Go south, pass Torver's Waite and avoid danger. It matters not if you take all day so long as you get there. Ask your lord to send half of his men to the aid of Sámr and then send another rider to Whale Island. We need half of their men to come here."

He nodded, "I will not let you down, lord."

I patted his shoulder, "I know. May the Allfather be with you. Open the gate!"

The double gates were unbarred. On the fighting platform, bowmen stood with nocked arrows. As soon as the pony galloped off, the bridge over the ditch was raised, the gates were closed and barred while we waited for the attack we knew would come.

We waited a long day. It was just after noon when we heard the battle of Hawk's Roost resume. To me, it sounded less intense for there were fewer battle sounds and we heard more shouts and chants. Fragments of songs drifted over but I did not think it was a full attack. I had an idea that this was part of Ubba's cunning or, more likely, his lieutenant Gangulf Gurtsson. I turned to Ylva, "What do you see?"

She smiled, "I read your thoughts, grandfather. You think that Ubba has men waiting to the north to ambush you when you go to the aid of Sámr."

"It is what happened last time but is Sámr safe?"

She shrugged, "I think so but even if his life was in danger, he would not wish you to go to his aid. You are the target of this attack. Sámr has endured the hard part. Ketil, Windar and Ráðulfr will be sending men south. Even if they only send half of their warriors that will be more than enough to aid Sámr." She turned to Erik, "Come with me and we will fetch food. Grandfather, sit on the barrel. You will need your strength soon enough."

The barrel was filled with ale and was tapped. She was right and I was no longer a young man. I sat. Haaken sat on the one on the other side. He laughed, "This is jest, Dragonheart, that the Allfather has two old men such as we standing a watch and preparing to face six times our number in Danish barbarians!"

I laughed too, "I would have thought that the prospect of such a saga would fill you with joy."

"If I thought I would be able to tell the tale then I would."

Without turning Aðils Shape Shifter said, "Do not be so pessimistic. We are Ulfheonar and such odds do not worry us."

"You are right, Aðils, let us embrace the moment."

We had eaten, supped and made water by the time the battle at Hawk's Roost died down. The chants ceased and there was another roar as battle resumed and then all went silent. I looked at the sky and saw that there were just a few hours of daylight left. Suddenly Ylva stiffened, "They come!" She donned her helmet and picked up her shield.

Although we could not detect any danger, we all trusted our witch enough to know that she would know that which we did not.

Aðils Shape Shifter shouted, "Stand too! Nock arrows. Prepare stones!"

Erik asked, "Why attack in daylight?"

Germund pointed to the water-filled ditches which masked the traps, "I am guessing that they fell foul of Lord Sámr's traps in the dark. They would wish to see our defences in daylight and then the main attack will be after dark. Don your helmet! If you wait until you need it then you will be too late." Germund had his shield around his back. He wore the scale byrnie he had worn when he had been a Varangian Guard and, in his hands, he held the double-bladed axe. I thought back to Olaf Leather Neck. He would be in Valhalla with Rolf Horse Killer and they would be watching events with keen interest.

I donned my helmet and drew Ragnar's Spirit. It seemed to sigh as it left the scabbard. I wondered how the Dragonheart Sword had fared at Hawk's Roost. Would I ever know? I rested my shield against the wooden palisade. Our bowmen had the ranges marked out. They would judge the moment to release their arrows. The Danes, if they had bowmen, would need to be closer than our extreme range for we were elevated on our fighting platform.

Aðils shook his head, "We can see nothing here."

He was right, "Haaken, you and Germund stay here."

We walked along the fighting platform to the north gate. This was a much smaller gate and here we had the protection of the Yewdale Beck. In the heat of summer, it might become a stream which could be leapt but after the meltwater, it was now a torrent. With the bridge safely removed they would either have to build one or find another way to attack us. With The Water on one side, the only other approach was from the side of Old Olaf. There we had cleared all of the trees to make a two hundred pace killing zone.

We reached Stig Karlsson who commanded the north gate. His bowmen, in the two small towers, were two paces above us. I looked up. "Can you see anything?"

"There is movement in the trees but the knoll of High Hollin hides them."

The knoll would have been a good place to build a stronghold but the one I had chosen was better. The wooded knoll was just six hundred paces from the palisade and the beck. Germund and Atticus had told me of stone throwers used by the Byzantines. They could have destroyed our walls but I knew that Ubba would not have them. The only war machine they could build was a ram and the beck was a barrier against that attack. I was convinced that they would attack the southern gate for it was flatter. The fact that it was the strongest part of our defences was the result of that weakness.

A sudden shaft of sunlight from behind Old Olaf glinted off metal and I spied the Danes. They were filtering through the woods on the slopes of the mountain. They would be beyond the range of our arrows but it would be difficult for their men to move on the stony scree covered slope. Even as we watched I heard slithering as an unwary Dane slipped on loose scree and rolled down the slope. He was four hundred paces from us but the lack of trees meant that his fall was unobstructed and we could see him. There was a crunch as his head hit the large boulder just three hundred paces from the beck. He lay still.

Aðils Shape Shifter turned to me, "They will leave men to watch this gate in case we relax our guard."

"I agree. Stig, be prepared to send one in two of your men to the south wall or the west wall if you hear the horn sound four times."

"Aye, lord!" He smiled, "My father will be watching from Valhalla and I will not let you down!"

We made our way back to the south gate but we walked along the west wall so that we could keep our eyes on the Danes scrambling along the tree line. They were well beyond the range of our bows. I estimated that they would have just an hour or so of daylight to scout out our defences.

Aðils shook his head as we neared the main gate, "We should have laid straw so that we could light it and illuminate the night."

"I think it would have made little difference, Aðils, for it would be easy to extinguish and would merely waste an arrow. Better to release blind when they attack at night. If only one arrow in five strikes a body then we will thin their numbers. Our defences are good. They will breach them but not this night."

I saw the first Danes descend from the slopes and move to the south of us. They were cutting off the road to Whale Island. I expected that. They formed a shield wall four hundred paces from our walls. Sámr must have taught them to respect our bows. The first ones we saw did not wear mail. These were the mercenaries, the expendables. When I saw mailed men and a standard from which was hung skulls and bones then I knew it was Ubba Ragnarsson. The last time I had seen him he had been clambering aboard a drekar. Around him were his oathsworn. I also saw a large warrior who wore no helmet but had a moustache and hair festooned with bones. Even at that distance, I could see that he had blackened his teeth. In his hand, he bore a war hammer. With a small axe head on one side and a hammer on the other, this was a dangerous weapon. The two stood apart from the others and I saw them pointing.

Ylva was next to me and she said, "They are wondering if you have a Valkyrie fighting for you."

I laughed, "More likely they are determining that I am still here and have not fled to Whale Island."

"So far, grandfather, your strategy is working. They had planned on an ambush and Hawk's Roost has not yet fallen."

I nodded, "But this is their main attack. See how they are exploring the ditches."

The one I assumed was Gangulf Gurtsson had waved his arm and ten lightly armed men ran forward. They passed the first of the white stones. Aðils had instructed his archers well and none sent an arrow in the direction of the Danes. The Danes ran with shields above their heads for they expected an arrow storm. I saw Aðils nock an arrow in his Saami bow. The first ditch was a hundred and twenty paces from us. Aðils shouted, "On my command kill the scouts!" He allowed the scouts to peer into the waterfilled ditch before he shouted, "Now!" His arrow and twenty others were not sent into the air but used a flatter trajectory. All ten scouts fell. One landed in the ditch and I saw Aðils shake his head in annoyance. That one body would fall and land on the spikes; it was a bridge. It was a weakness in our defences.

The Danes began to bang their shields with their spears and shake them at us. I turned to Ráðgeir, "Sound the horn, I think we can safely say that we are under attack!" The horn was to let Sámr know where the Danes were. We waited. The attack would come but not until dark.

We watched the Danes continue to filter down from the slopes. They were just going to attack the southern wall. We could, perhaps, have pulled men from the other walls but I could not guarantee that this was their only attack. Four blasts on the horn would bring more men to our aid.

The songs the Danes sang did not speak of their heroes; instead, they mocked the Clan of the Wolf. I saw Haaken One Eye shake his head in disbelief. His songs made men wish to fight. "These Danes have not one piece of word skill! If they fight as badly as they compose songs then you and I could face them all, Dragonheart."

I nodded, "And if I thought they would honour combat to the death then I would challenge Ubba!"

Ylva's voice was stern as she reprimanded me, "That would be reckless! They have no honour and we gain nothing by such an act of foolish bravery!"

I smiled, "You think I cannot defeat him?"

"Of course you can, but he would not fight fair. We are outnumbered and your plan is a good one! Doubt neither yourself nor Sámr!"

I put my arm around her and squeezed, "I am teasing. I have no intention of putting my life in the hands of a treacherous Dane. I will fight Ubba but on my terms and not his."

Clouds hid the waxing moon and that allowed the Danes to attack cloaked by dark night. It was the work of the Norns. Our target stones were rendered useless but we had the ditches as markers instead. They were filled with water and no man can step into water in the dark without making a noise. Added to that was the fact that there were spikes and stakes hidden beneath the water. Aðils had worked with the bowmen. As soon as we heard the first splash then he and the other bowmen, both men and boys, would send over arrows to plunge down. Many would be wasted but they would add to the injuries which our traps would cause. The rest of us would not be needed until they used ladders to scale the walls. We had not seen ladders but we knew they would have them.

Others had sharper ears than I did. Aðils did not wear a helmet and it was he heard the first Dane enter the water. He hissed,

"Ready!" It sounded like a serpent as the hiss rippled along the fighting platform.

We heard one cry and a Danish voice growled at the wounded man to be silent. We heard another noise as metal slid along metal. The Dane must have borne his wound stoically for he did not cry out.

"Now!"

When the command was given it sounded like a flock of birds taking flight. The arrows soared. The Danes were too busy feeling beneath the water for spikes to even think about the steel tipped arrows which were descending. This time there were shouts, screams and splashes as arrows, stones and spikes took their toll.

A Danish voice shouted, "They know we are here! Everyone, join the attack!"

There were clouds but the movement of so many men was visible. They had two more ditches to cross and these had not had their defences compromised. Some of the spikes and stakes were long enough to drive deep inside a man's body and rip into his bowels. The screams were almost painful to hear.

As they closed with the walls the onus was on me and so I roared a challenge, "I am Dragonheart! I wield the sword which was touched by the gods! Men of Cyninges-tūn ready your weapons. The Danes shall not pass!"

The roar from the walls was so loud that I am sure it stopped some of the Danes mid-stride. Then a Dane shouted, "He is an old man defended by women! Why do you fear him?"

In answer, Haaken began to sing. We had seen the skulls in the hair of some of the Danes. It was time to remind them of my victories!

The Danes they came in dark of night
They slew Harland without a fight
Babies children all were slain
Mothers and daughters split in twain
Viking enemy, taking heads
Viking warriors fighting back
Viking enemy, taking heads
Viking warriors fighting back
Across the land, the Ulfheonar trekked

Finding a land by Danes' hands wrecked
Ready to die to kill this Dane
Dragonheart was Eggles' bane
Viking enemy, taking heads
Viking warriors fighting back
Viking enemy, taking heads
Viking warriors fighting back
With boys as men, the ships were fired
Warriors had these heroes sired
Then Ulfheonar fought their foe
Slaying all in the drekar's glow
Viking enemy, taking heads
Viking warriors fighting back
Viking enemy, taking heads
Viking warriors fighting back
When the Danes were broke, their leader fled
Leaving his army lying dead
He sailed away to hide and plot
Dragonheart's fury was red hot
Viking enemy, taking heads
Viking warriors fighting back
Viking enemy, taking heads
Viking warriors fighting back
Then sailed the men of Cyninges-tūn
Sailing from the setting sun
They caught the Skull upon the sea
Beneath the church of Hwitebi
Viking enemy, taking heads
Viking warriors fighting back
Viking enemy, taking heads
Viking warriors fighting back
Heroes all they fought the Dane
But Finni the Dreamer, he was slain
Then full of fury their blood it boiled
Through blood and bodies, the warriors toiled
With one swift blow, the skull was killed
With bodies and ships, the Esk was filled
Viking enemy, taking heads
Viking warriors fighting back

Viking enemy, taking heads
Viking warriors fighting back

It must have enraged them for there was a sudden scream like of an enraged bull and we could actually see the wave of Danes as they threw themselves towards the walls. Our bowmen could now make out men and they slew them. Ladders rattled against the walls.

Ráðgeir, who commanded the western side of the southern wall, shouted, "Throw them back! Do not let them gain the fighting platform!" Darts and spears were hurled as our warriors on the wall made out the Danes. Even so the darkness helped the Danes and hid them. The first warrior who gained the top of the ladder made the mistake of finding Ráðgeir. Ráðgeir swung his sword backhand and the Dane's head was half severed. Dropping his shield, Ráðgeir leaned over and pushed the ladder from the wall. The ladder crashed, taking with it three men. He hacked at another warrior and then bent to retrieve his shield. A spear was hurled from the ground and it struck Ráðgeir in the neck as his head rose. It was a lucky strike but for Ráðgeir it mattered not. He died and, as he fell, he crashed into two men who were trying to raise a ladder.

Germund shouted, "I will take command of that wall, lord!" The Varangian Guard hurried down the fighting platform as fast as his leg would allow and even as the next Dane peered over the wood his axe swung and the Dane's head flew. Germund had fought in sieges and knew what to do. He swung his axe overhand and split the ladder in two. He turned to the townsfolk who were on the wall. "I am Germund the Lame and today you fight with the Emperor's Guard! All who reach this wall will die!" The men on the wall cheered.

I turned as a ladder slammed against the wall. A Danish shield was held above the warrior's head as he climbed. I put Ragnar's Spirit in my left hand and picked up a dart. The Danish sword waved before him as he tried to deflect the strike he knew was coming. When my sword hit his shield he looked up. I pulled back my arm and the dart flew into his right eye. He screamed and put his hand to the ruined orb. I swung my sword left-handed and hacked into his neck. Picking up another dart I leaned over and threw it at the next warrior who was climbing up the ladder. It hit his hand. His shield came down and Einar Larsson sent a stone to smash into his forehead.

Aðils Shape Shifter had climbed into one of the wooden towers over the gatehouse. He now directed the arrows and stones of our defenders. His Saami bow and his unnervingly fine eyesight struck warriors who were far enough away from the walls to think themselves safe. Ylva, Haaken and I were in the centre of the gatehouse. Each time Erik tried to edge forward we pushed him back. His task was to watch our backs. The three of us worked well together. Haaken and I had the strength to push away ladders while Ylva wielded her sword with such speed that it was almost a blur. What she lacked in strength she more than made up for in accuracy. As she struck each blow she screamed and it sent shivers down my spine. I could only imagine the effect it would have on the enemy. Soon her byrnie and her face were bespattered with the blood of the men she had slain.

Inevitably the Danes managed to make inroads. On the eastern side of the southern wall Sigiberhrt the Scar was commanding the men there. Erik suddenly shouted to attract my attention. I slashed my sword across the head of the Dane who was ascending the ladder and he tumbled to the ground then I turned.

"Lord, Sigiberhrt the Scar! He is surrounded."

Three Danes had managed to make the platform. Sigiberhrt the Scar was fighting hard. Even as I watched he rammed his sword up into the chest of a Dane but then one of the others hacked into his arm and the third into the side of his head.

"Aðils, the south-east wall!"

Aðils whipped around and an arrow flew into the back of one Dane almost before the words were out of my mouth. As the last Dane to make the wall looked up another arrow smacked into his forehead.

"Erik, sound the horn four times!"

I had seen that there were perilously few men on the wall Sigiberhrt the Scar had commanded. He should have called for help. Now it was too late. I left Ylva and Haaken to rush along the fighting platform. With my shield before me I ran to the ladder the Danes were using to climb into my citadel. In my head, I heard the voices of the Ulfheonar as they encouraged me. Where had they come from? I swung Ragnar's Spirit backhand and it hit the side of the helmet of the Dane who had just made the platform and whose sword hacked at my arm. The blow hurt but my blade knocked the Dane from the ladder. He fell into the ladder which was close to Ylva and that fell to the ground.

Leif Longshanks led the men sent from the east and north walls. They began to clear the Danes who had made the far end of the fighting platform. "Spread your men out along this wall. Send four to Germund. Leif, you take command here!"

"Aye, lord."

I returned to the gatehouse. As I reached it a Danish horn sounded twice. The Danes began to fall back. My men began to cheer until Germund's voice silenced them, "Pull up the ladders and bring them inside the walls! Let us deny them their use!"

Aðils climbed down from the tower, "I will see how many archers and slingers remain. They fought well, Dragonheart, but those Danes are determined."

Ylva sheathed her sword and took off her helmet, "Erik, come with me and we shall see to the wounded."

I shouted, "Have the dead removed from the fighting platform. Atticus, food and ale!"

Atticus would have been within my hall during the battle but now that the sounds of death had ended, he would be outside looking to see that his master was safe. His reedy voice came to me, "Aye, lord! I am pleased you are still alive!"

Haaken laughed, "It gives you confidence does it not, Dragonheart?"

"He means well. We held them." I took off my helmet and laid down my shield.

Haaken also took off his helmet and pointed to the body of Sigiberhrt the Scar as it was taken into the stronghold, "But at what a cost? Ráðgeir is dead also. The Danes can afford these losses."

"We knew we would have to hang on. When daylight comes then Sámr will come."

Haaken shook his head, "Sámr will want to come but we both know, Dragonheart, that he will not leave his family undefended. This Ubba and Gangulf are cunning. There will be men waiting to ambush them and there is but one way here. It is more likely that

Sámr will wait until men from the north reach us. I will do a head count." He sheathed his sword and left me alone.

He was right and even if Ragnar and Mordaf had disobeyed my orders and begun to march to our aid then they would not arrive until noon at the earliest. The same was true of Haraldr. We had the rest of the night and the morning to hold on. As I sheathed my sword, I heard a voice in my head. I had last heard it when I had been in Miklagård. Then I had been at the gates of Valhalla and about to enter. The voice was the Allfather's. The voice said, simply, '*Have courage, Dragonheart!*'

Atticus appeared at my shoulder. He had some bread and a horn of ale. Around his neck hung an ale skin. As I drank from the horn, I felt his eyes examining me. I drank half of the horn; fighting was thirsty work, and then wiped the foam from my beard, "I am whole, Atticus."

He nodded as he refilled my horn from his ale skin, "Yes, lord, but what of the price we have already paid? There are twenty bodies piled up and eight men are now in the house of women having their wounds tended. How long can we hold out?"

"For as long as it takes."

I did not bother with the bread. I was not hungry and when I had emptied the skin, he left me alone on the wall. Haaken returned and his face was grim. It confirmed what Atticus had told me, "We have lost one in three of our men. Eight of our best men now lie dead."

I nodded. The words of the Allfather still rung in my head. "And what is the alternative?"

His one eye stared at me and then he laughed, "Aye you are right!" I heard hammering from the south. "They are building something, Dragonheart."

"Aye, and while they build, they cannot attack. Let them build for when daylight comes that brings hope of relief." He looked at me and cocked his head to one side. I nodded, "You are right. This does not mean we will survive but, this battle is not about you and I but Ylva, Sámr, Erik and the others. We just need to show that we have the courage to stand for as long as we can and all will be well."

He pointed to The Water, "The spirits of the dead lie there and it is strange, Dragonheart, but as we fought, I felt as though Cnut,

Bjorn, Olaf and the others were behind me. I swear I could smell Olaf the Toothless."

I laughed, "And I felt them too." I did not mention the Allfather's voice but I added, "I heard their voices in my head. Their chants and songs as they rowed were all around me!"

Just then, far to the east, I heard a distant rumble. It was thunder and that might herald a storm. Was that the meaning of the Allfather's message?

Dragonheart
Chapter 20
The Sound of Thunder

"Is that the Allfather hammering, Dragonheart?"

"I think it is." I tapped the hilt of my sword. "That may mean hope or it may mean disaster but whatever it means we are powerless to do anything about it!"

"And that could be said of our whole lives, Dragonheart!"

Erik returned as did Aðils Shape Shifter. Aðils said, "We have used half of our arrows but worse than that we have lost eight good archers."

I nodded and looked at Erik, "Ylva is with the wounded. She said she will be back on the wall before the Danes attack."

The sound of hammering returned and this time it was not the gods it was the Danes. "And that may well be dawn. I think they are building a ram!"

"Then they have had to go a long way to find a decent sized tree!" We had cleared all of the large trees for more than half a mile around.

"A ram, lord?"

"Aye, Erik. They will use the branches to make bridges and then trundle it across the ditches. It will be slow but if they protect it with shields then they have a good chance of making our walls. We have good gates but a ram will break first one and then the other. The only way to defeat one is to use fire and we have wooden walls. If we use fire then we doom ourselves."

"Then all is hopeless?"

Aðils put his arm around Erik, "Not while the last of the Ulfheonar defend these walls. I will go and fetch a brazier, Dragonheart. You are right we cannot use fire when it reaches the walls but we can use fire before it does so. If we can ignite the wood then it will make those who push it fearful."

As he went Haaken said, "It will be like spitting in the wind. The wood will be wet. We would need oil."

"And you would do nothing?"

"You are right." He turned to Erik. "Keep your sword in your hand and remember all that you see. When this is over you will compose the song of this battle."

Erik smiled, "That task is yours, Haaken One Eye!"

He shook his head and I saw resignation in his one good eye, "Not this time."

When dawn broke, we saw that the Danes had lost many men. Their deaths had not been in vain, however, as many had died in our ditches and their bodies made places which could be used by the wooden bridges we saw next to the crudely made ram. They had fires burning and they were cooking food. I estimated that there were three hundred warriors before us. We had not slain three hundred and I knew that the Danes had men waiting to ambush those who would reinforce us. This time Ubba had been given good counsel and his plan was well constructed.

The walls were manned and the brazier in place when we saw the ram as it drew close. Ylva had joined us. Aðils shouted to his archers, "Now we can see the stone markers. See the men pushing the ram! They have shields above their heads but an arrow in the leg or the foot can be just as effective. When they reach the stones then use your arrows wisely!"

I was staring at the two leaders. I could now see them clearly and they were forming up with their hearth weru. All of them were mailed and they would follow the ram. Before the ram were the three rough bridges they had made. While they carried them, the men were protected. Once they laid down their burdens then Aðils and our bowmen would slay them. The ram had forty men pulling it and another twenty pushing it. Behind it were twenty more. The Danes knew they would lose men as they approached. They began to bang their shields and to chant. It was a single word, "Death!"

They repeated it and I heard a voice shout, "March!" The ram moved, slowly at first as the sixty men heaved at the war machine.

I, surprisingly, did not feel weary. I felt enervated for, as I looked along the fighting platform, I saw not despair but anger that the Danes had come to threaten the life of their lord. I saw courage etched on every face. I watched women, armed with hand axes and seaxes fetching food and ale for their menfolk. The clan was at war and that filled my Dragonheart with joy.

Aðils stood at the top of the western tower. He was two paces above me. The roof protected him from falling arrows but his chest and head were exposed. Here the shape shifter could not hide. He pulled back his Saami bow. The ram had not yet reached the marker stones and the Danes were busy heaving. The lead warrior had allowed his shield to slip or, perhaps, he thought himself safe. Whatever the reason Aðils took his opportunity. His arrow had a needlepoint and it slammed through the mail and into his chest. He fell and the ram stopped. The Danes must have thought all of my men were armed like Aðils and shields came up.

I heard shouts from the rear. I could not make out the words but the intent became clear. Ubba Ragnarsson and Gangulf Gurtsson led their column alongside the ram and then overtook it. I heard more words and the men with the bridges hurried forward. There were no targets for our bowmen. Perhaps a hand could have been pierced but that would not make the Danes stop.

Aðils shouted, "Wait until they place the bridges and then slay them." He continued to use his bow to great effect. All he needed was a glimpse of flesh. His second arrow hit the warrior who stood to the right of Ubba Ragnarsson. The two Danish leaders had full face helmets but the man Aðils slew did not. Another stepped forward to take his place and the column tightened as the shields were overlapped and heads ducked beneath their rims.

The first bridge was dropped over the ditch and there was a flurry of arrows. The four bridge bearers fell. The next two bridges were carried over. Now they were in range of our slingers too and we had more than enough stones. When one cracked into the hand holding one of the bridges the Dane let it fall and when he was exposed two arrows hit him. The bridge was stuck until another warrior could make his way forward to carry it. One bridge carried on. It was dropped in place. Three of the men carrying it were felled but the fourth dived into the ditch where he hoped he would be safe. Aðils' arrow pinned him to the dead man beneath him.

The column crossed the first bridge. Now they were within a hundred paces of the walls. We could hear the words of a chief, "Dwerg, carry the last bridge. The rest of you, shield wall!"

A warrior stepped from the column which changed to a double line of shields. The ram lumbered across the first bridge.

"Aim for their legs!"

Now that they had stopped moving the legs of the Danes were vulnerable. While Aðils continued to hit the flesh of the men our boys and bowmen sent arrows at the legs of the Danes. None fell although many were hit. When the last bridge fell and the four carriers were slain, I knew that we would soon be under attack.

The voice which had commanded the Danes shouted again, "First group, cross!" They had practised this or at least prepared for it. Eight men suddenly ran, with shields before them, across the first bridge and then the second. One was hit by Aðils but the rest formed a wall of shields. Neither flesh nor boot was visible. Arrows and stones rained upon them but to no effect.

"Second group cross!" As the second group ran, I saw that the ram was moving faster. The feet of the column had flattened the ground and soon it would reach the column.

I was expecting another group to run but instead, the voice shouted, "Axes!"

Three men rose from the seven who had formed a shield wall. One was hit by an arrow but the other two stood and threw their Frankish throwing axes. To my horror, I saw that their target was Aðils Shape Shifter. His body and head were exposed. One axe hit him in the chest. It split his mail and caused a bloody wound but it was the other which killed him. It split his head in twain and he tumbled, silent to the end, from the tower. His body lay before the gate. It would have to be removed before the wheels of the ram could move closer to the gate. Even in death, he was fighting the enemy. The two axemen had little time to enjoy their victory for Erik, Haaken and Ylva all hurled darts. Our archers and slingers took their revenge too and the men with the throwing axes lived just a heartbeat longer than Aðils Shape Shifter.

Haaken looked at me and held up two fingers. We were the last two Ulfheonar.

Just at that moment, there was a flash in the east and a few moments later the crack of thunder. It was almost as though the

Allfather was signalling the end of the Ulfheonar. It seemed to stir the Danes and they ran across the bridges. The bowmen and slingers wanted vengeance for Aðils and eight more were slain before they reached the walls. Now they were in range of our darts and javelins. Even the women threw them down. The Danes held their shields above their heads. With Aðils gone there was no one to direct the bowmen. I shouted. "Target the men pulling the ram!"

Haklang Larsson, one of the young boy slingers from the north wall, ran up to me, "Lord, my father sent me. There is fighting to the north. We have heard the sounds of battle."

I looked at Ylva who closed her eyes. When she opened them, she was smiling. "It is Sámr!"

I nodded, "But will he reach us in time?" I pointed; the ram was about to cross the last bridge. Even worse there were four ladders which had fallen into the ditch. Although it cost them two men to do so, the Danes recovered them and were lifting them in place. These were not mercenaries who prepared to climb. These were oathsworn warriors with mail byrnies. They would reach the top of the wall and we would have to fight them man to man. Less than ten experienced and mailed warriors remained on the south wall. We would have to die hard! The skies were darkening so that it was almost night as the storm clouds rolled across The Water.

Our bowmen and slingers had done well and it was only the men pushing the ram who remained. The Danes who had crossed already to make a shield wall now left a space for the ram. Two Danes died as they removed Aðils Shape Shifter's body. Once the ram hit the gates then they would enter the stronghold. The four ladders they had meant that we would have to fight them on the walls and there would be none to brace the gates. Aðils Shape Shifter had planned on fire arrows and he had died before he could use them. It was almost as though he spoke to me from the Otherworld.

"Haaken, the brazier! Use these javelins with me and we will lift it." He frowned and then realisation dawned. I put down my sword and we grabbed two javelins and placed them in the rings on the side of the brazier. I felt the heat from the hot coals. We headed to the palisade.

It was as we reached the edge that I heard the Danish command, "Axes!" I did not see the axe which hit my helmet but I felt it. I could not work out why I still stood for it had felt as though I had been kicked by a horse but the Allfather was watching me still. There was another flash in the east and another crack of thunder. The storm was growing closer. We reached the parapet and we dropped the brazier. As it fell the lighter coals dropped out. The ram had not yet reached the gate but the coals managed to spread themselves along its length. It was wet wood but the coals were hot. Some of them covered the men pushing the ram. One had his clothes set afire and, in his panic, he ran into two of his comrades who also began to burn. The ram was stopped and the bowmen and slingers on my walls, not to mention the women with darts, did not miss. The flames on the ram began to spread. It would not move now for two men lay dead under the front wheels.

The Danish voice shouted, "Climb the ladders, we have them!"

The throwing axes had taken another three warriors. I saw that Germund the Lame had just four warriors left with him. The rest were bowmen, slingers and women. "Ylva, stay here and direct the defence. Haaken, let us see what two old men can do to aid Germund."

Even as we ran, I heard Ylva say, "Erik, sound the horn five times." That call meant that every man had to come to the horn. Ylva was abandoning all the other walls. I prayed that Sámr won his battle for if not then the dead would have died in vain.

I saw that Germund the Lame was using his axe as a Varangian Guard. He swung it in a figure of eight. He took the head of one Dane who clambered onto the fighting platform but the Dane who had ascended the next ladder had slain the warrior guarding his right side, Reimar Yellow Hair. The Dane helped another up and the two of them advanced on Germund. Haaken and I had bodies to negotiate before we could get to him and we were too late. Even as he hacked into the arm, shoulder and chest of one Dane, a third Dane who had just ascended the ladder hacked across his neck. His head fell and then, a moment later, his body tumbled to the ground. The Varangian Guard had kept his oath. He had died defending his new home but he had slain many of our enemies.

The blow from the throwing axe had hurt me. I felt dizzy as I tried to reach the two Danes on the fighting platform. The rain began to fall as I heard another crack of thunder. I slipped. Haaken faced two of the Danes alone. His shield blocked the blow from one of them and he lunged at the thigh of the other. Bright blood spurted and I heard my friend shout, "I am Haaken One Eye. You face the last of the Ulfheonar save the Dragonheart you spineless Danes!"

He hacked at the head of the Dane before him. The one he had wounded now returned the compliment and chopped at Haaken's knee. I saw blood as his sword sliced into flesh and not boot. I regained my feet and swung Ragnar's Spirit twice. The two Danes fell but more were already climbing up the ladders and Haaken and I were the last two left alive on the southwestern fighting platform.

Haaken gave me a wan look, "That hurt." He seemed to see my helmet for the first time. "And you have a serious dent in your helmet! Does it not hurt?"

I laughed, "Soon it will matter not. Let us head back to the gatehouse and pray that Sámr arrives soon."

It was then that Ubba Ragnarsson and Gangulf Gurtsson clambered over the parapet. Ubba pointed his sword at me. "Your tricks will not avail you and when you are dead, we will take your witch and use her too. Then we will destroy all that you have built. This will be a burned out memory when we are done!"

I laughed, "You can never destroy what I have built for it is the Clan of the Wolf and it is part of this land. Can you destroy this land?"

Just then there was a flash over The Water and a crash a moment later. It lit up the sky and made the two Danes flinch. The Allfather had sent the storm to aid us and I swung my sword at Ubba. I took him by surprise and my sword hit his shoulder. My edge was sharp and I drew blood. That seemed to spark another eruption as the two Danes hurled themselves at us. I had the measure of Ubba but my vision was becoming blurred. I had to end this fight quickly. Haaken One Eye was close to the parapet and I had free rein to swing at Ubba's weak side. Haaken would have to fight Gangulf unaided until I had dealt with Ubba.

I punched with my shield at his face. He used his sword to block the blow and that suited me for it meant he could not strike back at me. I heard Haaken's shield boss ring as Gangulf swung at him. Ylva and Erik were spectators for they were behind us. If we fell then they would have to deal with these two warlords. Ubba was forced back and I found myself next to Gangulf. I pushed with my shield at his side and the swing he aimed at Haaken missed. It cost me for Ubba managed to stab at me. His sword scraped along my leg.

When he saw the blood, he shouted as though he had slain me, "I have the Dragonheart's blood!"

"Then have his sword too!" I feinted at his leg. He lowered his shield and I changed the strike to aim at his shoulder. I had already weakened and cut the mail links on his byrnie. Now Ragnar's Spirit sliced through the strap on his shield and into his arm. His fingers could not hold it and his shield fell to the ground. He grabbed his sword in two hands and, as he stepped backwards, he swung at my head. I willed my left arm to rise but it seemed slow to do so. I barely managed to block the blow. Why was my body failing me?

Stepping forward I lunged with the tip of my sword. He was not expecting it and my sword's tip tore open two links and slid along his side. It was a scratch but the blood flowed more freely and I could see the fear on his face. He stepped back again. Behind me, I could hear Haaken and Gangulf exchanging blows but I could do little about it. A grunt from Haaken told me that Gangulf had drawn more blood. The storm was now all around us but I could see even less. It was as though I was peering through a tunnel for my dizziness was far worse. I had to end this quickly. Ubba was waving his sword before him. He did not know from which direction I would strike. He did not know that I was hurt. I tried a simple trick and it worked. I stamped down hard with my left leg as I punched my shield at him. At the same time, I roared. His sword went to my shield and Ragnar's Spirit had a free swing to hack into the weakened mail on his left side. I sawed the blade backwards and I saw his ribs. His organs were exposed and I reversed my sword. Swinging hard, I sliced into his neck and his body fell to the ground.

Whipping my head around was a mistake. My vision blurred and I saw nothing. When I managed to focus, I saw Haaken on one knee. His left arm hung uselessly; Gangulf had breached his defences and incapacitated him. I saw Ylva stepping forward to defend him. Gangulf blocked Ylva's blow with his shield and swept his own sword upwards. Haaken must have been wounded again for the sword flew from his fingers.

The last survivor of my band of Ulfheonar smiled, "I will see you in Valhalla, my old friend. Farewell." Gangulf's sword took Haaken's head and then the Dane punched his shield at Ylva who fell over one of the many bodies which now littered the fighting platform. Erik bravely stepped forward. He was going to sacrifice himself for Ylva.

I forced my weary body forward, "Gangulf Gurtsson, face the Dragonheart or do you only prey on the weak and those who are already wounded?"

He laughed and turned to face me, "This will be the work of a moment and then the boy and the witch will die!"

"Erik, guard Ylva!"

"Aye, lord."

The Dane was unwounded. I had blood dripping from my leg and my head did not feel as though it belonged to me. My body was slow to react. The throwing axe had hurt me but I would not simply give up. Even as I stood to face him there was another flash and almost at the same time a crack which made my ears ring. It lit up the night and enabled me to see more clearly. I lunged at Gangulf's face. He could not lift his shield in time and he used his sword to block the blow. He did not have mail on his hands and Ragnar's Spirit slid along the back of his hand. Blood flowed; it was the first blood he had shed. I punched with my shield and hit his wounded hand. It was little enough but it would slow down his blows.

"This is the sword which was touched by the god. Can you not hear his anger? You have made a mistake, Gangulf Gurtsson. I know not why you sought me but now that you have found the Dragonheart you will wreak the punishment."

He swung his sword at my head but the wound had weakened him and the blow did not hurt my shield arm. I had no obstacle to my right and I aimed my sword at the side of his head. He had quick hands and our swords rang together. My dizziness was becoming worse and my vision was becoming blurred. I was not sure how much longer I could go on. However, I had to try. Erik bravely stood over Ylva's prostrate body but Gangulf would make short work of him.

He could see my discomfort and he took heart from it. "So, old man, you have been deserted by the Allfather! Your life will end now!"

He swung his sword backhand and caught me unawares. I partially blocked it with my shield but the power of the blow tore my leather strap and the shield flew into the air to land on the ground. I was weakening and so I held the sword in two hands. I had one chance. I had to bring my sword from on high and split open his head. Haaken's body lay before and, in my head I apologised as I stepped on to it. I would use my old friend to gain height. He would not mind for he was past caring. The sword felt like a lead weight. Perhaps the Allfather had abandoned me. I lifted it and shouted, "Ragnar's Spirit!" and I brought it down. As our swords touched there was a flash which lit up the whole world and a crack of thunder. All went black!

Ylva Aidensdotter
Chapter 21
The Sword in The Water

When I saw Haaken about to be killed I stepped forward to strike the Dane. With Ubba dead we just needed Gangulf to be slain and we would have won. His shield blocked my blow. Even as I raised my sword for a second strike his shield hit, first my sword and then my head. I found myself falling backwards. I blacked out briefly and when I opened my eyes, I saw Erik before me with his blade and shield to defend me. My grandfather was fighting Gangulf Gurtsson. He was a younger and fitter warrior. I saw blood trickling down the side of the Dragonheart's helmet and the dent in the side of his helmet was big enough for me to hide my balled fist. He was hurt. I tried to struggle to my feet and, as I did so, I was unsighted for a moment. I heard my grandfather shout, "Ragnar's Spirit!" as he raised his sword in two hands. As the two swords touched the Allfather sent a lightning bolt and it touched the two swords. The bolt threw the Dane's sword from him and then set his body on fire. He screamed and jumped to the ground below the fighting platform. I think that Haaken One Eye's body saved my grandfather for, when I reached him, he still breathed. I saw that the fall had killed the Dane for his body lay at an unnatural angle but it still burned.

Nothing else mattered save the Dragonheart. He could not die here. He was marked for death but I had plans. "Erik, help me take his helmet from him."

We slowly removed the helmet and I could see that the side of his skull was crushed. How he was not dead I did not know. I took a dagger and cut a piece of material from my dress. I bound it about my grandfather's head.

Just then I heard, from behind me, a cry, "It is Sámr Ship Killer! We have won! The Danes are fleeing south!"

I turned to Erik, "Find Arne the Fisher. I need his boat now! We must cross The Water!" The boy was going to argue. He was loyal beyond words and his bravery was quite remarkable. I smiled, "You will be with your lord until the end now go and wait by the boat for me. Have it taken to The Water." I went to move the sword from my grandfather's hands. It was hot to the touch. The blade was now blackened and burned but otherwise undamaged. His fingers gripped it and it would not release. *Wyrd.* I shouted, "I want four men to help me carry the Dragonheart!"

Snorri Gunnarson, Ulf Galmrson, Sweyn Olafsson and Harald Jorgenson rushed to help me. "Is he dead?"

"No, he still breathes. Keep his body horizontal and do not touch the sword for it is still hot. The Dragonheart will not relinquish his hold."

I descended first and the people of Cyninges-tūn stared in horror. I had no time for explanations. "He lives now make a passage we must get to Arne the Fisher's boat."

We headed for the gate. Men had opened it to let Arne and his sons carry the boat out. I saw, through the open gate, that the ram was still burning but as it was not on the Danish bridge, we could reach the beach.

"Ylva! Is he dead?"

I turned and saw Sámr. His mail was covered in his enemies' blood and he held the Dragonheart Sword in his hand. "He lives but I have no time to explain. Go to my hall. There are five horses there. Saddle them and take the bag that is on my bed. Meet me at the head of The Water. Come alone."

He spread his arm, "But what about this?"

"Now is the time of Baldr Witch Saviour. Let him take charge until you return. It will take but two days to do that which we must." There was a slight hesitation, "Trust me, Lord of the Land of the Wolf!"

He nodded, "Always."

Erik waited by the boat. I saw that Arne and his sons held it into the wind. "Snorri, place the body in the centre. Erik, can you steer?" He nodded. "Then take the tiller. Arne, your boat will be left at the head of The Water, I can say no more."

"And you need not, my lady. Will he live?"

"This is the last that any man shall see the Dragonheart. You are all privileged. Say your farewells."

They raised their swords as one and cried out, "Dragonheart." All were warriors and as brave as any yet tears were shed. In one night the last of the Ulfheonar had died and now the Dragonheart was leaving his land. The world would never be the same again. I climbed aboard and lowered the sail.

"Now Erik, head for the centre and I will tell you when to stop."

"Aye, lady."

I knew the exact spot to head for as it was where the wolf had met my grandfather. It was the centre of The Water and was the deepest part. As we sailed, I glanced back. The storm had passed. The last crack had been the one which killed Gangulf and the skies were now clearing. I saw the men of Cyninges-tūn as they slew wounded Danes and recovered our wounded. We had been hurt but we had survived. My life would change in that one moment. I had known it would for months, perhaps years. My mother and I had discussed it once she recovered from her illness. She would be sad and Sámr would have to help her for in one moment she had lost her father and her only child. There was nothing anyone could do about it. It was *wyrd*.

It was the spirit of Erika who told me we had reached the spot. I heard her voice in my ear. I turned to Erik, "Here!"

Erik turned the boat into the wind and we stopped.

I went to my grandfather. He still breathed but his eyes were closed. I said, quietly, "Now is the time, Dragonheart. Now you should let go of Ragnar's Spirit for its time in this world is over." I saw his fingers relax and I took the sword. I stood with the blade in my two hands. It felt hot but this was not the heat of a lightning bolt, this was the power of the sword. "Allfather, take the sword which the Dragonheart bore for a short time. Give him peace. When the Clan needs it, you will find a way to send it back to us." I dropped the blade into The Water. It barely made a splash but the air around me seemed to sigh. Above me the last of the clouds scudded away and a shaft of sunlight lit the spot where the sword had disappeared. "Now, Erik, take us to the head of The Water. We still have far to go."

Erik must have had many questions but he respected my silence. I took the mail from my grandfather's fingers and held his two hands in mine. I felt his dragon heart beating in his wrist. He was clinging on to life. He was the Dragonheart! It seemed to take an age to reach the beach at the head of The Water where I saw Sámr waiting with the horses.

"Erik, run the boat onto the beach. We have a burden to bear."

Sámr tied the horses and came down to help us. "The sword?"

"Is now at the bottom of The Water. None shall own it."

"And my great grandfather?"

"We have a journey to make. There will be just the four of us who go and only two will return. While I make him comfortable make a sling between Ada and Agnetha. They are gentle sisters and will make his last journey an easy one."

I wiped away the blood from my great grandfather. I used The Water to do so. It had powers. All the while I was aware of the presence of the spirit of my grandmother. It gave me comfort.

Sámr and Erik appeared behind me, "It is done."

"Then let us carry him carefully." The three of us carried him as gently as a newly borne babe. While the two of them tied their straps, I placed Wolf's Blood in his hands. He would have a weapon. Once he was secured in the sling and we had mounted our horses then Sámr and I took Ada and Agnetha's halters and led them. I headed towards Úlfarrberg.

I knew that Sámr had many questions but I was already weary. This had been my first real battle and it would be my last. I owed it, however, to Sámr to tell him all.

"Before I tell you where we go, I need you both to swear on the Dragonheart sword that you will never reveal where it is."

Sámr nodded, "For my part that is easy." He took out his sword and said, "I so swear!"

He passed the sword to Erik. There was fear in his voice but he was brave. "I swear the secret shall die with me!"

"We are going to Myrddyn's cave. It will be the tomb of the Dragonheart."

"But he lives!"

"Yet it will be his tomb. His life hangs by a thread. If we can get him to the cave….He was chosen by the Allfather. The spirits have told me all."

"You cannot leave him there alone!"

"Nor will I. The bag you brought contains all that I will need for my new life as the guardian of Dragonheart's tomb. The tomb shall be my home. I will not return to Cyninges-tūn."

"What? But your mother? The people!"

"My mother knows and she will care for the people. Only you two shall know where I am. You can visit in times of need but I need the power of Myrddyn and the Dragonheart to watch over the Land of the Wolf. Úlfarrberg will also help me to have the power to use my magic to keep the Land of the Wolf safe."

We rode in silence until Sámr said, "But you will be alone!"

"I will have the spirits. Sámr, you did not choose to lead the clan. That was decided by others. I did not choose my path. It was chosen for me. We have been close and we will remain so. My powers mean that I can read your thoughts and inhabit your dreams. Do not disregard your dreams for they come from me."

I had known this was coming since my father's death. I was the one who had been chosen to stay with the Dragonheart. I did not mind. The power from the cave would make me the most powerful volva but I would be alone. I glanced at my grandfather. I saw his chest rising and falling. His spirit was strong but he was dying. The blow from the axe had set in motion a series of events inside his body which even I could not stop. I could heal but I could not bring him back from the dead. The only hope was the cave of Myrddyn.

Erik was quiet but reflective. I heard words in his head. The spirit of Haaken One Eye was in the boy and that was *wyrd*.

It was dark as we approached the Lough Rigg. I dismounted, "I will go within for we shall need light."

I climbed the rough-hewn rocks which were the steps. I took the flint and lit the fire I had already prepared. The past year had seen me make many visits here. This would be my home for eternity and I wished it to be as comfortable as I could make it. Once the fire was going, I lit the brands which I had placed in stone sconces around the cavern's walls.

I returned outside. "We have one more journey for the Dragonheart to make." We carried him, reverently and carefully up the stones. The lights made the inside look like one of the White Christ's churches but this one was beautiful for it had been made by the Mother. The stone plinth which was prepared would be his resting place. It was at the height of my chest. I wondered if Myrddyn had made it for I had had nought to do with its construction. Once he was laid there I said, "We must remove his mail and then you need to leave me for I have preparations to make. I will let you in before dawn to say goodbye. You may camp outside. The rain has passed and you will be dry."

Even as they nodded, we heard a solitary howl from Úlfarrberg.

I smiled, "Our sentinels know that we are here."

The cave acted as a sounding chamber and I heard the voices of Sámr and Erik as I made my preparations. My grandfather was slipping away but he would not go until Sámr had said his farewells and there was something else which had to happen but I knew not what. Some things were denied even the Mother's handmaiden.

Erik's voice drifted in to the cave along with the smoke from the fire they had lit, "The Dragonheart knew you would come. He never doubted you, lord."

"This Dane and his lieutenant were cunning. They left a third of their men to ambush us. It was my hawk which warned us. We came as soon as we could but they fought hard."

"Will any escape?"

"Not this time for my father was already heading north with a mighty host. Along with Mordaf and Naddoðr they will slay all that they find. Should any manage to evade our hunters their tale will stop any from daring to breach the borders of our land. The Dragonheart saw beyond his own death."

"But he breathes! Surely Ylva can save him!"

I sighed when I heard Erik's words. If I could save him I would but even as I took the bandage from his head, I felt his life slipping away.

"If she could, Erik, she would."

"What will become of me, lord?"

I heard Sámr laugh. On the way to the cave, I had told him of the battle. "You are now a warrior of honour. The boy who bearded the Dane to save the volva. Atticus will need someone. You will live in the hall of the Dragonheart and you will become a warrior. You will take a wife and have children."

I stepped out of the cave to their campfire, "So cuz, you are galdramenn now?"

He laughed, "No, but even I can see that Erik here is destined to be a warrior."

I saw him smile, "And perhaps something of a singer too."

"Come, it is time to say your farewells and for all of us to speak our goodbyes."

The three of us stood around the Dragonheart.

I smiled, "I will be here forever and I can say whatever I wish, whenever I wish. You two should speak. Sámr?"

"Great grandfather you made me the man I am and I swear that so long as I live the Land of the Wolf will be a just land with no king and no prince. We will make our land a haven for those who flee evil and we will follow the old ways. You left us too soon but I will tell my son and my daughter the tale of the Dragonheart and I will visit with Ylva for I see in her your spirit. I know that I will hear your voice in my head and the sword you had made for me is part of you."

We both looked at Erik. He gave an embarrassed smile and said, "I know not from where these words came but they seem right."

The Dragonheart was truly named
With a sword and spirit rightly famed.
All enemies knew his heart was true
Each foe was dealt what he was due.
The land he made is a land which is strong
Filled with warriors who there belong
You have not died, you are just at rest
Of all the warriors you were the best
When the land has need you will return
With a sword from Odin, all will burn
We mourn you and we curse the Dane
But were ever the Danish Bane
Dragon heart who was the Viking Brave
Born to lead and taken as a Viking Slave
Dragon heart who was the Viking Brave
Born to lead and taken as a Viking Slave

I had promised myself I would not weep but I did along with Sámr and Erik. The three of us held each other in Myrddyn's cave as the Dragonheart left his body and went to the Otherworld.

Epilogue

My body juddered as Odin struck my sword and I found myself in a black world where I could feel nothing yet I could hear. I saw nothing but I felt no pain. My head, which had hurt, was now pain-free. I held, in my hand, Ragnar's Spirit and I gripped it tightly. I had been to Valhalla and I expected to see the light from the door for surely, I was dead. I needed the sword to gain entry. I heard fragments of conversations. They came and went like the sea surging onto a beach.

"Erik, help me take his helmet from him."

"Ylva! Is he dead?"

"Erik, head for the centre and I will tell you when to stop."

Then I heard a voice in my ear and it was Ylva. "Now is the time, Dragonheart. Now you should let go of Ragnar's Spirit for its time in this world is over."

I let go of the sword and I felt such a relief. It was as though a burden had been lifted from me. Then I felt myself sailing. I was a young boy and my mother and I were being taken to Norway. My mother was smiling for she had made the journey as easy for me as she could. Then I felt myself rising as I had in so many dreams and I found myself in a cave. It was like the cave where I had found the sword all those years ago. I felt light headed and sounds seemed to disappear. I caught two fragments more.

"The Land of the Wolf will be a just land with no king and no prince."

And the last thing I heard was, "Dragonheart who was the Viking Brave, Born to lead and taken as a Viking Slave."

Then all went black but I found I could use my legs. I saw again and, in my hand, I held Wolf's Blood. I knew it from the feel. I smelled wood smoke and I saw a light ahead. A door opened and there was Haaken One Eye, Aðils Shape Shifter and Germund the Lame. They each held in their hands a horn of ale. Haaken put his arm around my shoulders, "Now is the greatest Viking hero amongst us and Odin himself can reward you!"

I entered the warrior hall and I saw Odin himself gesture to a seat next to him. I was in Valhalla and my pain was over. I had saved my land and now it was passed to another. It was wyrd*!*

The End

Norse Calendar

Gormánuður October 14th - November 13th
Ýlir November 14th - December 13th
Mörsugur December 14th - January 12th
Þorri - January 13th - February 11th
Gói - February 12th - March 13th
Einmánuður - March 14th - April 13th
Harpa April 14th - May 13th
Skerpla - May 14th - June 12th
Sólmánuður - June 13th - July 12th
Heyannir - July 13th - August 14th
Tvímánuður - August 15th - September 14th
Haustmánuður September 15th-October 13th

Glossary

Afen- River Avon
Afon Hafron- River Severn in Welsh
Àird Rosain – Ardrossan (On the Clyde Estuary)
Al-buhera -Albufeira, Portugal
Aledhorn- Althorn (Essex)
An-Lysardh - Lizard Peninsula Cornwall
Balears- Balearic Islands
Balley Chashtal -Castleton (Isle of Man)
Bardas - Rebel Byzantine General
Beamfleote -Benfleet Essex
Bebbanburgh- Bamburgh Castle, Northumbria was also
known as Din Guardi in the ancient tongue
Beck- a stream
Beinn na bhFadhla- Benbecula in the Outer Hebrides
Beodericsworth- Bury St Edmunds
Belesduna– Basildon, Essex
Belisima-River Ribble
Blót- a blood sacrifice made by a jarl
Blue Sea- The Mediterranean
Bogeuurde - Forest of Bowland
Bondi- Viking farmers who fight
Bourde- Bordeaux
Bjarnarøy –Great Bernera (Bear Island)
Breguntford – Brentford
Brixges Stane - Brixton (South London)
Bruggas- Bruges
Brycgstow- Bristol
Burntwood- Brentwood Essex
Byrnie- a mail or leather shirt reaching down to the knees
Caerlleon- Welsh for Chester
Caer Ufra -South Shields
Caestir - Chester (old English)
Cantwareburh -Canterbury
Càrdainn Ros -Cardross (Argyll)
Carrum -Carhampton (Somerset)
Cas-gwent -Chepstow Monmouthshire
Casnewydd –Newport, Wales

Cephas- Greek for Simon Peter (St. Peter)

Chatacium -Catanzaro, Calabria

Chape- the tip of a scabbard

Charlemagne- Holy Roman Emperor at the end of the 8th and beginning of the 9th centuries

Celchyth - Chelsea

Cerro da Vila – Vilamoura, Portugal

Cherestanc- Garstang (Lancashire)

Cil-y-coed -Caldicot Monmouthshire

Colneceastre- Colchester

Corn Walum or Om Walum- Cornwall

Cymri- Welsh

Cymru- Wales

Cyninges-tūn – Coniston. It means the estate of the king (Cumbria)

Dùn Èideann –Edinburgh (Gaelic)

Din Guardi- Bamburgh castle

Drekar- a Dragon ship (a Viking warship) pl. drekar

Duboglassio –Douglas, Isle of Man

Dun Holme- Durham

Dún Lethglaise - Downpatrick (Northern Ireland)

Durdle- Durdle dor- the Jurassic coast in Dorset

Dwfr- Dover

Dyrøy –Jura (Inner Hebrides)

Dyflin- Old Norse for Dublin

Ēa Lōn - River Lune

Earhyth -Bexley (Kent)

Ein-mánuðr - middle of March to the middle of April

Eoforwic- Saxon for York

Falgrave- Scarborough (North Yorkshire)

Faro Bregancio- Corunna (Spain)

Ferneberga -Farnborough (Hampshire)

Fey- having second sight

Firkin- a barrel containing eight gallons (usually beer)

Fornibiyum-Formby (near Liverpool)

Fret-a sea mist

Frankia- France and part of Germany

Fyrd-the Saxon levy

Ganda- Ghent (Belgium)

Garth- Dragon Heart

Gaill- Irish for foreigners

Galdramenn- wizard

Gesith- A Saxon nobleman. After 850 A.D. they were known as thegns

Gippeswic -Ipswich

Glaesum –amber,

Glannoventa -Ravenglass

Gleawecastre- Gloucester

Gói- the end of February to the middle of March

Gormánuður- October to November (Slaughter month- the beginning of winter)

Grendel- the monster slain by Beowulf

Grenewic- Greenwich

Gulle - Goole (Humberside)

Halfdenby – Alston Cumbria

Hagustaldes ham -Hexham

Hamwic -Southampton

Hæstingaceaster- Hastings

Haughs- small hills in Norse (As in Tarn Hows)

Haugr- a small hill

Haustmánuður - September 16th- October 16th (cutting of the corn)

Hautwesel -Haltwhistle (Hadrian's Wall)

Hearth weru- The bodyguard or oathsworn of a jarl

Heels- when a ship leans to one side under the pressure of the wind

Hel - Queen of Niflheim, the Norse underworld.

Here Wic- Harwich

Hersey- Isle of Arran

Hersir- a Viking landowner and minor noble. It ranks below a jarl

Hetaereiarch – Byzantine general

Hí- Iona (Gaelic)

Hjáp - Shap- Cumbria (Norse for stone circle)

Hoggs or Hogging- when the pressure of the wind causes the stern or the bow to droop

Hrams-a – Ramsey, Isle of Man

Hrofecester -Rochester (Kent)

Hundred- Saxon military organisation. (One hundred men from an area-led by a thegn or gesith)

Hwitebi - Norse for Whitby, North Yorkshire

Hywel ap Rhodri Molwynog- King of Gwynedd 814-825

Icaunis- a British river god

Issicauna- Gaulish for the lower Seine

Itouna- River Eden Cumbria

Jarl- Norse earl or lord

Joro-goddess of the earth

kjerringa - Old Woman- the solid block in which the mast rested

Karrek Loos yn Koos -St Michael's Mount (Cornwall)

Kerkyra- Corfu

Knarr- a merchant ship or a coastal vessel

Kriti- Crete

Kyrtle-woven top

Lambehitha- Lambeth

Leathes Water- Thirlmere

Legacaestir- Anglo Saxon for Chester

Ljoðhús- Lewis

Lochlannach – Irish for Northerners (Vikings)

Lothuwistoft- Lowestoft

Lough- Irish lake

Louis the Pious- King of the Franks and son of Charlemagne

Lundenburh/Lundenburgh- the walled burh built around the old Roman fort

Lundenwic - London

Maeldun- Maldon Essex

Maeresea- River Mersey

Mammceaster- Manchester

Manau/Mann – The Isle of Man(n) (Saxon)

Mara and Mondrem -Delamere forest (Cheshire)

Marcia Hispanic- Spanish Marches (the land around Barcelona)

Mast fish- two large racks on a ship designed to store the mast when not required

Melita- Malta

Midden- a place where they dumped human waste

Miklagård - Constantinople

Mörsugur - December 13th -January 12th (the fat sucker month!)

Musselmen- the followers of Islam

Njörðr- God of the sea

Nithing- A man without honour (Saxon)

Odin - The "All Father" God of war, also associated with wisdom, poetry, and magic (The Ruler of the gods).

Olissipo- Lisbon

Orkneyjar-Orkney

Pecheham- Peckham

Peny-cwm-cuic -Falmouth

Pennryhd – Penrith Cumbria

Pennsans – Penzance (Cornwall)

Poor john- a dried and shrivelled fish (disparaging slang for a male member- Shakespeare)

Þorri -January 13th -February 12th- midwinter

Portesmūða -Portsmouth

Porth Ia- St. Ives

Portus Cale- Porto (Portugal)

Pillars of Hercules- Straits of Gibraltar

Prittleuuella- Prittwell in Essex. Southend was originally known as the South End of Prittwell

Pyrlweall -Thirwell, Cumbria

Qādis- Cadiz

Ran- Goddess of the sea

Roof rock- slate

Rinaz –The Rhine

Sabrina- Latin and Celtic for the River Severn. Also, the name of a female Celtic deity

Saami- the people who live in what is now Northern Norway/Sweden

Sabatton- Saturday in the Byzantine calendar

Samhain- a Celtic festival of the dead between 31st October and 1st November (Halloween)

St. Cybi- Holyhead

Scree- loose rocks in a glacial valley

Seax – short sword

Sennight- seven nights- a week

Sheerstrake- the uppermost strake in the hull

Sheet- a rope fastened to the lower corner of a sail
Shroud- a rope from the masthead to the hull amidships
Skeggox – an axe with a shorter beard on one side of the blade
Skreið- stockfish (any fish which is preserved)
Skutatos- Byzantine soldier armed with an oval shield, a spear, a sword and a short mail shirt
Seouenaca -Sevenoaks (Kent)
South Folk- Suffolk
Stad- Norse settlement (Singular and Plural)
Stays- ropes running from the mast-head to the bow
Strake- the wood on the side of a drekar
Streanæshalc- Saxon for Whitby, North Yorkshire
Stybbanhype – Stepney (London)
Suthriganaworc - Southwark (London)
Syllingar Insula, Syllingar- Scilly Isles
Tarn- small lake (Norse)
Tella- River Béthune which empties near to Dieppe
Temese- River Thames
Theme- Provincial Army Corps
The Norns- The three sisters who weave webs of intrigue for men
Thing-Norse for a parliament or a debate (Tynwald)
Thor's day- Thursday
Threttanessa- a drekar with 13 oars on each side.
Thuni- Tunis
Tinea- Tyne
Tilaburg – Tilbury
Tintaieol- Tintagel (Cornwall)
Thrall- slave
Trenail- a round wooden peg used to secure strakes
Tynwald- the Parliament on the Isle of Man
Tvímánuður -Hay time-August 15th -September 15th
Úlfarrberg- Helvellyn
Úlfarrland- Cumbria
Úlfarr- Wolf Warrior
Úlfarrston- Ulverston
Ullr-Norse God of Hunting

Ulfheonar-an elite Norse warrior who wore a wolf skin over his armour

Vectis- The Isle of Wight

Veisafjǫrðr – Wexford (Ireland)

Volva- a witch or healing woman in Norse culture

Waeclinga Straet- Watling Street (A5)

Walhaz -Norse for the Welsh (foreigners)

Windlesore-Windsor

Waite- a Viking word for farm

Werham -Wareham (Dorset)

Western Sea- the Atlantic

Wintan-ceastre -Winchester

Withy- the mechanism connecting the steering board to the ship

Wihtwara- Isle of White

Woden's day- Wednesday

Wulfhere-Old English for Wolf Army

Wyddfa-Snowdon

Wykinglo- Wicklow (Ireland)

Wyrd- Fate

Wyrme- Norse for Dragon

Yard- a timber from which the sail is suspended

Ynys Enlli- Bardsey Island

Ynys Môn -Anglesey

Historical note

My goodness me but that was hard to do. I have thought about this last novel in the series for over two years. I knew it was coming and I hope that I have done the Dragonheart justice. This is the last book but Sámr and Ylva appear in the New World series, albeit briefly. I may, some day, do a stand-alone book but it will not be about the Dragonheart. I hope that I have made my characters real and that you know how Sámr, Ylva, Mordaf, Erik and Atticus live after the cataclysmic end.

Some of my readers do not like the lengthy historical note section. You can find it on my website.

What I will say is that like them or hate them the Vikings were a unique race. Their descendants were the Normans but they were not the same as that hybrid of Norse and Frank. The true Vikings were pagans. They sailed further than any man. Columbus made the West Indies. The Vikings landed in New England and Canada! They were an uncompromising people and I hope that I have done them justice.

Some have questioned Jarl Dragonheart's longevity. There were examples of Vikings who lived as long. Harald Hadrada was one. They were hard men and their lives were violent. It was war which killed them and not the way they lived when at home. They were active and their diet seemed to make them live a little longer than might be expected. Meat, fish, cheese and ale must be a good combination! I think a vegan Viking would be a contradiction in terms!

The Vikings used foster fathers for younger warriors. When the first Vikings went across the Atlantic there was a German Viking who was a foster father to the leader of one the expeditions.

By 912 the Vikings ruled as far south as the Mersey. At the time this book is set Mercia was as large as it was ever going to get.

I used the following books for research:

- Vikings- Life and Legends -British Museum

- Saxon, Norman and Viking by Terence Wise (Osprey)
- The Vikings (Osprey) -Ian Heath
- Byzantine Armies 668-1118 (Osprey)-Ian Heath
- Romano-Byzantine Armies 4th- 9th Century (Osprey) -David Nicholle
- The Walls of Constantinople AD 324-1453 (Osprey) -Stephen Turnbull
- Viking Longship (Osprey) - Keith Durham
- The Vikings- David Wernick (Time-Life)
- The Vikings in England Anglo-Danish Project
- Anglo Saxon Thegn AD 449-1066- Mark Harrison (Osprey)
- Viking Hersir- 793-1066 AD - Mark Harrison (Osprey)
- Hadrian's Wall- David Breeze (English Heritage)
- National Geographic- March 2017
- The Tower of London – Lapper and Parnell (Osprey)
- British Kings and Queens- Mike Ashley

Griff Hosker
May 2019

Other books by Griff Hosker

If you enjoyed reading this book, then why not read another one by the author?
Ancient History

The Sword of Cartimandua Series (Germania and Britannia 50 A.D. – 128 A.D.)
Ulpius Felix- Roman Warrior (prequel)
Book 1 The Sword of Cartimandua
Book 2 The Horse Warriors
Book 3 Invasion Caledonia
Book 4 Roman Retreat
Book 5 Revolt of the Red Witch
Book 6 Druid's Gold
Book 7 Trajan's Hunters
Book 8 The Last Frontier
Book 9 Hero of Rome
Book 10 Roman Hawk
Book 11 Roman Treachery
Book 12 Roman Wall
Book 13 Roman Courage

The Aelfraed Series
(Britain and Byzantium 1050 A.D. - 1085 A.D.)
Book 1 Housecarl
Book 2 Outlaw
Book 3 Varangian

The Wolf Warrior series
(Britain in the late 6th Century)
Book 1 Saxon Dawn
Book 2 Saxon Revenge
Book 3 Saxon England
Book 4 Saxon Blood

Book 5 Saxon Slayer
Book 6 Saxon Slaughter
Book 7 Saxon Bane
Book 8 Saxon Fall: Rise of the Warlord
Book 9 Saxon Throne
Book 10 Saxon Sword

The Dragon Heart Series
Book 1 Viking Slave
Book 2 Viking Warrior
Book 3 Viking Jarl
Book 4 Viking Kingdom
Book 5 Viking Wolf
Book 6 Viking War
Book 7 Viking Sword
Book 8 Viking Wrath
Book 9 Viking Raid
Book 10 Viking Legend
Book 11 Viking Vengeance
Book 12 Viking Dragon
Book 13 Viking Treasure
Book 14 Viking Enemy
Book 15 Viking Witch
Book 16 Viking Blood
Book 17 Viking Weregeld
Book 18 Viking Storm
Book 19 Viking Warband
Book 20 Viking Shadow
Book 21 Viking Legacy
Book 22 Viking Clan
Book 23 Viking Bravery

The Norman Genesis Series
Hrolf the Viking
Horseman
The Battle for a Home
Revenge of the Franks
The Land of the Northmen
Ragnvald Hrolfsson

Brothers in Blood
Lord of Rouen
Drekar in the Seine
Duke of Normandy
The Duke and the King

New World Series
Blood on the Blade
Across the Seas

The Anarchy Series England 1120-1180
English Knight
Knight of the Empress
Northern Knight
Baron of the North
Earl
King Henry's Champion
The King is Dead
Warlord of the North
Enemy at the Gate
The Fallen Crown
Warlord's War
Kingmaker
Henry II
Crusader
The Welsh Marches
Irish War
Poisonous Plots
The Princes' Revolt
Earl Marshal

Border Knight 1182-1300
Sword for Hire
Return of the Knight
Baron's War
Magna Carta
Welsh Wars

Henry III
The Bloody Border

Lord Edward's Archer
Lord Edward's Archer

**Struggle for a Crown
1360- 1485**
Blood on the Crown
To Murder A King
The Throne

Modern History

The Napoleonic Horseman Series
Book 1 Chasseur a Cheval
Book 2 Napoleon's Guard
Book 3 British Light Dragoon
Book 4 Soldier Spy
Book 5 1808: The Road to Coruña
Book 6 Talavera
Waterloo

The Lucky Jack American Civil War series
Rebel Raiders
Confederate Rangers
The Road to Gettysburg

The British Ace Series
1914
1915 Fokker Scourge
1916 Angels over the Somme
1917 Eagles Fall
1918 We will remember them
From Arctic Snow to Desert Sand
Wings over Persia

**Combined Operations series
1940-1945**

Commando
Raider
Behind Enemy Lines
Dieppe
Toehold in Europe
Sword Beach
Breakout
The Battle for Antwerp
King Tiger
Beyond the Rhine
Korea

Other Books
Carnage at Cannes (a thriller)
Great Granny's Ghost (Aimed at 9-14-year-old young people)
Adventure at 63-Backpacking to Istanbul

For more information on all of the books then please visit the author's web site at www.griffhosker.com where there is a link to contact him if you wish.

Printed in Great Britain
by Amazon